Blackness Descended
On Invisible Wings . . .

Mara screamed as an ebony tentacle reached around the front of the horse and ripped its legs out from beneath it. The priestess crashed headlong into the foliage.

Logan jumped to his feet, a flaming red shaft of uncontrollable magicks in his hands. "Mara!" he called to her. "Run! I can take care of this thing!"

The priestess's eyes went wide. "Matthew! Don't! You need the book!"

Logan's flaming weapon transformed into the heavy, leatherbound volume. She watched in horror as the young man swung the massive tome like a sword, the screaming Darkness sweeping down toward him. Logan turned a nasty glare on her. Living Darkness exploded outward from Logan's skull in a geyser of twisting limbs and writhing appendages. He released a villainous chuckle as his squirming tentacles coiled about the priestess's throat and squeezed . . .

THE FINAL CHAPTER OF
STEVEN FRANKOS'S SPELLBINDING
TRILOGY!

The Jewel of Equilibrant
pulled Matt Logan away from his California home—
into a world of Darkness . . .

The Heart of Sparrill
gave him the powers he needed
to survive as a Spellcaster . . .

The Darklight Grimoire
will determine the final conflict
of magicks bright and dark . . .

Ace Books by Steven Frankos

THE JEWEL OF EQUILIBRANT
THE HEART OF SPARRILL
THE DARKLIGHT GRIMOIRE

THE DARKLIGHT GRIMOIRE

STEVEN FRANKOS

ACE BOOKS, NEW YORK

This book is an Ace original edition,
and has never been previously published.

THE DARKLIGHT GRIMOIRE

An Ace Book/published by arrangement with
the author

PRINTING HISTORY
Ace edition/February 1994

ISBN: 0-441-00013-4

ACE®
Ace Books are published by The Berkley Publishing Group,
200 Madison Avenue, New York, NY 10016.
ACE and the "A" design
are trademarks belonging to Charter Communications, Inc.

PRINTED IN THE UNITED STATES OF AMERICA

10 9 8 7 6 5 4 3 2 1

To Nestea,
the music of Mike Oldfield and Jerry Goldsmith,
and, one last time,
to my parents

·1·

Heartbeat

"Ride, Matthew Logan! *Ride!*"

Matthew Logan leaned forward on his yellow-and-green horse, wincing as a frigid wind bit into his contact lenses and brought tears to his eyes. The forest was a mass of green and brown blurs, vaguely discernible through the gloom of the night as the stallion thundered on. Other horses galloped beside his, their manes and tails whipped by the arctic gale. The four riders on either side of the young man all angled themselves forward, hoping to aid their mounts in reaching greater speeds. One was a large, muscular Rebel, another a lithe, darkly clad Murderer, the third was an ebon Guardian of Shadow, while the fourth was a slender, beautiful ex-priestess. Thromar, Moknay, Nightwalker, and Mara, Logan mentally checked off. They knew as well as he did that they only had so much time before the darkness of the night became permanent.

Logan flicked up his left wrist and glanced at his watch. Red light feebly glimmered back from the LED display window. There was no trace of the silvery specks of brilliance that had once dotted the crimson—they all had been replaced by a villainous blackness. But it was more than just blackness: This blackness seemed alive, sentient . . . radiating a dire feeling of anxiety that churned expectantly in Logan's gut.

Great, the young man sneered to himself, we're racing against time and my stupid watch doesn't work.

Logan paused. That was a stupid thing to say, he realized. Ever since I was pulled into Sparrill, my watch hasn't worked. The display had been replaced by the red and silver glow; now, however, this blackness was taking over . . . slowly, but surely. Getting closer.

"Logan!" Moknay suddenly called out. "Does your watch work?"

The young man felt a sudden burst of anger explode within him. "No!" he yelled, having just discovered it himself. "No, it doesn't work! Just like magic! Just like me!"

"But we need to know," Mara declared, her beautiful, long brown hair billowing in the wintry gale. "We need to know who is conjuring forth the Voices! We need to know if you can stop them! *We need to know what time it is*!"

"Time is but an illusion made up of countless riddles for which I may have the answers," Nightwalker remarked.

Logan gave the Shadow-spawn a furious glare. "Then *you* tell us what time it is!"

A frown crossed the Guardian's ebon face. "Alas, Matthew Logan, I am unable to do that. Only *you* may do that. Only a man from another world as you are may succeed. I am forbidden to exist in a realm of all Light or all Dark. I will cease to beeee . . ."

There was a hideous scream torn from Darkling Nightwalker's throat as darkness—a fluid darkness like that in Logan's watch—swooped out of the night sky. It instantly engulfed the Guardian of Shadow, leaving only the faint, residual tracings of his white hair and eyes.

It is true, Logan thought, gaping. Shadow can not exist in complete darkness. Then that meant the whole damn world would stop existing should the Dark get through and take control.

Goddamnit! he cursed. Somebody tell me what time it is!

The living darkness banked on ebon wings, sweeping over the steely-eyed Murderer. "Logan!" Moknay shouted. "Do something! Strand yourself here, but do something!"

Logan watched, frozen between choices as the malleable darkness consumed Moknay, swallowing even the reflecting glimmer of his strap of daggers.

"I can't!" Logan cried back. "I'm sorry, Moknay! I just want to go home!"

Thromar withdrew his heavy, bloodstained sword. "Friend-Logan!" the fighter boomed. "It's up to you to save us! It always is in the end! You know we'll lay down our lives for you, and you don't want that!"

Logan tried to reach out and grab the Rebel, yet the fighter's red-and-black mare was much too swift. "No, Thromar! Don't!" the young man screamed.

"We can only do so much, Matthew," Mara explained as the darkness dove for her. "Everything else is up to you."

"*Mara*!" Logan cried.

The young man watched in horror as the churning, alien darkness swarmed down and draped his remaining companions in a jet-black shroud. Oh, God! he sobbed. Not again! Not Mara! I already lost her once before! Why again?

Logan's thoughts were interrupted as his horse released a frightened whinny and reared backwards. The young man from Santa Monica was thrown from his mount, spilling ungracefully to the ground. Stunned, he glanced up to see a slender woman stagger toward him, hands outstretched imploringly. She was a pale crimson, yet hair as silver as Moknay's daggers spilled down the length of her bare back. She wore no clothes but made no move to conceal her nakedness. That fact instantly reminded Logan of the sprites, yet this woman was taller than the three sisters. She stumbled and almost dropped to the ground as Logan scurried to help her.

"Matthew Logan," she breathed, her voice betraying intense pain from some unseen wound.

As soon as Logan touched her, she swooned, spilling into his arms. Her breathing was shallow and harsh, and her breasts heaved as she took in what Logan feared to be her last breath.

"What . . . ?" Logan started.

"I have been raped," the crimson woman choked, her silver eyes filling with tears. "Help . . . me. Please."

Logan was overwhelmed by despair as he gently settled the woman on the lush carpet of grass beneath him. What was he to do? He could not heal her. He understood now the unseen wound from which she suffered, but that did not make it any easier to help her. Once again, he was completely powerless to do anything.

"How . . . What can I do?" he asked.

"They are after me," the woman gasped. "It was not enough what they did to me. They want to see me dead. They want to kill me."

Logan gently caressed the flowing silver hair, his blue eyes filling with tears. "But . . . But you're dying already," he replied, not knowing how he knew this.

The woman only nodded sadly.

A sudden cacophony split the night, and Logan looked behind him, icy terror filling his veins. The living horde of darkness had found him, and it had expanded to encompass the entire night sky. Faces appeared and disappeared within the churning tide of blackness, mutating, pulsing: faces of family and friends back home in Santa Monica, Moknay's face, Mara's; the face of

Druid Launce, and Cyrene, and the light blue ogre. A wormlike extension protruded near the base of the screeching darkness, grinning with Gangrorz's ebony eyes. The distorted, half-melted visage of Imperator Vaugen shrieked angrily at Logan, and an ebon-formed Groathit flung curses at the young man.

The crimson woman in Logan's arms screamed as the darkness obscenely caressed her legs, winding its way further up her ruby flesh. Logan backed away in revulsion as the blackness sucked the woman into its gaping, voidlike maw, reveling in her agony. Then, all at once, the myriad faces spit the woman back out, filling the night with triumphant howls and shrieks of laughter. Ice dotted the perfectly sculptured frame, and an expression of pain mixed with unrelenting determination was etched eternally on the woman's face. Logan gently lifted her head, ignoring the cold that burned his very hands. She was so still . . . so stiff.

There was no heartbeat.

Logan turned a fierce gaze at the hovering mass of darkness, allowing the coldness of the corpse to fire his anger. They had done this to her, he seethed. They had killed her, and Mara, and Moknay, and Thromar . . . and everybody else Logan had ever known! He would see them suffer. He would see them suffer even if it meant confronting them alone!

The young man watched the changing, flowing faces that scrawled across the shifting blackness. "All right, you bastards," he snarled. "I'll play games your way. Now . . . *What time is it?*"

The darkness screamed in fury, plunging straight for the young man as he held tighter to the motionless body in his grasp. There was still a chance, he told himself. Still a chance that he could win.

Darkness swarmed over him as the first of the visions reached him, and Matthew Logan screamed.

No hope! the young man shrieked. I can't fight *him!* That's the one person I can never fight! That's the one person I always have troubles dealing with!

Logan felt the strength flow out of him as he grappled with the ebon, mirror-image of himself. Its fang-rimmed mouth dove for his exposed throat, and Logan tried to push the mockery away.

There was no heartbeat.

Matthew Logan woke up. There was a cold lump of fear still in his stomach as he wiped streams of perspiration away from his face and found himself clinging tightly to the crimson Bloodstone in his arms. He glanced nervously across the silent camp and at his sleeping companions, fearful of the nightmare gradually fading from his mind.

"You are well?" a deep, ominous voice asked beside the young man.

Logan looked to his right and mutely stared at the bizarre figure beside him. Even in the gloom of the night, the man's stark white hair and blank, pupilless eyes reflected the flicker of light. Unsettlingly, his face and body melded in with the darkness, both an unnatural blackness that was not the hue of normal skin. A dark cowl draped his lithe frame as Darkling Nightwalker crouched next to the young man.

"You were disturbed . . ." the Guardian stated.

Logan nodded once, inhaling. "Nightmare," he answered.

Nightwalker's blank eyes gleamed. "An ill sign," he responded. "Tell me all you can remember."

Logan shuddered, consciously recalling the sights that had been mercifully retreating to his subconscious. "We were riding," he said, "and . . . and nobody knew what time it was. Then this darkness swept over everybody . . . including the red lady."

The young man glanced down at the Heart in his hands and frowned. A silence surrounded the clearing, broken only by the crackling of the campfire.

Darkling Nightwalker finally looked away. "Magic is a sub-conscious force," he said, low and ominous. "The ability lies within you all, yet it takes time to bring the control forward to the conscious mind. Without the conscious mind, there is no control. Magic becomes sporadic—dangerous to even the user— yet allows bridges to be formed; connections to be made; magical shock waves to be felt and translated as dreams. You yourself caused these shock waves once."

Logan tore his eyes away from the magical Bloodstone in his grasp. "My dream about Gangrorz's Tomb?" he queried.

Nightwalker nodded curtly, his white hair flashing in the glimmer of the firelight. "Indeed," he replied, "yet that was your doing. Tonight, what you saw was no true dream. It shall be very much real. It shall be what will happen to us should we fail to reach whoever is drawing forth the Darkness." The Shadow-spawn was silent a moment. "Tell me," he suddenly questioned. "Did I die?"

Logan jerked his head up with a start. Dream or no dream, how do you tell someone who was helping you that you saw

him die? It's not the most polite thing in the world to do . . .
then again, the young man mused, Sparrill—unlike his world—
was not covered in that imperceptible haze of masks and facades.
What things were—who people were and what they thought of
you—in Sparrill, things like that were usually pulled right into
the open with brutal frankness.

"Yes," Logan answered softly. "You . . . uh, were the first."

Darkling Nightwalker nodded. "And so it shall be," he agreed,
no trace of sorrow or despair in his deep voice. "Shadow is a
bastard child of both Light and Darkness. Should one become the
more dominant, I will cease to exist."

"Just like that?" Logan inquired, startled. "Bam! No more
Darkling Nightwalker?"

The Shadow-spawn nodded again.

"That's not fair!" Logan protested.

A faint flicker of a smile crossed the ebon lips. "You know as
well as I, Matthew Logan, that there are no rules in the millions
of multiverses that distinguish between fair and unfair. Whatever
happens, happens. Do you consider your plight here fair?"

"No, but . . ."

"Or your destiny should you remain?"

"No."

"Then why should I fight what will be?" questioned Nightwalker. "I cannot. I may only do as you do: try to alter events,
change the outcome of some seemingly unrelated occurrence.
There is no sense trying to fight the overall conclusion."

Logan narrowed his eyes, soaking in the information. "So we
have to prevent the Voices from coming?" he half asked. "Stop
them completely?"

"Halt their conquest," Nightwalker explained. "That is the first
step. They may arrive, but they must not be allowed to conquer.
That is when I—and all in this portion of Shadow—shall become
one with the Darkness. That is when we will hear what the Voices
have to say."

Silence returned to hover over the camp as Logan gazed at
the campfire. He found himself staring with glazed eyes at the
flames. Jumping, prancing shadows frolicked around the light of
the fire, yet when they trailed into the darkness beyond the fire's
light, they were consumed by the night.

"The disturbance in the Wheel is great," Nightwalker continued.
"It will not be difficult to shatter the dimensional barriers. A series

of events has led to this. Surely your own entrance triggered the entire chain."

Logan felt a surge of self-righteous anger swell in his breast. Ever since he had been in Sparrill, everything had gone wrong. Everything he tried to attempt, failed. Everything he tried to fix, shattered. He had never asked nor wanted to come to this other world, and he was sick and tired of being blamed for things that were not in his power to control.

"Now wait a second!" he fumed. "I never asked to come here! Where the hell do you get off telling me everything started because of my arrival?"

The fury in the young man's voice had no apparent effect on Nightwalker—as little ever did. "I am not blaming you directly, Matthew Logan," the Shadow-spawn replied. "I am simply trying to formulate an understanding of how simple it will be to break the walls between our existence and theirs and why that has come about.

"Your entrance," Nightwalker went on, "occurred during a normal tilting of the Wheel, when it was more or less closer to your world. That meant little—as it is a common action of the Wheel and an equally common action of Sparrill's to recruit, as it were, a new spellcaster. What happened to complicate things was your accidental—and not so accidental—discovery of the Jewel of Equilibrant. Since you were unable to keep its powers in check, the Wheel's already severe—but normal—tilt worsened. Add to that the resurrection of the Worm, and much of the Balance is gone. The Wheel is now tilting in the direction of the Dark at such a steep angle that summoning the Voices will be a relatively simple task since the ultimate Force is leaning that way already. Whoever is bringing the Voices into our realm will find the ordeal much easier than it should be."

"And it's all my fault," Logan sneered, sarcasm dripping from his words.

"I said nothing of the sort," Nightwalker replied.

You don't need to, Logan scowled to himself. That's one of the things I hate so much about this place . . . all the responsibility. It's really amazing to look back and see what little I had to do in Santa Monica. Survive, basically . . . but with all sorts of comforts: grocery stores, malls, Miller's Outposts, McDonald's. Others would do anything and everything for you. All you had to do was make the money to buy it. Here? Here survival wasn't the same thing as going to work and getting a paycheck. Here surviving meant fighting for freedom, fighting wild animals, fighting the weather, fighting for clothes to wear, fighting, fighting, fighting! Now stick yourself as the single most powerful person in the world and you've got *real* troubles. Not to mention responsibilities! Shit! I worked on a camera crew for a rinky-dink production company—I never wanted to be a Guardian for an entire land!

The young man's self-pity went momentarily slack as his blue eyes fell upon the morose Guardian beside him. Could be worse, Matthew, he told himself. Look at Nightwalker. He's a Guardian for an entire multiverse. His only purpose is to shoulder responsibility. That was the only reason he was created. How'd you like to be in his place?

Logan shifted the Bloodstone in his hands and felt a small tingle of pins and needles course through his palms, dimly reminding him of the disagreeing buzz that had plagued him when he had first arrived. At least the Heart still lived, he thought. Not like the personification in his dream—if that's who the red-and-silver lady was.

"You should try to go back to sleep," Nightwalker suggested, stepping quietly toward the fire. "This may well be the last night when the darkness is not tainted by something Darker."

A cold chill snaked its way up Logan's spine as he watched the Guardian of Shadow step away from the campfire and disappear along with the other shadows into the blackness beyond. He gave the Bloodstone another glance, searching for some kind of reassurance in its magical gleam.

There was no heartbeat.

A thin, white mist blanketed the campsite as Logan safely placed the Heart into one of his horse's saddlebags. A small nip of coldness in the misty morning air hinted at the coming of winter as the five gathered up their remaining supplies. A shiver crept past Logan's rather worn sweatsuit and brought goosebumps to his flesh as he pulled himself into the saddle of his yellow-and-green horse. Mara climbed into the saddle behind him, her slender arms entwining about his waist. Both trained their eyes on Nightwalker, who sat rigid in his saddle, his black flesh an obvious contrast to his horse's pure whiteness.

"They are not moving," the Shadow-spawn declared. "Whoever conjures forth the Voices remains stationary."

"That's good and bad," Moknay sneered, his grey eyes glinting like the steel of his daggers. "They're not moving away from us, but they're not moving any closer, either."

"Estimated location is west of the Ohmmarrious," Nightwalker added, invisible tendrils of sorcery probing the vastness of Sparrill.

Thromar swung himself into the saddle atop Smeea's back and frowned above his heavy, reddish-brown beard. "Then we've still got a ways to go."

Nightwalker clucked his mount forward. "I fear we will not make it," he proclaimed.

"Always the bearer of happy tidings," the huge fighter scoffed. "You know, Moknay, if I didn't know any better I'd say you learned all your grimness from Nightcreeper here."

Moknay pointed a menacing gloved finger in Thromar's direction. There was an unsettling fluidity to his motions. "I resent being compared to Nightwalker in any way, shape or form, Thromar," he growled. "Remember that."

Thromar released a low chuckle as he started Smeea forward. Moknay and Logan's horses followed, snorting mist from their nostrils. Logan watched as the trees and bushes of their campsite dropped behind them, their colors blending with the hazy fog. His horse only rode at a slow gallop, yet the blurring effect on the shrubbery was enough to pull a memory from the recesses of Logan's subconscious and remind him of his nightmare. An obvious shudder passed through the young man as he tried to blot out the terrifying image.

Mara's arms about him squeezed gently. "What's the matter?" she queried.

Logan shrugged, and a sharp flash of pain shot through the left side of his chest from a wound that had not quite healed. "I don't know," he replied. He tried to shut out the blurring foliage. "I suppose I shouldn't be so down. I mean, we did kill Gangrorz, right? And we found the Heart. Things should be all right—I should be going home now—but I'm not. Groathit's conjuring up these goddamn Voices and the most we can do right now is hope we reach him before he succeeds."

Mara's green eyes filled with wonder. "What makes you so sure it's Groathit?" she asked.

"I just know," Logan responded, teeth clenched. "He conjured Gangrorz back from the dead, didn't he?"

"Yes, but that doesn't mean he's the one conjuring the Voices."

Logan smirked. "No, it doesn't," he agreed, "but why wasn't he there when we confronted Gangrorz? Groathit's the kind of madman who would have wanted to watch us die."

"Maybe he knew something the Worm didn't," Mara suggested.

The young man shook his head. "I don't think it was anything like that," he said. "I just think Groathit wanted to find the most powerful weapon he could to use against me. Something Gangrorz said gave him the idea to conjure the Voices. That's why he wasn't there—he was already busy with plan two."

The tightened hold on Logan's waist transmitted more than just Mara's need to hold on. "But why?" she questioned, a horrified awe in her voice. "Does he hate you that much that he'd risk the entire world?"

"He hates me enough to destroy this whole multiverse," Logan retorted. "Look, you've never been around when Groathit's attacked, but you saw what he did the first time I came to Barthol's church. He's insane. He rants and raves and slobbers, and he's got the magic to back up most of his threats. I don't know. Maybe he's got some kind of paranoia or something. Maybe he just can't stand the fact that I'm supposed to be the next Smythe and I'm about ten years younger than him! Whatever his problem is, he'd rather see me dead than more powerful."

"Even if it kills himself?" Mara pressed.

Logan found himself nodding. "Yeah," he answered quietly, "even if it kills himself."

The pair went silent, and the morning was filled with the hoofbeats of the four horses. Sunlight began to break through the cover of mist, and Logan threw a swift glance behind him. Another day, he mused grimly. Another minute spent . . . another hour wasted. Perhaps all the time Groathit needed. So how much time did they have? And how much did they need?

Logan frowned as the fog started to disperse. Say, anybody know what time it is? he sardonically queried himself.

His name was Ridglee. He had spent a good portion of the last few weeks staring in a kind of enthralled revulsion at the tent that squatted off to one side. Apart from the rest of the camp, there was something about that tent that seemed to catch and hold the attention of all those who stayed there. Perhaps it was the darkness within, a blackness that could not be pierced by sun or torchlight. The only sounds that issued forth were faint, hungry burblings, accompanied occasionally by the scratchy voice of he who resided inside. Fortunately, the man whose tent this was had not ventured out for many days—which Ridglee did not mind in the least. He was not the least bit anxious to see the spellcaster with the spiky, blue-grey hair and blank, staring eye. He had heard rumors of what had happened to Joktan—how he had never returned when Vaugen had sent him for the wizard. How some of the servants had later found Joktan's sword outside the door to the sorcerer's chambers, half-fused into the floor. No, Ridglee was quite content if the magic-user wanted to hide away in his tent—now if only their Imperator would join him.

Ridglee jumped to his feet, tearing his eyes away from the ominous tent as confident footsteps sounded behind him. The opening to the Imperator's tent flew outward, and the Imperator himself strode out. The rising sun gleamed hideously off the blistered and red flesh, creating a disgusting contrast with the Reakthi commander's black chestplate. His right hand rested on the hilt of his sword, yet his left hand was clenched at his side, two fingers gone and the remaining three bent and gnarled. Fused flesh streamed down the Imperator's features, half closing one side of his mouth and drawing the other side back in a permanent sneer of hatred. Only the eyes remained the same. Only the dull grey eyes told who this man had once been—before his confrontation with the stranger and his band.

Imperator Vaugen waved his right hand imperiously in Ridglee's direction, and a number of the chestplated soldiers snapped to attention. There was a fire gleaming in the commander's eyes, Ridglee noticed. A determination that had returned to the steel of his gaze, and a half-smile stretched across the Imperator's distorted features.

A hoarse, dry voice rasping from a burned throat asked: "Has there been any movement?"

The Reakthi beside Ridglee, Trahurn, shook his head curtly. "No, sir," he responded. "There was a brief incantation performed during Ithnan's watch, but no other activity was reported."

The Imperator's smile widened, and his fused flesh stretched like clay. "He has not left the tent, then?" he queried.

"No, sir," the soldier replied.

Vaugen's eyes flicked to Groathit's tent, an icy fire burning in his gaze. "Very well, then," he rasped. His maimed hand waved them forward. "Withdraw your weapons and follow me."

Obediently, Ridglee extracted his sword and followed his Imperator. He caught the nervous glance Ithnan threw him, but could only shrug in reply. For days Vaugen had been warily eyeing the wizard's tent, growing more and more impatient as the troops remained stationary. They were—after all—in a foreign land, far west of their proper camp and stronghold. Should a troop of Guardsmen come upon them—or even a band of Sparrillians— the troops would be hard pressed to win. Supplies—and morale— would not last forever.

Vaugen stopped before Groathit's tent and waved his good hand. Trahurn threw open the entrance and backed away. Defiantly, the Imperator ducked inside, Ridglee and the others trailing him.

The light of the morning sun was instantly quenched as Ridglee stepped inside, and he felt his heart pound fearfully against his ribs as an unnatural cold pierced his armor. Squirming, writhing tentacles of blackness slithered and weaved about in the air, and the entire tent seemed about three times as long and two times as tall as it should have been. Somehow, space had been distorted, cramming a massive chamber into the dimensions of a tent. What extra room there was was filled with coiling, snaking tendrils of dark energy, and a foul, reptilian odor filled the musty air. More and more black serpents formed in mid-air, bubbling and gurgling like infants as they came into being. Pots and cauldrons churned with vile-looking fluids, and papers littered the floor and tables. Ridglee recognized the only book in the tent as the nefarious Darklight grimoire, recalling when the spellcaster had come demanding he be given the key to the library where it was kept.

A deep sense of foreboding built up inside the soldier as his eyes fell upon the scrawny figure in the far corner of the tent, hunched scribelike over notes and parchments. Thankfully, his back was to them, yet Ridglee could still see in his mind the sorcerer's wrinkled, taut face, his beaklike nose, and his eyes . . . The stories said that the stranger had wounded the spellcaster's left eye when Groathit should have been impervious to injury. Ever since, the wizard had been marred for life with a left eye that neither moved nor saw.

Imperator Vaugen clasped his hands behind his back and took a step closer to the wizard. "You have had all the time we discussed," he snarled, his rasping voice an animallike growl. "I will not keep my men here any longer. Come noon, we will be moving eastward."

Ridglee shivered as the bony shoulders beneath the silver chestplate jerked. "We will go nowhere," the wizard's scratchy voice reverberated throughout the tent. "We remain here."

Ridglee swallowed hard. Out of all his years as a soldier, he had only heard one other man talk to Vaugen like that and survive . . . but Imperator Agasilaus had long since been assassinated. Perhaps Groathit had the skill and sorcerous energies to back up his arguments, yet no sane man would defy a direct order from Imperator Vaugen when he had five armed soldiers behind him. The sorcerer wasn't that powerful.

Ridglee blanched. Was he?

The redness of rage began to scrawl itself across Vaugen's disfigured features. "You dare?" the Imperator wheezed. "When I give a command, I expect it to be followed without question."

"Then you are a most presumptuous fool," the wizard spat back.

The men in the tent were silent, listening to the pots and cauldrons belch and bubble. Ridglee felt perspiration form on his palm and around his sword hilt.

Vaugen neared the magic-user, grey eyes ablaze. "Listen to me, sorcerer, and listen well," he said. "I am your Imperator and this is my camp. So long as you are here, you will do as I say. You need what . . ."

"I need nothing from you!" Groathit snapped, still not facing his Imperator. The wizard paused. "You still do not understand what we strive for here, do you? Your feeble little mind cannot hope to fathom the . . . the ancient Darkness I seek to unleash. You are still caught up in your petty little games of conquest and treasure hunting. You are a fool."

Ridglee could feel the tension churning in the air between his deformed Imperator and the gnarled wizard. What good would mere weapons be against the sorcerer? Ridglee wondered. Vaugen surely did not think that five of them were enough to physically overpower the magician . . . there had been rumors about shape-shifting . . .

Oddly, the arrogance faded from Vaugen's voice. "We are wasting time," he whispered. "You said we would have power. You said we would not need Matthew Logan any longer. I have yet to see any proof."

The head of spiky, blue-grey hair turned slowly on the Imperator and his five men. Ridglee felt a skeletal hand snatch away his breath before it had left his lips. A wicked, insane grin was pulled across the wizard's face, drawing his skin tight along his skull. Triumph glistened in the wizard's good eye, yet it was the flare of living darkness that radiated from the socket of the left eye that sent Ridglee's mind reeling. The sorcerer no longer had an eye but had replaced it with a flickering, ebony globe of blackness. It crackled and sparked like flames as it burned in his socket, glaring in all directions at once.

"Here is your proof, my Imperator," Groathit mockingly replied. His left eye spat black sparks. "Now . . . we stay for another week or my next demonstration will not be so benevolent!"

Ithnan, Trahurn, and the others hurriedly scurried free of the accursed tent, eyes wild with fear. Only Vaugen and Ridglee remained inside, transfixed with a mixture of terror and awe at the spellcaster's jet-black eye and the churning, writhing darkness that continued to form out of thin air.

Twin daggers sparkled in Moknay's hands and his eyes flickered with a deadly sharpness as he watched the procession of uniformed Guardsmen march past. Thromar shifted in the brush next to him, his beady eyes following the Guards as they directed their mounts eastward. Moknay pushed the fighter's head down, eyes glinting.

"Keep your head down," the Murderer advised. "You've a knack for attracting trouble."

The large Rebel grinned with yellowing teeth. "Better to attract trouble than flies, Murderer," he responded good-naturedly.

Moknay shot Thromar an unfriendly glance and swung his gaze back on the troop of Guardsmen. Further to his left, Mara and Logan crouched in the foliage, watching with bated breath as the King's men went by. It would be just my luck, the young man thought darkly, to be discovered by Guardsmen. It wasn't bad enough that they had so little time to stop Groathit—or whoever—but the King's Guards had to still be searching for him, ignorant of the fact that the very world was in danger. To them, they still had a job to do, and an increasing number of soldiers had been passing their way.

"Word must have gotten around that we were near Lake Atricrix," Logan surmised.

"Or else they got word on the lake itself," Mara replied, her voice soft. "Your defeat of the Worm restored the waters."

Logan shrugged at the implied compliment, flinching as the wound the Worm had dealt him sparked upon his chest. Questioningly, Logan turned his eyes on Mara's chest, wondering how she fared. She had taken a blow meant for him and—for all purposes—

had been killed. It had been Logan and the Heart that had restored her, but the young man doubted his own abilities. Just how good a job had he done? Was it permanent? Was there still pain? How far could he trust magic?

The young man abruptly realized he wasn't so much inspecting the wound hidden beneath the priestess's clothing as he was admiring the contours of her body. With a slight twinge of red to his face, Logan turned back to the forest, tightening his grip on his Reakthi sword. Sometimes the wrong feelings and emotions spouted at the most inopportune of times.

"I've never liked hiding from Mediyan's dungheads and I'm not going to start now," Thromar was grumbling off to one side.

Moknay glided to his feet, his daggers instantly returning to his strap. "I think it's safe to continue," he remarked.

Logan pulled himself off his knees, brushing dirt from his sweat pants. He sheathed his sword and returned to his horse, pulling himself into the saddle. He helped Mara get on behind him, trying to ignore the warmth of her body against his. Nightwalker watched the four return from their vigil, his blank eyes gleaming whitely.

"They head eastward," the Shadow-spawn stated, "away from our goal."

Moknay sneered, and his upper lip and trim mustache turned upward. "Brilliant observation," he snorted. "I'm so glad you know the difference between east and west."

"This may cause complications," the ebon-skinned creature went on.

"Complications?" Thromar repeated, surprised. The fighter scratched his shoulder-length mane of hair. "Perhaps you were a bit too hasty, Murderer. Just what complications are you referring to, Nightcreeper?"

Darkling Nightwalker's face remained impassive; the distrust and dislike Thromar and Moknay held for the Guardian could not visibly dent the Shadow-spawn's composure. "A Balance must be set should we fail to stop the conjuration," Nightwalker explained enigmatically. "The factors will be to the east."

"I wish he wouldn't speak in riddles," Mara whispered into Logan's ear. "It makes me feel so damn stupid."

Logan grinned back at her. "Welcome to the club."

Dejectedly, Mara set her lower jaw on Logan's shoulder, pursing her lips unhappily. "But you don't understand, Matthew," she said. "I'm not a real fighter. The one thing I have as an advantage is all my studying—yet none of it has seemed to have helped. I can speak and read two other languages as well as our own, and it's done about as much good on our quests as a spear with no head."

The young man caught the familiar tone of inadequacy that tinged the priestess's words. "Hey," he remarked, "you can use your Binalbow, plus you helped get us out of Quarn's castle in one piece. You've done more than enough."

Logan grew silent as Mara drew her chin away from his shoulder, a slight twinkle in her emerald eyes. She really was concerned, the young man noted. This was his problem—his fault—and she really wanted to help him. But that was stupid . . . wasn't it? Back on Earth—in Santa Monica—people didn't act that way. They were too caught up in their own troubles. Logan had grown so used to keeping his problems to himself that he had always retreated in on himself when someone offered a helping hand. But Mara . . . There was something so very special about her that Logan wanted to . . . what? Burden her with his problems? No, not that. He wanted to make her happy, and, for all appearances, it looked like what would make her happy was to be able to share his troubles. To help relieve him of his burden . . . maybe just a little bit. But that *had* to be stupid, didn't it?

Or maybe, Matthew, a small voice sniggered in the back of his mind, maybe it really means you've fallen in love.

Logan couldn't help snorting at his own idealism. Yeah! he retorted. And monkeys might fly out of my butt!

A sudden, low whisper from Moknay drew the young man out of his thoughts. "Look!" the Murderer hissed.

Logan swung his head up and followed Moknay's pointing finger. A humanoid form lay in the shrubbery, still and unmoving. Its entire body was made up of crackling black energy, yet there seemed to be something wrong. The power was not active but dormant, as though it were dead. Where the two pinpricks of white light should have been, there was only darkness. Eyeless, the motionless Blackbody lay slung over a bush, its ebon arms thrown to either side.

Logan stepped off his horse, approaching the Blackbody in awe. That was something else that was wrong, the young man noted. Blackbodies passed through everything physical, yet this one lay draped over the foliage, as tangible as Logan or Mara. What the devil was wrong here?

"What's wrong with it?" Mara asked from Logan's horse.

Logan neared the still creature, blue eyes warily watching where its eyes should have been. Any second, he expected the white lights to blink back into being and the Cosmic being to reach out and send its jolting touch through his nervous system. But the Blackbody did not move as Logan stepped closer. A low humming sounded around the still form, probably coming from the inactive energy, but there was no movement.

Logan jumped as Darkling Nightwalker stepped up beside him, his own white eyes peering down at the unmoving figure of sorcery.

"It is dead," the Shadow-spawn declared.

"Dead?" exclaimed Logan.

"I didn't think that was possible," Moknay replied, trying to keep his composure so near to such powerful magic. "I thought it was only possible to destroy a Blackbody—I didn't think something like them could actually die."

Nightwalker watched the corpse sullenly before turning away and returning to his horse. "The Balance is gone; the Wheel may very well be on its side," he said. "In such a dire time, anything is possible."

The Wheel on its side! Logan blanched. Barthol had told him that when the Wheel tipped on its side, there was no hope of reversing it. Nightwalker couldn't be right! So maybe the Balance was gone since the Wheel was tilting so badly, but not on its side! That meant they had lost even before they had begun!

Tentatively, Logan reached out a quivering hand. The humming around the Blackbody's form seemed to seep into his fingers as he drew them closer, filling his hand and arm with a vibrating buzz of magic. Cold, hard marble touched Logan's palm as he settled his hand on the Blackbody's chest, once again showing himself that the creature's usual intangibility was gone. Trepidation grew in the young man's eyes as he moved his hand across the being's chest.

There was no heartbeat.

·2·

Voices

A magical window sparkled where, beforehand, there had been nothing but a blank wall. Beads of perspiration dotted the plump priest's forehead as he ran a hand through hair that was beginning to show signs of thinning. Faint sparks of luminance spattered the mystical chart, each accompanied by a bizarre, glowing symbol.

Squinting, Barthol leaned closer.

"Agellic's Gates," the stumpy priest breathed, "that's impossible."

Barthol turned away from the glimmering chart and looked down at the golden gemstone that rested on the table beside him. The color ran out of his face as he glanced at the other two in his study. The first figure was a towering mass of muscle, his rather monstrous-looking features pulled down in a perplexed frown of stupidity. The second was a diminutive, dark blonde clad in a green silk robe. A silver pendant of Lelah's Art dangled around her throat.

"What is it?" the blonde asked, her voice low so as not to break the tension in the air.

Barthol wiped droplets of sweat from his brow and stared back down at the gemstone. His reflection was thrown back a million times, and he could see a burning golden flame somewhere deep within the stone, yet he could not fathom its center. A faint flickering aura of yellow fire danced ghostlike about the surface of the Jewel.

"I'm afraid we should all be dead, Liris," Barthol declared, his voice filled with awe and fear.

Liris's blue eyes widened. "What?" she exclaimed.

The giant beside her blinked in puzzlement.

Barthol spun around and pointed a dimpled finger at his chart, but his eyes remained fixed on the glittering Jewel. "Somehow—

according to my charts, anyway—the Wheel is practically leaning on its side." Barthol held up a hand to prevent any outbursts from the priestess. "We've taken all the necessary precautions to see that the Jewel never leaked any energy, but the Wheel has tipped nonetheless. What's truly fascinating—in a horrific sort of way—is that it's stopped. Poised, even. It's just sitting there, on its side . . . waiting."

"Waiting for what?" Liris inquired.

The priest shrugged. "I haven't the foggiest," he admitted. "But what I don't understand is why there's been no reaction from the Jewel. We've had no discharges, no catastrophes . . . none of the telltale signs of unbalance."

Liris nervously fingered the pendant about her throat. "What can we do about it?" she wondered.

"That's why I've called you and Goar in here," Barthol responded, and his hand shook as he picked up a small tin from a nearby table. "I'm going to try to tap the Jewel—just briefly, mind you; I've no intention of winding up like Zackaron. Hopefully, I can find out who or what in the *Deil*'s stifling the Jewel—although I thought there was nothing this side of the multiverse that could do that. I'm going to want you to take this." He handed Liris the tin. "Should there be any trouble—even the tiniest hint of trouble—smother the Jewel with the powder that's inside. Goar, you will protect us should there be any physical trouble."

The bald giant stepped next to Barthol. "Goar do," it boomed, grinning with chipped and crooked teeth.

Barthol nodded once, inhaling deeply as he neared the glistening Jewel. By Harmeer's War Axe, the priest couldn't help thinking to himself, what in Imogen's name do I think I'm doing? I'm no spellcaster. I'm not even a magic-user. I've just a few tricks and divine privileges—why am I trying to tap the Jewel of Equilibrant?

Because, he answered himself, your charts show the impossible. Because you and everyone you know should be dead and dying. That's why you're tapping the Jewel. You've got to know what's going on—you've got to find out before everyone you love dies alongside the multiverse itself.

Nervously, Barthol stretched out a hand and lightly brushed the faceted Jewel. Gritty, tiny granules of dust flaked off the gemstone, residue from the last pinch of powder Barthol himself had put on. Only the flickering blue-black dust created by Zackaron could restrain the Jewel's energies when one was not a wizard—although

Barthol had heard the story of Logan and a certain talisman. But, then again, wasn't Logan destined to be the next Smythe?

The priest returned his thoughts to the gem before him and wiped off another layer of dust. Odd, he thought as he worked, the powder itself was a very fine mixture, yet the specks he removed were coarse, grainy motes. Some change in its makeup perhaps affected by the magic involved? he mused. Some chemical discharge quelled the sorcery?

Unexpectedly, a scream reverberated throughout the study, and Barthol leapt back, eyes wide. The grainy specks of dust came to life, sloughing off their false, blue-black disguise and transforming into a glaring ebony. Millions of tiny flakes shrieked from the Jewel's surface and from the interior of the tin, gathering together in the center of the room. Goar swung a massive fist toward the shrieking motes as they melded into a serpentine rope of jet-black sorcery.

"Goar protect!" Goar thundered.

Velvet power streamed from the forming snake of blackness, and Goar was flung bodily backwards. Liris released a frightened scream and dropped the tin of powder, narrowly ducking a small group of black clusters that howled down at her to join the larger mass. Barthol's own eyes were wide as he stepped back, staring as more and more of the ebony motes detached themselves from the Jewel.

"What are they?" cried Liris.

"Parasites," Barthol hurriedly surmised. "Some kind of energy parasite. They were covering the Jewel . . . not letting it react properly . . . like they purposely wanted to keep the Wheel's movements a secret!"

Goar pulled himself to his feet as the black helix expanded and grew. "Goar safeguard!" the giant rumbled, advancing on the blackness.

"No Goar!" Barthol warned, pushing Liris toward the exit. "We got to get out of here! Whatever these things are, they're no longer stilling the Jewel! Should there be any discharge . . ."

A troop of Guardsmen stationed in the northwest corner of Dentan gaped in surprise as the steepled church of Agellic erupted. An enormous column of golden-yellow flame shot upward, tearing through the marble roof and shattering the stellar windows. The castlelike battlements of the church crumbled into the cobblestone street, and dust spumed high into the air. Golden flickers of light remained dancing in the sky, like so many fireflies hovering over the destruction.

Among them shot a writhing stream of blackness that spun once, then vanished.

With the viscosity of molten rock, large bubbles broke the surface of the vile mixture and belched as they popped. Thick, fetid steam rose from the ruptured bubbles, filling the air of the tent with an almost corporeal stench of death. A warped smile drew across the wrinkled features of the Reakthi spellcaster as Groathit watched, enthralled, as the steam took substance, and his ebony eye flashed with malevolent energies.

The malodorous steam became darker, tinted with a blackness that slowly spread to encompass the rapidly forming creature. Something that may have been eye-stalks lifted from a bulbous head, and the mist congealed to create a shifting, writhing, worm-like body. Grotesquely, the sluglike being danced and hovered over the cauldron, its eye-stalks flickering in opposite directions. Abruptly, it trained its eyes on Groathit.

"You?" it asked, and its voice came from the bubbling, churning brew within the cauldron.

Groathit could barely contain his glee. "Yes, I," he replied. His left eye glistened like a black diamond. "Who are you?"

The maggot of smoke shifted, its eye-stalks twisting like tiny tentacles. "I am Servant to my Masters," it responded. "I am the envoy to those who speak in Darkness. I am the *Deil*, Ryth'ueyh; I have been sent to prepare you."

"Prepare me?" Groathit repeated, yet there was no haughtiness in his voice.

The miniature *Deil* spun dreamily through the haze and stink of the spellcaster's tent. "Know that I come before those who dwell in Darkness. It is my task to . . . approve. They who are my Masters are quite interested—for the stench of Purity is great in this multiverse. It seems my Brethren, he who is called Gangrorz, failed to fulfill his task."

The Reakthi wizard snorted in contempt. "Your brethren has most likely met his death a second time," he snarled.

Ryth'ueyh coiled and writhed as the cauldron boiled beneath it. "One of the many disadvantages of being the Servant rather than the Master," it rasped. "To work our powers and influence on the beings of your spheres we must become as you—steeped in flesh and mortality. For my Masters, it is not so."

The wicked, leering grin on Groathit's face widened. "And they are coming?" he asked eagerly.

The haze-formed *Deil* may have shrugged, or a gentle breeze may have wafted through its smoky figure. "Perhaps," was all it said. "It depends."

"Depends?" The Reakthi sorcerer screeched, his patience wearing thin. "Depends on what, beast? Speak!"

The *Deil*'s image blurred slightly. "On myself," it answered. "If I do not feel this world is ready for my Masters, they will not come. If I feel this world should belong to Darkness, we will use the door you have so thoughtfully opened."

"The Purity!" Groathit all but screamed. "What about the Purity? Your Masters hate such things as this! Sparrill is the very pinnacle of Beauty and Purity! Tell them! Tell your Masters this!"

Ryth'ueyh's voice seemed to hold an invisible grin. "I will consider it," the creature stated.

"Consider?" Groathit sputtered, his left eye blazing.

The smoke-form churned, and the eye-stalks jerked left then right. "Know you this, inferior organism," Ryth'ueyh declared. "In order to rule this realm, my Masters must keep the Balance aright. I have done this, shielding the movement of what you call the Wheel as it dipped ever closer to that which is the Darkness. After all, what good is a newly won kingdom when it has been ravaged by the war fought to possess it? No . . . my Masters will want this world and all its Purity intact, so I have taken it upon myself to use my Masters' magicks and keep stable the Wheel— allowing it to tip as far on its side as possible without destroying the Balance of this quaint little dimension." The *Deil*'s dark hue deepened. "This ploy was discovered what you refer to as a day ago. I lost a smaller version of myself in trying to escape."

Bony hands clenched at the wizard's sides, and his eyes dropped to glare at the floor. "No doubt to Matthew Logan," he growled, spittle dotting his lips. "Curse that insolent whoreson!"

"Petty rivalries?" Ryth'ueyh queried. "This is ill-befitting of one who wishes to serve the Darkness as I do." The misty worm floated gracefully away from the cauldron, limbs and feelers growing from its slowly changing form. "Now . . . there is one last step you must take before I leave to pass judgment on this world." The eye-stalks quivered. "Pick up that dagger . . ."

Hands trembling with excitement, the Reakthi wizard fumbled for the ceremonial dagger that lay nearby, grasping it in gnarled hands. His thin, bony frame shook as if on the brink of orgasm as he turned his eyes on the floating, shifting figure hovering before him.

"You must loathe and hate Purity as much as I," the *Deil* said, "and yet, you come from a world of both Light and Dark. You must show your worthiness by ridding yourself of all that is Pure and Untainted. Repeat these words: *Oud nkcy sylf ty ui to yei. V W'ewss gd'hcncy ewfnUd oud. W'ewss gd'hcency ewfnUd oud. W'ewss gd'hcncy. W'ewss.*"

Anticipation flowing through his veins, the Reakthi sorcerer repeated the alien words, forcing his tongue to make sounds that should have been impossible for the human throat. Easily, almost fluently, the strange chant spilled from his lips, filling the tent with his scratchy, grating voice. The pots and cauldrons joined in harmoniously, bubbling and gurgling in rhythm to the bizarre words. A wind picked up outside, beating at the tent flaps with a kind of otherworldly percussion. The frightened, muted voices from the soldiers outside dimly reached the spellcaster as he completed the incantation, and a wild fervor filled his body.

"Now," Ryth'ueyh commanded, "pluck out your right eye."

Muscles acted on their own accord—searing pleasure coursing through his elderly frame—and Groathit screamed in both ecstasy and agony as the dagger speared his normal eye. Blood streamed down his taut, wrinkled features as the sorcerer's uncontrolled hand dug the blade deeper, piercing the lens, severing the optic nerve, actually scraping the orbit of bone where the eyeball lay. With hideous, wet slapping sounds, the eye tore free, dripping with blood and vitreous humor. The rapture gripping the spellcaster released him as he turned his all-black, left eye on the churning, rotating *Deil* of smoke and steam.

"It is done," Groathit gasped, ignoring the crimson rivers that trickled down his face. "What now?"

Ryth'ueyh may have smiled. "We wait . . ." it said. Then added, "And listen."

The few clouds filling the sky were tinted red by the setting sun as Thromar dismounted, his eyes trained on the west. His reddish-brown hair seemed to glimmer in the light of the dusk as he turned away from the forest before them and faced his companions.

"I'd say we're about a day from Plestenah," he stated. "Maybe less. It's a pity we can't ride any faster."

"We'll ride our horses to death," Moknay grimly replied. "The damn things have taken us back and forth across Sparrill more than once in the last few months. Besides, Mara and Logan are riding tandem."

Thromar chuckled softly as he unstrapped his pouch of provisions from Smeea's saddlebags. "Concern for a handful of horses, Murderer?" he questioned. "That goes against your style."

Moknay grunted in reply. "Better to care for a horse than for a fellow man, Thromar," he retorted. "At least with a horse you know where you stand."

"And where you sit," Thromar joked.

The Rebel broke off a piece of bread from a loaf in his pouch and offered some to Logan and Mara. Mara nodded her thanks, but Logan declined. Instead, the young man turned away from where his companions were setting up camp and looked into the evening. *Two more days,* he mused gravely. *Two more days and we're only about halfway there. At the rate we're going, we'll never make it in time to stop Groathit—we'll probably get caught by Guardsmen anyway!*

Logan unexpectedly flinched as a blinding jolt of pain stabbed his right eye, sending his reflexes into a series of uncontrolled blinks. Eyes watering, the young man tried to hold his eyelid open to remove the object of his discomfort, wanting to blink all the more every time he felt his contact lens move. Something had gotten in his eye, he realized. It happened every so often. A speck of dirt, or some dust—something small enough to sneak in under his contact lens and begin to wreak havoc with his eye. And yet . . . the young man couldn't help but wonder about the suddenness of the assault, and the fact that—ever since he had come to Sparrill— his contact lenses had not given him any trouble.

Logan peered down at the limp contact lens caught between his forefinger and thumb. He didn't see any visible speck on the lens, but he wasn't about to replace it until he washed it with something.

Thromar was suddenly on his feet, a huge finger pointing in Logan's direction. "See?" he thundered. "See? Look! I *told* you he can take out his eye! I told you!"

Logan looked up wearily at the fighter, his vision half-blurred. *How something as simple as a contact lens could arouse such awe in the brawny fighter was beyond him,* Logan concluded. *Oh, well, probably the same thing as a pocket lighter to a caveman.*

Mara was suddenly standing beside the young man, her emerald eyes wide with surprise and amazement. "Matthew," she breathed, "what is that?"

Oh, God! Not Mara, too!

"It's my contact lens," the young man responded, a bit too tartly. "It's to help me see, that's all. Now will everyone stop making such a fuss over it?"

"What's it doing in your eye?" the priestess wondered.

"I *put* it there," Logan explained, trying to be patient but finding it difficult. "It . . . I just got something in it, okay?" He pointed at his horse. "Can you get me some water and stop staring?"

As Mara went to get a flask of water, Logan twitched as a sudden pulse of agony shot through his nerves and centered on the scar on his right shoulder. Muscles spasmed, and the young man felt his right hand tighten as pain brought agonizing life back into the wound on his palm.

"Matthew?" Mara queried, noticing his abrupt jerk.

Logan strained a breath through his teeth. "Ow, God," he hissed. "That hurt."

The young man tottered precariously on his feet as an insistent dizziness gripped him by the head. If Mara had not leapt to his side and placed steady arms before him, he would have surely pitched forward onto the ground.

"Friend-Logan?" Thromar questioned. "Are you well?"

Logan shook his head, feeling perspiration trickle down his face. "No," he gasped, "I'm not."

Moknay pulled himself to his feet, a dagger in either hand. "Where's it coming from?" he asked, recognizing the young man's abrupt sickness.

Logan brought a hand up to his forehead. "It's not . . . coming from anywhere," he answered, taking in another gulp of air. "It's my shoulder."

Moknay blinked. "Your shoulder?"

"The crossbow wound?" Mara asked, concerned.

Logan nodded. His eyes were still blurred by tears of pain, yet the agony in his right side was starting to diminish. A faint twinge of discomfort continued to pulse through his temples.

Mara's hand gently touched Logan's cheek. "Take off your shirt," she ordered. "Maybe we should look at it."

"No," Logan responded. "No, it's all right. It just . . . flared up."

Thromar stepped nearer, scratching his beard in worry. "It was a rather hurried dressing," he commented. "Perhaps Mara's right. It may have become infected."

Logan raised his head as the sickness abated. He wiped a river of perspiration away that had tickled his nose as it streamed down his face. "No, really," he said. "I'm all right."

"Are you sure, friend?" Moknay queried, the daggers gone but the caution still in his eyes. "You've suffered from spells like this before."

The unexpected fever and illness enshrouding Logan's brain gradually departed, leaving in its wake a disoriented turmoil buzzing through his mind. "Look, I'm okay," he tried to console his friends. "Nightwalker magically healed the wound, anyway. It can't be infected."

Daggers glistened across his chest as Moknay spun about. "Where is Nightwalker?" the Murderer inquired.

"He was right . . ." Mara started.

The priestess's voice trailed off as her green eyes scanned the foliage. There was no visible trace of Nightwalker or his white horse, nor could Thromar spot any clues in the surrounding vegetation. Nightwalker had—as he had often done before—mysteriously and completely vanished.

Blue eyes filled with confusion, Logan glanced about him. Nightwalker was gone, he noted. So why did he have such a bad feeling concerning the Shadow-spawn's disappearance? As fleeting as the dawn and as silent as the dusk . . . that's what everyone had said about Nightwalker, wasn't it? Why should the young man feel such an overwhelming trepidation concerning the Guardian's abrupt exit? Was it the fact that Nightwalker had healed Logan's wounded shoulder and hand? Did it stem from there? And the unexpected return of the pain? And why the hell couldn't he see out of his right eye?

"Holy shit!" the young man shouted, jumping back, arms spread wide. "I've lost my contact lens!"

"Your what?" Thromar wondered.

"My lens! My lens!" Logan howled, scanning the area below him frantically. "I must have dropped it when my shoulder acted up!" The young man dropped to his knees, his fingers sifting through the blades of grass. "Come on! You've gotta help me find it!"

"I don't even know what we're looking for," Moknay admitted.

"Friend-Logan's eye," Thromar replied, also crawling about on the carpet of greenery.

"Logan still had both his eyes, Thromar," the Murderer sneered.

"Yeah, but I can't see without it!" Logan confessed.

Mara unexpectedly interrupted the search, standing behind Logan with her head cocked to one side. There was an intense look of concentration on her lovely features as she strained to pick out something through the night. "Listen!" she demanded.

The force of the priestess's command instantly silenced the three men looking for the contact lens. Wonderingly, the trio lifted their heads, ears sifting out the sounds of the coming night. Only after a few moments, Logan resumed looking for his lost lens, figuring the priestess had imagined something. And, besides, what was more important than finding his lens?

That was when he heard the rumbling.

A few birds roosting in nearby trees took to the air with high-pitched screams; a gathering of insects ceased chirping. Trees began to shiver in an unfelt wind, and the rustling of shrubbery filled the forest as the deep-throated growl continued to increase in volume.

"I've got a bad feeling about this," Moknay murmured suspiciously.

"So did friend-Logan," remarked Thromar.

Unexpectedly, there was a terrified scream from everywhere and nowhere as the growing rumble became an ear-shattering yowl of energy. The leather saddlebags of Logan's horse flamed with a muted crimson glare, drenching the surrounding forest in a blood-red flare. A resounding crackle of power—like that of lightning—split the evening sky and echoed a thousand times over. A harsh, wicked gale as freezing as an arctic storm abruptly shrieked through the forest, burning Logan's eyes and stinging his unprotected face. Whispers seemed to fill the heavens—muted, bass, unintelligible raspings as if a hundred people were all buzzing in low tones among themselves.

Suddenly, the whispers became unified, and Logan felt Mara's hand on his shoulder, her long nails gripping his flesh in fear as the wheezing, asthmatic voices were abruptly understandable:

Rejoice. We have come.

Thunder shattered the heavy cloud cover above the mountains, and rain pelted the Hills of Sadroia. A growing, ominous roar of power sounded far to the east, creating an almost electric charge of fear in the sheets of water cascading from the sky. Screams echoed across the mountains as numerous mockeries of life scuttled, crablike, out of the open and into the multitude of cracks and crevices dissecting the hills. Only one figure remained, detached

from the rainwater that poured down his lean frame. His dark,
wild eyes were turned heavenward, and his brown, grey-streaked
hair clung to his scalp as more rain descended from the sky.
A frigid, deathly cold gale howled through the storm, hurling
raindrops westward, trying its best to dislodge the form that was
stanced atop the mountaintop. Even through the rain and clouds,
the dark eyes could see the sorcerous rent in the land—feel the
agonizing pain that burned up and down the borders of Sparrill.
And Zackaron could do nothing but watch . . . and weep.

Rejoice. We have come.

The chamber was in total chaos. High-pitched shrieks and terrified barks filled the room, starting off chain reactions of echoes
that rebounded up and down the underground structure. A hundred
little forms scampered around the chamber, gangly arms waving
and flailing above their heads. Little eyes, usually filled with
mischief, sparked with desperate fear as the monkeylike creatures
howled their fright. Thunderous agony roared outside, and the small
beasts screamed and ran. Only two of the little creatures remained
motionless, their black eyes tinged with despair. One's fur had gone
completely grey with age, and its dark eyes had lost some of their
glitter. The other was slightly larger, his pointed fangs just barely
visible beneath his brown fur. He grasped a dagger tightly in his
humanoid hand, yet he knew it was a useless weapon against what
transpired outside.

Munuc felt a shiver of terror race down his spine as a rasping
chorus of voices drowned out the howling of his own kind.

Rejoice. We have come.

Danica looked up from the wrinkled parchment, her narrow,
almost villainous-looking eyebrows knitted together in befuddlement. What sounded like a storm was brewing outside, yet she
knew from her own mystic foretelling that Plestenah was not
in for any ill weather for at least another two weeks. So what
constituted the thunderlike rumble from outside?

Questioningly, the sorceress got to her feet and walked to a
window. Darkness was steadily encroaching upon the town as
the sun dipped lower behind the western hills. Confused, Danica
returned to her worktable and passed a slim, delicate hand over
a glass orb. The globe glistened dully, faint sparks of magic
leaping from its surface. Unexpectedly, as Danica's hand finished
its mystical pass, what sounded like a shriek of lightning erupted

from outside, and the orb exploded. Blackness poured from the shattered globe, spattering shards of glass across the workroom. Danica emitted a startled shout as she threw herself backwards, trying to avoid the whizzing fragments of glass. Faint, whispering voices seemed to infiltrate her chamber as the blackness shifted and coiled itself together before passing through the roof of Fraviar's tavern.

Danica pulled her eyes away from the departing darkness and looked at her right hand. Large shards of glass had embedded themselves in her palm, and blood welled up around them. An incomprehensible fear shot through her system as she caught the faint glimmer of ebony that remained alive in the pieces of glass impaling her hand.

Rejoice. We have come.

Screaming, the wind rushed past the castle battlements, flinging its rage at the two figures overlooking the southern portion of Sparrill. In the lingering rays of sunlight, black and white metals gleamed with commanderlike pride, yet the faces of those who wore the chestplates reflected no pleasure. The clean-shaven Reakmor cleared his throat nervously, training his eyes momentarily on his leader beside him.

"Near as we can tell, sir," he said, "the disturbance seems to be originating from the foothills north of the Lathyn Mountains—close to Imperator Vaugen's fortress."

Imperator Quarn nodded, lost in his musings. His hand unconsciously stroked his silver goatee. "Yes," he agreed, "this bears Vaugen's stench." The Imperator abruptly turned on his partner, pale eyes flickering. "Learn all you can about the actual nature of this disturbance, Osirik, then report back to me at once."

Reakmor Osirik gave his commander a curt nod. "Yes, sir," he responded and militarily turned on his heel.

A sudden wave of darkness materialized far to the south, like a blanket of clouds or mist, yet it had no texture. Osirik froze as the sheen of blackness formed wraithlike over the Lathyn Mountains, writhing and surging like an angry sea. Semitransparent tendrils of ebony stretched westward, and the larger mass of darkness followed, undisturbed by the biting gale that shrieked past the castle walls.

"Sir . . ." Osirik started, turning back to face Quarn.

The Imperator held up a stiff hand, silencing the Reakmor without words. An expectation filled Quarn's lightly colored eyes

as the wind screeched like heralding trumpets.
  Rejoice. We have come.

Toadlike eyes blinked in wonderment as the rounded head poked
free of the shrubbery, saliva drooling from its rounded mouth. A
slender tongue darted around jagged fangs as the creature craned
its bulbous head about, its large, amphibious eyes glimmering with
excitement. Another of the monsters looked up from its hiding
place amongst the foliage, eyes filled with a malignant fire.
  They were coming, the Demons sensed. *They. They* who were
even more powerful than the Creator. *They* who had, in fact,
created the Creator as he had created them.
  And *they* were coming.
  Triumphant, soul-wrenching screams issued forth from the circular mouths as the Demons launched themselves into the coming
night, eagerly hurrying to the call of the Darkness.
  Rejoice. We have come.

Ridglee sprang to his feet, battle skills honed after many years
of service. His Reakthi blade felt comfortable in his left hand, and
his right hand flashed for the dagger at his side. A freezing wind
roared through the camp, threatening to uproot tents and knock
down people. Faint, whispering voices seemed to ride upon the
gale—unintelligible, deep, as if the words they spoke were too
important for Ridglee to hear and make sense of. Others of his
troop were on their feet, staring wild-eyed toward the east as if
they expected something to rise up out of the forest. Ridglee knew
better. He had been with the army too long to expect something
of a physical nature. He knew magic when he smelled it, and this
carried the stink of sorcery.
  The Reakthi noted that Imperator Vaugen had ventured outside
his tent to observe the sorcerous goings-on, his dull grey eyes
alive with his old determination and anger. Ridglee was unable
to decipher the expression on his commander's face, so distorted
was the flesh of his features. Instead, the soldier turned back to his
companions, his experienced eyes searching across the campsite
for whatever might come about from this magic.
  The sudden raspings on the gale became unified, speaking in
one voice yet many.
  Rejoice. We have come.
  A sudden movement behind the soldier caused Ridglee to wheel
around, weapons ready. Surprise flashed across his mind as he spied

Groathit arrogantly step free of his tent, his dark robe billowing in the scream of the wind. Dried rivulets of what appeared to be blood cracked and flaked down the sorcerer's right cheek, and Ridglee felt his stomach knot as he realized the wizard's right eye socket was as empty as the deserts of Magdelon. What may have been a misty slug hovered in the air behind the magic-user.

Groathit turned his flaring black eye on Vaugen, and a nefarious smirk played across his lips. "Well, Imperator," he queried sardonically, "did I not tell you to have patience?"

Vaugen scoffed at the sorcerer's confidence. "Patience?" he barked, and his voice was as brittle as ice. "Patience for what, wizard? I see nothing. Nothing save simple illusions of smoke and disembodied voices on the wind capable of an apprentice!"

The smoky form of Ryth'ueyh floated closer to the deformed Imperator. Its voice came from within Groathit's tent. "Voices they may be," it replied, "yet they are more."

Ridglee whipped around as a curtain of absolute blackness suddenly moved in over the camp: transparent . . . then opaque; intangible . . . then tangible. A few of Vaugen's younger recruits released shrieks of complete terror, and two men actually swooned from the sight. Ridglee, himself, fought down the preternatural madness that tried to take control of his mind . . . that tried to send him running into the night. In all his years as a soldier, he had never run, and he would not start now.

He gave the forest behind him a nervous glance. Besides, he told himself, night was falling—there could be no escape from the blackness now.

The mist-formed *Deil* turned its hazy eye-stalks on the sheet of blackness swirling and converging over the camp. "They are the Darkness," it went on. "And they are the Voices that speak in that Darkness."

A frightening smile pulled across the creature's face as its misty, steam-forged form began to solidify.

"And they are here."

·3·

Respite

The four were frozen with fright, heads lifted skyward as the natural darkness of night dogged the heels of the unnatural mist of blackness. Tiny particles of ice skittered across the forest floor, blown in by the freezing wind. Trees rustled and swayed as the gale tore through them, their branches creating high-pitched whistles as they severed the wind. No animal sounds reached the ears of the four, and Logan felt a shiver of dread rush through his system as he realized the natural sounds of Sparrill had once again fallen silent.

"We've failed," Thromar whispered, his voice ringed with shock.

A faint spark of resistance shone in Moknay's grey eyes. "We don't know that yet," he replied, although his tone denied his own statement.

Mara's hand remained tightly clamped on Logan's shoulder. "But you heard them," she said. "You heard them just like we did."

"I heard something," Moknay snapped, his fear of magic building to a tremendous height inside him. "I don't know what it was I heard, but I just heard something. Hearing things does not necessarily mean we've failed."

A deep voice sounded behind the Murderer: "No, it does not."

Logan jerked about, squinting his right eye to filter out the fuzziness. Darkling Nightwalker suddenly stood behind the quartet, his white horse nervously pawing the ground behind him. And yet, Logan noted, there was something wrong. A weary, haggard expression was drawn across the Shadow-spawn's face, and deep lines etched on his features told of an injury he had suffered internally—reminding Logan of the crimson woman in his dream. But there was more, the young man's half-blinded vision informed him. There was something else.

Then he realized it: Nightwalker's stark white hair and blank, snow-white eyes were darkening, showing the very faintest hints of grey as the coming night deepened.

"Where have you been?" Moknay demanded, and Logan momentarily feared the Murderer would demonstrate his surname.

"Elsewhere," was Nightwalker's response.

The Shadow-spawn stepped into the half-set-up camp, his movements sluggish. His tainted eyes scanned the four in front of him, and Logan felt cold despair fill his stomach at the look that was reflected in those eyes. "We must keep moving," the Guardian suddenly advised.

Logan and his friends could only blink, none of them moving.

Nightwalker spun on them, anger briefly fueling his motions. "Are you deaf?" he roared furiously. "I said we must keep moving!"

Logan jumped back as if trying to escape the ferocity of the command by physically moving aside. He had never seen Nightwalker display any anger before—hopelessness, yes, but never anger. He noted the same reaction showed on the faces of his companions as they mutely watched the darkskinned Guardian of Shadow.

None of the four made any move to mount their horses.

A sigh escaped Nightwalker's ebon lips, and he turned away from the motionless quartet. They deserved an explanation, the Guardian knew. If at least that much, they deserved some explanation.

"The Voices are here," the Shadow-spawn announced. "The spellcaster Groathit succeeded in bringing them into this dimension. Yet the wound goes far deeper than I thought. They have control over the Wheel, suspending it before it reaches its side, stopping it before the Balance is completely eradicated. Perhaps it was the only way they could arrive without destroying our entire multiverse, but, now that they have arrived, they will seek out the one thing that they have sensed even beyond their own dimensional wall."

"What's that?" Logan queried, and his voice quavered.

Nightwalker's grey-white eyes settled unnervingly on the young man. "You are holding it," he declared.

Although his hands were empty, Logan instantly knew what Nightwalker referred to and swung his half-focused eyes on his horse and the leather saddlebags at its side. The Heart, Logan mused. The Voices would go immediately for the Heart—just as they sent Gangrorz to do all those years ago.

"The emissions of the Heart are very distinct to the Voices," Nightwalker explained, "yet, just as it is for all others, the actual location of the Heart is very hard to detect. If we keep moving—remaining hidden—we may have a chance of surviving to the next tier."

"Next what?" Thromar blurted. "By Brolark, Nightwalker! We've failed! The Voices are here! Sparrill, Denzil . . . this whole damned world is defenseless! I'm afraid we stand no chance against such a Force even with Agellic on our side!"

Nightwalker's white-grey eyes touched the Rebel momentarily, and the Shadow-spawn felt the fighter's grief. Thromar was a warrior—a fiercely loyal fighter whose only true love was that of his land and of much of her people. He had risked many things, acquired many terrors, spilled much of his own blood to see that Denzil and Sparrill remained free—but now the battle had supposedly gone beyond the Rebel's skills. Now the war was a war of Forces where one side was not even going to show.

"There is much you do not understand," Nightwalker said, and there was no insulting, condescending tone in his voice. "Our foes are Voices . . . those that we hear whispered in the Darkness . . . yet look around you." Nightwalker waved an ebon hand through the darkening night, and a tiny bit of white returned to his eyes. "Voices we may hear, and Darkness we may see, yet neither can we touch . . . nor can they touch us. Both Light and Dark are insubstantial, and that third Force, that which is called Shadow, that too is not substantial. And yet, I was made to protect that which was spawned from the war between Light and Dark, so, until the Darkness is made physical, we need not fear them. It is their Servants who will pursue us; their *Deils* and Demons who will hound us. So long as we have the Heart, we have hope; so long as we are not discovered by the Masters, we have a chance."

"Chance? What chance?" barked Moknay. "What is this chance you keep talking about?"

"It lies to the east," Nightwalker responded.

The Murderer sneered at the elusive answer. "That's what you said before," he snarled, eyes glittering in the night.

"And that is all I shall say," Nightwalker retorted, "for now." The Shadow-spawn turned his tainted eyes skyward, staring into the stars. "If you will recall, Murderer," he went on, "I mentioned to you outside Agasilaus's fortress that there are certain future events which cannot be talked about for fear of altering such an event from actually happening. This is one of them—therefore, I can say no more."

The Guardian of the third Force pulled himself into his horse's saddle and looked down at the four gathered below him. "We must hurry," he said.

Logan remained still as Nightwalker's grey-white eyes trained on him. So many thoughts were rampaging through the young man's mind . . . so many fears. *So what have I gotten myself into now?* he asked himself. *It wasn't bad enough I had to fool around with the Cosmic Balance. Then I had to go in search of the land's magic itself; now I'm confronting a completely* other *Force from outside the Wheel's influence and all I've got to fight it with are a magical Bloodstone, a yellow-and-green horse, and a handful of friends.*

The young man's blue eyes flicked from person to person, reading the expressions that he saw there. Nightwalker wore a mask of concealed pain, trying to override his agony with a mien of determination. Thromar's heavily bearded features reflected great sorrow, yet something set a spark of hope twinkling in the Rebel's tiny eyes. Moknay's face was as grave as it always was, and his distrust of magic had dampened the usual sharp edge to his glare. The Murderer's own eyes were fixed on Logan, and an obvious hesitation showed in his half-stanced pose. So, too, was this hesitation evident in Mara, her green eyes aswirl with horror and her grip still tight on Logan's shoulder. They were all waiting for his response—for him to make the next decision. For him to bear the weight of the world on his shoulders.

Logan turned away from his companions as a familiar old anger started to burn in his breast. "I've gotta find my contact lens," he grumbled, and resumed his search although the night obscured the ground.

"You must do without it," Nightwalker shot back. "Even in such Cosmic turmoil, there is still a balance being set betwixt the major Forces."

Logan jerked his head up, eyes narrowed. "What?" he shouted in disbelief. "Because I lost my contact lens?"

"Know also that the Reakthi spellcaster, Groathit, has been robbed of half his vision," Nightwalker replied. "So long as a Balance exists, so do we."

Balance, Logan snarled, the rage inside him almost unbearable. Always some kind of fucking Balance . . . or Unbalance! Always something that supposedly makes some kind of goddamn Cosmic sense! Well, I've had it with this bullshit! Why don't I just take the Heart, pull out some magic, and send myself home? Or make Nightwalker do it? This isn't my world—it never was—and it never will be! I don't belong and I *can't* belong! I'm too used to cars, and traffic lights, and fast food restaurants, and lousy television shows! It's a wonder I've lasted this long as it is! It's a real, goddamn wonder . . .

The young man from Santa Monica listened as the anger in his thoughts gradually faded. A wonder, he repeated, gentler. A real, goddamn wonder.

Blue eyes—half-blurred with astigmatism—scanned the four figures around him. There's your wonder, Matthew, he told himself scornfully. There's your goddamn survival. These people. These . . . idiots who were so damn loyal! So damn helpful. There was no miracle to blame, or hidden secret to uncover. These four—and countless others—had been Logan's means of survival in a world where he did not belong. He couldn't leave them to face the Darkness alone. He just couldn't. He had to repay them that much; try to settle everything he had unsettled since coming there.

And Groathit! The young man's hands reflexively pulled into fists. Groathit was dead meat! He had always been at the root of Logan's troubles—always screwing things up for the young man when it finally looked like things were getting better. Well, Groathit was gonna pay. So he's got some more help—big deal! We beat the last errand-boy he sent after us, and we'll beat the next! And we'll keep beating them until I finally get a shot at that Reakthi bastard . . . and I'll do to him what I did to Gangrorz. I'll make him swell and pop, and I'll watch him explode all over the place. And then—then!—I'll go home.

Logan pulled himself out of his thoughts, training his half-focused vision on the dark Guardian. "Where to?" he queried.

Nightwalker smiled fleetingly. "Eastward."

The young man pulled himself off the ground and gave his companions a cursory glance as he stepped toward his horse. "So?" he questioned them. "What are you waiting for? Engraved invitations? Let's go to wherever Nightwalker says we have to go, then we'll head back and kick Groathit's ass from here to Santa Monica!"

A grim smile pulled across Moknay's features. "Here, here!" he seconded, and leapt into the saddle of his black-and-grey stallion.

The small, batlike bird spread out its leathery wings and brought itself down lightly on the stone walls of the palace, its taloned feet anxiously clawing the sides. A small piece of parchment strapped to its leg scraped the palace wall as the tiny creature paced back and forth across the battlements, its round, lidless eyes peering at the human forms around it.

The Guardsman on duty set aside his pike and snatched the winged beast off the parapet. He hurriedly untied the paper at its leg before releasing the scaly creature where it hopped back to the wall and glared at the humans with wild indignation.

"What's it say?" the Guard's partner asked at his shoulder.

The Guardsman reading the note went pale, licking his lips as he replied: "You'd better alert Viscount Faerlice. The king's not going to enjoy this."

"Why?" the partner wanted to know. "What's it say?"

A sudden voice sounded haughtily behind the two. "I believe that is information neither of you should know."

The two Guards turned about, eyes wide as they spied the royally cloaked figure stanced behind them. Dark brown eyes flared under a brow marked with scars, and a hand cuffed with lace shot out for the tiny note in the Guardsman's hand.

"Duke Paskal!" the Guard exclaimed. "I . . . Honestly, sir, I have been given permission! Viscount Faerlice wanted all messages screened so His Highness was only disturbed by the more serious reports."

Duke Paskal trained his dark eyes on the two Guardsmen, glaring at them as he would a lesser beast. Had the two men perhaps been dogs, Paskal surely would have kicked both just to hear them yelp.

"Indeed," Paskal sneered, and he snatched the note from the nervous Guard's hand. Dark eyes swiftly scanned the words. "And this you would classify as serious?" he queried contemptuously.

The first Guardsman blinked at the duke's question. "Something happens in Sparrill," he sputtered. "Commander Eldath feels it may very well be a Reakthi ploy or something worse . . . possibly concerning the Outsider. He requests aid, so shouldn't we . . ."

"No, we should not," Paskal interrupted, enunciating each word carefully as if the Guard had trouble hearing. "You are a Guardsman, louse, and your task is to guard—not to think. *I* will decide what to do . . . whether or not we shall send any aid to our men in Sparrill. And from here on in, any messages you receive will be brought to me—unopened—and not to Viscount Faerlice. Is that understood?"

The two Guardsmen lowered their heads, unable to look the duke in the eye. "Yes, sir," they meekly responded.

"Good," Duke Paskal retorted. "Now finish your watch."

The batlike bird watched the duke stalk off, scratching itself every so often with its beak. It didn't understand the sounds that had spilled from the human creatures' lips, nor did it care to. It had been created—as had all in its roost—by the court spellcaster to serve as sorcerously swift message-carriers to and from Magdelon. What the strange human things did afterward was not their concern, only this was the first time the strange batlike creature had ever seen one of the humans crumple up the message it had brought and fling it over the edge of the palace wall.

A cold desert wind snatched the parchment in mid-flight and swept it away into the night.

Logan peered through the darkness at his watch and frowned at the three-fourths of blackness that held sway over the display. He couldn't tell how much time had gone by, yet foam flecked the reins of his horse and some of the stars had faded from the sky. There seemed to be a little light coming from the east, but it could not be sunrise. This light was too dim—almost filtered—to be sunlight, and yet . . .

"What time is it?" the young man questioned out loud, and a sudden shock of déjà vu struck his system as he remembered his dream.

"I surmise it is close to dawn," replied Nightwalker.

"Close to dawn?" Thromar boomed. "Impossible! The sky's as dark as . . ."

" . . . the Voices themselves?" Nightwalker suggested the comparison.

The Rebel was silent.

Darkling Nightwalker's grey-tinted eyes fixed on Logan. "They are here, and they will begin to make this multiverse more to their own liking—starting with this land first," he explained. "Fear not, the sun will rise; yet, every day the Darkness is with us, the light of day shall grow weaker and weaker until it is finally blotted out for good. That is when I shall die."

Moknay glanced at the Shadow-spawn. "You'll die?" he repeated. "Are you saying you know when you'll die?"

"Not the exact time," Nightwalker responded, "but the precise moment, and that, as Matthew Logan already knows, is when this dimension belongs entirely to Darkness."

"But that's what we're setting out to prevent," Mara replied, her voice sounding directly in Logan's ear.

Nightwalker did not seem uplifted by the priestess's comment. "Yes," he agreed, sullenly, "this is what we're setting out to prevent."

Logan frowned at the Guardian's pessimism. Not that I'm being a hypocrite, the young man informed himself. I'm as pessimistic as hell, but now's just not the time for it. We're surviving on what might be a lie, and we don't need any extra pessimism to shatter that lie out from under us. Our chances are too slim to keep reminding ourselves of it—there's too little hope to begin with to lose it all to a sudden bout of dark thoughts.

The young man squinted ahead of him at the dark forest, trying to filter out the bad vision of his right eye and concentrate on the clearer vision of his left eye. How blurred the entire forest looked, the young man observed, and another shiver ran through him as he recalled his dream. He had to stop thinking about that dream, he told himself. It was just another kind of pessimistic thought that didn't help them any. They had to think of the Worm and his defeat at their hands, and Logan's sorcery at bringing Mara back.

Sorcery. The young man paused. What about sorcery? Why don't I feel that headache-causing buzz of disagreement anymore? Because the Voices are here? Are they dampening it even more so than Gangrorz did? Maybe. So why do I think there's more to it than just that?

Thromar held up a meaty hand, barely visible through the unnatural darkness of the coming dawn. "Hold up," the fighter ordered, drawing in Smeea's reins.

Logan reined in his mount, feeling Mara press against him as he leaned back. Before him flowed the clear waters of the Roana, reflecting the strained sunlight that rose from the east. Waterplants and flowers bobbed gently on the surface of the river, and the Bloodstone in Logan's saddlebag began to pulse with a rhythmic glow of crimson. The sky seemed to imitate that color, turning a deep red as the sun fought the blackness for dominance.

Logan noted Thromar was glaring unhappily at the sky.

"We'll have to cross her," the Rebel muttered to himself, "and it's not the first time we'll have to keep an eye on the sky above us."

Logan felt his head nod in agreement as a memory flashed through his mind: an earlier pursuit, round-mouthed Demons screaming after them. And there was another . . . Another memory that constantly resurfaced at this beautiful river—a memory that never failed to dampen the natural splendor of the Roana and cause Logan's chest to ache with guilt and sorrow.

The memory of Druid Launce.

Logan shook his head as if to clear the memory from his mind. Why didn't I trust him? he moaned to himself. Why didn't I believe he wanted to help? And why can't I remember the good things? Why do I only remember the bad? Guilt doesn't help anyone—certainly not Launce . . . not now.

The cold, icy wind howled as Thromar jumped from Smeea's back. "I suggest we cross her on foot—as quietly as we can," the fighter mused. "What do you think, Murderer?"

Moknay scanned the length of the river with eyes as grey as his daggers' blades. "It'll cost us some dry clothes, but it's the surest way of not being seen." He sprang off his own mount. "I'll go across first with the horses; the rest of you follow in groups of two."

Mara slid off Logan's horse, the young man following. They watched from the protection of the forest as Moknay slid into the crystal waters of the Roana, leading the four horses behind him. Logan clung tightly to the Heart, having removed it from its saddlebag, and Mara directed her Binalbow skyward, her green eyes searching for any indication of movement from the blood-red heavens. Gentle splashings accompanied the Murderer and the horses as they waded out into the river and quietly emerged on the opposite bank. Smeea shook her wet mane indignantly but remained silent.

A swift hand signal from Moknay sent Logan and Mara into the water. Cold instantly shot through Logan's legs, and he had difficulty holding his supplies above his head without visibly shivering. He tried to suck in his own breath as he waded further into the river, the icy waters reaching up to his stomach. The wet fabric of his sweatsuit wasn't helping any as it became saturated with the freezing waters and clung damply to the young man's skin. Cautiously, Logan threw a half-blurred look at the brightening sky above him, saw nothing, and reluctantly forged ahead.

The water was up to Logan's neck when he heard the warning whisper from Moknay. Immediately, the young man halted. Two dark shapes glided overhead, silhouetted by the struggling, blood-red sunlight. There was no mistaking the sticklike limbs and bulbous heads as the Demons swept over the river and continued on.

Logan remembered to breathe as he started to clamber out of the river, grateful to be free of that cold. All at once, the wintry wind blew over them and Logan feared his sweatsuit had turned to ice. Moknay handed the pair heavy blankets as he motioned Thromar and Nightwalker forward. Teeth chattering, Logan snatched the blankets from the Murderer's hands and hurriedly draped one over his wet frame. Swearing that his face was turning blue, the young man stepped into the safety of the trees and sat down, trying to control the shudders that ran through his body. He was somewhat surprised when Mara sat beside him.

"I think we're going to freeze," the priestess shivered, the ends of her long hair damp with water.

Logan was able to fight his chattering teeth to momentarily grin. "I know what you mean," he replied.

A sudden idea popped into the young man's mind which he almost cast out as absolutely ridiculous. At the last minute, he stopped himself. What's so ridiculous about it? he asked himself. It'd be innocent enough. We're both freezing our asses off—why not?

Summoning up his courage, Logan moved closer to Mara and wrapped that side of his blanket around the priestess, the other side still wrapped around himself. In response, Mara moved in, snuggling her cold and wet body against Logan's. An almost immediate warmth burned in Logan's frozen frame, and a grin bordering on stupid crossed his features. From the contented sigh of relief that came from Mara, Logan surmised the added blanket—and maybe his own body warmth—was helping warm her up.

Thromar stumbled into the wooded area, shaking water from his beard. "I'll be needing a keg of hot cider to survive this one," he grumbled, fighting with a blanket that barely draped his massive shoulders.

Nightwalker stood behind the Rebel, barely visible in his own dark cowl. Through his half-clear vision, Logan thought the Shadow-spawn looked much thinner and much frailer.

Moknay glided into the forest, a grey shadow in the unnatural dawn. "Let's keep moving," he urged the others. "I don't know why those beasts didn't sense us, but I'll not give them the chance to come back and correct their mistake."

"Have you no heart, Murderer?" Thromar queried, huddling in his blanket under a tree. "That water was as cold as a Reakthi's chestplate!"

Moknay glanced back at the sky. "Was it?" he responded. "I hadn't noticed."

"No, you wouldn't," muttered Thromar. "Not when you've ice water running through your own veins."

A dagger flickered in the blood-red sunlight as Moknay impatiently twirled the weapon in one hand. "We've had a moment of good luck," he stated. "Why tempt the gods?"

The large fighter grumbled something into his beard as he pulled himself to his feet. "Oh, I suppose you're right," he frowned.

Logan watched as the Rebel stood up, shaking more water from his chainmail vest. But I don't wanna leave! Logan protested silently. I've got my arm around Mara. You know how long I've wanted to do that? You know how much nerve that took? I don't wanna break it up! It's not fair!

There was a soft touch on Logan's left shoulder that, if Mara had not been on his right, the young man would have thought the priestess had lightly tapped him. Questioningly, Logan jerked around, squinting his right eye at the tiny figure that stood behind him. Even in the filtered light of the morning, her hair sparkled violet and her eyes reflected the same purplish twinkle. She stood only about five feet tall and wore no clothing; a faint smile was stretched across her lips.

"You needn't leave, Matthew Logan," Roana declared, her delicate hand on the young man's shoulder.

In shock, Logan turned his half-blinded gaze on his companions. From their own startled stares, the young man realized he was not the only one who saw the diminutive Guardian of Sparrill.

The violet-haired sprite turned her violet eyes on the others. "You were safe from the Demons because of like magic," she explained. "The Heart and my river radiate the same energies, so the Demons thought they sensed only the Purity of my river. You are relatively safe here. Until the Darkness sets out to destroy all Beauty—then no one is safe."

Darkling Nightwalker took a step toward the sprite, his tainted eyes worriedly locked on her small figure. "You are well?" he asked, and he sounded truly concerned.

"For now, Guardian," Roana responded. She turned her violet eyes back on Logan. "My sisters and I thank you, Matthew Logan, for undertaking the protection of the Heart. We are the Guardians of Sparrill and *that* is our task while the Voices prepare for battle; remember that should you need a Guardian. And, remember too, that, while you possess the Heart, you must also regulate its flow of magic. It is an easy task—simply direct the magic to where it will do the most good when the Bloodstone releases it. There is no sorcery involved on your part, and I thank you again."

The sprite gently brushed Logan's cheek with her hand as she stepped past the shivering five to the bank of her river. Her lengthy violet hair streamed out behind her as she dived into the waters, sending up an umbrella of silvery foam. Even once the crystal waters had settled, none of the five could see any trace of the diminutive sprite with the violet hair and experienced look in her eyes.

Thromar leaned back against a tree, his eyes glittering. "I think I'm in love," he sighed wistfully. "Be still, the raging fires of my heart!"

Moknay sneered. "Tell the fires of your heart to come out here and warm us up rather than dream about sprites and nymphs that you'll never have," he retorted.

Thromar frowned at the darkly clad Murderer, gathering some tinder with a sweep of his foot. "By Brolark," he cursed, "not only a murderer of men but a murderer of dreams as well."

Logan felt a smile pull across his face at the usual insult-trading between the two war-siblings as he tightened his hold on Mara. Dreams, the young man thought. Here's a dream. The most attractive girl I've ever seen in any world, and she's in my arms! I don't care if we ever leave here.

As if in response to Logan's happier thoughts, the rising sun strengthened its glare and burned through another layer of the blackness smearing the sky.

It was sometime around two in the afternoon when Logan awoke, finding Mara asleep on his right shoulder. He blinked a few times, wondering why his vision was so bad, then remembered he no longer had both contact lenses. This was going to play havoc with his brain, he told himself. It was massive migraine time if he didn't get another lens or take out his left contact, but that would leave him completely blind—and whoever heard of anyone saving the multiverse with an astigmatism? Hell, whoever heard of anyone saving the multiverse, period?

Logan squinted his right eye and looked up. The fire Thromar had started that morning had died to a few embers, yet it had dried most of the wetness from their clothing so that they weren't so uncomfortable. The horses, also, had put their brief rest to good use, grazing along the banks of the Roana to replenish their strength. The sky overhead shone a brilliant blue, dark clouds giving the only indication that something unnatural had occurred during the night.

Logan noticed Moknay was grinning at him from across the burned-out campfire. "What's so funny?" the young man wanted to know.

The Murderer's grin widened. "I was just remembering what you said about priests from your world," he chuckled, and his grey eyes indicated the sleeping form of Mara.

Logan felt the embarrassed rush of warmth that spread across his cheeks. "So," he retorted, "that's their problem."

Moknay smiled, his mustache turning upward. "Indeed."

Logan tried to think of something to say but his brain failed him. Besides, he finally told himself, why should I defend myself? Moknay's purposely teasing me 'cause he knows I'll put up a fight. So what's wrong about helping someone keep warm? It's innocent enough . . . even if my thoughts at the moment aren't!

The young man flinched at the blurriness that invaded his right eye and whispered a curse, rubbing at the contactless eye.

"Problems?" Moknay asked.

"This damn eye," Logan grumbled. "I can't really see out of it and it's driving me crazy."

Moknay slid to his feet, eyes glinting. "I may have something for that," he remarked and glided to where his horse was.

Logan watched with interest as the Murderer searched his saddlebags and finally came across something that he pulled free. Logan's blue eyes were wide as Moknay stepped across the dead campfire and handed the young man a black patch of metal with an attached strap. Curiously, Logan turned it over in his hands.

"What is it?" he wondered.

"It's an eyepatch," Moknay explained. "It used to belong to a good friend of mine—Teillo the One-Eyed. Finest craftsman and archer in all of Eadarus."

"What happened to him?" the young man queried.

"He lost his other eye."

Logan nodded. "Oh."

Moknay watched impatiently as the young man studied the eyepatch. "Well," the Murderer pressed, "put it on. It'll add flavor to your character."

Smirking, Logan slipped the eyepatch over his head and tugged it down so that the metal patch cupped over his right eye. It was comfortable enough, he noted, and it did stop him from seeing blurs. He probably looked like some mixed-up pirate wearing a sweatsuit and an eyepatch, but, thankfully, there were few mirrors in Sparrill.

"Help any?" Moknay asked.

"Yeah," Logan nodded, scanning the forest around him. His right eye remained open behind the cupped patch, yet he only saw blackness that was neither blurry nor clear. His left eye, meanwhile, was able to sweep the scenery and transmit clear messages back to his brain without being interrupted by fuzzy images from his right. Regardless of what he looked like, the eyepatch would save him many a headache.

Darkling Nightwalker abruptly entered the camp. Both Logan and Moknay glanced at him, neither aware that the Guardian had left the camp. A lean, weary expression was on the Shadow-spawn's face, yet his eyes appeared to be whiter than the previous night.

"Twice good fortune befalls us," Nightwalker declared, drawing his cowl around him as the freezing wind moaned through the forest. "While our foes sit and bicker, we will come ever nearer to our goal. Awake the others; we must take advantage of this opportunity."

Moknay retied the straps of his saddlebags, eyeing Nightwalker suspiciously. "How do you know what our foes are doing?" he questioned.

A vague smile appeared on Nightwalker's features. "As fleeting as the dawn and as silent as the dusk," was all he said.

The Murderer snorted. "More magical claptrap. All right, Nightwalker, we'll play things your way for now, but, when it comes time for it, your explanation had better be a good one."

Darkling Nightwalker nodded beneath his hood, his smile vanishing. "Believe me, Murderer," he replied. "I am thinking of the best one possible."

Logan swallowed hard; dark humor's one thing, he informed himself, but Dark humor was another thing altogether.

The afternoon sky began to darken as the unnatural blackness seeped free of the clouds and once again struggled with the sun for possession of the sky.

·4·

Collusion

Ridglee did not like the sniggering, mocking laughter that broke
from his Imperator's half-fused lips. Such laughter could only bring
trouble, the soldier concluded, when directed—as it was—at the
hideously gaunt figure in the silver chestplate and flowing robe.

Spellcaster Groathit clenched bony fists at his side, his left eye
blazing with a blackness that duplicated the mass of darkness
hovering over the camp. "What do you say?" the wizard shrieked,
and the wind shrieked along with him.

Clusters of grotesque creatures and shapes writhed about the
sorcerer, all dark of hue and glistening with mucus. These were
the Servants, Ridglee reminded himself. *Deils* that served the
Voices. Monsters with unpronounceable names like Shub'yiwg,
and Tuhauab, and Vsdaefn, and Ryth'ueyh. And humanoid
Demons stalked among the *Deils*, their large eyes aglow with
nefarious magicks given to them by the *Deils* around them.
And they all gathered about Groathit—all slithered about his
feet, cast their eyes and eyeless faces in his direction as though
he commanded them all. And Ridglee felt a shiver run through
him as he realized that, perhaps, Groathit did.

The wizard's eye flashed ebony. "When I ask a question, I
expect it to be answered!" he screamed. "What do your Masters
mean?"

The crocodilian snout of Uhayhoth—the *Deil* whose form
Groathit mimicked when shape-shifting—rose from the mass of
dark skin and slime. "Exactly what they say," the beast responded,
"for they are the Voices and ever do they speak the truth."

Imperator Vaugen laughed louder, rising from his seat and
striding toward the spellcaster. "So, wizard," he snapped, "all
your work seems wasted. All your time and energy spent for
naught. All your . . ." Dull grey eyes fixed deliberately on the

empty socket. " . . . sacrifices were in vain."

Ridglee feared for Vaugen's life as Groathit lowered his head, glaring into the sea of mutable forms before him. "You are quick to talk, my Imperator," the sorcerer snarled, "when I have such an array of forces around me."

"And I have another three troops joining us from the east, fresh with both men and supplies," Vaugen spat back. "Would you send your creatures against me, wizard? Would you order your powerless Darkness to consume me?"

"The Darkness is never Powerless," the monster called Lsuyryh said, its voice that of a beautiful young maiden. "The Darkness *is* Power."

"For all the good it does," Vaugen sneered, and his distorted lip curled backwards. "Mere power alone is worthless!" The Imperator turned on Groathit. "Had you any idea, wizard?" he howled. "Did you know what you would bring forth?"

"Of course I had no idea!" Groathit shrieked back, his eye blazing black. "Even in the Darklight grimoire there is not enough information concerning the Darkness to even hint at this complication! I knew the Darkness was powerful—I did not know that this Power was unable to assume any physical shape itself!"

The solidified form of Ryth'ueyh surfaced from among the other *Deils*. "Of course, inferior organism," it rasped. "That is why *we* were formed. That is why *we* carry out the wishes of our Masters."

"Because your Masters are incapable of any action themselves!" Vaugen raged, spinning on his heel and stalking off.

The serpentine *Deil*, Shub'yiwg, watched the Imperator leave, its thousands of eyes never blinking. "I do not like that creature," the *Deil* declared. "He does not realize the strength of my Masters and, therefore, must be a fool."

"Fool?" Groathit screamed at the tide of beasts churning and swelling around him. "I am the fool! I thought I could conjure forth the blackness—bring the Darkness itself to my side and rid myself once and for all of the threat of Matthew Logan! But I was wrong. I have received, instead, a squadron of shapeless beasts and a mist of darkness that radiates with sheer energy that can never be used!"

Perspiration broke out along the back of Ridglee's neck and a freezing dagger of fear speared his gut as a hundred thousand whispering voices seemed to fill the forest for leagues in every direction.

Perhaps if we took other forms.
Yes.
Other forms that already are.
Yes, already are.
This is possible.
Yes, this much is possible.
Other forms.
Others.

Groathit's left eye crackled with black sparks as he swung his lean head skyward, peering at the blackness above him. A ghastly smile spread across the magic-user's gaunt features as he examined the bodiless energy that hovered overhead, blacker than any moonless night Ridglee had ever seen.

"Other forms?" Groathit asked himself, and a gnarled hand stroked his chin.

When Groathit returned his gaze to earth, Ridglee felt the same madness try to grab hold of his brain as when the Darkness had first arrived. The sorcerer's remaining eye was locked on the ring of Reakthi gaping at him from about the camp, and the spellcaster's smile widened.

"That already are," the wizard repeated.

The *Deils* burbled and oozed about his feet.

Imperator Vaugen glanced up from where he polished his sword, the light of the tapers playing off the burned redness of his flesh. "Yes, Ridglee, what is it?" he questioned.

Ridglee licked his lips fearfully, not wishing to incur the wrath of his Imperator or of the man who had sent him inside. "It's the sorcerer, sir," the Reakthi replied. "He wishes to speak with you."

His eyes widening in surprise, Vaugen set aside his weapon. "And he did not simply barge in himself? How very unlike him." The Imperator rested his maimed hand across his lap. "Very well, send him in. Oh . . . and, Ridglee, such an esteemed guest surely needs an escort. Make certain he knows you are behind him when he enters."

Ridglee swallowed hard. "Yes, sir."

The soldier stepped backwards out of the Imperator's tent and faced the one-eyed magician waiting for him. For all the things he had seen—all the wars he had fought—Ridglee could find nothing that compared with the sight of Groathit's eyes. Never before had he felt such raw terror flow through his system than when he looked at the wizard's dark sockets—one black with emptiness, the other black with evil.

"Well?" Groathit wondered, his voice strained. "What did he say?"

"He'll see you, sir," Ridglee responded, holding the tent flap open for the lean spellcaster.

The Reakthi soldier threw his companions a worried look as he bent to follow after the sorcerer, feeling a line of perspiration run down the back of his neck and into his chestplate. It was good to wear chestplates again, the soldier decided, his thoughts straying. Imperator Vaugen had discovered that unarmored the Reakthi were harder to detect, but Ridglee still valued the sense of protection the armor gave him.

Ridglee almost ran directly into Groathit who was glaring at the soldier unpleasantly. "We will not be needing your presence, soldier," the wizard sneered.

"I've asked him inside," came Vaugen's voice from behind the spellcaster. "I believe I'll be wanting an audience for this."

Snarling, Groathit turned away from Ridglee and faced his Imperator. A horrifying pair, Ridglee concluded. One a user of mystic powers who has contorted his own frightening visage; the other a deformed soldier barely able to take his next breath without wincing in pain. By all rights, neither should be alive.

Imperator Vaugen took a confident step toward Groathit, a smirk on half of his face. "I believe Ridglee said you wanted to see me," he queried, and his rasping voice dripped with arrogance.

Fists were clenched at Groathit's side that turned his knuckles white. "Yes," the wizard said, the words obviously foul-tasting in his mouth. "I wish to make a proposition."

"A proposition?" Vaugen inquired, and if his eyebrows had not been long since burned off Ridglee was sure they would have risen in mock surprise. "You wish to bargain with me, wizard? To do business with a typical human creature? What happened to all your new friends? Your new power? I thought you said beforehand that you didn't need anything that I might have."

"I do now," the sorcerer responded, and Ridglee was shocked at the urgency in his voice.

"You do now," Vaugen slowly repeated, savoring the words. "How very interesting. And what, pray tell, do you need?"

The spellcaster shot Ridglee a nefarious backward glance. "You mentioned more troops," he said. "When will they be arriving?"

Vaugen stroked his chin with his three-fingered hand. "By the week's end, no doubt. Why?"

Groathit stepped closer to his Imperator, a gnarled finger jerking stiffly behind him. "You know what's out there," the spellcaster whispered. "You've sensed the power of what I've conjured forth. I think I may have devised a means for its use."

Vaugen tried to smirk again. "Oh, really? How?"

"The Darkness is unable to take physical form," Groathit answered. "That is, it is unable to create a real form for itself. It can, however, take another form. Another form that has already been made."

"You mean possess?" Vaugen questioned.

"More than just mere possession," Groathit replied. "It would need essentially all available space to contain just an iota of energy. Therefore, it wouldn't be so much possession as it would be . . . ownership."

"I see," nodded Vaugen. "Go on."

The spellcaster came nearer to Vaugen, an expression of determination scrawled across his features. His crackling eye lit his face with a blue-black glare. "By means of the Darklight grimoire, I have bound the Voices to me," he rasped. "They serve me and only me—in any way I wish. They will refuse to acknowledge this fact, yet they know it to be true . . . for I have the means of cancelling the spells which brought them here and that would, of course, send them back. But, now that they are here, they have the ability to take their war one step further. They can eradicate the Purity and Beauty they loathe—to destroy what we ourselves wanted to destroy."

Groathit's eye sparked. "They will kill Matthew Logan."

Vaugen stiffened at the mention of the name of the man who so horribly distorted his body.

"To accomplish this," Groathit went on, "they will need to take action themselves. Matthew Logan has already shown himself a formidable foe against their strongest Servant, Gangrorz. These lesser *Deils*—even as a force—will not halt him now that he has possession of the Heart. That is why it is imperative that we coerce the Darkness itself to act."

There was a long silence in the tent, and Ridglee began to feel a heavy unease become apparent in the air. The soldier watched quietly as his Imperator turned his back on his spellcaster, clasping his hands behind him. Groathit, Ridglee knew, was up to no good—that was obvious. But it was more than just what the wizard intended here. This act might have serious repercussions—might affect those Ridglee and his companions had left behind across the great seas to the east. Would Vaugen agree to what the spellcaster planned?

"Why do you come to me?" the Imperator finally asked, his burned throat causing his voice to be very low and strained.

"I need your men," Groathit responded, his eye churning with power.

Imperator Vaugen turned around, expressionless.

Groathit grinned. "The Voices need your men."

Ridglee felt dizziness grasp his head as he heard the spellcaster's words resound over and over again inside his skull.

Vaugen turned away once again, waving his maimed hand in a form of dismissal. "I will think on it," he stated.

The unholy glee fled Groathit's face. "You will think . . . ?" he sputtered. "What is there to think of? We must act now or . . ."

"I said I will think on it," Vaugen repeated, and Ridglee caught the taunting tone in his voice.

Mouth agape, Groathit glared at his deformed Imperator before spinning on his heel. Ridglee watched the sorcerer go before returning his gaze back to Vaugen, trying to voice his opinions concerning the wizard's plan. Yet how do I say it? the Reakthi wondered. Dare I speak my mind? Vaugen taunts Groathit, obviously. But will he agree to the wizard's ghastly proposition? All logic says no, and yet . . . more than just his features were disfigured by the stranger's blast. Since that day, Vaugen has been obsessed with the death of the one called Matthew Logan and may very well sacrifice the lives of his own men to this Darkness to accomplish this task. I only pray to whatever gods that watch over this land that I am mistaken.

Ridglee looked up and saw the dull grey eyes were trained on him, glittering in the light of the tapers. The Reakthi tried to say something—tried to think of a way to convince his Imperator to ignore the wizard's speech, yet he could only stare.

"You may leave, Ridglee," Vaugen commanded, "and speak not one word of what you heard here. Is that understood?"

The soldier tried to nod but only succeeded halfway. "Yes, sir," he breathed, and stumbled backwards out of the tent.

Groathit purposely ignored the slithering, pulsating creatures that dragged themselves into his tent, a thin trail of mucus drawing along the ground behind them. Eyes as black as the wizard's own trained on him, yet still the spellcaster ignored their presence. He had other things on his mind and did not wish to be disturbed. Once again his plans went awry, and, like before, games were being played—time was being wasted—giving Matthew Logan the time to gain the upper hand.

"We would have words with you, inferior organism," Ryth'ueyh stated, its eye-stalks weaving through the steam and stench of the tent.

"Do not interrupt me, beast," Groathit snarled back. "I am busy."

"Your petty little business can wait, inferior one," the *Deil* Vsdaefn replied.

Groathit turned on the two monsters, his black eye narrowing. Both *Deils* together were smaller than Gangrorz had been, and their shapes were not as fluid. Ryth'ueyh still held its sluglike frame while Vsdaefn resembled a hairless wolf with twin heads. Neither *Deil*'s lower body kept any constant form.

"Our Masters wish to send us out after the Purity that thrives here," Ryth'ueyh said. "You are holding us back."

Vsdaefn tilted one of its heads. "This is not possible."

"Not possible?" Groathit shouted back at the creatures. "Then why do you not go? Why do you not carry out your Masters' task? Because I *do* hold you back. Because I *do* have control over you." He snatched up the nearby Darklight grimoire. "So long as this is in my possession—and I have the means of banishing you back beyond the barriers—I hold total control over you and your Masters."

The two *Deils* were oddly silent.

Groathit continued: "I have learned from past experience that the one who now regulates the Purity you so badly seek is more powerful than you. So much so that he will no doubt destroy you without a second thought. Only your Masters will be able to stop him *and* destroy the Purity he holds. All you will do is delay him."

The spellcaster turned away from the monsters when a sudden idea struck him. Delay, he mused. Although a wizard, Groathit knew something of military strategy. If the *Deils* and Demons were to attack Matthew Logan, the accursed young man would have no chance to gain the upper hand. He would waste his time battling his enemies with no resulting victory while Vaugen wasted the wizard's own time. But during that period, perhaps it would be Groathit who gained the upper hand this time around.

The one-eyed sorcerer returned his gaze to the *Deils*, a morbid smile on his face. "Very well, then," he whispered, "I release you to carry out your Masters' wishes."

There was a very eager pace to the *Deils'* movements as they squirmed around and left, leaving a puddle of slime in their wake. Groathit turned away as soon as they left the tent.

"And sleep well the death that Matthew Logan shall deliver you," he added, and an unpleasant smirk crossed his features.

It had been more than a day since the departure of the hideous creatures, yet Ridglee still could not get their horrifying forms out of his mind. He still felt shivers when he remembered the voice of the one called Lsuyryh. How absolutely beautiful she sounded. It! How *it* sounded! Oh, gods! the soldier thought. How could anything that repulsive send such pleasurable memories and thoughts through his mind? It had made him think of Eoldea, the first woman he had ever had. And Orianna, and Dacia, and even that sweet young girl from Denzil—he never did learn her name, did he? And then . . . then he would look for the source of that voice, and he would see it, squatting there . . . disgustingly brown and mucid.

And the serpent one—Shub'yiwg—covered with eyes. Eyes that never blinked . . . never closed. Eyes that seemed to pierce the canvas of the tents, to probe into your most secret places and lay open your soul. Just what were these creatures? What had Imperator Vaugen allowed his spellcaster to let loose upon not only Sparrill but the other lands beyond?

Ridglee scanned the camp. It looked so empty now without the hill of dark protoplasm bubbling and frothing at its center. But the Darkness still hung overhead, trying its best to block out the light of the sun and plunge the camp into eternal night. And every now and then, faint whispers would sprout from everywhere and nowhere, rasping, gurgling, as if the blackness still spoke with its creatures even though they were no longer there. Or worse, spoke with the spellcaster, who—since his conversation with Vaugen two days before—had not left his tent for any reason.

The soldier got to his feet, trying to think of earlier campaigns and simpler days. He had first served Agasilaus when this whole campaign had first taken effect. There had been a cunning warrior! Ruthless, at times, but a cunning soldier nonetheless. Rumors ran that Agasilaus had only wanted the best for the Reakthi homeland— that he wanted to uncover the secret of Sparrill and return it to his own country. But that never came about, did it? Years later, Agasilaus was assassinated and Ridglee and his friends had been divided up like so much booty. The soldier still had no idea what had happened to his older brother, who had gone to serve Imperator Ikathar—or to the ones who had gone to Quarn or back to the stronghold. As a Reakthi, you were expected to serve and ask no questions . . . so why was it now—after all those years of faithful service—that Ridglee was beginning to question?

The flap to Vaugen's tent flipped open and Ridglee ducked behind a nearby tree. He watched with narrowed eyebrows as his Imperator strode briskly out of his tent, dull grey eyes warily surveying the camp around him. There seemed to be a moment's hesitation on the Imperator's part before he continued on, and Ridglee understood his uncertainty when he saw Vaugen duck inside Groathit's tent.

Cautiously, Ridglee stepped back into the open, fixing his gaze on the tent. There could only be one viable reason why Vaugen would go to the wizard, yet Ridglee could not be sure. He had to hear for himself the Imperator's acceptance of the spellcaster's plan before he so readily accused the two of their unholy cooperation.

Ridglee ducked behind the wizard's tent and placed an ear against the canvas. He could hear the muffled voices of the two inside—detect the pleased surprise in Groathit's voice and the unsure agreement of Vaugen's.

"What I do not understand," Vaugen was saying, "is why we do not capture a town? Hold all its populace captive and give them to the Voices? Why must it be our own men?"

"Because the process requires that the vessels be willing," the spellcaster's scratchy voice replied. "We must tell them that they will be acquiring helpful magicks to aid them in battle. Magicks that will leave them once victory is ours. Then, once the process has begun, everything of what and who they are will be wiped away and replaced by the persona of the Voices."

"If they must be willing," responded Vaugen, "surely there will be those who are unwilling. And they will later see a difference in their companions once the Voices have taken control."

"So we tell them that this process changes the body magicks in such a way that speech becomes unnecessary," Groathit answered. "They will believe that. They will believe anything that *I* tell them . . . and that you order them to believe."

There was a brief silence.

"But there is one who will not be willing at all," Ridglee heard Groathit go on. "That soldier who was with us when I first told you of my plan . . ."

"Ridglee?"

"Yes. He must be killed."

"No, I will not slay a loyal soldier," Vaugen retorted. "Regardless of what he heard beforehand, he will realize we only do what is best for our ultimate victory and conquest of Sparrill."

Ridglee pushed himself away from the tent, unable to bear another word from the two inside. He felt ill and had to force down bile that had risen in his throat, leaving a foul taste in his mouth. That taste seemed to reflect the horror the Reakthi felt. He was sickened by the revelation that his Imperator would sacrifice his own men to the experiments of his spellcaster and to some godless Darkness. But there was nothing the soldier could do. Warn his friends? Warn them of what? That their Imperator was mad? That he and his sorcerer were going to give up troops of men to the blackness that hovered over their heads? Not only would they think him insane, Groathit would surely kill him then.

Thunderous hoofbeats rent the stillness of the forest, and Ridglee peered around the wizard's tent to see a large army of unarmored men ride into the camp. Their Reakthi swords gleamed proudly at their hips, and the three troop leaders scanned the clearing expectantly, dismounting to await the welcome of Imperator Vaugen.

The entrance to the tent Ridglee hid behind opened and Imperator Vaugen stepped out, shadowed by Groathit. There was a smile of anticipation and triumph on the latter's features as Ridglee slumped back behind the tent and wept.

·5·

Stalked

Darkling Nightwalker turned his head away, his once pure white eyes now mottled with grey. Lines of despair were drawn across his ebon features as he turned his tainted eyes on the four behind him.

"We are undone," the Shadow-spawn declared.

Mustache curling, Moknay sneered. "Forgive me if I don't break down and cry," he snarled, "but what were we setting out to do?"

Nightwalker ignored the question, once again directing his grey-tinted eyes toward the northern forest. "Perhaps if we rode farther north," the Guardian thought out loud. "Perhaps then we will be able to skirt the troops and avoid the danger of being caught."

"Perhaps," Thromar agreed without really knowing why he did so.

Darkling Nightwalker looked at the others again, pointing a jet-black finger along the northwestern course of the Demonry River hidden in the distance by the forest. "You two," he instructed Moknay and Thromar, "scout along the banks of the Demonry—see if there is any place where the Guardsmen are not camped and where we may cross safely." The creature of Shadow swung his gaze and finger toward Logan and Mara. "The two of you, scout along the eastern shore of the lake itself. I will check this shore. Perhaps some sort of distraction will allow us the time and cover that we will need."

Matthew Logan took his single-eyed gaze off the figure of black flesh and white hair and glanced at Moknay. There was an unpleasant frown on the Murderer's face, and his eyes told Logan he did not like obeying Nightwalker's commands. Nonetheless, the darkly clad Murderer swung his horse around and started into the foliage, Thromar and Smeea behind him.

A light touch from the slender priestess sitting behind him drew Logan's attention back toward Nightwalker to see that the Guardian had already left as well. Hesitantly, Logan turned his yellow-and-green mount to face the east and clucked it forward, resting his right hand near the hilt of his Reakthi sword. They were deliberately risking their freedom for an answer to a question that only Nightwalker knew. That was why Logan could understand the perturbed look in Moknay's eyes—it was probably reflected in the young man's own eye.

"This doesn't make any sense," Mara voiced behind Logan, leaning closer to whisper in his ear. "This place is crawling with Guardsmen."

"Tell that to Nightwalker," Logan whispered back. "He seems determined that we get around this lake."

Mara pursed her lips, her green eyes searching the forest around them. "That's what doesn't make sense," she responded. "There's nothing north of Lake Atricrix except forest and sea."

Logan knitted his eyebrows together in thought and looked momentarily villainous with his eyepatch. "No towns?" he queried. "No cities along the coast or anything?"

"Nothing," Mara returned. "Nothing but Quarn's fortress and the Reakthi Stronghold."

Logan chuckled grimly. "And I don't think we're going there."

The two were silent as the yellow-and-green stallion broke through much of the protective greenery and skirted the edge of the forest. Beyond was the sparkling Lake Atricrix, its crystal-clear waters absorbing the blaze of the afternoon sun and redirecting it so that the surface of the lake flamed with golden light. The ugly, gnarled trees that had stood sentry around the lake's shores had grown taller and less crooked, straightening up like elderly men become young again. Their branches bloomed with light green foliage, an obvious contrast to the dark, almost green-black leaves they had earlier borne.

Intently staring at the lake, Logan was slightly startled when Mara's arms drew about him lovingly. "Look at it, Matthew," she breathed, and her voice was filled with pride. "Look what you did."

Yeah, the young man reminded himself, smiling inwardly, I did do that, didn't I? We saw it starting to clear up as soon as Gangrorz died, and now it's completely clear. Now Lake Atricrix—and even the Demonry River—were as beautiful and as pure as the rivers guarded by the sprites.

Logan frowned. Only this one was guarded by a number of troops, and they all wore the uniform of King Mediyan's Guardsmen.

The yellow stallion continued its slow pace around the southern shore of the lake, its green mane and tail billowing in the frigid wind. If it weren't for the constant reminder of the gale, Logan would have never have suspected that Groathit had succeeded somewhere in the west. For almost a week now, the five had been unhampered by any attack from Groathit's supposed new forces, and they had made fairly good time with their horses keeping a steady pace. It was only now—with the sudden discovery of Mediyan's Guardsmen camped out along the lake's shores—that the five had found anything to complicate things.

Mara watched the figures of uniformed men in the distance, their tents undulating in the wintry winds. "What are they waiting for?" she wondered.

"Me, probably," Logan answered.

"But why wait here?" Mara queried.

Logan shrugged, and a slight flash of discomfort radiated from his wounded chest. "Who knows?" he asked back. "It's got my signature written all over it. They know what I'm capable of doing whenever I get near anything—and a stagnant lake that suddenly becomes sparklingly clear has got to be the work of that stranger, Matthew Logan."

"They don't know anything concerning the Smythe and your purpose here?"

"Not when I first bumped into them," Logan replied, shaking his head. "They only knew I was important and that things like earthquakes, and unnatural floods, and unnatural rainstorms happened whenever I was around."

"So the sudden change in Lake Atricrix has been their only clue to where you've been," Mara nodded.

"And, like an idiot, I've come back," the young man said, frowning. He pulled his horse around. "Come on, let's get out of here. There's no way we're gonna get around this lake."

The young man pulled his horse back around and reentered the relative safety of the forest. Far off along the shores of the lake, he could faintly hear the Guardsmen—their muffled conversations, the uneasy pawing of their tethered horses' hooves, the wind beating against their tents. Gradually, however, the rustling of

the forest's vegetation drowned out the camped soldiers behind
the young man, and Logan began to feel a little bit of relief seep
into his tensed muscles as he and Mara returned to the place where
Nightwalker had separated their group.

The Shadow-spawn was already waiting for them.

"There's no way around the lake," reported Logan.

Nightwalker did not even look in the young man's direction.
His darkly tinted eyes were locked on the forest before him, silently
probing its greenness for the remaining two.

"Then we are undone," the Guardian repeated.

"But there isn't even anything north of the lake that could help
us," protested Mara. "How can we be undone?"

Darkling Nightwalker slowly turned to gaze at the priestess,
his eyes glimmering vaguely. "There is an army building to the
west," he replied, his voice low and ominous. "An agreement has
finally been reached by our enemies, and the Voices will have the
physical forms they'll need."

"Oh, great!" Logan exclaimed. "So we're supposed to go up
against an army of Darkness *and* Vaugen's men?"

"Vaugen's men will be that army of Darkness," Nightwalker
answered, and he turned away once more. "Treacherously, the
Imperator and his spellcaster have agreed to 'give' their own
troops to the bodiless blackness they have summoned forth. I
knew such a move would occur, and I set out to Balance that. I
set us eastward so that we could acquire the aid of Imperator Quarn
and his men, but now . . . now we are unable to get through."

"Now we are undone," Nightwalker concluded gravely.

Logan swung his good eye up as Moknay and Thromar rejoined
them, the latter's heavy sword out of its sheath and glittering in
the sunlight.

"Never seen so many Guardsmen before," the Rebel was muttering. "They must have every man that fat old Mediyan's ever
sent over here."

Moknay nodded sharply, smoothing his mustache with a
gloved finger. "Probably even pulled all the troops out of the
towns," he remarked. His grey eyes fell upon Logan. "You're
certainly capable of stirring up a lot of action, friend," he
quipped.

"Not my fault," the young man grumbled in defense, hating to
be reminded of his difference.

The Murderer smirked, swinging his gaze to the mute
Nightwalker. "So," Moknay declared, "are we undone?"

Nightwalker did not find the macabre humor of the Murderer humorous or even bothersome. "We are undone," he responded flatly, giving no indication if he realized that the outlaw was mocking him.

"Undone! Undone! Undone!" Mara cried from behind Logan, and she flung up her slim arms angrily. "We're undone and we haven't even done anything yet!"

"And neither has Vaugen's scumcaster," Thromar snorted, his weapon still out.

"That is where you are wrong," Nightwalker interjected, and he told the Rebel and Murderer what transpired in the west.

Thromar was grinning happily as the Shadow-spawn completed his explanation. Eagerly, the large fighter flailed his sword overhead. "So the battle remains on my kind of level!" he exclaimed.

"Even moreso than your battle against the Worm," Nightwalker went on. "Here it will be men against men—although some men are Darkness clothed in flesh."

"It makes a difference?" Moknay queried, an eyebrow raised.

"Yes," Nightwalker responded. "The Darkness will be basically animating these forms. They will not recognize a fatal blow—they will not mind losing an arm or a leg, or their heads. To them, the bodies of Vaugen's men are only garments, and they shall wear them so long as there is still use in them."

"Bring them on!" Thromar roared anyway. "I'll lop off their arms! I'll slice them in half! I'll cleave their skulls in two!"

Moknay folded his arms. "You'll probably talk them to death as well," he jeered, half a sneer on his lips. The Murderer faced Nightwalker, his grim mien replacing the sneer. "He'll be using all his men, won't he?"

The Guardian of Shadow nodded sullenly. "When messengers bring word that combat has begun, yes," the dark-skinned creature replied. "It will be disguised as an attempt to conquer Sparrill as Imperator Agasilaus conquered Denzil, but, of course, the true battle will be between the spellcaster Groathit and Matthew Logan."

"But only if we get that far," Logan muttered, strangling the reins that he held in his hands. "And we won't get anywhere unless we've got an army behind us."

"And we can't get through to Quarn," Mara finished.

"Not to say that's not for the better," Thromar commented. "We'd be asking Reakthi to fight Reakthi—and who's to say

Quarn wouldn't betray us if he saw Vaugen's men getting the upper hand?"

"Your prejudice runs deep, Rebel," Nightwalker stated, "but your fears are valid. We would have no word save that of Quarn himself."

Thromar snorted into his beard. "And a Reakthi's word is about as good as a sword forged in Magdelon," he growled.

"I take it that's bad?" Logan questioned, and the fighter's angry nod confirmed his suspicions.

Mara's eyes flickered emerald as she looked about the forest, thoughtfully running a hand through her long, dark hair. "If we went as far east as Lake Xenois, there's a chance we could reach Quarn's fortress undetected," she mused.

"That's an idea," Moknay nodded. "Thromar and I saw a troop of Guards head west—seems some of them are inspecting that mysterious cloud of blackness that appeared a few days ago—but most of them look to be camped around the lake. I doubt very strongly that there are any Guards left in all Sparrill to be stationed farther east."

"Except the possibility of scouting parties," Thromar suggested.

Darkling Nightwalker was slowly shaking his head, his grey-mottled eyes unblinkingly staring ahead. "There are varying levels of battle here," he remarked. "To travel so far out of our way would mean to lose our battle against time."

"So we don't," Logan interrupted, and there was a triumphant gleam in his uncovered eye.

"You've an idea?" inquired Moknay.

Logan couldn't help grinning. Damn right I've got an idea, he thought, and none of it requires that I use another drop of magic.

"We need enough of a force to fight a fortress of Reakthi, right?" the young man questioned.

There were agreeing nods from those around him.

"And we can't get through to Quarn." Logan didn't even wait for his friends to agree. "So we don't. We head in the exact opposite direction and get the army that we need."

"But there's nothing this far east, Matthew," Mara reminded him, almost apologetically since it would dampen his spirits.

"Mara's right, friend-Logan," Thromar added.

Logan's grin had now stretched from ear to ear. "We need to stop the Reakthi from conquering Sparrill," he dramatically continued on, "so we recruit that very same force that's been halting the conquest of Sparrill for however many years it's been."

Moknay's lips mirrored Logan's grin, and the Murderer's head began to bob up and down in admiration. "I'm beginning to see where you're leading, friend," he said.

"Well, I'm not!" Thromar indignantly boomed. "And I don't relish the thought of friend-Logan starting to talk like Nightwalker!"

There was an unbelievable pressure of hope building up inside the young man as he trained his blue eye on the large fighter, his grin unable to get any wider but still trying. "We need an army, Thromar," he explained, "and I know where we can get one."

"Where?" Mara questioned, her voice tinged with impatience.

Logan beamed triumphantly. "From the town of Eadarus," he declared, and the four were silent around him.

Commander Eldath apprehensively gripped the middle of his commanding scepter, feeling the silver rod grow slick with his own perspiration. Regent Nodabyus paced before the commander, his cloak of royalty flapping about his corpulent bulk as the freezing winds swept across the lake's surface. Other commanders were lined up along with Eldath, their faces all duplicating the look of anxiety that controlled Eldath's facial muscles.

"We have been camped here for a long time," Regent Nodabyus announced, and his voice was high-pitched and nasal. "Far too long a time." He turned on the gathered commanders. "Eldath, Marrack, you've seen to the deployment of both troops?"

Eldath nodded together with Commander Marrack. "My troop left two days ago to investigate the blackness, sir," the other commander said.

"And I saw mine off earlier this afternoon with Captain Dibri leading them, sir," Eldath reported, and he felt his knees knock together nervously as the regent looked briefly in his direction.

Regent Nodabyus gave the two commanders a curt nod, stroking the thick beard that covered much of his face. "His most High Paramount is displeased with the lack of results we have suffered here," the royal commander sneered. "I am here to change that." The regent's eyes once again glued on Eldath. "Commander Eldath," he went on, "you and your men have actually captured the Outsider and seen what he is capable of doing. Are you sure that what has occurred here is something within his power?"

Eldath licked his lips, wishing silently that his throat was not so dry and his stance not so uncomfortable. "I would believe so,

sir," he answered, and hated the unsureness that he let seep into
his own voice.

"You would believe so?" Nodabyus repeated, his voice echoing
the sneer on his lips.

"The last report we received on his whereabouts, sir," Eldath
recalled, "was from the troop stationed outside the town of
Plestenah. That was the last sighting we've had."

Regent Nodabyus resumed pacing. "And he was heading
east?"

"No, sir," Eldath replied. "West."

The regent halted, cocking his head to one side to stare at the
commander as if he were a very mockery of humanity itself. "West,
commander?" he queried. "Then what in Imogen's name makes
you think he's been here?"

Eldath could not control the quivering, wavering feeling in his
legs. "Because that report was over a month ago, sir," he stuttered,
and his scepter almost slipped out of his hand. "I believe he's been
here and there's an increased sighting of Reakthi activity to back
up such an assumption, sir."

"So what are we to do, commander?" Nodabyus snarled. "Ask
the Reakthi which direction the Outsider has gone?"

Commander Eldath lowered his eyes in embarrassment.

Regent Nodabyus swung his overweight form to face the lake,
folding his arms across his expanse of stomach. "We shall wait
here only until we receive word on Commander Eldath's missive
to the king," the regent ordered. "Or until our two scouting parties
discover anything to the west." He waved the commanders away
with a disgusted frown. "You are dismissed."

There was an almost collective sigh of relief from the gathered
commanders as they stepped away from the imperious regent,
losing his obese frame in the unnatural darkness that filled the night.
Eldath quietly wiped the slickness from his scepter, allowing himself to inhale deeply. Arrogance ran high among the Guardsmen's
officials—and the higher the official, the higher it ran.

Eldath felt the reassuring hand of Commander Marrack on his
shoulder. "Don't let him get to you, Eldath," his fellow official
advised. "The closest Nodabyus has actually come to a skirmish
has been on a map in one of Mediyan's studies."

Eldath jerked his head up to make sure the regent wasn't within
hearing range. "It's not that, Marrack," the commander admitted.
"It's just that I had him—the Outsider—a prisoner! And I lost
him. I can stand Nodabyus's taunts, it's just the fact that that fat,

arrogant shagshooter wouldn't even have attained the position he's at if it weren't for officials such as you and I to make significant achievements for him to take the credit for."

Marrack chuckled softly, also glancing warily over his shoulder. "Well said, Eldath," he agreed.

The two commanders were silent as they neared their respective camps. "Well," Marrack finally added, "if our men find anything to the west, it'll be because of us."

Eldath sneered. "And Nodabyus'll take all the credit."

Eldath stopped as his companion did, and the commanding Guardsman did not like the look of fear and bewilderment that sparked in Marrack's eyes. Eldath tried to follow his friend's misty gaze out toward the surrounding forest, and, instead, found his own eyes locked on a form that stood seductively beside a tree. Immediately, all thoughts of Commander Marrack and the fear that filled his eyes vanished from Eldath's mind as he gaped in puzzlement at the shapely figure watching him from the outskirts of the camp.

"Solange?" Eldath breathed, and something deep down inside him said that it was not.

The slender redhead pushed herself away from the tree, walking toward Eldath with that inviting roll of her shoulders that the commander had not seen in over a year. Memories came crashing down upon Eldath, burying who he was and what he was doing. All that mattered were all those times with Solange—the experiences that they had shared and the sensations that they had fired. And here she was—Solange—as beautiful and as exquisite as when Eldath had left her on the docks of Genymaen.

Eldath tried to force down the unbelievable joy that erupted inside him and ran to embrace his wife. His thoughts were chaotic, and an undescribable flame ran throughout his body as he held her tightly. "Solange," he repeated. "What are you doing here? How did you get here?"

Solange placed a finger against Eldath's lips, hissing at him to be silent. She stared at him with a deep longing in her brilliant blue eyes, and her voice was a throaty growl of passion. "Love me," she begged. "Now, please. Love me."

No such pleading was necessary on the part of Solange. Eldath's passion-inflamed mind threw all other thoughts to the wind, swelling with the single desire to possess the beautiful redhead before him. So overwhelmed by her presence—giddy that they were together at last—Eldath stripped free of his uniform, his eager

hands tearing away the brocaded gown Solange herself wore.
How beautiful she was; his mind reeled. Her skin a soft white;
her figure slim and lithe. He truly loved her, and . . . and she was
here. Wanting him. Needing him.

Solange pulled Eldath to the bed of grass along the shore of
Lake Atricrix, oblivious of the tents and campfires and activity
that must be going on about them. But Eldath's mind was filled
only with his love for Solange and the insatiable desire to be within
her—to show her how greatly he loved her by bringing her the most
unbelievable pleasure. This was the only thing that mattered, the
commander's clouded brain demanded. Love her. Touch her.

An ecstatic gasp escaped Solange's lips as Eldath thrust deep
into her. Her arms and legs entwined about him, holding him to her,
crushing his body against hers, pulling him deeper and deeper into
her. Disconnected thoughts and sensations raced through Eldath's
mind. He was detached from everything except the gorgeous redhead sprawled beneath him.

As Eldath pulled back to thrust again, his dimmed brain warned
him that something was wrong. Solange pulled at him, sucked at his
member as if that part of her were alive. Fiery tingles of pleasure
arced their way up Eldath's nerves, blotting out the wondering
thoughts of Solange, yet another warning broke through Eldath's
clouded brain: a strangely muffled scream. And another. And a
third. And more until a very chorus of screams and howls went up
into the night, filling the unnatural darkness above the lake with a
substantial fear. In confusion, Eldath turned away from Solange
and looked up to see the camp besieged by a horde of bizarre shapes
and forms, all of their eyes flaring with the same fluid blackness
as the night. Questioningly, the commander looked down at his
wife and screamed as Solange's body melted and swelled into
a dark-skinned bulb of flesh, stiff waves of cilia bristling across
its surface. Cold, oozing tentacles replaced Solange's arms and
legs, and her loving embrace became a murderous stranglehold.
Absolute horror pierced Eldath's mind as he tried to pull free, all
the more horrified when he realized he was still penetrating the
pulsating, pliable mound of flesh below him.

A gaping mouth suddenly tore across the glistening flesh and
swallowed Eldath whole. His last thought was of Solange.

Regent Nodabyus bolted free of his tent, his dimpled fingers
tugging at his sword. Hideous screams of the dying resounded
into the night, and the regent gaped in horror at the slaughter
that surrounded the lake. Heaps of dead Guardsmen ringed the

shore, their blood trickling into the crystal waters. Large, malleable creatures of throbbing flesh squirmed among the corpses, and gangly Demons shrieked their soul-shattering screams as they tore flesh and lapped at the spilled blood. Even the line of commanders that had just left lay dead, their bodies contorted and twisted and leaking crimson.

Nodabyus swung about as a gurgling, slithering sound resonated behind him. A grinning, eyeless, froglike being squatted at his back, mucus streaming from its wide nostrils. Overcome with horror and revulsion, the regent staggered back a pace, urging his muscles to raise his weapon although terror had sapped him of his strength.

The froglike monster hopped closer. "You have trespassed on sacred ground," it croaked, and Nodabyus could see the millions of steely fangs that lined its mouth. "For that you must be punished."

A denial exploded within the regent, and his deepest instincts to survive gave him the strength he needed. With a fear-induced warcry, the fat regent sprang forward, his blade coming down for the frog-thing's eyeless head.

Silver flashed in the light of the many campfires, and a silver-grey spear of muscle rocketed out of the frog-thing's mouth, catching Nodabyus directly in the forehead. Bone splintered as the steel tongue pierced the regent's skull, splattering crimson across the night. The sword fell from lifeless hands as the regent dangled above the ground, held erect by the barbed tongue bored through his head. It was only after the creature retracted its tongue that Nodabyus crumpled to the ground, a jagged hole carved clean through his skull.

The malleable slug of Ryth'ueyh crawled toward the dead regent, its eye-stalks questioningly jerking back and forth. "He was their leader?" the *Deil* asked the froglike beast.

The amphibious creature bobbed itself up and down in an attempt to nod. "He was," the *Deil* declared.

"Well done, BkhoiLhum," Ryth'ueyh answered. "We have surely demonstrated to these inferior organisms that the memory of our Brethren must not be defiled."

The two monsters turned their eyes and eyeless features on the lake, ignoring the corpses that lay strewn about the shores. Even in the unnatural gloom of the night, a secret kind of illumination seemed to light the lake, casting slim ripples of silver radiance out across its surface.

The mound of writhing cytoplasm that was Lsuyryh edged closer to its companions, its cilia waving rhythmically along its pulsating flesh. "They have infected it," the *Deil* observed, and its voice sounded reminiscent of Solange's.

Although eyeless, BkhoiLhum bobbed again. "Yes, what causes this?" it asked. "Why is the Tomb of the one our Masters favored above the rest so hideously tainted by Purity? Who has thus defiled his burial site?"

Ryth'ueyh remained silent, its eye-stalks twitching experimentally this way and that.

The wolf-headed Vsdaefn oozed gracefully to join its partners. "I am disappointed," the *Deil* remarked. "There remains no trace of he who was called Gangrorz by the Voices that speak in the Dark—there is only Purity here. Purity that leaves a foul taste in my mouth."

"Indeed," Lsuyryh agreed. "I like it not when Purity overthrows that which is Darkness."

Ryth'ueyh's eye-stalks quivered. "Yet," it began, "there is a familiar stench to this Purity. It is the selfsame Power we seek."

"And it lingers here still," the snakelike Shub'yiwg noted, slithering to join the congregation of *Deils*. "I can see where it has recently returned to this site. It has since headed south."

The twisting, coiling shape of Ryth'ueyh glided southward. "Your eyes have yet to fail us, Shub'yiwg," it remarked. "We go southward and destroy that which has defiled the gravesite of he who was the greatest of us all."

"Southward," BkhoiLhum repeated.

"And destroy he who is called Matthew Logan," Shub'yiwg added.

A double smile appeared on Vsdaefn's twin mouths. "So the Darkness commands."

The freezing wind screamed over the sparkling waters of Lake Atricrix, blowing the stench of death westward as the *Deils* gathered their army together.

·6·

Macrocosm

Like an ill wind blowing forebodingly at her back, the sensation of being watched once again came over Mara. It was like a creeping warmth on the back of her neck as unseen and concealed eyes trailed her movements, observing with an intense interest her every action. Hampered as she was behind Logan, the priestess could only glance to either side, probing the forest's surface for any hint of the mysterious watchers. Whether they existed or not, the blackness overhead was enough to give anyone a bad case of nerves, Mara concluded. Every morning it took the sun longer to burn the darkness away, and every evening the ebony fog rolled in ever earlier. Sometime during the night the priestess had thought she heard distant cries from the area of Lake Atricrix but had convinced herself it was due to an overactive imagination. And besides, they had left the Guardsmen's camp yesterday afternoon—surely they were too far to have heard any noises coming from it.

Mara clung tighter to the young man in front of her as the freezing wind moaned softly through the trees. The cold was growing worse, she noted. It was as if the icy winds had an invisible rapport with the darkness that tried to take over the sky, and when the blackness gained strength, so did the cold. So what would that make of the Voices' home? she wondered. A place of eternal night and freezing cold?

A primeval portion of her mind—a more instinctive part—disagreed. No, it corrected the priestess, this was not the Voices' home. It was the Voices themselves. *They* were the blackness and the cold . . . and an Evil that the young girl had never expected to learn of, let alone face.

Faint pink light of early dawn gradually pressed its way through the trees, and Mara swung her gaze heavenward. Even though the sky resembled the first rays of day, she knew the reddish-pink

light was that of a false morning. From the position of the
darkness-engulfed sun, Mara guessed the day was already some
three hours old. At least, that was what Thromar had estimated
when the five had awoken in absolute darkness. Internal clocks
refused to acknowledge the erratic actions of the sky, and Mara
had slipped free of sleep at the same time she usually did. Only
the heavens had refused to correspond, the true dawn concealed
by a coal-black curtain of foreboding. Now, however, the darkness was receding, breaking up into coiling patches of velvet, and
beams of sunlight filtered through the foliage, triumphant in their
early-morning battle.

The warmth felt good on Mara's face as the yellow-and-green
stallion beneath her made its way through the greenery of Sparrill.
A deep growl sounded ahead of her, and she recognized the sound
of rushing water as the small group neared the Jenovian River.
Abruptly, the hidden presence of skulkers once again sent invisible
spiders of fear crawling up Mara's back, and the young priestess
shivered uncontrollably.

Logan threw a backward glance over his left shoulder, squinting
behind his eyepatch. "Cold?" he asked.

Mara nodded, lying without speaking. She didn't need to tell
the young man what she was afraid of . . . it was silly. Just as
Logan was reluctant to confess his thoughts to Mara, so too did
she keep certain things to herself. Which certainly wasn't the way
to be truthful with someone, she scolded herself. Still . . . what
was the point in expressing a fear as unfounded as hers?

The priestess looked interestedly over Logan's shoulder as the
sound of rushing water grew louder. The constant shield of trees
and shrubbery dropped away as the four horses stepped clear of
the forest, facing the strong current of the Jenovian with equine
snorts. A similar expression was on Thromar's face as he eyed
the swiftly flowing waters, and Mara decided Smeea's protesting
snort equally summed up her rider's feelings.

"What now?" the large fighter queried, the displeasure heavy
in his voice.

Moknay half stood in his saddle, and his strap of daggers
flickered with silver fire in the sunlight. "I've no complaints
about following the river until we reach the bridge. It's not as
if we don't know where Mediyan's men are."

Thromar nodded robustly. "And I, for one, have had my share
of fording rivers." The Rebel glanced at his companions. "No
complaints, Nightwalker?"

Darkling Nightwalker shook his head weakly, his black features betraying hints of paling while his eyes continued to darken. "It makes little difference where we cross so long as we cross," he responded, and there was an unsettling weariness to his voice.

The frailty that steadily overpowered the Guardian frightened Mara. There was a very important link between Nightwalker and Sparrill, and the priestess did not like the weakness that sapped the Shadow-spawn of his strength. She could almost feel it doing the same to the land—draining its vitality; snatching away the beauty Lelah had bestowed upon Sparrill; sucking at its very core of power.

Mara's green eyes flicked down and rested on the leather saddlebags draping the hindquarters of Logan's stallion. In one of those pouches was the object that kept what little hope she had left glowing. So long as they had the Heart in their possession, they had the power to disrupt the Voices' triumph and the Reakthi's conquest. But should the Bloodstone fall into other hands, all was lost: Sparrill, Denzil, the Wheel, and Matthew Logan.

The priestess questioningly looked at the young man seated before her. There was something between them; she could tell. Whatever it was, it played havoc with her thoughts. At times she felt herself unworthy of Logan; at others, she felt herself needing to be by his side just to be there. What kind of illogical thoughts were these? That was one of the many things she had heard about love—it didn't have to make sense . . . ever. It just hit when the combination was right, and that made Mara realize the remote possibilities that had thrown them together. If something had changed slightly along the line—if Moknay had never stopped in to see Barthol—Mara would never have met the young man from another world. But these were all secondary, weren't they? Even if her pleasant feelings and sensations of some incomprehensible inner completeness were attributed to love, it was a love that could not last. Logan longed to go home while Mara was restricted to Sparrill. Even if there was some magical way for her to go with him, who's to say the priestess wouldn't feel as out of place as Logan did here? Oh, she'd be with him, sure, but—all romantic illusions aside—love just *didn't* conquer all, did it?

Mara blinked her thoughts away as the unsettling warmth returned to the back of her neck. Sneering to herself, the priestess jerked her Binalbow from her shoulder and leveled it at the forest, her slim hand resting on the controlling lever.

Her green eyes narrowed as she tried once more to see through
the curtain of greenery that was the woods.

Shub'yiwg's largest eye blinked in amazement as the serpentine
monstrosity ducked below the safety of the brush, its mucid flesh
bubbling and frothing like lava. The line of gangly Demons stanced
behind the *Deil* watched with anxious impatience, streams of drool
dribbling from their round mouths.

"Impossible," Shub'yiwg snarled, anger concealing the surprise
in its gurgling voice. "I have been detected. The female being
has sensed he who senses all." The *Deil* coiled in on itself, its
thousands of eyes glistening as it turned to face the small army
of Demons behind it. "There can be no further delay. We were to
wait till my Brethren arrived—we can do so no longer. We must
not allow them to turn the Purity on us."

There was a sudden shuffle from the farthest Demon, and
Shub'yiwg's many eyes went wide with shock. Yellow-white
blood splashed across the leaves as a second Demon crumpled
to the forest floor, its skull crushed. Eyes glittering like jewels,
the snakelike *Deil* rose to its full height.

"This is not possible!" the monster spat. "You should not have
been able to take *me* by surprise! Not me!"

A third and fourth Demon crashed into the surrounding
trees, both their heads crushed inward and yellow-white blood
fountaining from their mangled skulls. A fifth Demon released
a vengeful shriek as it pounced on its attacker, yet its cry was
cut short as it was batted across the forest and thrown into an
obstructing tree. Bones snapped and cracked audibly as the gangly
monster practically wrapped around the thick tree trunk, the ebony
glimmer fading from its large eyes to be replaced by the vacancy
of death.

Shub'yiwg turned hate-filled eyes on the advancing figure that
had so easily slain the small force of Demons. "You may reek of
Purity," the *Deil* growled at its assailant, "but you are not my
Task."

Black energy crackled about the serpentine form as Shub'yiwg
catapulted itself out of the shrubbery toward the line of horses.

Logan swung his head up at the sound of the high-pitched scream
that came from within the trees, and Mara's hand tensed around the
lever of her Binalbow.

"What was that?" the young man queried.

Moknay whipped his horse around, daggers in either hand. "Sounded like a Demon," he answered.

The screech ended abruptly, replaced by the rushing waters of the Jenovian River. Questioning glances were traded by all but Mara, who kept her eyes locked on the foliage. *If that was a Demon,* she mused, *then I was right all along: we were being watched . . . being followed.*

A sudden jolt of fear charged through the priestess as a coiling mass of energy and protoplasm launched itself from the forest, hundreds of eyes gleaming along its snakelike body. Instinctively, her Binalbow twanged, releasing twin shafts of wood that caught the writhing monster in its midsection. With a startled yowl, the pulsating beast crumpled to the ground, fifty or so of its eyes staring in stupefaction at the two crossbow bolts in its gut.

Darkling Nightwalker tried to pull his horse around, yet his ever-increasing weakness made it difficult to fight his horse's fear. "Mere weapons alone cannot quench the horror of what is happening!" he warned.

Feeling horror grip him around his own throat, Logan tried to calm his yellow-and-green mount as it screamed in terror at the snakelike monster. How Mara had gotten a shot off at the creature was beyond the young man's understanding. It was almost as if she was expecting something like that to happen.

Shub'yiwg ducked as silver flashed in the sunlight, and Moknay's daggers spun harmlessly into the greenery. With an enraged roar, the snakelike *Deil* rose up from the dirt, ebony spears of sorcery sparking about its body.

"You are to die," the *Deil* declared. "Champions of Purity and defilers of Gangrorz's Tomb, you are to die!"

Thromar snorted in contempt, unsheathing his blood-caked sword and ramming his heavy boots into Smeea's flanks. "I've heard that one before," he grunted.

Black energy spumed from Shub'yiwg's body as Thromar charged. Dark magic screamed, yet the huge fighter ducked the oncoming bolt with an agility that seemed impossible for such a big man. A victorious warcry echoed along the Jenovian's banks as Thromar's heavy sword slashed downward, catching a small section of the shifting monster and severing the flesh. The detached portion of cytoplasm continued to pulse and throb even though it lay separated from Shub'yiwg's main body.

Nightwalker narrowed his tainted eyes suspiciously, grey energy crackling about his hands. "More of them will be coming," he advised the others. "Matthew Logan, you must use the Heart. Our weapons alone are not enough. You know that."

Logan turned an angry eye on the Guardian. "No!" he roared. "I'm not going to use any magic! You said I wouldn't have to!"

"There will be more," urged Nightwalker. "We will be . . ."

"*No!*" Logan thundered, spurring his horse forward.

Mara clung tightly to the young man as he drove their frightened horse toward the writhing creature on the riverbank. Logan's Reakthi sword flashed in the morning light, streaking for the serpentlike monster. Ebony power flamed, and Logan careened from his mount, his sword spilling from his hands. With a curt shout, Mara felt the heat-filled blast of energy pluck the young man from his stallion and rip him out of her grasp.

"The Purity," Shub'yiwg snarled, pulling his lengthy body upwards. "I can see it. It is here . . . on this inferior beast of burden."

As the *Deil* rose up toward the leather saddlebags, one of its many eyes caught the sudden movement atop the horse. A surprised shout escaped the beast's mouthless form as Mara's Binalbow twanged, and two wooden bolts pierced the mutable form. Bubbling black acid began to drip from the viscid being as it toppled away from the yellow-and-green horse, writhing in pain.

"Impossible," the Servant rasped. "Mere weapons alone . . ."

Emerald eyes locked on the hideous mockery of life, Mara sent four more shafts shrieking into the pliable shape before her. For all she knew, this thing had killed Matthew! Killed him while she was right behind him! And she had been unable to do anything about it!

Shub'yiwg screamed as two more bolts slammed into its body, releasing another wave of sizzling black blood. With an agonized twist of its body, the *Deil* tried to flee back into the forest, yet another pair of bolts ripped through its gelatinous flesh.

"Masters," the creature gargled. "I am your Servant. Why have you deserted me?"

The tractile body jerked as more shafts tore through its mucid flesh, and the jet-black eyes all along its serpentine form winked out. With a wet slap, the *Deil* collapsed, its corrosive blood welling up around it like a miniature black pond.

Logan pulled himself unsteadily to his feet, lightly touching his bruised shoulder where the blast had struck him. "Okay, Nightwalker," he gasped, "what the hell happened? How come Mara was able to kill it?"

Mara wheeled around in the saddle, gaping at the young man. "You're all right?" she inquired.

Logan nodded slowly, trying to shake the dizziness from inside his head. "Yeah," he replied. He touched his eyepatch with disgust. "If I could have seen that blast coming, I probably could have dodged it."

There was a look of curiosity on Nightwalker's features as he watched the couple, and his grey-tinted eyes glinted with disbelief. Moknay noted the Guardian's perplexed stare, yet sneered at the implied ignorance. How many times before had Nightwalker feigned ignorance?

"What's the explanation?" the Murderer asked, and his tone suggested an immediate answer.

Nightwalker blinked as if he had not been concerned with that topic. "The explanation is plain enough," he responded. "So plain none of us even thought to consider it. The priestess's bolts are made from wood—the wood's from the forests of Sparrill."

"So they're part of the Purity of Sparrill," Thromar finished, his tiny eyes flashing proudly as he understood.

Nightwalker gave the Rebel a curt nod. "A small part but a part nonetheless." The Shadow-spawn returned his gaze to Logan and the confusion seemed to refill his eyes. "The rest of us, however, are not using such weapons." He glanced at the serpentine corpse. "There will be more coming," Nightwalker continued, "and Mara will not be able to slay them all. We need the magicks of the Heart, Matthew Logan. You must be prepared to use them next time."

Logan pulled himself into the saddle with Mara's help and jabbed an accusing finger toward the Shadow-spawn. "Bullshit!" he spat. "You said that this war would be on a more down-to-earth scale than our war against Gangrorz. That implied that I wouldn't have to use any magic."

Mara tried to back away from the young man as his anger spumed forth. Sometimes there could be so much fury inside him that it scared her.

"Look," Logan went on, "Mara killed one of these things with her Binalbow and Thromar took a chunk out of it as well. Doesn't that tell you that we don't need magic?"

"Mere weapons alone cannot . . ." Nightwalker started.

"Don't give me any of your philosophical crap!" snapped Logan. "Mere weapons alone *can* do something, so fuck you and fuck your magic!" The young man angrily clucked his horse forward. "Let's get out of here."

The yellow-and-green horse cantered away from the motionless *Deil*, trailed by Moknay's grey-and-black stallion. Thromar followed after them, sheathing his heavy blade. Nightwalker remained near the *Deil*'s cadaver, mutely staring down at it. Only the silent figure still lurking within the forest caught the pity that welled up in the Guardian's grey-tainted eyes before he pulled his horse around and shadowed the others as they rode farther downriver.

The blackness was seeping back into the sky as the sun began to drop behind the mountains in the west, and the arctic wind returned to moan through the trees. Frowning, Logan drew his handicapped gaze away from the unnatural darkness that was invading the heavens and scanned the clearing where they had made camp. It had been too dangerous to camp on the river's bank where they would be easily seen, so the five had returned to the protection of the woods. Morosely, the young man noticed Thromar was the only one left in the clearing—not that he blamed the others for leaving. He had really blown up that morning, hadn't he?

Thromar noted the young man's one-eyed gaze and offered him a piece of beef jerky. "Would you like something to eat, friend-Logan?" the fighter queried.

Logan shook his head slowly, trying to blink his single eye into focus. Being half-blind was a real bitch, the young man thought sourly. Maybe that was why he had snapped like that. Cut down to one eye really gave him a headache, even with the eyepatch. Not only could he probably have avoided the *Deil*'s blow earlier, but his depth perception was really screwed up thanks to his missing contact lens.

He should probably apologize for acting like such a grade-A asshole.

"Where did everybody go again?" he asked Thromar.

The Rebel shrugged haphazardly. "Moknay and Mara are at the Jenovian," he said. "Moknay wanted to shave; Mara wanted to freshen up. Imogen knows where Nightwalker went."

Logan gave the surrounding forest a cursory glance. He really didn't blame Nightwalker for running off again. The Guardian had a purpose, to protect Sparrill and all the other worlds of the multiverse from the Darkness, and Logan had refused to follow the Shadow-spawn's instructions. But screw that! He had been told that no magic was going to be necessary on his part! For once he thought he was going to get through this battle without fearing the imprisonment that would follow should he use too much magic—

then Nightwalker hits him with that "mere weapons alone" crap again. Besides, Logan wasn't planning on using any magic until he came face to face with Groathit . . . then he'd use magic!

The young man turned away from those thoughts and scratched at the days' growth of stubble that had accumulated on his cheeks and chin. He probably looked lousy, he decided. About a week's worth of stubble, an eyepatch over one eye, and a sweatsuit in tatters. He should have probably gone with Moknay and Mara to the river to clean himself up a bit, but maybe his pride kept him away. He had acted like a prize fool that morning, and he realized it would be difficult to face his friends again without feeling awkward and embarrassed at his previous actions.

Shrugging, Logan got to his feet and informed Thromar he was going to join the others at the river. The blackness overhead was steadily deepening as the young man stepped into the foliage. The deep growl of rushing waters sounded just on the other side of greenery, replacing the uneasy and unnatural silence of the forest life. Unexpectedly, Logan caught a flash of blurred movement on his right and whipped out Moknay's dagger, arm extended. Hampered by his blind right eye, the young man almost skewered the darkly clad figure that stepped lightly out of the greenery, a wicked grin on his features as he spritely hopped back a pace.

"I'd really wish you'd stop trying to return my dagger," smirked Moknay, and his strap of daggers flickered in the diminishing sunlight.

Logan sucked in a breath of relief, squinting his good eye at the Murderer. "Do you have to do that?" he demanded.

"Do what, friend?" Moknay asked back, and his grin betrayed the innocence in his voice.

"Walk so damn quietly," Logan complained.

"Part of my job," the Murderer quipped. His grey eyes fell upon the dagger once again, and a questioning eyebrow shot up. "Going to the river?"

Logan nodded.

Moknay smiled at a private joke, and his eyes sparkled like the daggers across his chest. "Don't take too long," he smirked. "I don't want anybody getting separated once this darkness rolls in completely." He was a grey shadow of the unnatural dusk as he started back toward their camp. "Oh," Logan heard him call out, "and tell Mara to hurry up, too."

Logan just kept nodding at the uncharacteristically cheerful Murderer. He didn't seem to hold Logan's outburst of anger against him, the young man mused. Might be the fact that they were heading for his hometown—and it had been a long time since they had been in Eadarus . . . a real long time.

Distant thoughts of the beginning—of Logan's arrival and his moments of near madness—ran rampant in his mind. He remembered first meeting Moknay—left alone in a town Thromar had called a thieves' quarters and almost getting the crap beat out of him by three drunks. He recalled the confrontation in the tavern between him and Groathit, and how arrogant the spellcaster had been . . . so sure of himself . . . It had cost him his eye. Now . . . Now it was going to cost the spellcaster much more. Now he was going to lose the one thing he couldn't bear to lose—the final battle with Matthew Logan.

Smiling in projected triumph, Logan stepped clear of the forest and stood by the Jenovian's banks, his thoughts still locked on Groathit and his many schemes. His single eye caught the movement by the river's edge and his thoughts were shattered by the slim, red-and-black-clad form kneeling beside the waters.

Mara smiled a greeting before dunking her head back into the river and then snapping back up, her long, wet hair cracking like a whip across her back. The fabric of her black tunic was sticky with water and clung to the slender curves of her upper torso with the grip of epoxy. Spots of moisture also dotted her red slacks as small rivulets of water trailed down her long tresses, across her shoulders, and down her back.

A sudden hot flash ran through Logan and he swore he must have blushed down to his knees.

"Coming to join me?" Mara queried.

Logan tried to find his tongue but realized somebody must have taken it. "Uh . . . I . . . um . . . just to shave," he finally got out.

Mara nodded and smiled, ducking forward once again to further wet her hair. Logan was bombarded by droplets as the priestess jerked up once more, tossing her head back and splaying liquid across the riverbank.

Logan knelt beside the beautiful girl, wetting Moknay's dagger in the cold river. Mara didn't seem to hold his earlier fury against him either, he noted. In fact, she seemed rather pleased to see him— although he couldn't understand why after he had acted like such a buffoon. And why couldn't he think of anything clever to say? Why did he have to feel so damn awkward when he could be making witty, charming conversation? Because someone had muddled his brain and his tongue, that's why! So blame it on the magic.

Shaking his head to sort out the jumbled thoughts that lurked there, Logan set about ridding himself of the stubble growing about his face like crabgrass. A faceful of water struck him as Mara sent a playful splash at him, an enchanting smile on her lips. Logan looked up at her, water dripping from his black hair, and he gave her his best Moknay-sneer.

"You still haven't kept your promise to me," the priestess scolded, combing out her wet hair.

Logan flinched as he scraped the underside of his jaw with his dagger. "What promise?" he asked back.

"You were going to tell me about your world, remember?"

Logan smirked and almost cut off his nose. "There's not much to tell," he replied.

Mara eyed the young man, a deep flame of some secret emotion burning in her emerald gaze. "Not much to tell?" she repeated. "Not much to tell, indeed. There's something there that's enough to make you want to go back."

Logan couldn't fight logic like that. "Yeah," he agreed, "but what's there is just what I'm used to. That's all. What's there is *my* world. Nothing else. Sometimes I wonder *why* I want to go back—other times I *have* to go back. My world doesn't have much to offer except for the fact that it *is* my world. I know where I belong there—I know what I'm supposed to do. Here, I'm not so sure. Here, I get so damn confused." He glanced over at the priestess. "And I don't like being confused," he concluded.

Mara nodded sharply, water dripping from her hair. "So I've noticed," she smiled.

Logan finished his dagger-shave and attempted to use the rippling waters of the Jenovian as a mirror. The reflection that peered back at him almost startled the young man. His cheeks and chin were still dark with stubble only his Norelco Tripleheader back home could get at, but his bare-bladed attempt was adequate. Still, his black hair had had time to grow and was no longer the well-groomed, half-the-ear barbershop job it used to be. In addition to his longer hair, the eyepatch did add a certain touch of spice to his looks, and Logan almost felt like placing his dagger in his mouth and snarling piratelike at his image. Give me a dark cape and a bandana and I'd fit right in, he thought with a grin.

But you don't fit right in, the anger inside reminded him. You're a stranger, remember? An outsider? A man who doesn't belong here at all and who's been given the ungodly task of carrying a world's responsibilities on his shoulders. Do you want that,

Matthew? Do you? Of course not! So stop smiling and get back to camp. Your *real* world's still waiting for you.

An unexpected second splash of water knocked the young man's thoughts aside and quenched his anger like fire. In shock, he turned his single eye on Mara, who was smiling with a lustful bout of mischief in her eyes.

"You know what?" she teased the young man. "You think too much."

The cheerfulness that sparked in Mara's eyes—and that had gleamed in Moknay's as well—chased the fury away from Logan's thoughts. Like catching a contagious disease, the young man smirked back.

"Oh, yeah?" he questioned, and sent a wave of water back at the priestess.

Mara shrieked as the cold water drenched her but retaliated with a backhanded slap that sent more water cascading into Logan. Silvery bubbles spumed in the light of the dying sun as the couple batted liquid at one another, playing a very wet game of catch with the Jenovian's water. Soaked, Logan hardly realized how hard he was laughing as he turned away from the river and jumped at Mara.

"Wanna play that way, huh?" he asked.

Playfully, Logan lifted Mara up and attempted to toss her into the river. With a yelp, the priestess grabbed onto the young man's sweat jacket and pulled him in after her. Crystal-clear waters sprayed as the pair splashed into the Jenovian, laughing loudly at their own silliness.

Mara flicked one last splash at Logan. "See?" she said with a laugh. "I told you you think too much."

The smile that was stretched across Logan's face almost hurt as he stared into the beautiful green eyes before him. What is this? part of his mind asked, stunned by the happiness. What the hell is this we're feeling? But Logan ignored his own wonder, overwhelmed by the joy burning inside him and decided sometimes he *did* think too much.

All at once, Logan's hand was on Mara's arm, and their touch became an embrace, and their embrace a kiss. And even the coldness of the Jenovian could not dampen the burning desire flaring to life in both of them.

"I believe this is the prelude to their primitive reproductive coition."

Logan broke away from Mara's soft lips and turned on the speaker. He felt a stab of fear penetrate his heart as he spied the dark shapes of cytoplasm writhing on the shore, each flanked by two Demons. Abrupt shock dampened the many emotions whirling through him, and the young man's loving embrace with Mara became a grip of mutual fear.

The two *Deils* slithered closer, their black eyes trained on the couple waist-deep in the river. Although shifting and mutating like Gangrorz, Logan noticed the smaller creatures held distinct shapes. The first, he observed, resembled a giant, featherless bird, yet a mass of small, wiry tentacles squirmed where a beak should have been. The other beast resembled a crocodile only in the constant shape of its snout, and, for some odd reason, also reminded Logan of Groathit.

"Are these the inferior creatures that dared defile the Tomb of our Brethren," the bird-thing queried, its voice a high-pitched shriek, "and those who dealt Shub'yiwg the Sleep of Death?"

"So says Ryth'ueyh," the reptilian monster answered. Its ebony eyes slid downward on its crocodilelike features. "Odd, I seem to detect something strange about them."

"Yes," the other agreed, "a disorder in the air. An Unbalance."

Tiny rivers of sweat accompanied the dripping riverwater down Logan's face as he watched the two *Deils* writhe and churn before him. He still had his sword and dagger, but Mara was weaponless, and she was the one who had killed the first *Deil*. Maybe he had been too harsh on Nightwalker—maybe some kind of magic was going to be needed. But . . . dammit! Why'd they have to attack now? Why when he and Mara were so blasted vulnerable?

Logan withdrew his sword and took a step toward the *Deils*. "Back off," he threatened, blade extended. "I'm the one you're looking for, so if you don't want to end up like your 'Brethren,' I'd suggest you get the hell out of my way."

The crocodilian *Deil* turned an amused gaze on its companion. "Are we being threatened by this insignificant organism, Tuhauab?" it queried mockingly.

There was an unsure gleam in Tuhauab's ebony eyes. "I do not know, Uhayhoth," it muttered. "This Unbalance . . ."

Uhayhoth barked a harsh laugh that seemed to generate from the depths of its protoplasmic form. "Unbalance!" the monster venomously spat. A taloned hand formed out of its malleable slime and ordered the quartet of Demons forward. "Kill him!"

Logan pushed Mara behind him as he leapt to confront the four Demons. Shrill, soul-shattering screams issued from the

monsters' mouths as they launched themselves toward the river,
claws glinting in the departing sunlight. Teeth clenched, Logan
drew his bruised right arm across in a sweeping arc of steel. One
of the creatures shrieked in pain, yellow-white fluid ripping free
from its chest. Another hastily retreated, narrowly avoiding the
Reakthi blade. The third Demon was not so swift, and Logan
felt his arm go rigid with shock as the sword slammed into the
side of the Demon's skull, lodging firmly in the skull. Pale blood
splattered the young man's hand as the fatally wounded monster
spilled to one side, crashing into the fourth Demon and knocking
it into the Jenovian.

"Pathetic creations!" howled Uhayhoth, barbed limbs sprouting
from its back. "No wonder your Creator was destroyed!"

One of the uninjured Demons looked up, its large eyes flickering
with the nefarious magicks of the *Deils*. A twisted, malevolent
sneer crossed its circular mouth, and saliva trickled down its chin
as it redirected its attack and lunged for Uhayhoth. The crocodilian
Deil toppled backwards in surprise.

Logan reached behind him and grabbed Mara's hand, sprinting
out of the river. They were fighting among themselves, he mused
with a grim smile. The Demons had been created by Gangrorz, and,
no matter what had happened to the Worm, remained fatally loyal
to him. Not even another *Deil* could talk about the Worm in such
condescending tones without sparking into life the faithfulness the
Demons held for their deceased Creator.

With a warcry, Logan dove from the Jenovian River, tearing
his sword through the inconsistent muck of Tuhauab's body. The
monster screamed in astonishment, losing its balance and spilling
into the forest beside its companion. The remaining Demons
seemed momentarily confused as the two humans ran into the
foliage while their leader and Creator's Brethren continued to
struggle along the riverbank.

An enormous, crablike pincer formed out of Uhayhoth's bulk
and snapped the neck of the renegade Demon. "Stop them!" the
Deil thundered, and the two surviving Demons knew what would
happen if they disobeyed.

Green and brown blurred as Logan bolted through the greenery,
shoving aside branches and brambles that obstructed his path. He
kept one hand securely gripped to Mara's, his Reakthi blade in
the other as he pushed shrubbery aside. He could hear the loping
gait of the Demons in pursuit as he broke through the trees and
back into the clearing of their camp. Moknay looked up as the

pair hurried in, their fear scrawled across their faces.

"Moknay!" Logan cried out. "We've got to . . ."

The young man felt his voice crack and die as his eye spotted the coiling, oozing shapes of protoplasm that stood in a semicircle about the camp. Numerous pairs of black eyes trained on him and Mara, and an overwhelming wave of despair washed over him.

"Welcome, Matthew Logan," a slug-shaped *Deil* greeted him. "We have been awaiting you."

A heavy silence fell upon the camp as the tension leaked from Logan's stance, and his arms fell to his sides. Bushes rustled behind him as the two Demons charged in, briefly startled by the appearance of more *Deils* and the surrender of their intended prey. Hopelessly, Logan lowered his Reakthi sword, yet refused to let the weapon drop to the ground in total submission.

"We tried to stop them," Thromar sadly apologized. "Our weapons weren't enough this time."

The maggoty shape of Ryth'ueyh slid forward, its black eyes flashing from atop their stalks. "Of course not," it responded. "Mere weapons alone cannot stop the Force of those who speak in the Darkness."

A swift blue eye jerked to the leather bags strapped to his horse's flanks, and Logan saw that the *Deils* had yet to uncover the Bloodstone. That was what they needed, he decided. He would be unable to reach Mara's Binalbow in time, let alone use it right to wipe out all the *Deils* that filled the camp. He had to get to the Heart and pull out a stream of magic. Not a whole lot—these *Deils* were certainly weaker than Gangrorz if one was attacked by a Demon—but just enough energy to blow these bastards into so many little pieces of slime.

Mucus dripping to the ground in writhing, squirming blobs, a disgusting, wolflike creature neared Logan and Mara, fixing the eyes of its twin heads on the two. "What is to be done?" it questioned.

Ryth'ueyh twisted its eyestalks in thought. "Perhaps it would be best to contact our Masters," it mused. "We would not want to incur their wrath by doing something incorrectly."

Logan jerked his head up toward Thromar and Moknay, a burning determination in his one eye. The two opposite the young man read his expression but frowned at the young man's desire to fight. It was suicidal, the returning gazes seemed to say. Their escape depended entirely upon the Bloodstone and Logan's possession of it—unfortunately, any type of distraction would probably prove to be fatal.

There was a murderous flicker of icy fire in Moknay's grey eyes as his gloved hands darted for the many weapons hidden within his cape. "What the *Deil*," the Murderer said with a shrug, "you only live once." And double blurs of silver lashed out from his hands.

The sluglike Ryth'ueyh screamed as one of Moknay's triple-bladed throwing knives passed dangerously close to its protruding eyestalks. With a provoked roar, the creature spun toward the darkly clad Murderer as Logan sprang.

Using the anger that had earlier burned within him, Logan propelled himself across the clearing, scrambling for his yellow-and-green horse. Black eyes instantly turned on him, and the wolflike Vsdaefn stretched out a coiling limb. The *Deil* shrieked in agony as its tentacle split in half, severed cleanly by Thromar's massive sword. Corrosive black ichor spurted into the evening air, striking the forest floor and burning into the grass like ebony acid.

The other *Deils* reacted, Ryth'ueyh extending a clawed arm toward Logan. "Stop him!" the monster ordered. "He must be stopped!"

"Uglier bastards than you have tried!" roared Thromar, lashing about viciously with his ichor-smeared weapon.

Ryth'ueyh drew back its limb as Thromar's sword sliced the air close by. With a hideous scream, one of the Demons threw itself at Thromar, black fire burning about its claws. It screamed a second time as one of Moknay's daggers speared its forehead, spreading yellow-white blood across the trees. The other Demon also toppled backwards, two daggers lodged in its skinny throat.

"An Unbalance!" the birdlike Tuhauab screamed behind Logan. "Beware the Unbalance!"

Logan was half-relieved when he reached his horse and fumbled with the cover of his saddlebags. Blinded on the right side by his patched eye, the young man failed to see the froglike monstrosity that leaped toward him, a silvery tongue ejecting from its fang-rimmed maw. An unexpected shove pushed Logan to the ground and away from his horse. Blood spattered the campsite as Thromar dropped to his left knee, BkhoiLhum's steel tongue stabbing into his right thigh.

Cursing in pain, the bearded Rebel slammed his sword down, and sparks flew as metal clashed with metal. BkhoiLhum emitted a garbled scream as its tongue splintered. Silvery-black fluid seeped from the frog-thing's mouth as it withdrew what remained of its tongue, still howling its misery as blood clogged its throat.

Mara flipped into the campsite, snatched up her Binalbow, jerked the lever twice, and sent four shafts of wood into BkhoiLhum's eyeless face. Black streams of lifefluid squirted from the froglike being as the *Deil* toppled backwards, its tiny forearms twitching spasmodically. A hind leg formed out of its shifting bulk long enough to convulse once, then stop.

"This is not possible," Vsdaefn snarled at Ryth'ueyh. "Another of our kind has been vanquished by these inferior organisms! How can this be?"

"Because the Balance is no longer tipped in your favor, beast," a deep, ominous voice declared imperiously behind the *Deils*.

Logan picked himself off the ground, swinging around to catch sight of the cowled figure behind him. Darker flecks of grey marred Darkling Nightwalker's hair and eyes as he steadied his weakening form against a nearby tree. Lines of sorrow and of pain dug deep furrows in the Shadow-spawn's features, yet the clenched fists at his sides revealed a fierce will to survive.

"What know you of the Balance?" snapped Ryth'ueyh in contempt.

Nightwalker smiled back at the creature, and even Logan felt a shiver run down his spine at the cruelty of the grin. "You are not the only Servants, beast," he growled. "Even in Chaos there must be some Order, and, so long as a Balance exists, you and your Masters have not yet won."

"What do you mean, inferior one?" Vsdaefn boomed. "What Servants do you speak of?"

Nightwalker raised a darkly clad arm and a painful hum vibrated across the clearing. Invisible shock waves of energy streamed throughout the campsite, creating an audible buzz that threatened to burst the eardrum. Crackling energy stepped free of the foliage, their raw power drawn into humanoid shapes of unearthly blackness. White eyes flared on each of the figures, narrowed with intense hatred at the gathered *Deils*. Slowly, as a whole, the army of Blackbodies turned to face Logan.

"*For a third time you who hold sway to the entire multiverse have brought forth a portion of the Macrocosm,*" one of the creatures told the young man, yet it seemed to speak with all their voices. The horde of Blackbodies turned on the *Deils*. "*We—like yourselves—are Beings of the Megacosmos . . . and Servants. Yet we serve the Balance . . . something you have sworn to destroy. We will not allow you to do so—even if it means our own destruction and that of the Wheel.*"

Ryth'ueyh seemed to forget all about Logan and his friends. "Come, then," the *Deil* barked. "Come and face your nonexistence!"

As black power crackled on both sides, Logan helped Thromar to his feet. "Are you all right?" he worried.

Thromar nodded quickly, his face pale behind his beard. "Right enough to ride, friend-Logan," he replied, "which is what I suggest we do."

Returning the nod, Logan leapt onto his yellow-and-green stallion, pulling Mara up behind him. Thromar, his face contorted in pain, dragged himself to Smeea and clambered into the saddle, the right leg of his pants already heavily soaked with his own blood. Energy arced and forked around them like ebony lightning bolts as the four horses galloped free of the clearing.

Blackness flooded the sky as the sun disappeared behind the western hills, and the freezing wind whipped over Logan's wet clothing and made him shiver. A low moaning on the wind seemed to whisper the name of the destined champions in the war that had just started behind them.

"How'd you know they'd help?" Moknay called to Nightwalker, the rumble of battle fading in the distance.

"It is their Task," answered Nightwalker, and that was all he said.

Fine, Logan thought, snorting to himself at the Guardian's silence. Don't explain—at least you bought us the escape necessary and saved me from using magic again. Judging by the way you sometimes work makes me think you did that on purpose just so I wouldn't have to use magic, but that's stretching things a little too far, isn't it?

And as the quartet of colorful horses rode through the unnatural darkness that was not yet night, no one was able to see the deep remorse and sadness that filled Darkling Nightwalker's eyes like the ever-strengthening grey of weakness.

And the arctic wind moaned again: *Deils*, it seemed to say. *Deils*.

7

Brothel

Logan stood off to one side, losing himself in the shadows. Mara was at his arm, yet he did not even notice her, his eyes glazedly fixed on the three figures highlighted in the glare of Sparrill's moon. Unable to bear with the grief, his mind was oddly detached from the scene and, thereby, growing numb. Smeea uneasily snorted, pawing anxiously at the dirt. Her red eyes momentarily flicked upward to train upon the three forms outlined by the yellow-green glow of the night. The darker forms of Moknay and Nightwalker were like ominous specters surrounding the half-seated figure of Thromar, and the dim beams of moonlight only made the fighter's face appear paler.

Darkling Nightwalker walked lightly away from where the fighter sat and approached Logan with silent steps. A deep look of loss reflected in the Guardian's eyes as he faced the young man from Santa Monica and shook his head sullenly. "He has lost a lot of blood," the Shadow-spawn said, his deep voice hushed with pity. "He will not last the night."

A bead of moisture invaded Logan's uncovered eye and the young man tried to blink it clear. "No," he choked, and the denial he had wanted to fill his words became a strained plea. "Can't you do something?"

Nightwalker shook his head once more, empty, white eyes downcast. "I can do nothing now that the Voices have spoken in this multiverse, Matthew Logan," he replied. "My powers wane as theirs increase. You yourself said you felt the magical repercussions in your own wound."

Logan nodded, briskly glancing at the torn shoulder of his sweat jacket and the dried blood that still clung there in caked patches. "Can't we at least get him to Eadarus?" the young man queried. "Maybe someone there can . . ."

"He hasn't the strength to stay on his horse," Nightwalker interrupted.

"But we can't just let him die like this," protested Logan. "It isn't fair."

Darkling Nightwalker's grey-tinted eyes filled with remorse. "Remember what I said before, Matthew Logan," he stated. "There are no rules in the millions of multiverses that distinguish between fair and unfair."

The sorrow that swelled so greatly in the young man gave way, and the tears flowed freely from both his eyes. Mara's already tear-stained face turned to look at him, yet, so deadened by his grief, Logan did not feel her reassuring touch on his hand. So many thoughts were racing through his head he was hardly able to grasp one when another would replace it.

Thromar's dying.

He's been with you from the start.

He's going to die.

Your fault.

Save him.

Thromar's dying.

Caught up in a stupor of despair, Logan came closer to the dying Rebel and inwardly cringed at the crimson pool that formed beside the fighter's right leg. A weak smile revealed yellowing teeth as Thromar glanced up at the young man's approach and tried to conceal his pain and enfeeblement.

"I hope your eyes are not leaking, friend-Logan," he remarked. "I'd hate to think I brought tears to any of my friends."

Logan barely stifled the anguished sob that tried to escape and sniffed instead. "Thromar . . ." he began, but his voice betrayed him and quivered woefully.

"Come, now, friend-Logan," said Thromar, smiling, but his eyes had lost most of their twinkle, "I've taken worse. A mere flesh wound! By the time you and Moknay return from Eadarus, I'll be better than ever."

Logan knew as well as the fighter that that was a lie. There would only be a very cold, physical shell left of the Rebel by the time anyone returned from Eadarus. And yet, Thromar refused to acknowledge the nearness of his own death for the benefit of his friends. He wanted them to continue on without him . . . to consider him just another casualty in the coming war with the Darkness, but . . . he was more than that. He was Thromar, the loyal, fierce Rebel, who somehow still carried an air of innocence about like him a curious child and always had a chuckle or two about anything. How could Logan forget him? How could Logan go on knowing *he* had killed his friend? Knowing he was at fault yet again? The young man had already suffered through the death of Druid Launce—had felt the druid's body go limp as they both had grasped the oaken staff of Launce's trade. And now Thromar was dying in much the same way, having taken a blow meant for Logan . . . just like Mara had done.

The young man looked back at the priestess standing in the shadows. Mara, he mused. He had saved her, hadn't he? He had brought her back to life when she had taken a blow meant for him. Surely he could duplicate the process? If he could pull Mara back from death, why couldn't he heal Thromar's leg?

Weigh the consequences, another part of his mind advised. First, Roana told you that tampering with such Natural occurrences could upset the Balance. Bringing one person back to life was one thing— making a habit out of it was another. Logan might knock the whole Balance back in favor of the Darkness if he used the Bloodstone, or, worse, he might permanently strand himself here . . . trap himself forever in Sparrill all because he had used one iota of magic too much. Did he dare risk not only his own return, but the Balance of the Wheel itself?

"You're damn right I will," the young man grumbled out loud, turning swiftly on his Nikes and striding to where his horse stood.

There was a living shadow at his back as Logan reached out for his saddlebags, and Moknay's gloved hand was suddenly on the young man's shoulder. "I know what you're thinking, friend," the Murderer said, "yet I'm not sure it's the right thing to do. You'll be attracting the Voices like moths to a taper."

Logan spun on Moknay, a fiery rage burning in his uncovered eye. "I don't care!" he snapped. "I'm not going to let Thromar bleed to death!"

Moknay was silent as Logan untied the leather straps and lifted the cover of one of the pouches. Crimson light blossomed forth from the saddlebag, so brilliant that even Logan was forced to turn away. A crackling of power came from within the sack like the blinking of a neon light, and Logan threw a questioning look at his friends behind him. Moknay had backed away, his grey eyes alert with his mistrust of magic; Mara was wide-eyed, the shadows she had been concealed in banished by the red glow that came from Logan's saddlebag. The bewilderment in the young man dampened, however, when his quizzical gaze fell upon Thromar and he saw how deathly pale the Rebel looked in the ruby flame.

Squinting his good eye, Logan turned back to the scarlet flare of light spuming from his saddlebag. Tentatively, he reached inside the leather pouch and lifted out the Bloodstone. Crimson radiance burned anew as the Heart came free of its encasement, alive with a halo of sanguine energy. A chorus of nearby crickets began to chirp gleefully, adding to the hum of power emanating from the gemstone. A sudden gasp pulled Logan's eye away from the Heart and back to Mara.

"Regulate the Heart," she breathed.

Logan blinked. "Huh?"

"Don't you remember what the sprite told us?" she questioned. "You have to regulate the Heart since you're in possession of it. Whenever it releases any energy, you have to direct it to where it would do the most good."

And it would require no magic on his part, Logan finally recalled. So the Bloodstone's curious glare was its signal for release. The young man could use the discharge to heal Thromar and not even worry about upsetting the Balance or damning himself to Sparrill. It couldn't have been at a more opportune moment.

Logan squinted his uncovered eye at the Heart, peering through the haze of light surrounding the gem like a rosy fog. Okay, he thought, you need to be regulated—I'll regulate you.

As if a thing alive, the aura of brilliance encasing the Heart leapt skyward, bent inward, and dove into Logan. There was an intense tingle of pins and needles all throughout the young man's body as the sorcery filled him, causing his hair to stand on end in something like a static electric charge. The young man momentarily feared the sudden coalescence of energy inside him—worried that it wouldn't leave him when he sent it elsewhere—but then he turned toward Thromar and forced his doubts aside.

A vermilion mist of power outlined the young man from Santa Monica as he knelt beside the Rebel, crimson tendrils of force crackling about him. Scarlet sparks jumped experimentally from the young man's fingers as he delicately touched the wounded leg, and—just like it had been with Mara—he could see the internal damage.

Through the magicks of the Bloodstone, Logan saw past the fighter's flesh to the muscle beneath, probed further through the shredded sinew and split veins, and looked at the very bone itself. The frog-thing's tongue had reached the femur, chipping the bone in three places. Blood-red fire streamed from Logan's hands and shot into Thromar's leg, repairing the bone, reconnecting the severed femoralis vein, healing the torn muscle, and closing the ragged tear in the flesh. A tiny pink scar was all that remained of Thromar's wound as Logan got to his feet, still glimmering with the aura of the Heart's magicks.

"By the bubbling brew of Fraviar," Thromar breathed in awe. "Friend-Logan, did you know you were glowing?"

The fighter finally passed out from loss of blood.

An ebon hand was on Logan's shoulder as he stared down at his unconscious friend in concern. "You have done all you can," Nightwalker informed him. "With the Voices here, not even the Heart's magicks can replace the blood lost in battle. For the Rebel to live, we must depend upon his own internal system and a magic of another sort."

Moknay was nodding grimly. "Necromage," he murmured, and the freezing wind brushed past them as if to accent the word.

Logan turned his good eye on Nightwalker and his carmine halo cast coral shadows across the Guardian's black flesh. "So what am I supposed to do with the rest of this stuff?" he wondered.

Nightwalker shrugged beneath his cowl, turning away from the young man. "Sparrill will need all the strength she can acquire to stave off the Darkness and all the magic available to silence the Voices," he declared, then added as an uncertain suggestion: "Cast it out across the land."

Sounds logical, Logan surmised, and he certainly didn't like the idea of keeping all this energy bottled up inside him any longer than he needed to.

Just as the young man was about to disperse the Heart's fluxion, an idea sprang to mind. There was one other thing that needed to be done before he got rid of the power churning inside him.

Multitudes of rays unexpectedly lashed out from Logan's coruscating frame, seemingly undirected and wild. Even cloaked by the unnatural darkness, the forest came alive with scarlet incandescence as brilliant beams of crimson sorcery speared across the trees and bushes around the five. Moknay instinctively flinched as many of the bolts whizzed for his chest, striking the daggers that were strapped across his front. Each blade fulgurated with a sudden burst of cerise, then the flare vanished, drawn into the weapon itself. Other shafts of sanguine sorcery arced for Smeea, touching and filling the many weapons Thromar kept at her side. The Rebel's own sword was illuminated by a streak of power, and the weapons at Logan's belt gleamed with a vermilion sheen. Finally, Mara's own sword and dagger scintillated the color of blood, her Binalbow mirroring the gloss.

Okay, Logan thought proudly to himself, now we've got more than just *mere* weapons . . . now we've got magic weapons. All right, he ordered the remaining magic, you know where Sparrill needs the most help. Go!

A titanic column of red magic leapt up from out of the young man and whistled into the night sky, briefly dispelling the heavy curtain of blackness. Smaller branches of radiance split from the main body, forking out in different directions to add their magic to Nature's defense. One of the rays arced back down and shrieked into Nightwalker, illuminating the Guardian in a bath of ruby light. The Shadow-spawn stiffened, then turned a faint smile toward Logan, much of the grey fleeing from the emptiness of his eyes.

"The Balance struggles still against the Darkness," Nightwalker said, voicing thoughts he would have otherwise kept quiet about, "and your actions, Matthew Logan, have helped restore some Order to the Wheel's tilt. Nonetheless, I can sense that—no matter how hard we try—we cannot fully restore the Balance so long as the Wheel is held in check by the Darkness. This is one of the tasks that must be accomplished if we are to defeat the Voices."

Moknay flicked at one of his daggers and frowned as its silvery blade briefly sparkled red. "Be that as it may," the Murderer stated, "we need to get Thromar to a healer of some sort before trying to right the Wheel and all such other magical claptrap. Might I suggest we keep moving?"

The renewed strength in Nightwalker seemed to lighten his usually dark mood. "Compassion fits you well, Murderer," he noted. "You should not be so afraid to show it."

Moknay sneered both at the emotions he let slip out and at Nightwalker for observing them. It had been many years since the Murderer had worked with others, and there had been reasons for that . . . many reasons. Reasons such as the good feelings that accompanied Moknay when he was with friends—true friends— and how deeply those feelings cut when those friends died or departed or became enemies. It had been Logan's absolute unique-ness to Sparrill that had piqued the Murderer's interest, but now— in recalling parts of his past—the return to Eadarus no longer sat well with the darkly clad outlaw.

"I am a Murderer, Guardian," Moknay snarled venomously at Nightwalker, drawing fully back into the character he professed to be, "not some compassionate fool who lets his emotions guide him. Perhaps I may sound as if I care for Thromar's well-being, yet—need I remind you—if he dies, we'll not be far behind." Moknay turned on his heel, his cape billowing behind him like a living part of the night. "Now . . . let's move."

The four horses broke through the darkness of the forest and clopped over the stone bridge spanning the Jenovian River, Smeea bearing the still form of Thromar draped over her muscular back.

A frog croaked beneath the bridge, and Logan's sword flickered crimson in reply.

Just because he was the only one who truly knew what transpired, Ridglee was not alone in feeling fear's cold hand clamp benevolently on his shoulder like an old friend. There was a look of awe mixed with primeval fear in Ithnan's eyes as he watched the first of Vaugen's new troops. None of the thirteen men moved, frozen like statues of flesh. The stink of burnt flesh remained thick in the air, and Ridglee forced himself to look once again at the eyes that had been seared away by the sorceries brewing inside the human forms. Lapping tongues of darkness roared in the empty sockets now like fiery ebon embers of evil. Even unaware of what Ridglee knew, Ithnan sensed something terrible had occurred—something that was perverse and definitely above the young Reakthi's level of comprehension. He turned a bewildered look on the older soldier beside him, yet Ridglee could not meet his gaze.

"What's happened to them?" Ithnan questioned out loud.

Ridglee shrugged as if it were not important. "They've been given magic," he replied, and he scanned the camp to see where the one-eyed spellcaster lurked.

Groathit stood just behind Vaugen, a malicious smile drawn on his lean, gaunt features. The black flame of his own eye sparked and crackled like a guttering torch as he admired the new troop and the burning darkness that lapped from their eyes.

"You've sent for more men?" the wizard rasped quietly to the disfigured commander standing in front of him.

Imperator Vaugen nodded once, his dull grey eyes alive with a deep suspicion of his new soldiers. "The message was sent," he snarled in response. The Imperator leaned back, his eyes surveying his other men as he whispered to his spellcaster. "They know something is wrong," he noticed. "They'll not be willing to undergo the process."

Groathit's black eye flickered. "Then we should have done as I said, shouldn't we have?" he mocked. The jeering turned to sudden fury. "I told you they should all be taken at once, but you would not listen to me. You hardly ever listen to me."

"I am still in command here, wizard," Vaugen spat back, and his fused lips stretched as he attempted to sneer. "Remember, you would have no 'army' unless I had willingly given up my own men—and there were no guarantees this idea of yours would work. I was not about to lose all my warriors only to find the human body too weak to accept the transfusion."

Groathit mocked a sigh. "And now you fear the others will not be willing," he growled. The spellcaster stepped away from the Reakthi commander with contempt. "You are pathetic."

Arrogantly, Groathit made his way into the center of the ring formed by Vaugen's normal soldiers. An imperious sneer crossed the sorcerer's lips as he actually sensed the fear and apprehension radiating from the warriors. And I am considered a member of this pitiful race? he mused. No longer. Now I am more. Now I am a part of the Darkness itself—the vision of my left eye proves this is so. Since I control the Darkness, they cannot control me— like they did these lesser men. It was only just that the Darkness blotted out whatever pathetic little man existed beforehand. In the overall scheme of things, the lesser man never made a viable difference.

"Listen to me," Groathit addressed the gathered troops. "You have been witness to the first step in the Reakthi conquest of Sparrill. With these magicks—magicks that your friends have received and now control—we shall crush the Sparrillian resistance and take their land as our own. We shall be able to obtain the Heart of their land and return it to our own desolated homeland where our world shall once again become rich and fertile. But this can only come to pass if you follow your friends' example— only if you accept the magic into yourselves." The sorcerer's eye crackled dramatically. "Remember . . . *you* make the difference, and, without you, the Reakthi shall never reach their allotted place as rulers of the vast empire we are destined to have."

Smiling, Groathit inspected the faces of Vaugen's troops and was pleased to see some of their fear had drained from their expressions. So easily fooled, the wizard grinned to himself. So quick to accept the foolish notion that they were needed . . . and so equally eager to take up that task. Disgusting.

Good speech, sorcerer, Ridglee mentally congratulated Groathit as men began to approach the mystically endowed soldiers. The older Reakthi had watched the change in Ithnan—had seen the younger soldier's uncertainty diminish as the words of the wizard reached him and reawakened his pride to be a Reakthi. So where had Ridglee's pride gone? Where had his loyalty gotten to? Perhaps both had been wounded throughout the many years of battle with nothing to show for their fights. Perhaps they had finally been crushed when shown the harsh reality of it all by overhearing the collusion between Imperator and spellcaster. Perhaps that was what had happened to his pride and loyalty—but there was little Ridglee could do to revive them now. They—like the Reakthi empire Groathit had mentioned—were dreams long dead that were slowly being malformed and twisted into a nightmare by the gnarled magician standing behind the disfigured Vaugen.

Ridglee caught the spellcaster's black eye trained on him and felt his lips pull down in a frown at the skull-like smile that materialized across Groathit's face. Smirk, sorcerer, Ridglee cursed silently to himself, you've every reason to—you've won, damn you. You've won.

As if he could read Ridglee's mind, Groathit's smile widened.

Logan forced the memories from the front of his mind as his horse made its way down into the lush valley, heading for the walled city at its center. The sun was just dissolving through the blackness polluting the heavens as Moknay dismounted and peered ahead at his hometown. He ran a thoughtful finger across his mustache.

"What I don't understand is why we have to sneak in," Mara wanted to know from behind Logan.

Moknay's eyes glittered in the first rays of sunlight as he turned away from Eadarus. "They'll know who we are," he replied, "and they'll not take kindly to Logan walking in and asking for help—help for you, or for Thromar, or for himself, or for all of Sparrill. They'll probably know everybody and their mothers are out looking for him and they won't be pleased that he's possibly brought them in after him and to the town itself." A grim smile passed fleetingly across the Murderer's features. "The first time Logan was in Eadarus was the first time I've actually seen Mediyan's men venture inside the gates."

"So they won't willingly let us in because of the danger Matthew might bring to them?" Mara pressed, her eyes reflecting her bewilderment.

"Essentially, yes," responded Moknay, "and I'm not sure how they'll react to my return, knowing—as they most certainly will—that I've been accompanying Logan."

A frown crossed Mara's lips. "Rather selfish people, aren't they?"

Moknay's grim smile reappeared. "Not so much selfish as self-preserving," he quipped. "The people of Eadarus don't take stupid chances. To them, all chances are stupid."

"But we've got to get Thromar inside and somehow get them to help us against the Voices," Logan argued, a deep feeling of fear rising up inside him as his once oh-so-brilliant plan now looked as if it were about to fall apart. Why hadn't he considered the attitude of Eadarus's people? Three of the bastards had tried to kill him just because he had bumped into them!

"I'll go in," suggested Mara.

The priestess's words broke Logan's concentration and he whipped about on his horse to make an adamant reply; Moknay beat him to it. "Definitely not," the Murderer told her. "You've no idea what that town's like."

"I've been pretty careful so far," Mara protested, perturbed by the concern the two men displayed.

Moknay sneered his familiar sneer. "Sparrill's finest, my dear," he retorted, and there was no mistaking the deadly seriousness in his tone. "You'd be robbed, raped, and rotting before the sun set tonight."

Mara went silent, her emerald eyes flashing with an unspoken ire. She could never prove her worth if they continued to treat her like some fragile piece of crystal dinnerware! She had already agreed to herself that she wouldn't rush blindly into danger just to show her abilities to Logan and the others, but she wasn't getting anywhere playing by *their* rules either.

Grey eyes gleaming, Moknay returned his gaze to Eadarus. "I suppose there's nothing better to do than to sneak in myself and see if I can find some help," he mused out loud.

The deep voice of Darkling Nightwalker sounded behind the three: "But by that time it may be too late for the Rebel, and you yourself said they may not welcome you with open arms." The Guardian's pale eyes glanced at the walled city below them. "I would go in myself, yet I fear the strengthening Darkness may momentarily sap me of my magicks, and I would be revealed."

"If there was somebody we could trust outright to help us . . ." murmured Moknay, and his hands moved for his weapons when he mentioned the word "trust."

Logan suddenly glanced up, a strange grin on his face. The many memories flooding through his mind as he sat and stared at the town had given him the possible answer. "Bella!" he exclaimed, and the others looked at him questioningly. "If we can find Bella, she'd help us!"

An odd look came over Mara's face, and the green of her eyes may have flashed a little greener. "Bella?" she repeated. "Who's Bella?"

"A friend of Thromar's," Logan rapidly explained, the excitement building up inside him. "I'm positive she'd take us to a necromage."

"If we can find her," Moknay reminded the young man of the grave reality.

Nightwalker dismounted, an ebon hand taking the reins of Logan's horse. "I shall wait for you here," he informed them. "Hurry, we are running short of time."

The mention of time brought a vivid picture to Logan's mind of his frightening dream, and he threw his watch a curious look. Beneath the tattered sleeve of his sweat jacket, the digital display window was entirely black, only spotted in places by pinpricks of scarlet light. The young man knew that as the Voices' power grew the darkness of his watch would grow and the starlike points of red light would be swallowed up by the blackness. It was probably then that Nightwalker would cease to exist.

Logan shuddered to himself as he followed Moknay and Mara on foot, the former leading Smeea by the reins. His stomach knotted in expectation as the high wall surrounding Eadarus crept closer, seeming to grow with each step. Even though it was Moknay's hometown, Logan knew from firsthand experience that it was a cold and heartless place. In the first few moments Logan had known him, Moknay had callously killed three men, a Reakthi Reakmor, *and* had started a rather severe brawl just to serve as a minor distraction. Questioningly, Logan's blue eyes rested on the dark form of Moknay leading the black-and-red mare closer to Eadarus and somewhat understood the Murderer's obvious unease. In the time he had been with Logan, Moknay's dark nature had lightened considerably, and perhaps he feared he was no longer good enough to survive the harshness of Eadarus's back streets and alleys.

"Fair warning," Moknay whispered back to Logan and Mara as they stepped through the massive front gates. "Hold onto anything you may value . . . such as your lives."

The three walked into Eadarus, Smeea's hooves clattering upon the cobblestones of the street. The memories racing about Logan's skull intensified as he spied the winding roads, heard the vendors calling their wares from the canvas shops lining the streets, and watched the riders and carts rumble around them. Dark, skulking shapes lurked in the shadows, and someone swiftly raced across a rooftop of a nearby house before jumping down and disappearing into a back alley. Suspicious eyes fixed on the trio and their wounded companion draped across his horse, and Logan felt a trickle of perspiration wind its way down the back of his neck. He shot Mara a glance and saw the anxiety raging in her green eyes mingled with a weird kind of relief. Perhaps the priestess was now thankful that the two men had not let her venture into the city alone.

The canvas shops soon gave way to women, and the buildings along the street closed in, narrowing the cobblestone roads. Logan remembered thinking on his first visit that this was definitely not the better portion of town, and nothing seemed to have changed from his last visit. Darkly clad figures still crept along the sidewalks, weaving in between the hookers and whores like shadows. A few of the figures were so self-assured they had removed their hoods, leaning confidently up alongside the buildings, picking their teeth with stilettos or cleaning under their fingernails with daggers. Ugly scars ran across their features in contrast to the inches of makeup the prostitutes smeared on their faces, and both groups watched with equal interest the three that led the red-and-black mare down the street.

Logan's attention was diverted by the familiar structure farther down the street and by the nearby silversmith's shop. He almost expected to see the demonic form of Groathit burst from the tavern, red eyes blazing as he scanned the street for Logan. Or to see Moknay bodily hurled across the street and into the silversmith's shop.

Groathit, the young man thought, and fury bubbled up inside him. Damn Groathit! Damn his persistence!

The young man jerked himself to a halt when someone purposely stepped in his way. Telling himself he wasn't about to bump into anybody else in Eadarus, Logan looked up at the smiling face of a roguish character, three teeth missing from the man's exaggerated grin. A hideous pink line of scar tissue wound its way down the fellow's brow, severed his right eyebrow in half, then continued farther down his right cheek. Behind him were four more menacing-looking men.

The leader of the rogues continued to peer down at Logan. "Well, now," he said with a grin. "Wot's we got here, then?" His smile vanished. "'Fraid we's don't likes people from Droth in Eadarus. We's gonna have t' ask yer friends and you t' leave."

Fear clogged his throat and Logan was unable to make a response. Fortunately, a grey form interceded between them, and the rogue found himself staring eye to eye into the steely glare of Moknay the Murderer.

"Best to leave him alone, friend," Moknay growled, and his face was unpleasantly expressionless. "He's with me."

The rogue was only momentarily displaced by the Murderer's nefarious stare. To strengthen his previous threat, he threw his four companions a bemused look. "You's hear that?" he chuckled. "The man from Dorth's wit' him."

Unexpectedly—to Logan, anyway—the rogue whipped back around, a dagger suddenly in his hand and plunging for Moknay's solar plexus. Mara stifled a gasp as the blade glinted silver in the light of the rising sun, then vanished into the shadows between the two men. Logan's own hand went for his sword as he expected to see Moknay slump to the cobblestones, a victim of Eadarus's viciousness, yet the young man was surprised when the look of shock crossed the lead rogue's face, and he started to crumple to one knee, his hand still locked in the shadows of Moknay's chest.

Icy fire flared in Moknay's eyes as he tightened his grip on the rogue's wrist, twisting ever so slightly. The tip of the man's blade practically rested at Moknay's gut, almost piercing the fabric of his grey tunic, yet the Murderer had been prepared. He knew not to take chances in Eadarus, and he had been more than ready when the five had stepped forward to confront them. He threw the other rogues a malicious sneer as their leader dropped to the street, his wrist snapping with an audible crack.

Moknay shoved the injured rogue away from him and two daggers materialized in either hand. "I suggest next time you listen when I offer a bit of advice," the Murderer snarled. "But maybe you can make up for your insolence by answering me a question."

"We's ain't gotta tell you nothin'," the injured rogue spat, clutching his broken wrist to his chest.

A grey boot flashed in the morning light and kicked the rogue's fallen dagger into the air. Silver screamed as the blade spun dangerously close along the side of the man's head and lodged in the baseboard of a cart that was just behind his right ear. "Then perhaps I'll cut the words from your throat," Moknay suggested.

One of the other rogues stepped forward; probably the youngest of the five, Logan surmised. "What do you want to know?" he asked.

"We're looking for a woman by the name of Bella," Moknay replied. "She operates around here."

The youngest rogue pointed to a building just a few yards ahead of them. "She should be in there," he told them.

"Shut up, Stearck!" the leader of the five ordered. "We's no reason t' be helpin' this bastard!"

Moknay looked down at the leader before glancing back up at the young rogue with a macabre grin. "He's right, you know," he told Stearck as he started for the building. "Just as I had no reason to spare *this* bastard's life."

An almost invisible kick sent the lead rogue toppling from his knees and crashing to the cobblestones, unable to stop his fall with his snapped wrist. The remaining rogues watched with a mixture of admiration and fury as the three strode farther down the street and tethered Smeea outside the brothel where Bella worked.

Logan threw the five rogues behind them a nervous glance as Moknay tied Smeea's reins to a tethering post. There was an unhappy grimace on the Murderer's face as he looked back at the five.

"They'll be onto us soon enough," he muttered grimly.

"Who will?" Mara questioned, astonished by the sudden display of cruelty and resulting swiftness.

"The rest of the town," Moknay answered. "That younger fellow recognized me—his friends probably did as well. No one in their sane mind would deliberately confront me."

Mara raised her eyebrows. "Are you that notorious?"

The Murderer smiled at her disbelief. "There are two people in all of Eadarus you just don't mess with," he explained. "I'm one of them—the other one is Roshfre."

Roshfre, Logan mused. Thromar had mentioned both Moknay and Roshfre the night before they had entered Eadarus for the first—and only—time. "Everyone from Moknay to Roshfre could be there," the Rebel had said, "all just as willing to slit your throat!" And if this Roshfre was as dangerous as Moknay, Logan certainly didn't want to run into him without the Murderer by his side. Even then, who was to say who would be the victor should the two disagree?

The young man suddenly noticed his friends were watching him, and a slightly sardonic smirk raised Moknay's mustache. "What are you waiting for, friend?" the Murderer inquired. He waved a gloved hand toward the brothel's door. "You're the only one who knows what Bella looks like—Mara and I will wait out here with Thromar."

A large lump of fear rose in Logan's throat, and he had to swallow hard to force it down. What had he just been thinking about leaving Moknay's side? What if this Roshfre fellow was inside here? What if Logan bumped into him accidentally? Hell! Who needed Roshfre? What if Logan bumped into *anybody* in there? Even someone like that rogue leader?

Hesitantly, Logan took a cautious step toward the door. It was only a whorehouse, he thought, trying to console himself. Just walk in, tell one of the women you're looking for Bella, then leave. No big deal, right? So why the hell are my knees knocking together?

Logan opened the door and stepped inside, losing Moknay and Mara as the wooden portal shut behind him. A few streams of sweat made their way down his face as he inspected the massive hall, surprised by the elegance he found there. A few women reclined about him and threw him friendly glances, and the young man couldn't get over how attractive some of the whores were. Well, why not? he wondered to himself. Cyrene had told him about the infertility of all women until they were married—why shouldn't some want to enjoy that freedom? In Eadarus it was probably something of a very special trade—like Mara's one-time religious order. Things were different in Sparrill than in his own world, Logan had to keep reminding himself. And which world had the right to say what was right and what was wrong?

A gorgeous redhead pulled herself off a nearby couch and approached the young man, fluttering dark eyelashes at him. "Can I do something for you?" she asked pleasantly.

Logan smiled back, feeling very self-conscious. "I'm looking for someone," he replied.

"Aren't we all," a dark-haired woman said, laughing, from a chair.

Logan felt the warm rush of embarrassment start to flood his cheeks as he cleared the nervousness from his throat. "No, uh . . ."

he started. "She . . . um . . . works here. Bella? Know her?"

The redhead raised an eyebrow, accenting the makeup around her light green eyes. "Bella?" she queried. She suddenly extended a slim hand. "My name's Halette; I'm not busy at the moment."

"Huh?" blinked Logan; then he caught the knowing glimmer in her eyes. "Oh! It's not for me! It's . . . I've . . . There's a friend of Bella's outside and it's pretty important I talk to her."

Halette smiled, her painted lips sparkling red in the light of the brothel. "A friend, huh?" she said as if she had heard that line before. Her extended hand suddenly took Logan's and she started up the flight of stairs to their left. "Come on, then."

Dumbly, Logan trailed after the redhead, his hand clamped in hers. He couldn't stop his eye from roving up the back of the woman's tight green dress, noticing the slender legs that peeked from long slits in the sides and how eagerly the fabric clung to the shapely curves of her backside. Still, the young man was here for a purpose—with Moknay and Mara waiting for him outside.

The sultry frame of Halette seemed to blur as the young man pictured Mara. That kiss they had shared had been so sudden, so unexpected—and, then again, neither had pulled back or resisted. Although unplanned, somehow it wasn't. Logan—dare he admit it?—loved Mara; at least, that's what it felt like, and, maybe—just maybe—she returned that love. But . . . what did it really matter? Some things just couldn't be . . . no matter how badly one of them may want it.

Halette stopped and rapped sharply on a closed door, throwing Logan another beautiful smile as she waited for the door to open. A moment or two later, the portal cracked open and Bella peeked out, her black hair in something of a mess and some of her makeup rubbed off.

"Yes, Halette?" she questioned. "What do you want?"

Halette pulled Logan to her side, draping an over-friendly arm around his shoulders. "You've a visitor, Bella," the prostitute remarked, "and a rather cute one at that. Said he's a friend outside."

Bella glanced at Logan, no trace of recognition sparking in her eyes.

"I'm a friend of Thromar's," Logan hastily explained.

A wild expression of joy overtook Bella's features. "Thromar?" she all but squealed. "Here? Back in Eadarus? I'll be right out!"

The door slammed shut in Logan's face.

"Whatever you said was the right thing," Halette congratulated him. "Now . . . what about yourself?"

Logan tried not to look at the redhead's exquisitely dressed figure. The pent-up feelings inside the young man raged fiercely, demanding gratification. A gorgeous redhead is practically offering herself to you for a few paltry gold pieces and you're acting like some goddamn saint! his desires ranted. Sex, Matthew! Raw sex! Panting people! Sweating bodies! The whole deal! Think about it!

Logan tried to push aside the detailed images his mind was conjuring up as he stood nose to nose with Halette. "Sorry, but I've got business elsewhere," he apologized. "Can I take a rain check?"

"A what?"

The young man forced a smile. "Maybe some other time, okay?"

Halette shrugged her shoulders, and other parts of her moved just as nicely. "Sure," she replied, and left the young man outside Bella's room.

It was about then that the door flew open and Bella hurried out, grabbing Logan's hand and yanking him down the stairs after Halette. The two hit the hall at a run and bolted out the door, Bella practically dragging the young man behind her. A weary relief washed over Logan as he exited the brothel but was stopped short when Bella halted in front of him.

"Where is he?" the whore questioned.

Dreading the worst, Logan looked past the woman and saw no one remained at the tethering post. No Thromar, no Smeea, no Moknay, and no Mara.

Apprehension began to chew at the young man's stomach.

"What's the matter?" an amused voice behind them probed. "Lose something?"

Logan looked back to see Halette seductively leaning in the doorway, a mocking smile on her lips. Her slender arms were crossed across her full breasts and one leg was free of her dress, a very nice tan revealed in the light of the morning sun.

The trepidation expanded to horror as Logan saw that none of the five rogues were anywhere to be seen either.

A finger was suddenly waggling accusingly under his nose. "Is this some kind of trick?" demanded Bella. "If it is, I see nothing funny about it."

Halette sniggered. "I do."

Logan threw his one-eyed gaze up and down the narrow streets. "No tricks," he told the two whores. "Look, I came here with Thromar and two friends. Thromar's been hurt—badly. We need to get him to a necromage before . . ."

"Necromage?" Bella interrupted in horror. "Someone's killed my Thromar?"

"No," Logan interrupted back, "he's not dead yet, but he will be unless we can get somebody to help his body replenish its store of blood. That's why I came looking for you. We were hoping you'd help."

"I'll help," Halette said, "but it looks like we'll have to find your friends first."

"And I's know where they are," a voice said at Logan's side.

The young man turned to his right and stared into the scarred face of the lead rogue, his broken wrist still held close to his side. That same, missing-toothed grin remained on his ugly features as he took another step closer.

8

Daigread

The rogue threw Bella and Halette a friendly leer of perversion before fixing his dark eyes on Logan, the smile on his lips stretching into a mocking smear of teeth. The scar that snaked down his face pulled back along with his facial muscles as he leaned his stubble-strewn face closer to Logan's.

"Yeah," he repeated smugly, "I knows where yer friends went. Not's t' say I'll be tellin' you without some . . . er . . . compensation fer me hand."

Logan's hand instinctively jumped to the hilt of his sword, his face a mixture of concern and disgust. What had happened to his friends while he was inside the brothel? Had this bastard done something with them? And what about Thromar? How much time did they have left before the magic Logan used on the Rebel faded and the loss of blood finally killed him?

"What did you do with them?" the young man snarled, letting his disgust and rage overpower his worry.

The rogue took a step back, eyes widening in mock surprise. "Me?" he exclaimed. "Who's t' say I did anything with 'em? I just said I knows where they are. It's just that I'm not the kind o' guy who'll give out information fer free, if ya catch me meanin'."

Spiked heels clicked against the cobblestones of the street as Halette stepped past Logan, her slim hands shooting out for the rogue's collar. His rusting vest of chainmail clinked as the prostitute drew him close to her, her heels giving her an inch advantage in height. "Yorke," she snarled at him, "you don't screw with a whore unless you're willing to pay. What did you do with his friends?"

For some reason, Yorke was intimidated by the redheaded hooker. "I'm tellin' ya," he answered. "I's didn't do nothin' with 'em. Stearck told 'em where the nearest necromage was—that's all."

"Then why didn't they come and get me?" demanded Logan, half freeing his Reakthi weapon.

"Didn't have the time," Yorke returned with a secret grin. "Now can ya be lettin' go of me shirt? Yer wrinklin' the material."

"He's lying," Logan accused, his one eye narrowed at the rogue in angry suspicion.

Halette shook Yorke by the collar, making his chainmail tinkle like bells. "Well, Yorke?" she asked. "What else have you forgotten to tell us?"

"Come on, Halette," the rogue begged. "How's a fella t' make a proper livin' if yer always beleaguerin' me t' tell the truth fer free?"

"Lie all you like and charge people for it," the prostitute retorted. "Now speak up, or I'll let my young friend here make me a new pair of earrings from your private parts."

Yorke lost his smile as he stared into the green eyes of the redhead before him. "Fine, but yer sister won't like it," he said.

"Never mind my sister, Yorke," Halette commanded. "Talk."

"All right, all right!" the rogue responded. "Roshfre's men took 'em, okay? Now let go o' me shirt!"

Halette released the rogue's collar and Yorke plopped unceremoniously to the cobblestones. "Ouch!" he complained. "Did ya hafta go droppin' me, sweetcheeks? Can't yer see I's an injured man in need o' some tender lovin'?"

"Go crawl back in your hole, Yorke," Halette threatened, "or else stop your whining." She turned her gaze on Logan. "It looks as if you're going to have to see Roshfre about your friends."

"I'm afraid he has no choice in the matter," a new voice suddenly said behind them.

Logan spun to see a group of six men stanced at their backs, weapons out and confident smirks on their faces. Each wore dark clothes of their own choosing, yet a red strip of cloth wound around each one's right arm as if to signify something important about them.

"Stand aside, Halette," the leader of the men ordered. "This doesn't concern you or the others—it's the stranger we want."

"If this is Roshfre's business, it concerns me," the prostitute replied, defiantly facing the six men.

Questioningly, Logan started to look in Halette's direction. Just what connections did the redhead have with Roshfre that allowed her to talk like that to his men and coerce common rogues like Yorke to tell the truth? Whatever ties there were, they must have been pretty strong. Maybe Halette was Roshfre's favorite whore . . . and she had taken a very obvious liking to me? Oh, great! the young man groaned inwardly. If his men don't kill me, Roshfre will!

A hand was around Logan's throat suddenly, and something sharp pricked his right cheek. He could feel the warm, foul breath of Yorke on his neck as the rogue struggled to hold his dagger in his broken-wristed grasp, and the momentary shock of the move froze Logan's muscles. In addition, the young man could sense the terrified pace of Yorke's breathing, and some of the rogue's trepidation began to rub off on Logan.

"Now yer not thinkin' o' bumpin' off ole Yorke here just 'cause he's keen t' what's goin' on, now were ya?" the thief queried, and he forced a chuckle. "No, I's been thinkin' we's all liked t' see Roshfre . . . or there ain't gonna be no stranger for you t' take. Ain't that right, Halette?"

The redhead threw the rogue a nasty glare but nodded. "Of course, Yorke," she answered, "but release my friend. I'll see you aren't harmed."

"Sez you!" barked the thief. "You may be Roshfre's sister, but I's ain't worth harpy turds! Ain't no doubt in me mind that these fellas had orders t' quiet anyone's who mighta seen somethin' they's don't wan' 'em t' see."

The captain of Roshfre's men stroked his heavy beard. "All right, Yorke," he sighed, "you've made your point. Now, move; it's not polite to keep Roshfre waiting."

Uncertainly, the rogue relaxed his hold about Logan's throat and let the young man angrily tear away. Ire flamed in Logan's eye as he shot Yorke a vicious glare but turned quickly away to look at Halette. Roshfre's sister, huh? he questioned himself. Made sense.

"Bella?" Halette was asking her companion. "Are you coming?"

"If this has anything to do with my Thromar, you can swear to Brolark I am!" the dark-haired whore proclaimed.

Logan blinked as Roshfre's men led them down the cobblestone street. A short, stocky hooker with black hair; a tall, gorgeous redheaded whore who just happened to be the sister of the second most dangerous man in all of Eadarus; and an untrustworthy rogue who'd sooner stick a dagger in the young man's back than help him. And Logan had thought ebon-skinned Guardians and light blue ogres had been strange partners?

Logan edged his way to Halette's side. "I don't mean to be insulting," he whispered, "but isn't this Roshfre something of a dangerous fellow?"

The redhead threw the young man a charming smile as she continued down the street. "Roshfre?" she repeated. "No, she's my sister."

Behind him, Logan could hear Yorke mutter: "Face it, Yorke, this just ain't yer blasted day."

A rat gave Logan a red-eyed stare before whipping around and darting back into the darkness. The young man had never been this far into Eadarus before, and now he was actually making his way under the city, stepping carefully down cobblestone stairs and further into blackness. Algae clung to the walls and steps, making the stones slick and treacherous, and the musty stench of the underground passage filled Logan's nostrils with disgusting, sewerlike smells. Most of Roshfre's men walked ahead of them, Halette with them, her high heels clacking noisily against the slippery staircase. Bella and Yorke followed behind Logan, and the young man kept throwing wary glances in the latter's direction. Yorke's idea of self-protection included killing anybody who happened to threaten his existence, and more than once Logan expected the rogue's dagger to be back at his throat. Yorke would obviously lie, cheat, steal, and murder to keep himself alive—which seemed to dampen Logan's spirits. If all the people of Eadarus were like this—and it seemed they were—the young man's hopes of gathering an army behind him would be cut down quite brutally.

Roshfre's men rounded a sharp corner in the staircase, and yellow-orange light suddenly filled the underground corridor. The stink of the narrow hall fled through hidden vents in the walls, and the stairs ended at level ground. Torches lined the wall, spreading their naked light across the stone chambers that undermined Eadarus. Muffled voices sounded around one corner, and the bearded captain halted at the bottom of the stairs, waving Logan forward with his unsheathed sword.

"Move along, stranger," he commanded.

Logan gave the bearded captain a sneer of defiance and began down the surprisingly clean passageway. The voices that reverberated throughout the corridor grew louder, and Logan felt his heart jump in shock as a curt shriek from Mara filled the hallway with a hundred echoes.

"Hey!" Roshfre's captain exclaimed as the young man unexpectedly bolted ahead of them, his hand on his Reakthi sword.

Logan charged around a corner and burst through a set of double doors, sword out and ready. Nearly half a dozen men leapt to their feet at the young man's intrusion, daggers, knives, swords, and tridents all in their hands. Only the figure at the head of the table remained seated, calmly eyeing the young man with icy blue eyes. Moknay and Mara stood behind her chair, appearing unhurt; a dagger was lodged in the wall between them.

Roshfre got to her feet, the torchlight sparkling off her long red hair. Unlike her femininely dressed sister, the bandit wore all black clothing save for a red sash about her waist that was of the same material as her guards' armbands. A mace dangled at her hip.

"You must be Matthew Logan," she said evenly. "I've heard a lot about you."

Logan clenched his teeth, letting the anger have full control. "Let go of my friends," he demanded.

Roshfre took a silent step toward the young man, holding out her hands to show that they were empty. "But as you can see," she answered, "I don't have hold of them."

"Don't play bullshit games with me!" spat Logan, his fury blinding him to the table of rogues and cutthroats all armed and watching him with mistrust in their dark eyes. "I'm sick and tired of bullshit games! Now let go of my friends!"

Roshfre smiled, first at Logan, then at the men seated around her. It was about then that her men arrived, their bearded leader in front. Halette, Bella, and Yorke remained among them.

"You heard the man," Roshfre shrugged to her many men. "Let them go."

Uncertain murmurs ran up and down the length of the table as Moknay and Mara stepped out from behind Roshfre's chair and toward the safer, more open center of the room. A relieved smile was half-drawn on Mara's lips as she came closer to Logan, but the lithe, redheaded form of Roshfre suddenly slipped in front of her and edged up to the young man.

"We'll take you instead," Roshfre said, silver flashing in her hand.

Logan gave the dagger that had materialized near the tip of his nose a hate-filled glare before looking back up at the woman wielding the blade. This was the third time in less than an hour that he was being threatened, and, frankly, he was getting sick of it.

"Fuck you," he said bluntly, and stepped arrogantly around Roshfre's weapon to join his friends.

A thick silence descended upon the underground chamber as Roshfre's men growled and snarled anxiously among themselves. Their leader blinked away what surprise she had let show in her eyes as she turned to watch Logan. "Either you're very brave or very stupid," she decided.

"Bravery and stupidity," Halette quipped from the doorway. "The two sides of a one-sided coin."

Roshfre glanced fleetingly at her younger sister. "Shut up, Halette," she ordered before returning her attention to Logan. "Well?" she asked the young man. "What is it?"

Logan swung his one-eyed gaze on the redheaded cutthroat, purposely ignoring her query and demanding back: "Where's Thromar?"

Mara lightly touched his arm, fearing there would be a limit to Roshfre's tolerance. "They said they'd get him to a necromage," she told Logan, yet there was little conviction in her voice.

"I can assure you we will not let the Rebel die," Roshfre added.

"Oh, no, of course not," Logan sneered. "Not until you've bled him dry of all his money and provisions."

"Oh, good shot!" Halette cheered him on.

"Need I remind you, Matthew Logan," Roshfre sneered back, her calm exterior crumbling, "this is my town and these are my men. You are here—alive—on my request; you are hardly acting like a proper guest."

"Maybe because I'm not being treated like a guest," Logan barked. "Look, we came here for help and all we've gotten are hassles! You bastards turn your back on everything that doesn't immediately concern you or your fucking little town! You didn't give a damn who I was or what I might do until it caused a few problems here; *then* you acted! You want to know something? There's a goddamn army building up out there. There's a whole fucking army of inhuman soldiers massing together in the west under Groathit and you probably don't give a damn about that either! You won't give a damn about it till they're at your gates and knocking down your goddamn walls!"

"It's no use, friend," Moknay put in, his voice level. "They wouldn't listen to me—I doubt if they'll listen to you."

Logan shot the Murderer a swift glance before returning his single-eyed gaze to Roshfre and the men around her. "No, they wouldn't," he agreed with a snarl. "They'll just plug their ears and close their eyes. It doesn't matter what happens to the rest of the world so long as Eadarus is safe, now does it?"

"Now you just hold . . ." one of the men at the table started.

"No, *you* just hold on!" Logan furiously roared. "Don't you realize anything that's been going on? There's an army massing to the west! The *west*! They're not going to come at you from the east—they're gonna come from both directions and crush you! Just the same way you lost Denzil!"

"He's got a point," Yorke stated.

The captain of Roshfre's men nudged the rogue into silence.

"You talk a good war," a man wearing a bandana remarked, "but why should we take your word? The word of a stranger?"

"Then don't take his word," Moknay answered for the young man. "Take mine. We're not dealing on the scale of a simple Reakthi attack, Xile. We're dealing with events on a Cosmic scale—Forces of the Macrocosm."

The thief called Xile raised an eyebrow beneath his bandana. "Like with the Wheel?" he probed.

"You know about the Wheel?" Logan asked back.

"Doesn't everybody?" Yorke inquired, once again receiving a sharp elbow from Roshfre's captain.

"Mystical claptrap," a hulking brute of a man snorted, answering the rogue's query. "Meaningless drivel meant to waste our time with lengthy sermons and give some sort of purpose to a priest's life."

"You weren't with us when the Jewel of Equilibrant discharged in Plestenah, Frayne," Moknay evenly responded. "Or in the Hills of Sadroia."

Roshfre's bearded captain nodded his head slowly. "We received word on some strange things going on there," he mused, "apart from the increase of Guardsmen in the region."

Another bandit echoed the captain's nod. "Weren't there some kind of reports, Marcos?" he asked the captain. "Lights or something?"

Marcos scratched thoughtfully at his beard. "Yes," he answered, "some months back, I believe it was. Visible flashes of light seen as far off as Wailvye."

The man called Frayne snorted once more. "So now we're supposed to take the word of an Outsider and the shallow proof of flashing lights as valid fact?" he grunted. "Roshfre, slay these fools and let's get on with our business."

Logan narrowed his good eye at the larger man, feeling his anger
boil with renewed vigor. This Frayne was a thief—a murderer of
perhaps some hundred people—yet Logan's fury gave him the
courage to approach the skeptical criminal and jab an accusing
finger beneath the man's nose. "You won't have any business to
get on with if you don't listen to us," he gritted.

"Are you threatening me?" Frayne rumbled, pushing himself
away from the table and rising to his feet.

"Get rid of him!" another cutthroat shouted. "He's not part of
this council! We don't need to listen to him!"

"*Daigread*!" someone else exclaimed. "*Daigread*!"

A sudden eruption of shouts and curses were thrown up from the
gathering, and Logan stepped away from the unexpected outburst.
It seemed to the young man that everyone was shouting and yelling
in his general direction, many echoing that one word he had heard
moments before the chaos had begun. He noted Mara standing
close by his side, her eyes wide with trepidation as she watched
the cursing, howling brigands. Moknay stood behind her, a grim
frown on his features while his eyes were locked exclusively on
Logan. Yorke, Bella, and Halette watched curiously as Roshfre
stepped back to her place at the table and tried to call her men
back into order.

"Silence!" the redhead finally screamed, bringing her mace
down upon the table and splintering wood.

The gathered thieves went quiet, all eyes turning on their leader.
"The rite of *Daigread* has been suggested, and I adhere to it," the
woman announced.

A few men tried to protest but a sharp glance from Roshfre
shut them up. She looked down at Logan, and the young man
was unable to read the expressions hidden within her eyes. "At
the rise of tomorrow's sun, we shall hold the rite of *Daigread*,
which will tell us whether or not Matthew Logan and the words
he speaks are worthy of our attention."

Skeptical grumbles sounded from the men at the table as Roshfre
left the chamber through a back door. Most of her thieves began
to file out of the room, throwing glances at Logan and his friends
as they departed. Some wore mixed expressions—others showed
nothing but hatred and distrust of the young man. Questioningly,
Logan looked at Mara.

"What the hell is this *Daigread*?" he wondered.

The priestess half shrugged. "It's a corruption of an older tongue,
I think," she replied. "It means something like 'death festival.' "

Logan swallowed hard as a sudden gloved hand fell upon his shoulder and Moknay peered at his friend with obvious concern lurking in his grey eyes. "It's the initiation into Roshfre's band," he explained. "If you succeed, they'll have no choice but to listen to you."

The young man nodded, understanding now the comment about not being part of their council. Roshfre and her men would not recognize him—and the things he had to say—unless he were part of her group, and only then would they listen to what he had to say with the little bit of objectivity that could make the difference.

Moknay's face showed no signs of humor. "Do you think it's too late to try Quarn?" he queried.

The anger had drained out of him, leaving him very weary and very scared. Silently, Logan peered at the candle flickering beside his bed, his eye glazing over as he stared without blinking. He could hear the cacophony of Eadarus outside the walls of his room but he didn't pay it much attention. His thoughts were locked on the coming morning and the odd ritual of *Daigread*. Moknay had told him it would be a challenge of both his wits and his skill that nine out of ten men from Eadarus never survived. To be a part of Roshfre's band, one had to compete in this cold-blooded ceremony, and—should there be more than one applicant at the time—compete against one another. Logan had it lucky—or so Moknay had told him—there was no one else foolish enough to want to join Roshfre's band. Still . . . what did Logan know about fighting? He knew certain aspects of weapons . . . big deal. He knew how to swing a sword and shoot a bow . . . so what? What if he did make it through the *Daigread* rite? That meant he still had to face one of Roshfre's own men to the death—and with his luck it was probably going to be that big, thick-headed hulk, Frayne.

There was a light tap on Logan's door, and the young man blinked himself free of the hypnotic candle flame. The door slowly creaked inward but it was not Mara outside but the lean, roguish Yorke. Logan's hand instantly went for his sword.

"What do you want?" he demanded.

The rogue smiled, yet even with its missing teeth, his grin held no mockery. "Nothin'," he replied. "Just came by t' wish yer luck. Takes real guts t' make a stand like ya did."

"Or lack of brains," muttered the young man, remembering what Halette had said.

Yorke's smile widened. "Naw, not really," he responded. "I's been thinkin' 'bout all them things you was sayin'. Are they real?"

"Of course they're real!" Logan exclaimed. "You think I'd be stupid enough to take this *Daigread* thing if they weren't?"

Yorke scratched the stubble on his chin. "An' there really is an army massin' in th' west?" he wondered.

Logan eyed the rogue with a skeptical gleam in his eye. "Yeah," he answered, "but why should you care?"

"Why shouldn't I's?" Yorke asked back. "We's not all o' part o' Roshfre's band, ya know. Some o' us prefers t' think fer ourselves, and, t' do that means we gotta look out fer ourselves too."

"You mean you'd actually go against Roshfre's wishes?" the young man queried.

"Agellic, no! Nothin' as drastic as that, but I's could do what I's wanted t' do. See, Roshfre may have lots o' things under her control, but one thing she ain't got is me . . . not that she'd wants me anyways. But that's all right with me 'cause it leaves me t' live me own life th' way I's sees fit." The rogue unhooked something that looked like a wound rope from his belt and offered it to the young man. "'Ere's a little somethin' t' help ya through yer ordeal t'morrow," he explained. "'S not much—just some fancy-ass whip I's stole off o' some fool who thought it'd be all right strapped t' his horse while he was in a brothel. Might come in handy if they make ya face somethin' ya don't wanna get too close to facin', if ya catch me meanin'. 'Sides, I's can't use it with me wrist broken."

Logan stared down at the coiled whip as the rogue started out the door. An uncertain and befuddled call from the young man halted the rogue. "Yorke," Logan inquired, definite puzzlement in his voice. "Why are you doing this?"

The scarred rogue threw the young man an awkward grin, and a sparkle of wild mirth glistened in his dark eyes. "Why not?" he quipped, and stepped out of the room, shutting the door behind him.

Logan got little if any sleep at all that night. There was some time in the early morning hours around two where he may have drifted off into a fitful bout of slumber, but anxiety and nerves kept him awake the rest of the night. There was still no hint of dawn when the door to his room creaked cautiously open and an

almost invisible figure slipped inside. Having given up trying to
sleep some three hours before, Logan jerked himself up, searching
the dark room with his one eye.

"Who's there?" he wanted to know.

"Shhh," someone told him. "We've not much time."

Logan squinted and vaguely caught the caped form that was
Moknay. "Not much time for what?" he asked.

"To get out of here," the Murderer answered.

The young man from Santa Monica blinked at the darkness
around him and tried to look in Moknay's general direction.
"What about this *Daigread*?" he questioned. "We can't leave
till . . ."

"Forget about it," the Murderer whispered. "We need you alive
to lead an army, friend. If you take *Daigread*, your world and
mine will both be short one Matthew Logan."

"But we need to get their help," pressed Logan. "If this *Daigread*
thing is the only way I can do it . . ."

"And if slitting your own throat were the only way, would
you do that?" Moknay interrupted. "Look, friend, I know you
thought this was a good idea—I did as well for a while—
but Roshfre and her men just aren't listening to reason. I've
stayed up all night trying to talk them out of it—got through
to a few but didn't have the time for the majority. They know
something bad's happening but they want to go back to being
ignorant. Your being here has hit them with the truth that they
might be needed—or that, sooner or later, they'll get involved—
and they don't want that. If you die during *Daigread*, it's just
another man's failed attempt to join Roshfre's band—but it also
silences you and the truth you're speaking. Do you follow my
logic?"

"I think so," Logan uneasily replied.

"Good." The Murderer nodded. "Now get your things together
and let's get out of here."

Logan pulled his Nikes on in the dark and slid out of bed,
wrapping his Reakthi sword about his waist. Even accustomed
to the blackness that filled the room, the young man was barely
able to see the outline of furniture and of Moknay as the Murderer
easily navigated the chamber and glided soundlessly across to
the door. As quietly as he could, Logan trailed, yet every step
he took seemed to set up a series of groaning and moaning in
the floorboards that tried to alert anyone to the young man's
presence.

Logan stopped outside the room, throwing a strained whisper toward Moknay. "Wait a minute," he breathed. "I forgot something."

The Murderer threw the young man a questioning glance that was lost in the night as Logan tiptoed back into his room. In the ebony void, Logan found a chair and groped blindly across its back, half smiling when he touched the coiled whip Yorke had earlier given him. A startled shout almost broke from his lips as Logan's hand also brushed the warm and pliable flesh of someone's face.

"You must stay, Matthew Logan." A deep voice pierced the night.

Logan tried to slow his heart, which was pounding furiously against his ribs in shock. "Nightwalker?" the young man barely choked out.

"It is I, Matthew Logan," answered the night. "The army of Darkness grows, and it is imperative you stay and convince these people of your task. There is no time left for any other alternative."

"If I stay, I'm dead," Logan whispered back.

The room went silent for a moment, and Logan wondered whether Nightwalker was still there.

"You must waste time to save time," the Shadow-spawn finally responded. "Therefore, you must remain."

"Don't start with your goddamn riddles," the young man snarled. "Don't you understand that if I stick around, I'm going to get killed?"

"What of the Rebel?" Nightwalker asked back.

Logan paused. Yeah, what of Thromar? If they left now, they'd be leaving without Thromar, and only Roshfre and some of her men knew exactly where the fighter was. But if they didn't leave— and Logan went through with this *Daigread*—Thromar would have company at the necromage's.

"Logan," Moknay hissed from the doorway, "what's taking you so long?"

"Nightwalker's here," the young man explained.

The Murderer slid back into the room, his grey eyes piercing the veil of blackness. "There's no one here but us," he replied. "Are you sure it was Nightwalker?"

Surprised, Logan waved a hand around the seat he thought Nightwalker was occupying. To his befuddlement, the chair was empty. "But . . . he was!" the young man sputtered. "Just a second ago . . ."

Moknay nodded once, stroking his mustache. "As fleeting as the dawn and so forth," he remarked. "Did he have anything important to say?"

"He said we've got to stay," Logan reported.

"Didn't you explain what's going to happen if we do?"

"I tried," the young man answered, "but he said we've got to waste time to save time. He also said we'd be leaving Thromar behind."

"Thromar," Moknay murmured. "I'd almost forgotten about him. Damn! Nightwalker has a point—we would be leaving Thromar, but I think it's safe to assume Thromar would have wanted us to go on without him."

"But they might kill him," Logan protested.

The young man could not see the Murderer's frown through the blackness. "Maybe, maybe not," he replied. "One thing's for sure—if you stay, you die."

Logan suddenly straightened up, tightening his grip on Yorke's stolen whip as if for added strength. "Says who?" he queried. "Maybe I can last out this *Daigread* thing long enough for Nightwalker to do something—or maybe I can even win."

Moknay smirked. "If you use magic."

Logan glared at the Murderer, his prideful boasting mutating into a sudden anger. "No," he snapped. "With no magic."

A flicker of an idea sparked the steely greyness to life in Moknay's eyes. "Wait a moment, friend," he grinned. "I haven't any clue as to what Nightwalker meant by saving time by wasting it, but if you can hold out for at least the first half of *Daigread*, I might be able to find out where Thromar is. Then, once he's safely out of Roshfre's grasp, you and Mara can make your escape."

The young man rubbed at his right eye hidden beneath his eyepatch. "Well," he muttered, "I guess it'll have to do. We don't have much of a choice."

The Murderer whirled around, his cape fluttering through the night like a sheet of grey mist. "I'll try to hurry," he said. "Just don't get killed until I get back."

Logan frowned at the Murderer's humor. "Oh, ha ha."

A crowd filled the enormous chamber, quiet despite their unruly appearance. Torches crackled noisily along the sheer walls, throwing shadows throughout the massive underground arena. The vast size of the chamber sent resounding echoes across the room as Logan followed the procession of men out into the center of the ring. Through the soles of his tennis shoes, the young man could feel odd indentations in the stone floor, and his single eye had already caught curious depressions half-concealed on the ground as they zigzagged before him.

The murmurings of the crowd died as Roshfre stepped down into the arena, her long hair glittering in the torchlight. Her red sash shone just as brilliantly as she raised her arms and wordlessly demanded the audience's attention.

"We would have a newcomer," she declared, throwing a finger in Logan's direction. "This man here has dared to accept the challenge of *Daigread* and will soon face what all of you here once had to face."

Logan scanned the scarred and dark faces of the mob. There were so many people here—even some women among them. This *Daigread* couldn't be all that horrible if all these people had survived it to join up with Roshfre, could it?

Look again, Matthew, the young man's darker side rasped. These people looked like the kind who'd bite the heads off their own cats and boil them for dinner.

A serious case of butterflies made the young man feel as if he had just eaten boiled cat as well.

"As you can see," continued Roshfre, "he is not from Denzil nor is he from Sparrill, but we must not let that stand between us. Events may be transpiring and he must be allowed to speak his mind as our equal—for now we will let his skill and ruthlessness speak for him." The redhead jerked up her left hand, cold blue eyes ablaze. "Let *Daigread* commence!"

The low grumblings of gears and machinery sounded in Logan's ears, and the young man was surprised to see slabs of stone press up through the floor. At certain junctions in the ground, thick sheets of rock growled upward, grinding and rumbling into place with the aid of unseen mechanisms. Rock slammed together as select slabs formed corners and angles, and the huge arena reverberated with the groan of machines as a maze suddenly filled the once empty chamber.

The bearded captain of Roshfre's men tapped Logan on the shoulder. "You've just got to make it to the other side," he explained. "Sounds a lot easier than it is."

Logan gave the only entrance to the stone maze an apprehensive glance.

Marcos leaned closer, adding in a whisper, "Moknay told me about what's going on. If what you say is true, Imogen won't let you fail." The captain started to back away, then finished with a grin: "Just watch your feet."

Great, the young man mused sourly to himself, I've got the protection of a mythological god to watch over me. Somehow that just doesn't quite cut the pressure down any. Still . . . if Roshfre's own captain believed in what the young man had to say, there was a very good chance Logan could get their support if he survived *Daigread*—even though Moknay was going to try to show up before he reached the end of the maze.

Clutching tightly to the coiled whip in his left hand, Logan stepped into the maze and was cut off from the rest of the chamber. The stone slabs that had pushed their way up from the ground towered some eight feet high, blocking out the young man's view of the crowd. He had noticed that the seats of the arena had been placed high along the wall, and most of the bandits had filled the topmost rows. They probably had a pretty good view of him while he blundered around below them. Wonderful! An audience to watch him die.

The young man started cautiously down the first corridor and followed the corner to the left. He still felt indentations in the floor, indicating that other blocks of stone were underfoot, probably allowing whoever operated the devices below to create a different maze for every participant of *Daigread*. With a twinge of paranoia, the young man also noted small apertures in the walls themselves, reminding him of the trap in *Raiders of the Lost Ark* that shot darts.

There was a sharp retort somewhere ahead of him like something metallic snapping, and Logan glanced up. His impaired vision barely caught sight of the spiraling silver blur that drove for his throat as he threw himself to the floor, narrowly ducking the dagger that had launched from the far wall. There was another machinelike clang, and a score of steel shafts jabbed out from the opposing walls, ready to impale anyone who had dodged to either side to avoid the blade.

They saw the same movie, huh? Logan sneered sarcastically to himself. Well, if that's the way they're gonna play it; *Daigread* was going to be a bunch of tricks and traps that were obviously being controlled from somewhere below. Since they all come from there—and since my first escape was downward—Marcos's curt warning was more important than I thought. I've just gotta watch my feet.

Logan came to a branch and decided to go right, keeping his ears open and his eyes trained on the stone floor. He made a few more turns without mishap before coming to a dead end. Frowning, the young man backtracked as best he could and went left at the first junction. There was about a fraction of a second between when he noticed the line of small holes spanning the floor before him and the movement of his leg. Sensing a trap, the young man transformed his next step into a wild leap, half flipping, half rolling over the tiny openings. A roar of energy sounded somewhere below ground as jets of flame sprang from each hole, creating a blazing wall of fire behind the young man that almost singed his Nikes.

"Must be going the right way," Logan grumbled to himself. "They're trying to kill me again."

Mara watched from high atop the stands, her hands longing for the feel of her Binalbow. She watched in disgust at the gathering of thieves and brigands, their eyes aglow at the chance to see death played out before them. If she had her Binalbow, they'd see death! she told herself. Just what kind of lowlife slime thrilled at seeing a man struggle desperately for his life? And all for the initiation into a band of cutthroats who probably didn't have a bit of loyalty about them. Why, they probably wouldn't listen to Logan even if he did make it through!

Logan halted at a three-way branch, staring down each corridor suspiciously. The hall on his left had ominous-looking markings criss-crossing the stone floor, telling Logan that something decidedly nasty was waiting for him. The corridor on his right showed no such visible signs of danger, while the usual small holes dotted the walls of the passage ahead of him.

Shrugging, Logan uncoiled Yorke's whip and continued forward. Better to brave rocketing daggers and shooting darts than God knows what, he concluded. Shit, if my life wasn't at stake, this *Daigread* might even be fun.

Distracted by his own thoughts, Logan failed to notice the tiny button set in the rock floor and accidentally stepped on it. A click sounded below the floor, instantly activating some hidden machinery. Immediately Logan was on guard, carelessly diving forward and hoping no pits decided to open up in front of him. Instead, what sounded like a chorus of serpents filled the stony maze, and foul-looking, greenish-grey mist spumed from the rows of holes in the wall behind him. Logan didn't need to inhale to know that the haze was probably as poisonous as it looked, and he scrambled forward frantically, holding what breath he had managed to trap in his lungs.

Roshfre turned away from the maze, nodding at the thief Moknay had addressed as Xile. "He's gotten farther than most would have wagered," she stated.

The bandit nodded agreeably, his bandana flapping. "A bit clumsy, but he's still alive."

"That is what counts, isn't it?" Halette smirked from nearby.

A cutthroat seated beside the prostitute grinned over at her, jerking a finger at a larger man sitting below them. "Not if ya ask Thumbs," he responded.

Mara turned a questioning glance along with Halette at the balding rogue called Thumbs. Catching the mention of his name, the slightly obese thief turned and smiled a decaying smile at the women; it was when he turned back around that Mara noticed his left hand was devoid of all fingers except his thumb.

A line of perspiration streamed across Logan's brow as the young man gave the stone corridors a perturbed glare. How much more of this was there? he wondered. The arena had looked large, but certainly not large enough to hold all the yards he had already walked. Maybe the maze was sending him around in circles?

Something triggered within the walls and Logan looked up too late. A weighted net spun out from a trap door, catching the young man and knocking him to the ground. Startled, Logan grappled with the mesh and only succeeded in entangling himself further. With an exhausted curse, the young man released his stranglehold on the net and looked around.

Stupid, stupid, stupid! he cursed himself. I wasn't paying attention and got trapped for it. Now what? Is the game over if I can't get out?

In reply to the young man's unspoken question, there was a hungry growl of gears, and a portion of wall rose up. A dark form stalked free of the shadows, the hairs along its back stiff and bristly. Blazing yellow eyes trained on the young man as the creature cautiously emerged from its prison, its body lean with starvation. Long, foxlike ears flattened across its skull as it spied Logan and halted. The claws of its overly large forepaws glittered in the light of the torches, and its back legs tensed as it prepared to spring.

Logan gaped at the animal confronting him, once again resuming his useless struggle with the net. Damn them! he cursed the thieves of Roshfre's band. Damn them and their *Daigread*!

With an enraged shout, Logan managed to free Moknay's dagger in the confines of the net as the wolflike beast jumped. Crimson magic unexpectedly blossomed from the dagger's blade, severing the net and momentarily blinding the animal. Yowling, the creature's leap went out of control, and it slammed into a wall with a bone-jarring thump.

Logan scrambled to his feet, uncoiling Yorke's whip. "All right," he sneered at the creature. "Hold it!"

The animal swung around, shaking its head free of the dizziness of impact and the weakness of hunger. "*But hungrrrrry*," a faraway voice informed Logan.

The young man blinked, fixing his single eye on the scrawny creature. "What?" he exclaimed.

"*Hungrrrrry*," the plaintive whine sounded again, and the wolf-like thing's eyes flickered weakly.

Logan stared at the starving animal stanced before him. It—like the anthropoid creature Munuc—had talked to Logan in a sort of telepathic fashion, not really speaking but being heard nonetheless. That meant—to Logan anyway—that the creature was certainly intelligent.

"What are you?" Logan questioned it, his hand still tight around Yorke's whip.

"*Ealhdoeg*," the creature replied. "*Hungrrrrry ealhdoeg.*"

The word was familiar, Logan recalled. He had never seen the creature's kind before, but Mara had described their appearance and their curiously high level of intelligence. What she hadn't told him was that they were capable of speech.

"You're hungry?" Logan asked the creature back, and it answered with a weary nod of its canine head. A malevolent smirk crossed the young man's lips as he pointed farther down the corridor. "There's a whole army of men just beyond these walls," he explained. "They're probably the bad men who locked you up and didn't feed you. If you help me get out, you can eat all you can catch."

And make for the perfect distraction when—and if—Moknay shows up, the young man added silently to himself.

"*What is distraction?*" the ealhdoeg queried.

Logan raised his eyebrows in shock, then remembered that Munuc was able to read his thoughts as well . . . but that had been with the help of Druid Launce's staff! And now there was no staff in sight! Was it the ealhdoeg's intelligence or perhaps the outburst of Natural magic from Logan's sorcerously enhanced dagger that allowed for this odd conversation to take place? And why had the blade's magic reacted in such a way? Whatever the reason, the young man was being offered an ally that had far superior senses than humans and could probably lead the young man out of the maze with his life intact.

Roshfre got to her feet, peering into the stone maze stretched out below her. A puzzled frown was on her lips as she tried to see over the obstructing slabs of rock that made up the *Daigread* chambers.

"What's he doing?" Xile wanted to know.

Roshfre's frown expanded. "It looks like he's . . . talking to it."

"Talking to it?"

"That's what I said, damn you!" the redhead snapped. A fiery gaze fell on Mara. "Just how strange is this stranger-friend of yours?" she demanded.

A smug smile crossed the priestess's lips as she turned away from the redheaded bandit and returned her stare to the arena below. Already Logan was more than halfway free.

Logan and the ealhdoeg took a careful turn around a right junction, the former smiling at the surprised reactions he could hear coming from the crowd outside the stone walls. *So no one's made friends with an ealhdoeg, huh?* he mused. *I bet that's got 'em puzzled—not to mention pissed. I'm certain there can't be much farther to go.*

"*For food?*" the ealhdoeg asked.

Logan looked down at the scrawny creature padding silently beside him. "Yeah, for that," he said. "I can't wait to see the look on the guy's face that I'm supposed to fight when I walk out of here with an ealhdoeg at my side. God, I hope it's that jerk Frayne."

An asthmatic, high-pitched laugh came from the wolflike beast next to Logan as if it understood the joke as well, and the two rounded another corner of the maze. Abruptly, the ealhdoeg's telepathic chuckle rose to a vocal howl of pain, and blood spattered across its fur as a crossbow bolt slammed into its frail, hunger-starved body. Horrified, Logan looked up, searching the walls for the point of emission.

Blocking the rest of the passage was the large frame of Frayne.

"You wanted to see my face, Outsider," the cutthroat snarled, loading another bolt into his crossbow. "Well, here it is."

The shock numbing Logan's system began to wear off as he looked down at the twitching form of the half-starved ealhdoeg, blood trickling from its chest to form a scarlet pond beside it. Strength exploded in Logan's muscles as his horror turned to rage, and his rage turned to hatred.

Logan's whip cracked once, snapping the crossbow from Frayne's grasp. Cursing, the larger man went for the dropped weapon, but a second retort from the whip drew a bloody gash across his arm and he retreated a step.

Logan clenched his teeth so hard it hurt. "You goddamn son of a bitch," he growled, insanely launching himself at the bigger thief.

Silver flashed in Frayne's hand, and Logan narrowly avoided the dagger thrust at his stomach. The young man jerked his own sword free of its sheath, yet Frayne swerved, moving with Moknay's agility. A meaty fist drew up from the ground and slammed into Logan's jaw, knocking the young man back against the wall. Somewhere below ground, mechanisms hummed and gears clicked into place.

Xile jumped out of his seat, his hand on his sword. "What in Agellic's Gates does that bastard think he's doing?" he demanded.

"Killing a nuisance," the thief beside Halette retorted.

"He's cheating!" Xile argued. "He wasn't free of the maze yet!"

Roshfre placed a reassuring hand on the bandit's arm. "Calm yourself, my friend," she soothed. "Frayne is only a little overeager."

The bandana around Xile's forehead snapped like Logan's whip. "Overeager, my ass!" he spat, leaping down the seats of the enormous arena. "I'll not have the ritual of *Daigread* desecrated by that chomprat's droppings!"

There was an odd glitter of comprehension in Halette's eyes as she fixed a rigid gaze on her older sister. "You engineered all this, didn't you?" she said. "You told Frayne to cheat."

Roshfre's own silence condemned her.

Functioning on nothing but the raw strength of his own hatred and fury, Logan drove in again, his red-tinted sword clashing with Frayne's normal blade. So blinded by his intense rage, Logan was not even aware that the walls were steadily closing in, the thundering of their gears sounding alongside the clanging of swords. A tremendous frustration built up inside Frayne as he backed against one of the moving walls, desperately searching for an opening in Logan's wild attack. The thief was having a hard enough time trying to keep the Reakthi blade away from his flesh while Logan drove in with the strength and fury of a berserker. Crimson-tainted steel was everywhere, and the fleeting thought of losing to this Outsider ignited Frayne's own personal madness.

A meaty hand pushed in past Logan's blade, jabbing a cruel finger into the young man's good eye. With an agonized scream of rage and pain, Logan crashed backwards, blinking repeatedly to clear his only eye with its contact lens still in place. Frayne watched as the young man tried to clamber to his feet, one hand covering his uncovered eye.

"One thing about Eadarus," the large cutthroat said, grinning in triumph, "we don't play very fair at all."

The anger fuming inside Logan burned the pain from his eye as he raised the eyepatch over his contactless eye. "Neither do I," he retorted, using his astigmatic vision of his right eye to land a wicked kick to Frayne's groin.

The large bandit went down, and Logan realized for the first time that the walls were closing inward. Hastily, the young man started to sprint for the corridor that must lead to an exit when a huge hand lashed about his ankle, dragging him to the floor and knocking the sword from his grasp.

"You're not going anywhere," Frayne said, the agony still scrawled across his face from Logan's kick.

The grinding of gears boomed louder as the walls closed in for a crushing finale. Panic overtook the young man's anger, and Logan rammed his Nikes repeatedly into Frayne's face, trying to reach his fallen blade. Regardless of the pain, the larger man held on. A narrow corridor was all that remained as the opposing walls continued their steady advance, and a claustrophobic terror grabbed Logan about the throat.

No! he screamed to himself. *It's not fair! I'm not going to die! No!*

The young man's hand came across Frayne's deserted crossbow and he whipped around, jerking back the trigger. Frayne howled as the wooden bolt tore across his shoulder, yet his grip did not weaken, retaining its viselike hold.

"Nice try," the thief growled, fumbling with his free hand for a dagger.

Logan threw the useless crossbow at Frayne and watched in panic-stricken helplessness as the cutthroat avoided the weapon and held up a dagger, its blade gripped between his fingers. A malicious grin twisted the thief's features as he cocked back his arm to throw the knife and shrieked as the ealhdoeg's fangs ripped into the muscles of his back. The crossbow bolt still protruded from the animal's side, yet a wild light shone in its yellow eyes as it tore out great chunks of the bandit's flesh. As Frayne's grip finally fell away from his ankle, Logan was thrown off balance and sent rolling down the last corridor. Frayne's hideous screams were abruptly cut short as the walls slammed closed, crushing both Frayne and the ealhdoeg in their fatal embrace.

Logan pulled himself to his feet, still trying to blink the vision back to his left eye. His anger was depleted and he was too weak to be terrified. He only felt sick and weary as he half walked, half staggered out of the *Daigread* maze and collapsed in a tired heap on the floor.

Marcos helped pull the young man to his feet. "You did it," the captain declared. "You passed *Daigread*!"

The vision of both his eyes blurred, Logan stared blankly at the bearded Marcos and at the others who were gathering around him in a curious ring. As if they were the distant crashing of waves, the young man dimly heard shouts and yells exploding from the crowd that he knew existed somewhere but couldn't quite tell where at the moment. He briefly caught sight of the red bandana that Xile wore, and he stole a glimpse of Halette—or was that Roshfre? He thought he saw the red-and-black garb of Mara, but he couldn't be sure in the wild chaos that surrounded him.

"Spellcaster!" someone screamed angrily. "He cheated!"

"He won!" someone else shouted. "He's earned the right to join!"

"Kill him!"

"It was fixed!"

"No strangers! People from Droth can't be allowed in!"

"He deserves to be initiated! Let him!"

"Never!"

The various accusations and demands were lost in the overall turmoil of the arena as Logan felt consciousness slipping away from him. Why won't these people shut up? he pleaded silently. I didn't get any sleep last night and I need it now.

A voice Logan had never heard before unexpectedly broke through the chaos of the chamber and the young man looked up with blurry eyes to see a lean, long-haired man approach the bottom of the arena, Moknay's grey form stalking behind him.

"*Silence!*" the newcomer commanded, and, miraculously, there was.

Half-dead, Logan felt the stirrings of a faint memory spark within his skull and even in his weary state he began to piece things together. The pale, long hair. The robe. The authority in which he carried himself.

The Smythe?

Logan passed out.

·9·

Army

Consciousness returned in weak threads, pulling Logan up out of the darkness of oblivion. Feeling sorely drained of both strength and emotions, the young man pried his left eye open and came face to face with a dead man.

With a startled shout, Logan jerked away from the corpse lying beside him, rolling off the narrow bed and landing with a thump on the wooden floor. His still bedpartner grinned down at him lifelessly, eyes wide and unfocused, its skin beginning to turn the sickening yellow hue of death.

"Welcome back to the legions of the living," someone quipped behind him.

Logan spun on the floor, warily eyeing the robed figure in the doorway. His weary brain recalled a distant memory of seeing this man once before—bringing with it a memory of *Daigread*—and the young man unsteadily pulled himself to his feet, his single eye locked on the man before him.

The gaunt figure stepped into the room, his long, dirty-white hair streaming down around bony shoulders. A greenish-grey robe draped his lean frame, yet he loomed over Logan by almost a foot. A strange, almost maniacal grin was stretched across thin lips, and disturbing, black-brown eyes fixed on the young man.

This was not the Smythe, Logan concluded, dimly recalling his brief shock before passing out and feeling slightly cheated by it. Whoever this man was, he was tall like the Smythe, and his hair and gangly frame bore a close resemblance to the deceased spellcaster, but he was not the Smythe.

"Who are you?" Logan demanded. "Where am I? And what the hell's going on here?"

The stranger released an insane snigger. "Oh, yes," he chuckled, "the Rebel told me you excelled at asking questions."

Rebel? Logan asked himself. Thromar?

The man stepped toward Logan. "My name is Dirge," he introduced himself, "and you are at my home. Unfortunately, there weren't enough extra beds." He indicated the dead man that continued to silently laugh in Logan's direction.

The young man blinked in quiet bewilderment. Who was this man who looked like the Smythe—but wasn't—and had brought him out of Roshfre's underground labyrinth—alive? Or was he still under the city and in the grasp of the redheaded thief? And what of those who had accompanied him?

"Where are my friends?" Logan asked out loud.

Dirge pointed a bony finger heavenward and Logan felt a momentary panic tug at his mind. "Upstairs," the lean man answered, and Logan's relief was not fast in returning. "They've been waiting for you."

Logan squinted his good eye at the strange man stanced before him. "Waiting for me?" he repeated. "Waiting for what?"

"More questions, eh?" Dirge grinned. "Waiting for you to end the commotion, of course. Half the crowd this morning was ready to slit your throat after you survived *Daigread*."

"So why didn't they?"

"I stopped them," Dirge proclaimed, proudly straightening himself to full height.

Logan raised his eyebrows, a skeptical mien drawing across his features. "You stopped them?" he retorted sardonically. "Why the hell should they listen to you?"

Dirge leaned down toward the young man, placing a finger beside his beaklike nose as if it were their secret. "There is one thing even the fiercest and bloodthirstiest rogue in Eadarus does *not* do," he declared, "and that is argue with a necromage."

Necromage! Logan realized. This man was the necromage to whom Roshfre had sent Thromar. And Moknay had brought back the necromage rather than the Rebel for what reason? Had something happened to Thromar?

"How's Thromar?" the young man chanced.

Dirge beamed, dark eyes flickering. "Strong as a dragon's breath," he quipped. "He'll be back to his normal strength in at most a week's time. That's the reason I had to meet you— and not as a business call. Your healing of the Rebel's leg was utterly astonishing! Where did you learn such intricate mystical weaving?"

"I didn't learn it anywhere," Logan sneered, perturbed by the mention of magic. "I'm just stuck with it."

"Stuck?" Dirge exclaimed. "I should hardly say stuck! It's an absolute wonder, what you've accomplished! I couldn't let such a blazing new talent get killed by a band of unruly cutthroats, eh? The Murderer and I hurried back as quickly as we could and stopped Roshfre before she could do anything particularly sadistic to you."

Logan ran a tired hand through his black hair, inhaling deeply as if that would help replenish some of his diminished strength. "And they're all upstairs now?" he questioned the necromage. "Waiting for me?"

Dirge nodded curtly. "Yes, yes," he answered. "You're officially one of Roshfre's men now. There was some bickering over the validity of your escape . . ."

"Validity of my escape?" Logan thundered. "What the hell do you mean, validity of my escape? I went in—I came out! That's all I was supposed to do!"

"Indeed," agreed Dirge, "so they came to the conclusion that Roshfre's own act of treachery—planting that Frayne fellow inside the maze itself—cancelled out any sorcery you may have used to charm the ealhdoeg."

"But I didn't use any magic!" the young man fumed.

"You know that, and I may know that," the necromage responded, "but try to tell that to a bunch of superstitious cutthroats, eh? You'll wind up with more than one dagger up a bodily orifice."

Logan drew back his lips in an angry snarl as he glared at the gaunt necromage. Ever since he had stepped into Eadarus he had been bombarded by a remarkable barrage of apathy and selfishness. The people of Eadarus were so damn uncaring for the overall safety of their world and here was Logan—running around like a chicken with his head cut off—risking his damn life in damn *Daigread* mazes to get Sparrill's own people to fight for her!

Sparrill's finest, Logan snorted. Hah!

The young man released an exasperated sigh and hoped that maybe Nightwalker would come up with a secondary plan now that his was falling through. "So now what?" he asked Dirge. "They want me to go upstairs and say what I said yesterday?"

"Basically, yes," Dirge said, "although we're still not sure they'll really listen to you. The Murderer thinks that maybe a handful of men will come with us even if it means breaking relations with Roshfre, but some men are better than none."

Logan raised his eyebrows. "Us?" he asked.

"Most assuredly," replied Dirge, his head bobbing up and down and sending his lengthy hair flying. "I'll not sit idly back and watch the destruction of my land and world. I mean, death may be my business, yet I've no intentions of meeting my employer, eh?"

"Oh, great," muttered Logan, his voice lacking all emotion. It wasn't bad enough that the young man's ploy had crumpled before the onslaught of indifference in Eadarus; now he was going to get stuck with a handful of renegade rogues, a half-sane necromage, and his usual group of four friends—all slightly worn from their previous battles.

They'd be dead before they got anywhere near Groathit!

Logan walked tiredly to the door. "Well," he said resignedly, "we might as well get this over with. The sooner we get out of here, the sooner we can come up with another plan."

Dirge responded with a wild grin that made Logan shiver nervously as he followed the bony necromage out of the room and up a flight of wooden steps. The mortician's home was unsettlingly dark and narrow, reminding Logan all too much of the *Daigread* maze, and he flinched as if he expected weapons to shoot out at him when the floorboards underfoot creaked beneath his weight.

"You do a lot of this, eh?" Dirge questioned cheerfully.

Logan looked up. "What?"

"Saving the multiverse," Dirge specified. "You do it a lot?"

The young man from Santa Monica felt an insane bubble of laughter take root in his throat and couldn't prevent the chortle of misplaced mirth as he trailed the necromage up the stairs. Matthew Logan, the young man told himself, hero of the multiverse and champion of a million worlds . . . even though he doesn't want to be. Jesus! What does it take to get out of this place?

The flicker of insanity died and the weariness briskly crept back in to engulf the young man as he completed the lengthy climb to the ground floor. Voices—familiar and unfamiliar—began to resonate from further down the corridor, and the prancing glare of torches started to dot the narrow hallways with orange-red bursts of illuminance.

Logan rounded a narrow corner and entered what he guessed to be Dirge's equivalent to an embalming room. The wide chamber was filled with tables and huge slabs of granite, and odd devices and charts lay scattered about the shelves and floor. The sharp angles of the room sent the myriad voices within echoing back and forth across the chamber, but all went quiet as the young man stepped into the doorway. It seemed everyone's gaze hung on Logan as he entered the room behind Dirge, and he could suddenly feel the heavy weight of responsibility clamping down around his shoulders. He could not miss the cynical and mistrusting glare in the eyes of all those who were not his friends.

Dirge cleared his throat loudly. "I believe Roshfre's newest member has something to say," he declared.

Logan took a deep breath of air and scanned the faces of the thieves and bandits filling the embalming room. A necromage's workshop, the young man thought, frowning to himself. What a charming place for my plan to finally die.

It was outside, hiding in the bushes around the walls of Eadarus. It could see the unnatural, bad magic that filled the sky—that caused the afternoon sun to disappear in a wave of blackness before it had vanished behind the mountains of the west—and somehow it knew that that was wrong. It could sense the horrible manifestation of Evil in the west, the birth of a hundred new creatures every day, and the death of the normal creatures as they were crushed within their own physical shells. Bad magic was alive and growing beyond the rivers and trees, it knew that. But there was something else alive and evil—something else that moved with a form all its own yet was as black and as bad as the darkness that quenched the sun. These other things reeked with the stench of entropy—these other things did not belong within the Forces of the Wheel either. They belonged outside— they belonged apart from the Wheel where their hideous smell of death and corruption would not be smelled. Where their unnatural presence alone would not silence the singing of the birds and the crying of the insects. For this was bad magic—truly bad magic.

And one such creature had crept past the beings that lived behind this unnaturally formed mountain of stone; one such creature loped secretively down the paths and avenues called streets; one such creature had fooled its way past the Guardian of neither good nor bad magic; and one such creature was undoubtedly forging its way toward those who were friends and seeking to slay them as its Masters slayed to the west.

And the thing lurking in the brush outside Eadarus longed to act, yet knew that now was not yet the time. And it hoped it was not making a mistake.

*   *   *

"Look, maybe I've made a mistake," Logan snarled, his hand tightly clenched around the hilt of his sword and his teeth grinding together in anger. "I thought maybe you bastards would give a shit about what was happening—I thought the rumors about you being 'Sparrill's finest' were true. But now I see that they're not. Now I see that *you're* not. You're nothing but a bunch of uncaring, selfish pickpockets who think that life is nothing more than stealing from one another while someone else's stealing from you." The young man glared at the assembled thieves in Dirge's embalming room. "I've told you what's been going on," he continued, "and I don't care whether you believe me or not. I never wanted to come to this goddamn place, and I'm getting out of here the moment I'm able. That's probably when Groathit's dead—now whether I kill him or he kills me really doesn't matter anymore. If I win, I go home, and anything else that happens here afterward I could care less about. But, if he wins, you'll find yourselves probably begging your good-for-nothing King to save your butts when you're the only city left that hasn't fallen to Groathit and Vaugen!"

Logan turned to stalk out of the room but stopped in the doorway, swinging around again and fixing his single eye on Roshfre with an intense glare of rage. "I came here to warn you and hoped that you'd care," he growled, and his voice was low and threatening, "and all I've gotten is trouble. I hope that you remember that when the Darkness takes you over."

With a furious turn of his heel, the young man strode out of the chamber and back down the corridors of Dirge's workshop. He didn't really know where he was heading, but he just didn't give a damn at the moment. He was sick of Eadarus and he was sick of Sparrill. He wasn't accepted; he was accused of being an Outsider and a stranger; and, what's worse, he just wasn't believed. Roshfre and her men refused to acknowledge what he said—even though he was a member of her band now—and all on the basis that he had no proof.

Proof? They wanted proof? How about the darkness that had already turned the afternoon to evening? Or the sheet of blackness that was seen by virtually everyone in eastern Sparrill and western Denzil as it materialized out over the mountains near Vaugen's fortress?

Soft, hurried footsteps sounded behind Logan, and the young man felt some of his fury drain away from him as Mara caught up to him, a delicate hand touching his shoulder. "You shouldn't have let your anger get the better of you," she said. "Moknay thinks you may have convinced a few more men before you blew up."

Logan sneered, not at the priestess but at the group he had left behind. "I don't care," he snapped. "What good is a few more men? Murderous cutthroats or not, even they won't last five minutes against the army Nightwalker said Groathit was building."

Mara gently turned the young man around, her emerald eyes probing deep into his own blue eyes, trying to see past the ire and frustration that churned there. "Matthew," she stated, "we need all the help we can get. Ten men are better than five."

"Just as a hundred men are better than ten," the young man retorted.

The priestess bit her lower lip in thought, catching the faint spark of disillusionment in the young man's eye. "Maybe you're just asking for too much," she tried.

Logan felt her comment drive straight through his heart as she uncovered one of the reasons for his anger, and he doubled the protection around himself as he snapped back, "Yeah, the story of my life."

The young man was going to spin back around and stomp off down the hall when there was an unexpected explosion of stone, wood, and mortar. White clouds of dust spumed into the air as an entire portion of wall crashed inward, accompanied by a thunderous clap of power. Pelted by shards of rock, Logan careened to one side, Mara falling with him. Dirt found its way into his nose and mouth, coating his tongue and throat with dusty grime and forcing him to cough.

A dark form rose up from the destruction, a pair of black eyes piercing the curtain of debris. Its second pair of eyes were blank, no longer guttering with the malevolent energies of the Darkness. Dirt adhered itself to its gelatinous frame, and dried and caked ichor splashed along its naked back and encrusted the split skull of its second head.

With a vengeful snarl, the *Deil* Vsdaefn leaped into the hall, its second head dangling lifelessly from its neck.

"The Purity, Unbalance!" the monster roared. "Give me the Purity!"

Choking from the dust, Logan tried to clamber to his knees, his only eye squinted to keep the dirt out of his contact lens.

Vsdaefn stalked into the house, its wolflike limbs throbbing and pulsating like living clay. "Your ploy succeeded, Unbalance," the *Deil* admitted. "I am all that remains of my Masters' Servants—

and, for that reason alone, I shall not fail them!"

Blinded by the swirling clouds of rubble, Logan attempted to pull himself to his feet, his hand groping futilely for his sword. Noises sounded elsewhere, confusing the young man momentarily until he could see the silhouettes of other people rushing to his aid. Vsdaefn turned his head on the approaching brigands and released an enraged snarl, squirming tentacles forming from the muck on its back.

Roshfre skidded to a halt in Dirge's narrow hallway, her cold blue eyes glittering with a moment's surprise. "What in Imogen's name is it?" she queried, her hand on her mace.

Moknay tried to fight his way through to the front of the crowd, his gloved hands embracing his strap of daggers. "A *Deil*," he explained. "One of the Voices' Servants. Now get back!"

"What?" one of Roshfre's men inquired. "And let you have all the fun, Murderer? I was here first."

The wolflike *Deil* tensed as the thief launched a slim dagger toward the creature's throat. With a fiendish growl, Vsdaefn lunged to one side, avoided the weapon, and shot back up, streams of ebony force rocketing from its eyes. Roshfre dropped to the ground to escape the blast as the man beside her erupted into a million particles of blackness. Saliva oozed from Vsdaefn's remaining mouth as it swung its attention back to Logan, its eyes guttering and snapping like a torch's flame.

"The Purity, Unbalance!" it howled. "Give me the Purity!"

Logan managed to extract his sword yet was unable to find the balance to stand. "I don't have it!" he shouted back.

Vsdaefn paused, cocking its only remaining head to one side in question. "You lie!" the monster said. "I can smell the stench of Purity about you!"

The young man brandished his blade, noting the faint crimson tinge to the Reakthi steel. "You wanna come closer and find out where it's coming from?" he sneered at the *Deil*.

Roaring, Vsdaefn leapt, batlike wings sprouting from its pliable spine. Logan threw himself back to the ground, his sword up for protection. The wolflike creature banked sharply, blackness gleaming in its eyes.

"Get back!" Moknay was still yelling. "Normal weapons don't hurt it!"

"The Purity!" Vsdaefn bellowed again. "I want it!"

Logan risked a glance up as wiry limbs stretched down for him. Yelling in fright, the young man kicked himself backwards, his sword automatically chopping downward. Red fire licked along the edges of the Reakthi blade, and Vsdaefn shrieked in pain as one of its tentacles dropped to the floor, slithering and squirming like a decapitated serpent. Logan scrambled madly to his feet, his single eye locked on the flying monstrosity before him.

"This is not possible!" the *Deil* yowled, eyes blazing. "Die, Unbalance! *Die!*"

The enraged beast folded its wings, making a sudden, crazed dive for the young man and the band of thieves behind him. A mind-numbing shriek abruptly ripped from the creature's mouths—both living and dead—as Mara jumped up from where she lay, her scarlet-glimmering sword driving deep into the *Deil*'s bowels. The wings melted across the monster's back as it spiraled to the ground, thick, black fluid gurgling from its wound in corrosive waves.

Vsdaefn hit the wooden floor near Logan, fixing angry dark eyes on the priestess. Gnashing teeth sprouted all across its back and sides, and a twisting horn rose up from the viscid flesh of its forehead.

"You shall die!" the creature swore. "You shall all die! And my Masters will speak again!"

The young man glared down at the *Deil* as it tensed to spring in Mara's direction. Ruby light exploded as the heavy Reakthi blade pierced the creature's mucid form, releasing a fountain of sulfuric ichor. Vsdaefn screamed in agony, its pulsing, mutable legs crumpling beneath its own weight. Pleading, groping hands surfaced from the beast's frame as glimmering red sorcery ravished its tractile shape. Sorceries crackled as the *Deil*'s Darkness clashed with the Purity of the Bloodstone, and one of Vsdaefn's eyes exploded, spattering the far wall with black fluid.

A pitiful moan escaped the wolf-thing's dead mouth as it turned weakly on its side, its remaining eye trained on Logan as magicks roiled inside it. "You shall die, Unbalance," it predicted. "When the Darkness speaks, you shall die."

The creature's tongue suddenly swelled and burst, splashing Logan with its dark lifefluid as it slumped to the wooden floor, devoid of life. The darkness of its remaining eye dimmed and went out, and the glossy sheen to its naked flesh faded.

"By Brolark," Marcos breathed. "That's what a *Deil* looks like?"

Logan jerked his sword free of the monster's malleable flesh and wiped some of the sizzling ichor from his face. "Not really," he replied. "They keep changing shape. The Worm didn't have any constant shape at all."

"It seems something's been added," Thromar stated from the back of the crowd. "That sword didn't glow red when I owned it."

"A necessary step," Moknay told the Rebel. "Logan used a flux of the Heart to make all our weapons more than mere weapons; it was the only way we could fight these bastards."

"And you agreed to wearing a strap of magical daggers?" Thromar boomed with laughter. "Good for you, Murderer! Maybe there's a little courage left in that cowardly little body of yours!"

Moknay swung grey eyes on the bearded fighter, but the scowl on his features was one of mock anger. "You know, Thromar," he sneered, "I liked you better when you were unconscious."

Logan wiped a stream of the *Deil*'s blood from his sweat jacket as he turned an inquisitive eye on Roshfre. The redhead was quietly staring down at the hideous shape of Vsdaefn, her emotions hidden behind the iciness of her eyes. Others of her band were more openly gaping, but others still wore strange smirks and faked frowns of disapproval as they observed the dead creature at their feet.

"You wanted proof," the young man commented, sheathing his Reakthi sword. "There's your proof."

Roshfre swung her head up slowly to gaze directly into Logan's eye, but it was not she who answered.

"Probably just another spellcaster's trick!" a bandit accused. "Darkness's Servant, me mother's ass! Looks like a wolf!"

"A talking wolf?" someone else argued.

"Faked! More sorcery!"

Raw strength accompanied the intense revival of anger as Logan spun away from the shouting, cursing group of brigands. Again! he screamed to himself. They were at it again! Even faced with the corpse of a goddamn *Deil*, they still tried to ignore it! They were lying and they knew it, but it was Logan's word against their reluctance to help—and not even the dead body of a fucking *Deil* was going to make these bastards see the truth when they didn't want to!

"Matthew," Logan heard Mara call to him as he strode angrily through the opening caused by Vsdaefn's entrance. "Matthew! Where are you going?"

The young man refused to answer as he stepped around the rubble and debris of what remained of Dirge's wall and out into the cobblestone streets of Eadarus. The rage inside him was so overpowering that he couldn't stand another minute with those self-righteous assholes! Imagine! They saw one of their own men get blasted into so many pieces and they still wouldn't believe him! What kind of idiots did they have living here, anyway?

Lord, I just want to go home!

Logan jerked himself to a surprised stop when he suddenly saw the torches and men blocking his way, their numbers filling the back streets of the town with roguish grins and stolen weaponry. At first Logan thought they had been attracted by the *Deil*'s destruction of property, but then he saw how orderly they stood and how disciplined they were as they milled about the street. These were not the faces or actions of men who had come running to defend their precious little town—hah! They probably didn't give a damn if Dirge's house exploded into so much junk. No one cared in Eadarus.

The puzzlement must have still been on Logan's face as he recognized one of the men at the front of the horde of townsfolk, and his eyebrows raised in bewilderment.

"Yorke," the young man asked the rogue, "what is all this?"

Yorke grinned, the torch he held snapping and popping. "I's had a talk wit' some o' me friends," he replied, "an' this is the army yer lookin' fer. We's may not be as good as Roshfre's men, but we're willin' t' fight."

A grin slowly spread across Logan's lips as he scanned the score of men massed in the darkened streets. Waste time to save time was what Nightwalker had said, and Logan couldn't help but grin.

He had his army.

Ridglee shivered in uncontrollable terror as the night filled once again with the low moaning cries of the Voices. Even those men who were no longer men—the soldiers so eagerly "given" by Vaugen and Groathit—showed signs of mourning, their glaring eyes dripping tearlike sparks of energy. A freezing wind groaned alongside the blackness's sorrow, sending rippling tendrils of cold through Ridglee's hair and against his flesh that caused goosebumps to rise from both cold and fear.

Gone. All gone.
Lost. Forever lost.
What good are Masters with no Servants?
The Purity is strong here.
The Purity.

Accursed Purity.
They have been destroyed.
Our eyes, our ears, our limbs.
Destroyed.

Ridglee turned a questioning glance at the tent squatting off to one side of the camp. Over the rasping, wheezing voices that sprouted from the dark—and the harmonizing howl of the wind—the Reakthi soldier could hear another voice: the scratchy, throaty growl of the spellcaster. With a determined expression, Ridglee cautiously made his way closer to the wizard's tent, ears straining to blot out the Voices and the wind.

"You have no further need for them," Groathit snarled from within his tent, his voice twinged with impertinence. "You have forms of your own. Why should you need Servants to carry out actions you yourselves are now capable of carrying out?"

Listening intently to the sorcerer's odd conversation with himself, Ridglee almost jumped when the roiling cloud of living blackness overhead answered the wizard's question, speaking with its many different voices. Just as many separate voices came from within the wizard's tent as well as from outside.

Who did this thing?
Yes, who?
Who?

Ridglee could almost see the skull-like smile that must have been stretched across Groathit's lips. "Matthew Logan," the spellcaster breathed, hatred thick in his voice. "Only he is capable of such a feat. Only he can control the Purity with such skill."

Purity. Accursed Purity.
It must be destroyed.

"But he will grow in power," Groathit continued from his tent. "Matthew Logan will become one with the land—one with the Purity. He will try to slay you as he has slain your Servants."

A ghastly chill scurried ratlike up Ridglee's spine as a hundred thousand whispering laughs filled the night's unnatural blackness.

Darkness cannot die.
Darkness can never die.
Light and Dark can only banish one another.
Banishment.
Does not the Night always return to banish the Day?
We cannot die.
We cannot.

"Then he will banish you!" Groathit screeched from behind his walls of canvas, and Ridglee could picture the veins along the wizard's neck popping out in anger. "You have felt what he has done to your Servants—he will do likewise to you! You must destroy him!"

We will destroy the Purity.

Yes, the Purity.

"Matthew Logan is the Purity!" the sorcerer screamed furiously. "Kill him and the Purity withers! Destroy him and the Purity dies!"

The death of the Purity?

Of the Purity?

Then we shall find this being who is one with the Purity.

And we shall destroy him.

Ridglee jumped as footsteps sounded behind him and whipped about to see the younger Ithnan making his way toward his post for the night. The younger Reakthi threw Ridglee a curious glance and jerked a friendly thumb back toward the main body of tents.

"Ridglee," he queried, "why are you still up? You weren't on guard tonight, were you?"

Ridglee ran a hand through his hair, almost feeling the grey that tinted the edges. In his younger days he would never have been surprised from behind. "No," he answered Ithnan, "I wasn't on duty. I . . . I just don't feel tired."

Ithnan smiled with the youthful ignorance of a young man anxious to fight for his people and what they believed in. "Well, get some sleep," he advised. "We move as of tomorrow's dawn."

Ridglee nodded reluctantly as he began a slow walk toward the tent where he was bunked, his hand resting on his sword hilt out of habit. He noted with cold horror the numerous, sleepless men stanced about the camp—unmoving, silent—horrible magicks burning inside forms they had taken from their rightful owners. And there was an added shiver as Ridglee realized the Darkness had stopped its pitiful moaning, and the wind was left to howl alone.

The naked flames of the lanterns threw odd shadows across Nightwalker's ebony flesh as the Shadow-spawn stood at the head of the table, half-hidden in his dark cowl. The tavern was filled with as many of the men they could fit inside and still more clustered about the windows and doors, eager to hear the plan of battle. A select group of people sat about Nightwalker, most of their eyes trained on the Guardian who had entered the town only moments before. Only Logan allowed his gaze to wander from the dark-skinned Shadow-spawn, curiously scanning those about him.

Mara sat to the young man's left, Thromar, Bella, Dirge, Halette, and Roshfre's captain, Marcos, finishing that side of the table. Across from Logan were Moknay, Xile, Yorke, the young Stearck, Yorke's second-in-command—a man called Scythe, and another of Roshfre's men, a brigand named Hach. All in all, they were a dangerous-looking bunch—even Logan with his eyepatch—and even more such men surrounded their table and filled the tavern. The young man from Santa Monica could tell many of the men mistrusted the darkly clad Nightwalker—their fear and unease of magic sparking their caution, yet Logan and Moknay continuously added details to Nightwalker's speech, hoping to calm any misgivings the men Yorke had assembled to help fight their war.

"It will not be long before they begin moving," Nightwalker was saying, his deep, low voice resounding about the rogue-filled tavern, "and even I will not be certain as to their first move. Situated as they are west of the Ohmmarrious River, they may choose to strike first at the town of Plestenah or Frelars or Gelvanimore. They may even march as far west as Prifrane."

"How's many men have they got?" questioned Yorke.

Darkling Nightwalker shrugged beneath his cowl, his white eyes reflecting the light of the tavern. "They gain more every day," he answered, "and I know not the number of them that have been shells for the Darkness."

"So we's don't know if they's got enough men t' attack all four towns at once?" the rogue wondered.

"I would not expect them to do that," Nightwalker replied, "regardless the number of men. That would be spreading their forces far too thin."

"But it's definitely going to be one of those towns?" Stearck queried.

"It would be logical enough," Moknay responded. "Although Groathit has a far worse plan in mind, he's got to keep up the facade of actually attempting to conquer Sparrill."

"What do you mean?" Hach probed. "What facade?"

"If Groathit's plan succeeds," the Murderer explained, "there won't be any Sparrill left to conquer. That's why Logan's so important to us—Groathit wants him."

Scythe sneered. "Then what's stopping us from giving him to the Reakthi whoreson?"

"Because what the spellcaster has set in motion threatens to destroy all semblance of Balance," Nightwalker put in. "Unless Matthew Logan is able to halt the sorcerer, the entire Wheel and this multiverse of Shadow will be engulfed once more by Darkness; we will cease to be."

"Just like that?" Xile inquired.

"Just like that," Mara answered. "Our multiverse was formed out of the war between Darkness and Light. Now the Darkness has pushed its way back in after being forced out by the Wheel's creation and the Balance that was established. It's planning to retake the Shadow it helped create by destroying what Light exists here—in Sparrill, I would guess that's the Heart."

"And that which you call the Heart is the greatest manifestation of Light in all the multiverse," Nightwalker added, confirming Mara's statements. "That is why they have started here. Just like your Reakthi foes, the Voices hope that once the strongest falls, the rest will be quick to follow."

"That's what they think," Marcos snorted, stroking his heavy beard assuredly.

"Do not become overconfident," warned Nightwalker. "They still far outnumber us—not only in manpower, but also with the Force of Darkness on their side."

"Which is why I suggest we follow the main roads," Thromar interjected. "From what we do know, we can guess that they'll have close to the amount of men of their fortress, right? And more troops are joining up with Vaugen and his scumcaster every day— unnoticed because the bastards are probably not wearing their chestplates. What I suggest is we follow the road northward and pass through Debarnian and ask the townsfolk for aid. I'm certain at least a hundred men will join us there. Then we can continue westward and ride through Plestenah, gathering up even more men. We needn't worry about Mediyan's Dungheads—they're probably still camped around Lake Atricrix."

"What makes you so certain these people will just up and leave?" Scythe wanted to know. "I'm a little uneasy myself 'bout leaving Eadarus unguarded."

Logan's smirk that had been on his face since he had stepped outside Dirge's workshop strengthened. "You leave that to me," he told the rogue. "There's a friend I have who once told me that if I ever needed anything guarded, she'd help out."

"She?" repeated Scythe, disdain in his dark green eyes.

"Ever hear of the three sprites?" Logan queried, his smirk growing smug. "They *are* Guardians."

Surprised murmurs spread across the clustered tavern and Logan felt a weird kind of pride rise in his breast. These people, he noted, were almost afraid of him. They had heard of the things he had done, seen some of them with their own eyes, and they—the heartless, treacherous rogues of Eadarus—feared him. In a way, it made the young man feel pretty good. Besides, after all that trouble they had put him through, he deserved a little respect!

Nightwalker took his seat at Logan's table, the grey starting to seep back into his empty eyes. "I believe the Rebel's plan is our best hope for vanquishing the Darkness and silencing the Voices," the Shadow-spawn declared, "but we must move out tomorrow. We are so very far away from the towns in peril."

"No problems," Yorke grinned. "Scythe and I's seen t' most o' the supplies already. The Murderer'll tell ya—people in Eadarus work real fast."

"Or else they don't work at all," Scythe finished, wickedly grinning.

Moknay's grey eyes strayed on the rogue called Scythe, noting a familiarity in the thief's demeanor that reminded the Murderer of his early days. "The noon tomorrow should be sufficient," Moknay said.

"And might you be wanting a few more good swords?" someone asked from the doorway.

Although the interior of the tavern was swarming with cutthroats and brigands, the atmosphere had been one of relative silence, but now that quiet grew to enormous proportions. Logan turned a quizzical eye on the clustered doorway and blinked his single eye repeatedly when he saw the lithe, redheaded form in the entrance. There was a sparkle of understanding in Roshfre's blue eyes as she stepped up to the young man, the sea of rogues parting magically to allow her room. Many of the redhead's men trailed her into the bar, adding to the already large grouping of men in the room.

"I believe even Roshfre's capable of making a few mistakes," the redhead proclaimed, "and if it takes a band of ugly rogues and freebooting mercenaries to open my eyes, then so be it. Besides, I can't let you people take all the credit, now can I? So what do you say, Matthew Logan? Can you still use me and my men?"

A triumphant smile pulled across the young man's lips as he took a hearty gulp of ale even though he didn't like the stuff.

"You bet your ass I can!" he exclaimed happily, slamming his mug down to accent his cry.

Roshfre threw the young man a questioning smirk. "Bet my what?" she queried.

Halette jumped up from her seat, mirth glowing in her green eyes. "Sounds like my kind of wager!" she shouted. "Any takers?"

·10·

March

"Still no word from Captain Ureis, sir," the sandy-haired Guardsman reported.

Captain Dibri of King Mediyan's Guards nodded curtly, tightening his grip on his scepter of command. "Has there been any answer from Commander Eldath?" he queried.

"No, sir," came the reply.

Dibri paused for a brief thought as he trekked through the vegetation of Sparrill. "That will be all," he finally said. "Thank you, Aelkyne."

The sandy-haired Guardsman called Aelkyne started to step away from his captain but hesitated before resuming his place in the ranks of men. Worried eyes trained on the perplexed face of Captain Dibri as the Guard asked, "Excuse me, sir, but do you think something's intercepting our birds?"

Dibri ran a frustrated hand through his hair, his gaze locked on the brightening sky above the treetops even as he marched. "I don't know what to think, Aelkyne," he sighed with confusion. "I know something's not right but I can't rightly say what."

"The only reason I ask, sir, is because none of our missives to the King are being answered either," Aelkyne remarked.

Dibri answered with a hapless shrug, his eyes still glued to the heavens. There was an unsettling chill in the captain's stomach— a close relative to the freezing wind that moaned softly through the trees. Even though used to the warmer climate of Magdelon, Dibri knew that the polar breeze was far too cold to mark the Sparrillian winter. Either they were in for very harsh weather, or something much more sinister was in the making.

The commanding Guardsman squinted as he peered into the firmament. Although the blackness had only just faded away, the sun was almost at its zenith, turning the sky a glorious blue.

Nonetheless, Dibri could see no hint of the darkness he and his troop had been sent to find, and he wondered if the roiling cloud of ebony had continued its swift westward direction and had utterly destroyed his homeland of Magdelon.

Well-trained ears picked out the clash of steel on steel over the wind's groans, and Dibri tore his gaze from the sky. Other Guards behind him jerked rigid, their hands on their weapons. The scream of a man in agony pierced the walls of foliage and drifted away on the breeze.

"Forward," Dibri ordered his men. "Quick, on my say-so."

The troop of Guardsmen started forward once more, weapons freed and muscles tensed. As the sounds of battle grew nearer, the force of the cold wind strengthened, its howls attempting to silence the cacophony of war. The chill in Captain Dibri's stomach spread to the rest of his body, and the Guardsman threw his men a brief glance. There was no telling who fought ahead of them, so why did the captain have this disquieting feeling that he would lose much more than just a few men?

Eyes locked on the curtain of greenery, Dibri was momentarily distracted when his boot landed in something wet and slippery. Revulsion shot through his bowels as he glanced down and saw the red pools staining the forest floor. The headless upper torso of a man lay at Dibri's feet, strips of sinew and flesh still clinging to its bones. Internal organs lay scattered about its base, and a line of entrails snaked back into the woods like a grisly marker, all wet and glistening with blood.

His disgust slowly fading, Captain Dibri poked at the hideous remains with his sword, turning the carrion over. Bronze glinted in the late-morning sunlight, and Dibri bent down to pick up a scepter similar to his own. Even smeared as it was with crimson, Dibri knew it belonged to Captain Ureis.

A dry leaf crackled; Dibri jerked himself rigid as a shadow passed over the sun. A chestplated figure emerged from the brush, blackness exploding in its eye sockets. Its face was pale and expressionless, and its form seemed lean and underfed. Although a Reakthi sword dangled sheathed at its hip, blood coated its hands rather than its blade.

Steel split the air as Captain Dibri took a measured swing at the malnourished Reakthi, his sword catching the soldier across the face. There was no blood from the open wound that ripped across the warrior's face, only a cadaverous dark glare that emanated from beneath the Reakthi's flesh.

A fist punched through Captain Dibri's chest and tore its fingers through his beating heart. Spatters of blood struck the young Aelkyne across the cheek as a living, seething tide of darkness rolled in overhead like thunderclouds.

Rejoice, a hundred thousand voices rasped, *we have come*.

A crackling halo of black energy radiated about the head of Groathit, highlighting his blue-grey hair with ebony fire. Dried blood remained caked about the empty socket of his right eye and black sorcery gleamed in place of his left. A ghastly smile was drawn on his face, stretching the wrinkled flesh taut, and the dark aura of power flashed off his exposed teeth.

Imperator Vaugen refused to acknowledge the shudder of horror that filled his maimed form. Not even the freezing gale that shrieked through the forest seemed to affect the crackling ring of blackness around the sorcerer's skull, and the wizard's own frame had been growing leaner—similar to the bodies of those men who had been given to the Darkness.

"I do not understand you, wizard," the Imperator spat, trying to disguise his fear with anger. "First you have me gather all my men together in one place, then you separate them again. If these are the workings of a rational mind, I cannot fathom them."

Groathit cocked his head in Vaugen's direction, and his smile seemed to read the fear that lurked in the Imperator's dull grey eyes. "I did not expect you to fathom them, my Imperator," smiled the sorcerer, "which is why I did not bother to explain them to you. We have half our forces—why are you so distraught?"

"Why?" echoed Vaugen. "Why? Because you sent more than half of those endowed with the Darkness eastward and have us traveling in the opposite direction! Tell me, wizard, what is to the west? What possible reason might you have to take us away from our goal? What madness has allowed you to separate us from those who are the Voices?"

"We are not separated from the Voices, my Imperator," Groathit replied, and his halo of blackness sparked. "They are with me, and I am with them."

Vaugen tried to hide his surprise. "What?" he barked angrily. "I thought you said it was impossible for any man to hold even an iota of energy without giving up his own self. How can you be with them and them with you?"

"I knew you would not understand," Groathit mocked, "but then, I am not just any man." His arrogance burst full into life.

"*I* am the reason the Voices are here, fool, and so long as the Darklight grimoire is in my hands, *I* am the reason they remain. If such is the case, they can never control me since it is I who controls them. This very fact alone allows me to speak with their Voice and wield their Darkness without fear of losing myself in their evil.

"As for the reason for our westward trek," the spellcaster continued, "Matthew Logan is out there . . . somewhere . . . and for all my magic, I cannot find him! So let him come to us— and come to us he shall! In the meantime, I have a personal score to settle with someone else—someone else who destroyed my chance to slay Matthew Logan and snatched victory from my very hands! The accursed worm who dared to humiliate me when triumph had been mine!"

Vaugen pulled his cloak about his crippled frame as the freezing wind of unnatural cold screamed through the trees. "Who do you mean?" he demanded. "Say what you will and be done with it!"

Groathit's left eye erupted as he swung a furious glare on the disfigured Reakthi commander, but something inside him quelled his fury. "The sorcerer Zackaron," the spellcaster breathed. "While Matthew Logan comes to us, I shall have my revenge on the sorcerer Zackaron."

"The madman?" Vaugen queried, and there was no hiding the surprise in his voice this time. "You are seriously going to enter the Hills of Sadroia to find and kill a man whose mind rivals that of a newborn infant? He is insane, wizard!"

Groathit's smile reappeared across his skull-like features. "And who is to say that insanity itself is not a source of power?" he inquired. "Truly, if you are insane—and do not doubt the extent of your own abilities—who is to say there is little you cannot accomplish?"

"And what of Matthew Logan?" the Imperator retorted. "How is he to find us if we lose ourselves in the Hills?"

"Who said anything of we, my Imperator?" Groathit responded, his imperious, mocking tone returning to his voice. "*I* will be in the Hills while *you* shall wait for Matthew Logan's arrival in the town of Prifrane."

Vaugen's burned and deformed features grew red with rage and he jabbed his maimed hand at the spellcaster. "And what are we to do, wizard?" he screamed, his voice brittle. "Rent a room in a nearby hostel?"

Groathit turned his black eye on the foliage before him, contemptuously turning away from his enraged Imperator. "The town of Prifrane will be ours," he stated, matter-of-factly, "as will the town of Plestenah."

"With half our force?" Vaugen screeched. "You expect half my men to take two towns? My whole force could not take Eadarus!"

"The town of Prifrane will be ours," Groathit steadily repeated, "and it is there that you shall wait for Matthew Logan while I dispose of the sorcerer Zackaron."

Vaugen was going to say more but held his tongue. The anger slowly burned out of his disfigured frame, replaced by bewilderment glowering in his dull grey eyes. Perhaps what the wizard had said before held true. Perhaps if one were insane there was little they did not fancy themselves capable of accomplishing.

Perhaps Groathit was insane.

Logan threw a look over his shoulder at the horde of men, horses, and carts that dropped steadily behind him as his yellow-and-green mount rode into town. Other horses trotted beside his, their riders all wearing miens of determination. Mara's grasp around the young man's waist spoke of her own ambition, and Logan felt a similar resolution build in his chest. They needed to convince the townsfolk of Debarnian that they needed their help and needed it now. It was Moknay who had suggested they leave their army outside of town and meet them the following morning on the opposite side of town—the sudden appearance of a mass of rogues possibly throwing the trust of Debarnian's populace. So only seven rode into town: Moknay, Thromar, Roshfre, Yorke, Xile, Mara, and Logan: Nightwalker, of course, would show up when he knew things had been resolved.

The arctic wind howled forlornly down the cobblestone streets as the six horses cantered into the village. There was an uneasy stillness to the usually busy roads, and caution instantly sparked to life in Logan's eye. Half-blinded as he was, the young man kept his head moving from side to side as he alertly scanned the town, prepared for whatever ills the wintry wind might carry.

A few townsfolk left their shops and homes, curious gazes trained on the seven riders. Questioningly, Thromar dismounted, beady eyes flicking from building to building. A frown scrawled beneath his heavy reddish-brown beard as he turned his gaze back to those of his group.

"I saw more life at the necromage's workshop," the Rebel quipped. "What the *Deil*'s going on?"

"For some reason that curse carries so very much more meaning nowadays," Xile flippantly shot back, his bandana whipping in the gale.

Moknay, grey eyes aflame, pulled his horse's reins about, directing the grey-and-black stallion for another portion of town. "I'd suggest we head straight through to Barthol," he declared. "Get our answers there."

Thromar shrugged as he clambered back upon Smeea, following the line of horses that wound through the cobblestones. More stares met the seven from windows and doors, and a blacksmith nearby even stopped his hammering to watch the small group pass.

An unsettling knot formed in Logan's stomach as his yellow-and-green horse rounded another corner. Why was everything so quiet? he wondered. Had something already happened here that frightened the townsfolk into submission? Was this a trap? Had Vaugen and Groathit already been here? Was the town already theirs? Or was there another reason for the nervous silence and wary gazes that radiated from the structures of the town?

"Agellic's Gates," Moknay breathed, and Logan jerked his head up in question.

The impressive, spiraling steeples of Agellic's church lay in ruin, small portions of them still rising above the debris. Enormous chunks of marble and ivory littered the street, dust still swirled into the air by the freezing wind. Shards of glass glittered like transparent daggers amongst the rubble, and surrounding buildings still bore pockmarks from where shrapnel had blown into them.

"By Brolark!" exclaimed Thromar.

Yorke flashed a frown, his facial muscles pulling downward around his scar. "I's take it the person we's were meant t' meet ain't gonna be meetin' us here?" he probed.

Emotions deadened by shock, Mara dropped off Logan's horse and began a slow, almost trancelike walk toward the destruction. "What could have happened?" she wondered.

Logan dismounted, grabbing the priestess's arm. "Whoa, hold on," he suggested. "Let's find out before we get too close."

A gruff voice sounded behind the young man, almost startling him out of his own shock. "You looking for something?"

Logan spun, facing the blacksmith who had watched the seven ride past his shop. The large man still held his heavy hammer in his hand, and soot and grime besmeared his perspiring face as he peered down at the young man from Santa Monica with distrust.

"What happened here?" Mara queried. "What happened to the church?"

"Destroyed," the blacksmith responded bluntly.

Logan managed to find his voice. "By whom?"

"Why do you want to know?" the large man demanded.

Soft, catlike footsteps sounded in the cobblestones as Roshfre dismounted, stalking toward the blacksmith with a purposeful glimmer in her eyes. "Destroyed by whom?" she repeated, her slim hand resting near her mace.

The blacksmith's gaze flicked from Roshfre to Moknay. "No one knows," he answered. "There was an explosion from inside. Leveled the entire building."

"No one survived?" Mara asked.

The blacksmith went silent again, the hesitation alive in his stare. "What's your purpose here?" he asked back.

"There's seven o' us an' one o' him and he's askin' the questions?" Yorke smirked, a malicious gleam in his eyes even though he suffered from a broken wrist.

Thromar leapt from Smeea's saddle, approaching the blacksmith with open hands. "We come in peace," the Rebel said, "and were looking for our friend who was the priest at this church. Mara herself was one of his priestesses."

The heavyset blacksmith peered closely at the dark-haired Mara, unable to keep the suspicion in his glare when he looked into her emerald eyes. The sorrow etched on the priestess's face seemed to soften the man's reluctance and he threw a meaty hand down the street.

"The priest still lives," he answered. "He has been living at the home of Baynebridge the lapidary with the only other survivor. He still will not tell us the exact cause of the explosion but has warned us all to be on our guard. Forgive me if I was harsh."

Mara gave the blacksmith an acknowledging nod, wiping a tear that had formed in one eye. Barthol was alive despite the destruction of the church—thank Imogen for that!

The line of horses clopped noisily down the street, stopping when they reached the small shop of the lapidary. Curiously, Logan poked his head in the doorframe and discovered exactly what a lapidary was.

Numerous jewels and gemstones filled the tiny store, sparkling and glittering with polished resplendency. All manner of odd equipment stood behind a flimsy wooden counter, and tables were strewn with chisels and other strange implements that Logan could not even begin to guess the purpose of. A young man with dazzling blond hair leaned over one of the tables, intent on the work before him. What looked like a pair of crude glasses dangled on the end of his nose.

Moknay slapped Yorke's hand away from a brilliant purple stone as he said, "We're looking for Baynebridge."

The man behind the counter flashed the Murderer a smile almost as sparkling as his hair. "I am he," he replied.

Moknay drummed his fingers impatiently on the countertop. "We need to see Barthol," he insisted.

The blond-haired Baynebridge stopped short, suspicion filling his eyes. "I'm afraid he's not here," the lapidary answered. "Agellic's church was destroyed a . . ."

Gloved hands shot out and grabbed the lapidary by his leather apron, drawing him close to glowering grey eyes. "I've had my share of difficulties for one month, friend," Moknay sneered, the daggers strapped across his chest glimmering silver and red. "So you get Barthol out here or I'll show you a type of carving you've probably never thought of using on your gemstones."

Roshfre's eyes held a glow of mirth more familiar to her younger sister's eyes. "Now, now, Moknay," the redhead scolded. "Don't mess him up too badly; I like his looks."

"Moknay?" repeated Baynebridge, the fear that had exploded in his eyes vanishing. "Why didn't you say so? Barthol was hoping you might show up one day . . . if you were still alive."

"If we were still alive?" the Murderer echoed in question, an eyebrow raised.

Moknay hesitantly released his hold upon the blond gemcutter's apron and let him step to the back of his shop. There Baynebridge opened a small door and disappeared inside, reverberating footsteps sounding as the lapidary walked up a flight of wooden steps.

"Can we trust him?" Xile wanted to know.

Yorke smirked. "Looks like we's gonna hafta."

Tense minutes plodded by, adding to the uneasy air that pervaded the town of Debarnian. Abruptly, footsteps once again sounded on the unseen stairs, yet they were more in number and the urgency in them was evident to even Logan's hearing.

The door swung wide and Barthol hurried out into the shop, anticipation drawing deep furrows in his features. The young

lapidary trailed behind him, a slim blonde woman bringing up
the rear. All anxiety died as the chubby priest bounded across
the counter, wrapping pudgy arms around the lithe form of the
Murderer.

"Moknay, my friend!" Barthol cried. "I never thought to see
you alive again! When that darkness came in from the east—and
my charts started reading impossibilities—I thought you surely
dead at the hands of the Worm."

Moknay answered the priest's eager greeting with a curt returning pat on the back, refusing to show any more emotion than
necessary. Although cold indifference burned in his eyes, the Murderer's sneer had been replaced by a slightly concealed smile.

"The Worm had no hands, Barthol," Moknay retorted. "Such
faith. And you call yourself a priest?"

"And Mara!" Barthol exclaimed, entwining his limbs around
the dark-haired priestess with the same enthusiasm. "I feared the
worst for you! But look at you! Agellic's Gates! I do believe
you've grown even more beautiful than before!"

Logan was startled when Barthol flung himself at him, warmly
welcoming the young man back to Debarnian. "And you, Matthew
Logan!" the priest cheerfully shouted. "It's good to see you're
still up and about! You're taking care of my Mara, aren't
you? By Harmeer's War Axe, young fellow! How did you
lose your eye?"

Logan sneered at his own stupid misfortune. "I dropped it."

Barthol was only momentarily taken aback by the young man's
comment before his enthusiasm returned with renewed vigor.
Pleasantly, the slightly overweight priest greeted the others gathered in the lapidary's shop, unaffected by their roguish looks and
untrusting appearances. After all, Logan reminded himself, one of
Barthol's best friends was Moknay the Murderer.

Moknay settled his hands on Barthol's shoulders, trying to
restrain some of the energy spuming from the priest's rotund
frame. "Before you overwhelm us all with your happiness," the
Murderer advised, "would you first explain what the *Deil* happened
to your church?"

Barthol's beaming smile faltered and a look of remorse entered
to quench the sparkle in his eyes. "It was most catastrophic," he
answered. "According to my charts, something had forced the
Wheel on its side. At first I assumed you had been defeated by
the Worm and that had done it, but then I realized something had
actually kept the Jewel itself from sensing the severe jar in the

Balance and I knew it couldn't be Gangrorz. I was going to tap the Jewel—just a little bit, mind you!—and wound up accidentally discovering some kind of energy parasite or something or another that had been coating the Jewel and quelling any discharge. Due to my poking around, whatever this thing was fled and the Jewel was no longer stilled. There was one vast *whoom*! and I was a priest with no church!"

Logan's blue eyes went wide, something akin to skepticism forming in his gaze. "And you survived a blast from the Jewel?" he queried, a nervous hand on the hilt of his sword. He had seen what had happened to a common thief who had been too close to the Jewel when the gemstone had blossomed forth with a double discharge of energy, and there was no way Logan was going to believe anyone could survive a discharge resulting from the complete sideways tilt of the Wheel.

"Mainly due to accident, my boy," Barthol explained, a bit of red tinging his face. He motioned to the young woman behind Baynebridge. "Liris dropped the tin of powder that Zackaron created to keep the Jewel in check moments before the Jewel discharged. Dropping such a container of powder raises quite a cloud of dust—fortunately in our case it was magical and was created solely for the purpose of holding back the Jewel's magicks. It was only this delicate curtain of magic dust that kept that Jewel from frying Liris, myself, and Goar into so much Cosmic refuse. The rest of the church—I'm sorry to say—wasn't so lucky."

The uncertainty remained alive in Logan's blue eye as he lightly fingered the handle of his Reakthi blade. "So how did you survive the collapse of the church?" the young man queried.

Barthol's saddened expression worsened and his next words were soft and difficult. "Goar protected us," the priest explained. "He practically shielded us from falling debris until Liris and myself were safely outside. Unfortunately, he stepped out from around the protective shield of dust to do so. Goar may not have been very bright, but he was certainly a loyal friend."

Logan bit his lower lip, feeling depressingly rotten and regretting his sudden bout of caution. Another loyal friend was dead, the young man mused, and he had practically forced the information out of Barthol. Goar was another now added to the long list of the deceased—all gone because of their loyalty to either friends or cause: Druid Launce, the Smythe, Cyrene . . .

Moknay's grey eyes remained empty of emotion. "And where is the Jewel now?" he inquired.

Baynebridge ducked down behind the counter, standing back up with something swaddled in cloth. Delicately, the lapidary unwound the surrounding fabric to reveal the massive golden gemstone, yet immediately Logan could see something was wrong. The light of the sun illuminated the smooth facets of the enormous Jewel, and hot white reflections bespattered the walls of the shop, yet the tiny fire that burned deep inside the Jewel was not there. As if blown out by the freezing wind, the golden flame that rested deep within the heart of the Jewel of Equilibrant was gone.

Logan stretched out a questioning hand to touch the golden gem. It reminded him so very much of the unusual corpse of the Blackbody they had seen and the lifeless body of the red woman in his dream. Like both of these, the Jewel had seemingly lost the beat of life that should have been pulsing within it, yet, as the young man could surmise himself, with the Voices here—and the Balance all but nonexistent—it only made frightening sense that the golden fire should be dead.

Xanthic fire glimmered weakly inside the multifaceted Jewel as Logan's curious hand touched the crystalline sides. Yellow light fluttered back to life, dimming, strengthening, dimming, only to strengthen once more. Startled, Logan drew his hand away but the fire that had so suddenly ignited inside the Jewel remained aglow. Weakly—barely perceptible at all from certain angles— the golden flame flickered at the Jewel's heart.

"How'd you do that?" Xile queried, the thief's fear of magic obvious in his surprised backward step.

Logan shrugged, trying not to get angry at the insinuation that he had anything to do with it at all. "I didn't do anything," the young man replied scornfully. "I just touched it."

"The Unbalance," Barthol murmured. "You've given it a bit of hope."

"What's an imbalance have to do with anything?" questioned Roshfre.

"Not an imbalance," the chubby priest corrected, "an Unbalance. An imbalance is simply a lack of balance; an Unbalance is the act of changing or altering that balance. Our young friend here is such an Unbalance, and the Jewel recognizes his potential."

. Wonderful, Logan sneered to himself. Even a goddamn gem can tell I'm different.

"That's partly the reason we're here," Mara told Barthol. "Matthew's found the Heart and wants to use it to go home— before he does, though, he's sworn to kill Groathit."

"A marvelous idea," Barthol agreed, "but one not quite so simple in the carrying out. Mind if I ask why, my boy?"

Logan strangled the hilt of his sword. "Because every time I get ready to go home, Groathit comes along and messes everything up," he snarled. "The reason there's no Balance is because Groathit's pulled the Voices into this world and is helping them destroy everything just to get to me. I figure I've got nothing to lose if I go up against the bastard—only trouble is, he has an army backing him up."

"And now so do we," Moknay went on, briskly retelling the priest of their trials in Eadarus and of Nightwalker's discomforting pessimism in relaying the news to them.

Barthol's face was pale as the Murderer's words sank in, but his head nodded up and down approvingly. "Oh, yes, most certainly," the priest responded. "I'm sure I could convince them to go. Why, Brolark! I could have the whole damn town join you! Women and children! I warned them something was afoot and they've been waiting on my word for action! Imogen, yes! You'll get your help, Matthew Logan! And this time for certain we'll send you home!"

Logan allowed a small smile to stretch across his lips as he gazed longingly into the mirrorlike interior of the Jewel. Twice before he had had such hopes as the ones Barthol exclaimed, but now he had a war to win before he could even consider going home again.

No, the young man decided, for now I'll just keep the optimism in check.

The wine from the celebration and the water of the tub both brought warmth to Logan's body as the young man stepped from his bath, toweling himself dry. As he wiped the moisture from his body, he noted with a little drunken pride that his physical condition had not deteriorated since his arrival in Sparrill. So he wasn't able to jog in the mornings anymore, or play raquetball, or use the Nautilus machines, nonetheless, horseback riding and sword fighting seemed to fill the gap. In fact, maybe it was the overabundance of wine in his system, but his body looked in better shape than before. Okay, so there was a faint scar trailing up his left forearm, and double scars on his right shoulder and hand, and an almost-healed wound on his chest, but he still seemed to be in damn good shape. Hell, he had to be! He had passed *Daigread*, hadn't he?

It's strange, the young man mused as he finished drying off. I'm being hailed a hero here for things that I'm to blame for anyway. I was the reason the Wheel started tilting, but now I'm praised for stopping it. Groathit brought forth the Worm to kill me—causing a lot of Natural distortions—and everyone's cheering me for killing the bad guy that I got resurrected in the first place. And now, even though Groathit's done it again just to get to me, the whole damn town of Debarnian *wants* to fight with me so they can help right the world and save the multiverse.

Logan released a drunken snigger. Oboy! Save the multiverse! Again!

There was a funny buzzing in his head as Logan slipped into a white silk robe and tied it shut. Some march tomorrow morning, he chuckled to himself. I'm supposed to be leading the men of two towns—oh, excuse me—warriors of two towns, and I'll probably have a hangover!

Logan threw himself on the feather bed of Debarnian's finest hostel and peered up at the ceiling without his eyepatch. Even though the wine that swirled through his head caused his vision to be slightly out of focus, the young man could still tell his right eye was far worse than his left. What a stupid thing to go and do, he berated himself. Drop your contact lens. Dummy! Then you're gonna go lead an army into battle and hopefully go home and you'll never see this place again and you can get another contact lens and stop dragging around this stupid sword and not have to worry about being chased by some goddamn wizard who wants you dead and you won't attract any more magic 'cause you'll be home where there isn't any magic and you'll see everybody you left behind back there and live happily ever after, amen.

The young man from Santa Monica abruptly sat up, his eyes narrowed in thought. The lightheadedness the wine gave him seemed to slacken as he swung his feet onto the floor and stepped out of his room, tugging his robe tightly about him. Determinedly, he strode down the hall to the next door and lightly rapped against it. The noise of the people downstairs continued to filter up through the floorboards, but only the stoutest remained below—Thromar probably among them. Logan was grinning to himself about the Rebel's drunken expression that must have been on his face when the door opened and Mara looked out, clad in a similar robe to the young man's.

"Matthew?" the priestess queried, her voice tainted with wonder.

Logan pushed himself past the dark-haired woman, quietly
shutting the door behind him. "Shhh," he instructed. "I'm on a
secret mission."

Silk rustled as Mara placed her hands on her shapely hips, her
lips pursed in amusement. "Secret mission, indeed," she scolded
the young man. "You're drunk."

Logan threw the door behind him an apprehensive glance as
though it would reach out and impale him with splinters. "Shhh!"
he retorted. "That's the secret!"

Mara laughed, a glorious twinkle filling her eyes as she trained
her vision on the young man. Playfully, she plopped on her own
bed, looking up at Logan warmly. "So what's the mission part?"
she queried.

A portion of Logan's boldness—brought on by the wine—weakened. Hesitantly, the young man looked away from the priestess's
beautiful gaze and out a window at the unnatural night. "I was
thinking," he answered.

"That's the mission?" Mara laughed.

Logan's seriousness increased, almost smothering his drunken
audacity. "No," he replied softly, "it's just that . . . tomorrow we
march for Plestenah, and that might be where Groathit's going to
strike first. If it is, in about three days' time we'll be at war. That
means tonight's the last night we'll have to talk."

The young man chanced a look at the priestess. Her smile
remained on her lips, but something—an emotion Logan could
not recognize in his drunken state—welled up in her emerald
gaze. Gracefully, she rose from the bed and stepped to Logan's
side, entwining a silk-clad arm about his.

"What do you want to talk about?" she asked.

Logan shrugged, and silk chafed against silk. "I don't know,"
he muttered. "It's . . . I was thinking before about all the people
I left behind in my world and—if I make it back—how I'll get
to see them again. That made me realize all the people I'd leave
behind in this world . . . and I won't ever get to see again."

Logan's blue eyes fixed on Mara and locked on her green eyes,
and the young man was lost in the emotions that shone there.
Befuddled, Logan sat on the edge of Mara's bed, the wine from
the celebration not helping him think any better than his own
confused heart.

Mara's hold about his arm squeezed a little tighter as she sat
next to him. "You *do* want to go back, don't you?" she queried.

"Yeah," responded Logan, but the certainty faded from his voice when he added, "but . . . I guess you can't have everything."

Once more blue eyes fixed on green, and the emotions in Mara's gaze reflected in Logan's. As before, without thought or word, the two drew nearer, their lips touching and fusing. Gently, their kiss pulled them onto the bed, magically untying the sashes of their robes, filling the hostel room with the force of their love.

All traces of the wine's intoxication were burned from Logan's system as he drew his lips away from Mara's and stared into her eyes, caught up and consumed by the feelings that raged inside him. Words tried to pass his lips but his throat constricted, denying the young man his voice. He wanted to say so badly how he felt—how much he cared for the beautiful woman with him—but part of him would not let him speak. To speak such words would cause the hurt and sorrow he was already so familiar with—to say such things would only magnify the hesitation he was feeling about going home—to mouth such phrases could only hurt Mara when he finally did leave her . . . and that was the one thing the young man never wanted to do. Yet, then again, to leave and not say what he felt could hurt her just as deeply.

The words broke free: "I love you, Mara," Logan declared. "God, do I love you."

Mara smiled back, her eyes glimmering brightly. "I love you, Matthew Logan," she replied.

Then there was no more time for talk.

Fraviar frowned at the confused look that sketched itself across his sister's features as she turned away from a small book at her table and consulted another of her heavy tomes. Concerned, the hulking tavern-owner of Plestenah pushed himself away from his seat and neared his sibling, draping an enormous arm around Danica's slim shoulders.

"What is troubling you this time, sister?" he asked, scratching the bushy black mustache that perched beneath his rather large nose.

Danica looked away from her books to peer out the window facing the west. Her soft brown eyes were filled with trepidation, and she gave her own bandaged hand a worry-filled glance. "I'm not certain," she answered her brother truthfully. "There look like more stormclouds moving in from the west."

Fraviar shrugged massive shoulders. "Is that all?" he boomed.

"By the bloody blade of Thromar! What's a little rain now and again?"

Danica turned her fidgeting gaze on Fraviar, her delicate hands pulled into fists. "But there's no indication of rain in any of my spells," the wizardess argued. "Damn me! I wish I was more in tune with Natural magicks!"

The muscular tavern-owner returned to his chair, his bleary blue eyes watching the nervous pacings of his sister. "And you fear these stormclouds are the same ones that passed overhead before?" he inquired.

Danica nodded, curtly and abruptly.

"But why are they coming back?" Fraviar wanted to know.

"I can't tell!" Danica shouted in frustration. "I'm not a Natural magic-user! But I can tell you one thing—it's not to drop rain on us!"

"Well, then," answered Fraviar, "they're not Natural themselves. Does that help?"

The sorceress didn't answer as she cast another glimpse out the window at the encroaching blackness. "I'm afraid these 'clouds' are in some way associated with the earlier nights and later days we've been having. The gods know we've been having varying distortions in all levels of magic." Danica turned a serious eye on her brother. "Is Servil back yet?"

"By Harmeer's War Axe, Danica!" the tavern-owner exclaimed. "The man just left yesterday morning! He may be fast, but he's not that fast!"

Danica swung a fearful glance on the roiling darkness that steadily advanced over the treetops of Sparrill's forest. Terror turned her blood to ice, and a shiver crawled up the back of her silver gown as she resigned herself to wait. They would have to hear what Servil discovered, she decided. Only then would the sorceress know what they were dealing with.

A cold wind beat at the window.

Servil remained low in the greenery, the freezing wind screaming through the leaves and his lengthy brown-gold hair. His short bow hung in his hand, and his quiver of arrows felt good against his back as the animated darkness moved in closer. The scout still could not see what the blackness was made of—if it was made of anything at all—but his keen, hunter's ears had picked up the sound of men marching his way. Many men—numbering over two hundred.

The darkness passed over Servil's hiding place, and cold fear gripped the scout's throat. It felt as though a million eyes had suddenly passed over him and ignored him, having seen him, nonetheless. Particles of ice began to skitter across the forest floor as the blackness rolled in, and frost decorated the foliage with snowy white petals. Servil's own hair drew flakes of ice, and the unbelievable cold drank the strength from his limbs as the scout pulled himself to his knees.

Steady, militarily paced footfalls broke through the screams of the gale, and Servil ducked back under cover as a massive troop of Reakthi tramped through the brush. The scout noticed in bewilderment all their chestplates seemed to hang on underfed frames, and darkness—as livid and as ominous as that overhead—churned where their eyes should be. Many of their hands were stained with blood, and others suffered from grievous wounds that they either ignored or did not know they had. There were no horses among the many men, and carts were pulled by Reakthi, who exerted no extra strength to drag the heavy vehicles eastward. From the weapons and provisions stacked high in the carts, Servil knew these soldiers meant war.

Darkness exploded behind the hidden scout and a white-chestplated Reakmor emerged from the shrubbery, blackness burning from its eyes. Bloodstained hands blazing with velvety magic reached for Servil's face as the scout leapt to his feet.

Rejoice, the Reakmor said, and an infinite chorus echoed him from above, *we have come*.

·11·

War

Darkling Nightwalker screamed.

Logan jerked about in the crude saddle of his horse, electric fear jolting through his nerves. Even the gathered cutthroats of Eadarus froze at the sound and the townsfolk of Debarnian also swung their attention on the Shadow-spawn. For three days they had ridden, neither taxing their horses nor wasting their own strength. Cart-loads of food and weapons rumbled behind the makeshift army, supplies from the farmers and blacksmiths of Debarnian. Hopes ran high among the hurriedly gathered troops, and Logan himself was surprised to find himself remotely optimistic. Perhaps his bright outlook concerned the young woman who rode behind him and what they felt for one another and had shared. That aspect alone helped keep the young man's mind off the coming battle, but now, as Nightwalker's scream filtered away on the polar wind, Logan's anxieties returned.

"What's the matter?" the young man asked the Guardian. "What happened?"

Nightwalker's expression was pained, and he kept one hand to the side of his head. "They attack," he said. "They win."

"They who?" Thromar wanted to know. "The Voices?"

Nightwalker tried to nod, but the movement proved too painful. "Ahead," the Shadow-spawn replied. "At the town of Plestenah."

Both eager and apprehensive mutters jostled one another from the warriors grouped behind Logan. An unexpected spear of ice pierced the young man's chest, filling him with a sudden fearful realization of what he was doing. You're going to war! he howled at himself. You're going to throw yourself into a full-scale battle with hundreds of men on both sides and hope that you survive to pull out of it! What happens if you don't? What happens if you get killed?

Although the young man's optimism was instantly slaughtered by the abrupt revelation, his darker, more realistic side came to his rescue. *What of it?* it demanded back. *If I die, I die . . . everyone dies . . . Sparrill dies. If I win, I go home. You know it's come down to this. I can never leave so long as Groathit's running around trying to come up with more ways to kill me. I've either got to kill him or never go back. Since this war is the only way I can get that chance, I'll just have to risk it.*

The young man swerved in his saddle, fixing his single eye on Nightwalker. "Is Groathit with them?" he interrogated.

"I cannot tell, Matthew Logan," Nightwalker responded. "I am sorry."

Xile turned a questioning look at the forest that lay ahead of them, his bandana trailing out behind him. "What's the plan, then?" he queried.

Logan spotted the scowl on Thromar's face as he turned to watch the Rebel. "I'd love to attack from both the front and the rear, but Plestenah's built on the damn river and crossing the Lephar would take just too damn long." Thromar's frown lengthened. "We'll have to improvise," he decided. "Xile and Marcos, take your men around the northern edge of town—we should be less than a league from it by now; Roshfre, take your troop as far south as you can go—follow the river if you have to. The rest of us will charge straight in from the east. Taking them on three sides just might do it. Now Plestenah doesn't have any walls, so it'll be street fighting at its worst."

"What I live for, Rebel," remarked Scythe, and a number of Eadarus's rogues macabrely chuckled.

Marcos withdrew his sword, and the sound of steel sliding free of leather sounded over the wind. "You heard the man!" Roshfre's captain thundered. "Ride!"

A large detachment of men split from the main group, Xile and Marcos leading them into the foliage. A smaller squadron branched to the south, and Logan caught a last glimpse of Roshfre's flowing red hair as she drew her forces into the forest. There was a moment of awkward silence before Logan realized he was officially in charge of the remaining men and rammed the heels of his Nikes into his horse's flanks.

"Hoo hah!" Logan could hear Yorke exclaim nearby. "We's gonna have some bloodshed!"

The young man swallowed hard as the rogue's words succumbed to the thunder of hooves and the wailing of the wind. The greens and browns of the forest blurred with the acceleration of Logan's horse, and, somewhere ahead of them, Logan thought he saw a patch of darkness hovering above the trees.

This is it, the young man concluded, a hand clenched tightly about the hilt of his sword. This is war!

Perspiration wound down her face as invisible shock waves of force shunted through Danica's body. The muscles of her arms were rigidly locked in outstretched positions, hands up, fingers splayed. Strands of brown-gold hair draped into her face, slick with sweat. Her eyes were closed in intense concentration, and her lips spoke words that were inaudible to those around her.

Must keep trying, she told herself. Must not give in. Keep it up—keep struggling or the entire town will be overcome. They've already broken through my shield on the southern bridge—I must not let them cross the western bridge!

Fraviar reaffirmed his grip on his heavy sword, turning his eyes briefly away from the horde of dark-eyed creatures that pounded furiously at the invisible barrier that kept them from the town. The tavern owner's bleary blue eyes cast a worried glance at his sister's silent torture before resting on the lean scout Servil. Although a hideous wound still smoked upon the man's left shoulder, the archer stood tall beside Fraviar, his bow drawn and an arrow nocked.

"They're not human, you say?" Fraviar questioned.

"Can't be," Servil replied. "I placed three arrows through the throat of a Reakmor and he kept right on coming. Not fast though. Slow. I was able to outrun the lot of 'em."

Fraviar frowned at the inhuman Reakthi battling at the magical defenses of the bridge. "Hmmmph," he grunted. "Even ready for the bastards, and they're getting the better of us. How goes the battle at the southern end?"

"Not well," Servil answered sullenly. "Last word was we were being pushed toward the center of town. They don't notice any wounds we deliver 'em, and their sheer number would have over-whelmed us already if your sister wasn't holding 'em back."

A dark curtain seemed to drape over the sun, and blackness moved in overhead, whispering, rasping laughter sprouting from within like thunder. A cold lance of energy suddenly drove through Danica's chest, shattering her concentration and piercing her soul.

With a scream, the wizardess arched backwards, crashing to the street as her magical shield ruptured.

No victorious warcry came from the horde of Reakthi that trampled across the stone bridge, eyes crackling darkly. Voices echoed from the heavens, mocking, taunting whispers that brought a flurry of fear to Fraviar's stomach as he charged forward to meet the enemy.

Steel rang loudly as Fraviar's sword struck the bronze chestplate of the nearest Reakthi. Black energy exploded from the soldier's eyes, and a fist cocooned with sentient darkness swung at the tavern owner's head. Battle-honed reflexes sent Fraviar ducking out of the way only to drive his sword upward, penetrating the flesh below the warrior's armor. Fraviar could feel the steel of his weapon slice through vitals and dig its way through bone, yet the Reakthi he fought displayed no pain. Expressionless, the soldier grabbed again, and Fraviar felt black fire burn on his right cheek.

The blow sent a combination of icy fear and burning agony coursing through the large man's frame. Reeling, Fraviar staggered backwards, his grip on his weapon faltering. He could hear the screams of the townsfolk around him and glanced back to see the impenetrable force of Reakthi advancing.

Gentle hands helped Danica away from the line of battle. The sorceress dazedly looked into the eyes of Servil, hardly recognizing him in her delirium.

"Couldn't do it," she gasped. "Couldn't . . . Too strong. Couldn't hold them."

"You did your best," the scout answered softly. "It's up to your brother now."

Danica tried to protest as Servil left her side but could not find the strength to do so. There was an empty feeling in her heart, a sensation of desolation and abandonment. Just as she knew she could not hold back the forces by herself, she knew that Fraviar's hastily grouped fighters could not stop the Reakthi's inevitable conquest. Perhaps the people of Plestenah had been enough to turn aside a squadron of Mediyan's Guardsmen, but these warriors were not the King's Guards. Nor were they simple men. Danica could sense the otherworldly magicks brewing inside them—the overwhelming stench of chaotic power rumbling overhead. These Forces could only be from beyond the Wheel's influence—the Forces of Darkness that thrived apart from the Balance, and, now that they were here, what had become of that Balance? Surely some signs still existed, or all would have been Darkness by now.

Seized by vertigo, Danica tried to focus her vision on the battle raging about her but was unable to see the fighting. All she could see was the unearthly cold that filled the air and the deadly shroud of blackness that was its home.

The headless body swayed precariously on its feet before dropping to the cobblestones, a mist of coiling, writhing darkness fleeing its demolished shell to rejoin the mass of blackness boiling overhead. Exhausted, his sword heavy in his hands, Fraviar watched the darkness lift into the heavens.

Whatever spells animated these Reakthi—whatever magicks controlled their muscles—they could not be physically harmed. These soldiers were all but dead. They showed no emotions, betrayed no hint of pain. Like a sea beneath a storm, they kept advancing, wave after wave of the chestplated bastards crashing down upon the town, sweeping up more and more men with every step. But if someone hacked and slashed enough, one of these Reakthi whoresons would fall apart, so utterly dismembered that it wasn't even any good to whatever controlled it. Then that blackness would flee skyward and add to the darkness already frothing above the village.

"Fraviar!" someone yelled. "Down!"

The tavern owner blindly obeyed, ducking without a word of question. Black sorcery screeched over his head and cleaved through the wintry wind, striking a house and exploding into black flames. Quizzically, Fraviar looked toward the direction of the blast, and his eyes went wide. More Reakthi were marching in from the south, pushing back the decimated ranks of townsfolk. A cold lump of fear took root in the tavern owner's gut as he realized the Reakthi soldiers had broken through the men stationed at the southern end of the town and were now trapping the remaining fighters between their dark-eyed forces.

"Pull back!" Fraviar shouted. "They come from behind!"

"Then the southern end has fallen!" someone else cried.

"I don't think they politely stepped aside and let them through!" A sarcastic reply sprouted from the weary fighters.

Such a bleak response, mused Fraviar. They knew just as well as he that their fight was now hopeless. They were impossibly outnumbered to begin with, and the added sorceries involved gave the people of Plestenah little chance of victory.

There was a sudden uproar from behind the troops of Reakthi advancing from the south, and their eastern flank went down. Thunder boomed angrily from the blackness overhead as the dark-eyed Reakthi turned to meet an army of mounted fighters. Familiarity sparked in Fraviar's bleary eyes as he recognized the lean figure of the Outsider, Thromar's friend from another world. His sword flamed with an aura of crimson power as he cut a bloodless swath through the horde of Reakthi, and a mighty group of forces rallied at his back, as grim and as ugly as if he had all of Eadarus behind him.

Terror was coursing frigidly through Logan's veins as he charged his horse directly into the chestplated figures marching before him. Red fire leapt up and down the length of his sword as he swung downward, splitting flesh and chopping through bone. He could feel Mara loading and firing her Binalbow behind him, and Moknay's grey-and-black stallion reared up close beside his own horse, its rider's hands a blur of grey cloth and silver steel. Thromar's booming warcries filled the streets of Plestenah, and grey shafts of power shrieked from Nightwalker's trembling hands. All assortment of weapons materialized in the scarred hands of the rogues of Eadarus, drawn from hidden sheaths and concealed scabbards. Weapons of a more ordinary sort filled the hands of the townsfolk of Debarnian, and a weary cheer met the ragtag army as they charged madly into the heart of the battle.

The apprehension alive in Logan's nerves expanded as he saw Reakthi who were trampled by the horses' charge rise from the ground, unaware of their crushed limbs and open wounds. More chestplated soldiers stalked toward the small army, living darkness crackling from their eyes. One staggered back as Mara's Binalbow twanged in Logan's ear, yet the Reakthi kept coming, ignoring the twin shafts of wood that speared through his neck.

"Matthew!" Mara cried out in fright. "They're not dying!"

"Keep at it!" the young man screamed back.

But they're not dying! his own mind shouted again. How many times do you have to stab one of these things to make it fall down? How many times do you have to chop off limbs and heads to make these bastards stop?

Scarlet sparks exploded as Logan's sword bounced off the golden chestplate of a nearby Reakthi. Through his half-sight, the young man could see much of the battle going on about him. Reakthi were everywhere—massing clumps of black-eyed warriors, hands and weapons flickering with sentient darkness as they pressed their way through Logan's men. It seemed to the young man that his yellow-and-green horse was a lonely island in a frothing sea of Reakthi, and Moknay—who had been so close beforehand—now fought a mile away, another lonely island.

Blackness glistened around the shriveling, bony hand of a soldier as it tried to push past Logan and reach toward Mara. There seemed to be some wild glimmer in its eyes, the only hint Logan saw that these warriors were controlled by conscious lifeforms, and Mara involuntarily cried out as she saw the skeletal hand reaching for her leg.

Logan released an enraged shout, bringing his sword up and severing the Reakthi's hand at the wrist. No blood sprayed as the limb split, and the Reakthi continued to grope toward Mara's leg with its jagged stump. All at once Mara realized the thing was not reaching for her but for the saddlebags at her rear.

Thunder exploded from overhead.

The Purity, a million voices rasped in rage and ecstasy. *It is here.*

The Purity.

Destroy it.

Destroy the Purity.

Oh, shit! Logan swore to himself. I brought the goddamn Heart with me!

A hundred hands were suddenly reaching for Logan's horse, and the terror in the young man's veins burned with its cold. He heard Mara scream again in fright, saw the worried look on Moknay's face oh so far away from him, noted the absolute horror scrawled on Nightwalker's features. What the hell could he do? There were too many of them!

Red power fountained from the leather saddlebags, catching four Reakthi in its crimson bath of light. Instantly, the soldiers crumpled to the street, the blackness in their eyes extinguished. A furious, warbling shriek reverberated from the darkness overhead, and more hands groped for Logan's horse.

"Matthew!" cried Mara.

Logan tried to find an escape route through the ocean of hands grabbing for his mount. "Stay on the horse!" he warned the priestess. "We're safe up here! Just stay on the . . ."

A bony hand hooked onto Logan's sweat jacket and another grabbed his sword arm. There was a moment of panic as the young man felt his center of gravity shift and he spilled to the Reakthi-engulfed streets. Chestplates and glowing dark eyes surrounded him, and Logan struck out blindly, swinging his sword back and forth with a sudden strength forged from fear. Voices echoed about him: mocking him, taunting him, demanding his death for so foolishly safeguarding the Purity and daring to wage war against the Darkness.

Agony swarmed over Logan's senses as a Reakthi blade drove through his side and his own sword clattered to the street, its red flame flickering in the freezing winds.

Steel flashed again and again from Moknay's hands as the Murderer tried to steer his horse in the direction of Logan's stallion. Ruby energy continued to pulse from the concealed Heart, dropping any Reakthi who got too close, but for every three that fell, five more joined the surge of bodies. A look of horror that was all too easy to read filled Mara's expression as she straddled the horse alone, her eyes scanning the multitude of chestplated soldiers for any sign of Logan. Moknay's own eyes failed to spot the young man, having caught a glimpse of him once but losing him in the chestplates and dark sorceries.

Black flame licked the side of Moknay's leg and the Murderer thrust downward, plunging a dagger through the throat of a Reakthi. Darkness flamed in the warrior's eyes as it reached up a scrawny hand blazing with magicks, and Moknay kicked the soldier away from him in a mixture of fury and fright. Damn them! he cursed to himself. Fatal wounds meant nothing to them! It was just as Nightwalker said! You could cut off their arms, their legs, even their damn heads and they'd keep on coming like they didn't notice the loss!

A warhorn screamed on Moknay's right and grey eyes flicked to that side to spy Xile and Marcos thunder into view. Almost immediately, a volley of enemy arrows riddled the two troops, and Marcos was among the first to fall from his steed. Jeering laughter boomed from the heavens as another rain of missiles whistled about the fighters, killing both horses and men alike. There was a grey explosion from Nightwalker's weakening frame and the Reakthi archers scattered.

The Murderer sneered as the last mocking rasp of laughter faded on the arctic gale. They had been fools to think they could take the Darkness's soldiers by surprise when the Darkness itself loomed over their heads. Gods knew how many inhuman eyes lurked within that impenetrable black cloud of force! They had not only

been ready for Xile and Marcos, they had probably been waiting
in eager anticipation. Damn them! For all their careful planning—
for all their gathering of men—the Voices were still beating them!
But Moknay would not give in to the despondency that rose in his
chest. After all, he was the Murderer . . . not the murdered!

Chestplated men fell without a sound beneath the powerful
hooves of Smeea as the mighty red-and-black mare pushed
forward. Her rider lashed out on either side, his sword in his
right hand, a flail in his left. Wounded Reakthi staggered, yet
always regained their balance to come at him again, black eyes
burning. Sweat streamed down the Rebel's tremendous muscles,
and his rusty vest of chainmail tinkled at each swing of his
brawny arms.

Thromar's tiny eyes peered through the churning mass of limbs
and armor and spied the close-cropped black hair of Fraviar. With
a resounding yell, the Rebel drove Smeea forward, trampling more
soldiers who blocked his way. Bones splintered and snapped
beneath the horse's charge, and Thromar's weapons knocked
aside any Reakthi who did not fall to the fury of his mount.

Fraviar swerved as he heard the heavy hoofbeats strike the
cobblestones and a smile stretched across his face as he saw the
Rebel thundering toward him.

"Ho, friend-Fraviar!" Thromar boomed, his flail crushing a
Reakthi's skull who was only briefly stunned.

The tavern owner's smile was fleeting as he returned his
attention to the struggle going on about him. "I should have
known better than to throw a fight and not invite you, eh?" he
questioned.

Thromar roared with laughter, weapons flailing. "I'll forgive
you this time if you'll forgive the number of friends I've brought
with me!"

The mirth drained from the tavern owner's eyes as he decapitated a Reakthi and still had to duck a returning blow. "You should
not have come, friend-Thromar," he declared somberly. "The town
is lost. We fight a battle already decided."

"By Harmeer's War Axe!" the Rebel retorted. "It's not bad
enough I have to ride with Moknay the Murderer! You're starting
to sound as grim as he! In fact, everyone's starting to sound as
grim as he!"

"We are outnumbered," Fraviar continued, the seriousness in
his voice reflecting his grief. "For what these creatures lack in

intelligence and skill, they make up for in number and dexterity."
The tavern owner's blade flashed silver. "The town is theirs,
friend-Thromar. We fight for no reason."

"We fight for our freedom! Our land!" exclaimed the Rebel,
shocked by the hopelessness in his friend's voice.

"We fight against magicks beyond our understanding!" Fraviar
shot back, angry at the stubbornness he knew he would find in
the Rebel. "As much as I hate to say it, we must retreat."

Thromar looked down at his friend, trying to probe the despair
in the tavern owner's eyes. Fraviar's gaze remained strong as he
stared back at the Rebel. The town of Plestenah was lost—there
was no sense to lose lives as well.

"I'll give the signal to retreat," Thromar finally agreed, the
enthusiasm fading from his voice. "What of the townspeople?"

"Most have fled already," Fraviar replied. "Those to the south
are beyond our help."

With a dismal nod, Thromar turned Smeea away. A retreat, the
Rebel knew, would cost them more men. While the scattered forces
of Logan's army tried to regroup itself and pull out, the possessed
Reakthi would continue to swarm all over them. But whether they
pulled out now or fought on, they would still lose much more than
just the village of Plestenah.

Barthol tried to stand on the seat of his wagon, squinting into
the darkness that covered most of the town. Even though he waited
in the forest east of Plestenah, the noise of battle reached his ears,
and the others gathered about the wagons watched and listened
nervously to the clamor of war.

"Can you see anything?" Liris asked over the scream of the
wind, the bagged Jewel resting in her lap.

Barthol squinted again, and a frown crossed his lips. "Not a
thing," he answered. He sat back down in the cart with a strained
grunt. "I don't like it, Liris," he added in a hushed voice. "Rewyt
has completely slipped Wheelward and I can't even find a trace
of IukIan. Such ill omens as these can only indicate that now is
hardly the time to start a war."

"Barthol," the blonde priestess responded, "your charts are in
Cosmic turmoil. If you couldn't understand them beforehand, do
you honestly think you can understand them now?"

"What good am I if I can't?" the priest retorted, and he slapped
the sword at his side in disgust. "I can't rely on my blade as the others can. What use am I if I can't read the signs of my charts?"

"What use are any of us?" Halette asked sardonically, a bow gripped in her hand. "We sit on the outskirts of town and see to the provisions while everybody else gets slaughtered."

"We've our responsibilities," Liris answered the prostitute. "There are people fleeing the town who will need our help— injured that will need tending to."

Halette pursed her lips, training her green eyes on the village that existed somewhere beyond the curtain of foliage. "I like excitement," quipped the whore. "Tending to the injured's about as exciting as making love to a dead man."

A shrill note pierced the veil of the forest, and Barthol jerked his head up, eyes wide. "That's the signal for retreat," he stated.

"That means we've lost," Bella understood.

"Turn the carts around," Barthol ordered those about him. "Get ready to bolt; pick up whatever survivors you might see."

Frost dotted the leather sacks of food and weapons in the wagons as the darkness filling the sky moved eastward. Horses pawed the ground in nervous agitation as the force of the wind grew stronger, and the signal to retreat broke through the screams of the gale once again. Anxious eyes looked over shoulders as those guarding the carts readied themselves to move with the first sign of survivors.

None came.

Logan staggered to one knee, his fingers curling about the hilt of his sword. The form of a Reakthi stalked toward him, blackness blazing from its skull. There was an abrupt roar of energy and the soldier exploded from the inside, arms, legs, and head rocketing off in separate directions. A humanoid form of dark mist lingered in what might have been surprise as its physical form was torn forcibly from around it before wafting heavenward.

Friendly hands helped Logan to his feet, and the dull throb in the young man's side subsided. Questioningly, Logan threw his one-eyed gaze behind him and found himself staring into the disturbed eyes of the half-mad necromage, Dirge. A wild smile was drawn on the lean man's lips and heavy streams of perspiration wound down his bald forehead.

"I trust you are mentally coherent?" the magic-user queried.

"Huh? What?" Logan sputtered, his mind trying to chase off the impending unconsciousness. "How did you . . . ?"

"Make him explode?" Dirge completed. "I'm a necromage, remember? These may not be normal Reakthi, but they're still normal bodies. I believe what I did has something to do with internal gases. I tried plugging up their airways, but that didn't work. Damn things aren't breathing, wouldn't you know?"

The haze of confusion still hovered about Logan's brain. "Can you . . ." he started.

"Do it again?" Dirge finished. "'Fraid not. Takes a lot out of me to put a lot into them."

"No!" Logan snapped. "Can you see Mara?"

The necromage craned his neck upward, and he reminded Logan of a human stork. "Can't see her," he reported. "Want me to pinpoint her heartbeat? I can do that, you know."

Logan beat down the final remains of his bewilderment by slashing at a chestplated figure close by. "Yes," he answered Dirge. "Find her! She's in danger!"

"Oh, I should hardly say so," came the calm reply. "She's safe so long as she stays on the horse. The Heart's fluxion."

The young man from Santa Monica turned his eye on the necromage, determination fueling the muscles of his arm. "Was that what it was?" he wondered.

Dirge waved a hand at an approaching Reakthi and the soldier collapsed, the muscles of its legs no longer obeying the orders from the Darkness inside. "Eh?" he asked Logan back. "Oh, yes! Yes! The Heart's flux! The girl and your horse are the safest ones out of the lot of us! Or should that be *your* girl and *the* horse, eh?"

Logan was too busy swinging his sword to even think about being embarrassed. "What about my side?" he inquired. "What'd you do to it?"

"I finished the job you started," replied the necromage. "You have a wonderful knack for really tightly woven mystic stitching. I'd really like to see you work more often."

"What?" the young man exclaimed. "I didn't do anything!"

"Whether you know it or not, yes, you did," Dirge corrected, grinning as if he knew the answer to a riddle. "Magic's a subconscious force. There's lots of things you can do without realizing it."

A sneer crossed Logan's features as he tore a gash of flesh off a nearby Reakthi's cheek. Great! he snarled to himself. I can work magic without knowing that I'm working magic! I wonder how many times I've done that! None that I can think of offhand, but, just like Dirge said, they're things you do without even realizing you're doing them!

A high-pitched note screamed out over the din of battle, star-tling Logan out of his thoughts. Someone was giving the signal to retreat! But why? Were things that bad? Unhorsed as he and Dirge were, the young man was unable to see over the heads of the many Reakthi, and his halved vision frantically scanned the waves of soldiers surging around him. We can't leave now! he protested. I haven't found Groathit! If we're retreating, I'll never get another shot at him!

"Dirge!" the young man cried out in his desperation. "Can you detect Groathit's heartbeat?"

The necromage looked up, his brow furrowed with creases. "I can't detect a heartbeat unless I've heard it before," he explained. "Sorry."

"What about magic?" Logan tried again. "Can you tell if some-one's using magic?"

"Oh, most certainly!" Dirge replied. "But I wouldn't be able to tell with *this* much sorcery going on!" He waved a bony hand at the raging battle about them. "I'd never be able to tell one source from another!"

Logan scowled, drawing his attention away from the mob of Reakthi warriors. Even if I could find Groathit—if he's here—what the hell could I do? Everybody else is retreating, and that was the reason I brought the Heart with me. I just didn't expect the Darkness to start grabbing for it. Aw, shit. Leave it to me to mess things up every time.

Sword gleaming red, Logan fought his way eastward . . . or what he hoped was eastward. Occasionally a horse would pass close by, yet Logan would be out of range before he could call out to the rider. The streets were a flurry of motion, catching Logan up in their movement and throwing him northward, then southward, then eastward again. Friends and enemies became a blur of figures, and the young man's impaired vision barely helped him navigate his way through the churning tide of people.

"Dirge!" Logan shouted. "Are we heading the right way?"

No reply came from behind the young man as Logan swung about to find he was—once more—alone. A hand crackling with blackness grasped at the young man, and Logan lopped off two fingers before he spun back around, forcing wobbly legs to carry him through the maddening horde of fighters.

An unfriendly grip clamped around Logan's collar and lifted him bodily into the air, swinging him around so that he roughly landed on a horse's haunches. Befuddlement briefly turned the young man's world upside down as he tried to collect his senses and looked into the glittering eyes of the rogue called Scythe.

"Why walk when one can ride?" the cutthroat grinned, and the murderous glint in his eyes sent an involuntary chill down Logan's back.

"Thanks," the young man breathed, relieved to be above the crushing wall of Reakthi but not so certain he wanted to be with this psychopathic outlaw.

Scythe hurled what looked like a steel boomerang, catching a Reakthi some ten feet away in the throat and half severing the soldier's head; the warrior turned in their direction and fixed blazing eyes on the rogue.

"What's the idea of sounding the retreat?" Scythe questioned. "I was just getting started."

"*I* didn't sound the retreat!" exclaimed Logan, afraid that this man would blame him for the withdrawal.

"Somebody did," Scythe responded, and another sicklelike plate of steel shrieked from his overhanded throw.

Logan hurriedly scanned the narrow roads of Plestenah and winced when he saw the majority of Reakthi. What had started out as a street filled with horsed fighters ended up as a deadly procession of Reakthi on foot. Numerous wounds of fatal width and depth crisscrossed the chestplated soldiers, but—just as no blood seeped from the torn and shredded flesh—the warriors seemed not to care. Instead, they pressed on, hands and eyes flickering with the same malevolent energies that brewed above them. Snow dusted the rooftops of many of the surrounding buildings, and ice skittered among the cobblestones as the raging wind howled through the village. Somewhere in the distance, Logan could hear the crackle of flames.

"Shit," Logan breathed at the carnage around him. "We were wiped out."

Scythe snorted. "No reason to retreat."

The young man returned his attention to the eastern section of town. "Did you happen to see what happened to my horse?" he interrogated.

"I think the girl got it free," the rogue responded, and another sickle of steel whizzed from his hands. "Must have—I've never seen anyone that good with a Binalbow."

A small tingle of pride mixed with jealousy crept into Logan's overriding fear as Scythe's black-and-white mare stampeded madly out of town. Oddly, many of the Reakthi dropped back, either afraid or unable to come near the horse. With a cheerful whoop, Scythe sent his mount leaping over a demolished fence and galloping free of Plestenah. Logan threw the village one last look as smoke from burning structures filled the already darkened sky with added blackness.

Strange how the Reakthi seemed to let them by, the young man mused.

The blood drained from her face as Danica carved an invisible path through the chestplated forces, unseen barriers erected on either side. Darkness blossomed in their eyes as the malnourished figures struck at the solid walls of sorcery, ebony roaring from their fists. Angry rumbles of thunder rocked the blackness overhead as more and more of Plestenah's defenders scurried through the avenue drawn up the middle of the enemy's line. Those soldiers that did slip a crackling black hand through the protective shields stumbled backwards, arrows thunking into their bodies from Servil's short bow.

Fraviar slapped the archer across the back. "Go!" the tavern owner ordered, pushing Servil forward.

Servil hesitated, looking back at the sister and brother behind him. "What about you?" the scout asked.

"Never mind about us!" bellowed Fraviar, his sword reflecting the velvet light from the unnatural fires that bloomed behind him. "Go!"

Long strides sent Servil hurrying after the last of Plestenah's survivors, the uncertainty growing in his breast. Concern lit his eyes as the scout tossed a worried glance over his shoulder to see clusters of dark-eyed Reakthi descending on the lone pair. They'd never make it, he told himself, but, then, they probably knew that the moment Danica started casting. A sacrifice of two people to ensure the escape of the small army that had come to their aid seemed an unfair trade to the scout. After all, Danica and Fraviar were his friends.

A grumbling boom of anger ripped from the living night roiling through the sky, and a hundred thousand whispering voices howled their rage.

The Purity escapes.
Stop it.
Stop the Purity.
Destroy it.

Servil's fear increased the adrenaline racing through his system and his long-legged stride grew quicker, carrying him through the cobblestone streets with the grace of a young deer. Brown-gold hair streaming, the scout bolted out of the village, afraid to even cast one last look at the friends he knew he would never see again.

"Which way?" Mara shouted, lost among the greens and browns of the forest about her.

Nightwalker swayed feebly in the saddle of his snow-white mount, his eyes tinted a bleak grey. "Eastward," he croaked, and the finger that pointed trembled like a hand struck with palsy. "We must fall back toward Debarnian, where the Purity itself can aid us in battle."

Yorke threw an unpleasant look at the foliage behind him, his left hand grasping his sword. "They're gonna be after us soon enough," he said. "What's that red thing ya got glowin' in yer saddlebags, anyhow?"

Mara spurred the yellow-and-green horse to her right, eyebrows knitted above her eyes with determination. "None of your business," she retorted.

"If it weren't none o' me business, I's wouldn't be askin'," the rogue responded, digging his heels into his horse's own flanks. "Had them Reakthi buggers droppin' like bloodpetals in th' grass!"

"It's something that can help us," the priestess answered vaguely, "but only Matthew can use it. Are you sure you didn't see him?"

"Look, if I's seen 'im, I's woulda told ya!" Yorke protested. "He still has me blasted whip!"

A branch tore past Mara's shoulder and the priestess instinctively flinched. Cold terror as she had never known before had flooded her nerves when the hideous Voices had rained from the heavens bemoaning the loss of the Purity as it rode safely out of town along with her. And—somewhere—Matthew was still without a horse, possibly wounded and most certainly sought after . . . if not by the Darkness then by Groathit himself. What she wouldn't give to be able to turn the stallion around and search for him, but she had a primary responsibility to see to the Heart's safety. And now she couldn't even find Barthol and the rest of the carts of food and bandages!

"Does anybody have an idea as t' where we's goin'?" queried Yorke. "'Cause I'm lost."

Mara turned an angry glare back on the rogue. "Would you just shut up!" she yelled at him.

Shrugging, Yorke went silent as the three horses rushed madly through the brush. Foam dotted the mouths of the creatures as they galloped swiftly away from the conquered town, hooves kicking up clods of dirt that dissolved in the gale.

Faint murmurs barely heard over the thunder of hooves reached Mara's ears, and she swung a questioning look in Nightwalker's direction.

"Lost," the Shadow-spawn mumbled, his expression one of agony. "The Darkness grows. The Balance falters. Shadow fades. I die."

A cry of concern spilled from Mara's lips as Nightwalker careened backwards off his horse and landed limply in the dirt. So hurried that her actions were almost clumsy, Mara jerked her horse to a stop and leapt to the ground, racing back to where the Guardian lay.

"Nightwalker!" she cried.

The Shadow-spawn tried to lift his head, failed, and slumped back to the carpet of leaves and grass. "The Darkness grows," he gasped again. "Shadows fade." Eyes that were once pure white fixed on Mara, and the grey that invaded them told of their despair. "I am dying."

Mara pulled the Guardian upright, her hands clenched around his cowl. "No," she said. "No! You can't!"

A hand of glistening ebony touched the priestess's hand, and the contact was faint and weak. "There is a book," Nightwalker choked. "A book that the spellcaster wields. He is heading westward with his remaining troops. Tell Matthew Logan . . . Tell him that he must get this book and use the incantations within to restore equilibrium to the Wheel. This must be done before the Darkness can be destroyed. Only then will the Light be saved—only then will Shadow return."

The cowl that Mara gripped in her hands dissipated, and Nightwalker's form melded with it. In stunned silence, the priestess stared down at the patch of restless shadow cast by the trees of the forest and at the place where Darkling Nightwalker had been last.

The Shadow-spawn was gone.

Logan could not explain the creeping dread that filled his stomach as he glanced down at his watch to see the last faint spark of red shudder and wink out. Complete blackness now shone from the display window of the young man's timepiece, eerily illuminating his face with an ebony glow that closely mimicked the storming darkness overhead.

"I've got a bad feeling about this," the young man muttered to himself.

"As well you should," Scythe remarked. "We've just lost a war."

Logan looked up at the rogue riding before him, wondering whether or not he should explain. Deciding it wouldn't be worth the time, the young man peered back down at his watch. No more red or silver, he thought. What did it mean? That the Darkness had won and there was no stopping it? No, that couldn't be it. Scythe's comment was just as broad as that assumption. We haven't lost the war—just a battle. We're still alive—we're still kicking. That counts for something, doesn't it?

There was no mental response from the young man's own mind, and that did little to soothe the jittery nerves inside him.

Scythe threw a look over his shoulder. "Someone's coming," he advised. "From the south."

Logan jerked to his right as heavy hoofbeats reached his ears over the wailing of the freezing winds. Leaves scattered as a horse leapt through the shrubbery, rivulets of blood still dribbling from the sword wound tearing along its left side. A dull glaze sheened its eyes with a ghastly glitter, and its side did not heave with exertion as it drew up alongside Scythe's black-and-white mare.

"Thought I recognized your heartbeat," Dirge exclaimed happily, flashing Logan a proud grin. He wiped a river of sweat from his bald brow. "Look who I found. Not the girl we were looking for, but a find nonetheless, eh?"

For the first time Logan realized there was a limp figure draped over the rear of Dirge's wounded horse, red hair billowing in the arctic gale. Unconsciously, Logan finally noticed how slender and frail Roshfre actually was.

"What's wrong with her?" the young man asked. "Is she alive?"

Dirge blinked before laughing as if he eventually understood the joke. "Of course she is!" he answered. "I wouldn't have taken the time to bring her with me if she wasn't, now would I, eh?" He affectionately patted the horse he rode. "Her horse, I'm sorry to say, isn't."

Scythe turned a wary eye on the necromage, and Logan was glad to see a little unease enter the rogue's grim mien. "If that horse is dead, how come you're riding it?"

"I couldn't find a live one," replied Dirge, shrugging.

Logan could tell Scythe was not at all pleased by the animated cadaver galloping alongside him but spoke before the rogue could say another word. "What about the rest of Roshfre's troop?" he wondered. "Why didn't they help?"

"I believe they tried," Dirge said, giving the unconscious redhead a backward glance. "Southern end was thoroughly wiped out, though. Lost the whole lot of them. Basically sent them to their doom when we had them go south."

Great, Logan morosely thought. An entire troop of men wiped out because we didn't know the situation inside the town when we attacked. And God knows how many men survived the initial charge into Plestenah, or what had happened to Xile and Marcos . . . or Mara . . . or Moknay . . . or Thromar . . . or anybody!

God! the young man cried desperately to himself. If that was war, Matthew, this must be defeat.

·12·

Despair

Blue-white light ripped the sky in a jagged streak. Heavy droplets of water cascaded from the heavens, thrown eastward by the freezing winds. Thunder cracked above the snow-capped peaks of the Hills of Sadroia, echoes rumbling deep within the mountain range.

Shivering from the cold, Ridglee looked up at the cloud-filled sky and knew that the darkness of the clouds was accented by the unnatural darkness that lurked behind them. Raindrops pattered against his chestplate as he stepped out of his tent. He scanned the hastily erected camp through the curtain of rain, frowning when he came to the lone figure squatting—hunched over—on a large boulder. A sizzling black layer of energy surrounded the lean spellcaster like an outer skin; although he sat in the middle of the storm, the aura of sorcery kept him dry and warm.

Easy for him to order us to wait out the storm, Ridglee thought foully to himself as he glared at the wizard. Groathit was growing just too damn powerful for the soldier's likes. His earlier announcement that Plestenah had fallen did not thrill the experienced warrior—instead, it drew a cold sword of fear through his heart. It was not a Reakthi victory, Ridglee mused. It was a victory for that blackness that did not belong in this world. And now the sorcerer smugly ordered the troops—troops that should have been ordered by Vaugen—to make camp and wait out the storm. By then, the unholy darkness should return while its "soldiers" continued their eastward march.

The soldier's unease and anger coalesced into a raging determination that sent his booted feet stalking through the muddy ground. His eyes kept flicking back to the gnarled figure sitting beneath the mountain range, overpowering even though dwarfed by the hills behind him. Ridglee's teeth clenched as he ducked back into another tent, unannounced and unrequested. Dull grey eyes, the color of a Reakthi blade, swung up and fixed on the warrior's. Fused flesh pulled as far away from the teeth beneath as possible, and an unsavory scowl marked Vaugen's disfigured features.

"You were not asked here, Ridglee," the Imperator grated, and his voice was a gravelly rasp.

A conditioned fear rose in the soldier's throat as he defiantly faced his commander. All his adult life he had been trained to strictly obey the word of the man who wore the black chestplate—regardless of who he was. Now, however, the Reakthi was going against that law. Now he was going to face his Imperator—not as a captain whose word was not to be doubted, but as a man who was being influenced by an insane sorcerer and who—gods protect them all—was succumbing to the madness himself.

"I wish to speak, my Imperator," Ridglee stated, and he cursed the nervous quiver in his voice.

The area of flesh that had once housed an eyebrow rose above Vaugen's right eye. "Speak, then," he responded simply.

Ridglee cast an anxious look over his shoulder, toward where he could still hear the rain striking the ground outside. "About the sorcerer, sir," he began.

"What about him?" the man in the black chestplate demanded.

"I fear his decisions," the Reakthi admitted, curbing what he truly thought of the spellcaster. "You are the leader of these men, my Imperator, not the wizard. I do not think his choices are best for us."

"You don't, hmmmm?" queried Vaugen. "Not even though the wizard's plans have brought us the conquest of Plestenah?"

"But we did not conquer Plestenah," Ridglee argued, and he could see the shock that registered on Vaugen's face because of his disagreement. "Groathit's creations did. There was not a Reakthi among them."

"They were Reakthi, Ridglee," Vaugen replied, much too calmly for the soldier's likes. "They wore the chestplates and carried the swords. They were as Reakthi as you or I."

"They were Darkness," the warrior argued. "They were inhuman shells that don't even resemble men any . . ."

"They were Reakthi," Vaugen interrupted, clenching his undamaged hand at his side. "Why are you questioning my command, Ridglee?"

"It's not your command I'm questioning, sir," the soldier replied. "It's the command of the spellcaster—the fact that he is commanding when you should be."

The Imperator jerked to his feet, rage burning in his eyes. "What?" he shrieked. "You dare imply that I have lost command of my own men? I am Imperator! I command here! No one else!"

"Then why do we wait out the storm on his orders?" Ridglee pressed.

"We wait out the storm on *my* orders!" Vaugen screamed. "They were my orders! Mine, do you hear me? Mine!"

"Then what reasons did you have for ordering such a . . ."

"Again?" Vaugen roared. "Again you question my word? Ridglee, if you were not such an experienced soldier, I would have you drawn and quartered! Get out! Get out of here and thank whatever gods you believe in that I don't have you slain for insubordination!"

Ridglee glared at the grey-eyed Imperator before backing cautiously out of the tent. There *were* hints of madness to his train of thought, the soldier concluded. Madness that blinded the Imperator's ability to see that Groathit *was* in command and Vaugen had simply let that happen. But it was the same with Ridglee, wasn't it? He had known about the Imperator's agreement with the spellcaster and had let his fellow soldiers be deceived. Just like Vaugen, he had allowed that to happen.

Feeling as bleak and as gloomy as the clouds that spread rain across the sky, Ridglee stepped back into the storm. His eyes instantly locked on the hunched figure across the camp grinning knowingly in his direction. It was almost as if the wizard knew everything that had gone on inside the Imperator's tent—and, perhaps, he did. There had been no messenger—no way of knowing what had occurred in Plestenah—yet the spellcaster had known in full detail, almost as if he had been there himself. But that, Ridglee knew, was impossible. Groathit had been here, at camp, sitting in the rain without getting wet.

The soldier turned on his heel and strode through the downpour, frustration and fear battling inside him. He needed to talk to someone—tell someone who would listen that their Imperator was falling into insanity, their sorcerer already mad, and their fellow soldiers betrayed. Ridglee had been a fool to remain silent. He should have warned his friends—told them what Vaugen and Groathit planned. Instead, he had kept silent, his fear whispering that no one would believe him and so nothing would be done. And now regret flooded the warrior's thoughts—filling his mind with a hundred different variations of alternate worlds where he had said something, or where something had been done, and things had turned out differently than what they were at the moment.

Ridglee stepped into Ithnan's tent, knowing his trust was well placed with the youngster. Although sometimes reckless, Ithnan listened to what Ridglee had to say—looked up to the older soldier like he would an older brother. Indeed, the two had a kinlike relationship that very much reminded Ridglee of his own previous relationship with his older brother who now served under Imperator Ikathar.

"Ithnan," Ridglee whispered, keeping his voice down despite what he suspected the wizard outside was now capable of.

Stanced near the far end of his tent, Ithnan turned to glance at his comrade. Sparks as black as velvet crackled in the younger soldier's empty sockets and his already withering features were as blank and as expressionless as the stones of the Hills around them.

Overwhelming terror clutched Ridglee by the stomach and he felt violently ill. Vainly attempting to hold back his sickness, the soldier staggered from the tent and burst back out into the rain. Tears of disgust, rage, and horror mingled with raindrops as Ridglee stumbled back to his own tent, emotions in turmoil.

From his rock, Groathit smiled.

Baynebridge threw a wary glance over his shoulder at the night-filled forest behind him. "Are they following?" the lapidary queried.

"Of course they're following," Xile retorted. "They've destroyed the blasted town! Why shouldn't they be following?"

Thromar pulled Smeea to a stop, his eyes probing the darkness. "On foot," he muttered. "They can't ride horses. Notice how all our mounts got skittish around so many of the bastards?"

Grunting in discomfort at the burn on his left side, Hach pulled his mount to a stop. "I was too busy fighting for my life," the thief remarked impolitely.

Xile wiped at his sweat-soaked bandana as he reined in his stallion beside the others. "So where the *Deil* are the others?" he wondered out loud. "And the carts?"

Thromar shrugged, uncharacteristically quiet. "Retreats are never organized," he sullenly declared.

"I can't even tell where we are," Hach complained. "For all I know, we could be ready to ride off the edge of Dragon's Neck!"

"Stop complaining, Hach," Xile ordered. "You complained under Roshfre's command and you're complaining now."

"I like complaining," the cutthroat answered back.

"Shouldn't we keep moving if they're following?" Baynebridge asked, his movements as nervous as his horse's.

"What's the point?" asked Thromar.

"So they don't catch us!" the lapidary exclaimed. "So they don't kill us!"

Thromar dismounted. His keen senses smelled the hint of moisture in the air, the telltale signs that a storm broke to the west and might push its way as steadily east as the Reakthi soldiers, but he did not voice this. Nor did he voice a reply to the terrified Baynebridge.

Xile jumped down from his horse. "They're not on horseback," he informed the gemcutter. "I believe we're safe for the moment."

Baynebridge's eyes widened as Hach—hampered by his wound—also clambered to the ground. "We're not going to stop for the night, are we?" the lapidary screeched.

"I don't know about you, but I am," Hach snorted. "My ass hurts, my arms are sore, and my side feels like it's on fire."

Xile shot the complaining bandit a disapproving look before glancing back at the blond lapidary. "I can assure you they won't catch up with us in a night," he said. "Besides, there's no point in running 'til we drop."

"Perhaps there's no point in running at all," Thromar morosely proclaimed.

The freezing wind screamed through the night as Xile turned an inquisitive eye on the Rebel. Such somber tones coming from the fighter did not sit well with the thief. He had heard tales of Thromar's deeds—heard firsthand the Rebel's enthusiasm and boasts. The despair that now overtook the huge fighter worried Xile, and he wondered just how deeply this loss affected the Rebel's childlike optimism of the world.

"My feet stink as well," Hach said, continuing his complaints.

Moknay jerked his horse to a halt, senses straining to pick out sounds over the harsh wail of the wind. The young Stearck stopped beside him, his head cocked to his right.

"What is it?" the young rogue queried.

"Heard something," the Murderer responded and went silent again.

A low rumbling filled the blackened forest, the tumbling of wooden wheels accompanied by the thunder of hoofbeats. Instantly, Moknay's heels jabbed into his horse's flanks, propelling the stallion into the foliage. Stearck's reaction was a bit slower, and the young outlaw had barely started to move before Moknay was already out of sight. The rumble grew louder as the two horses exploded out of the shrubbery, dashing directly in front of a cart of Debarnian design. Releasing a startled shout, Halette jerked the wagon to a hasty stop, the heavyset man on horseback that accompanied her also stopping.

"Agellic's Gates!" the prostitute cursed. "You two scared the life out of me!"

"Where's Barthol?" Moknay wanted to know.

Halette shrugged, and Stearck tried not to stare in admiration. "How should I know?" the whore shot back. "Damn wagons ride about as smooth as the crags of the Lathyn Mountains! Shattered a wheel a few leagues back and got separated. Would've been stranded for sure if Fjorm hadn't have happened by."

The Murderer's steely grey eyes passed over the heavyset blacksmith from Debarnian before returning to the redhead driving the cart. Eyebrows narrowed when Moknay noticed the still body lying among the supplies of the wagon.

Halette followed Moknay's gaze. "Thumbs," she explained, nodding her head toward the motionless man with the missing fingers. "Took two arrows in the chest; don't know if he'll make it."

"He's a member of Roshfre's band," Stearck murmured in youthful awe. "He'll make it."

"Speaking of which," Halette commented, "have either of you seen my sister?"

Moknay's gaze of icy grey answered her query without words.

"That good, huh?" Halette quipped. "Any other time I'd offer to make things batter, but I'm a little out of sorts today. Want a rain check instead?"

The Murderer's eyes fell on the whore. "A what?"

Halette shrugged—something Stearck suspected she liked to do. "Don't ask me," she told Moknay. "It's something I learned from your friend from elsewhere."

The Murderer nodded back and leapt from his horse, a gloved hand sifting through the provisions in the wagon. "I suggest we stop for the night," he said. "We'll not find anyone in this blackness but we might hear someone if they pass close by."

"Where were you heading?" Fjorm asked.

"Back to Debarnian," replied Moknay. "I only hope the others have as much sense to head back that way."

"How many do you suspect we lost?" the blacksmith probed.

"Over half," the Murderer answered.

Fjorm persisted: "What do you think our chances are of saving Debarnian?"

Moknay remained silent as he inspected the wounds on the man called Thumbs, frowning at his own speculations, his grim mien even grimmer.

Halette pursed her lips at his silence. "That good, huh?"

Yorke watched with a superstitious caution as Mara flipped open the saddlebag's cover, flooding the forest with crimson brilliance. Scarlet light splayed itself across the priestess's face, causing her to squint but emanating a warmth that cancelled out the cold of the wind. Tentatively, she reached her hands into the leather bag and grasped hold of the pulsating Bloodstone.

"What the *Deil* are ya doin'?" Yorke questioned.

The Heart came free of the saddlebag, ruby flames flickering across its surface. "Trying to help," Mara answered the rogue.

"Tryin' t' help how?" Yorke asked back. "I's thought you said the only person what could use that thing was that Logan fellow."

"I did," Mara responded, eyes locked on the blazing gem in her grasp.

Yorke scrambled to his feet and backed away from the priestess. "Then I'll ask ya again: What the *Deil* are ya doin'?"

Mara ignored the rogue's magical fear and set the fluxing Bloodstone on the ground. The entire area was bathed in a powerful red glare, and, somewhere close by, a cricket experimentally chirped. Carefully, the priestess drew a finger along the side of the radiating Heart and hoped she guessed right when she suspected the sudden blossom of energy indicated another flux.

The Heart's power flow was irregular—she remembered that much from her reading—so there was nothing to stop it from being such a release of power. What she feared was her inability to help—but hadn't the sprite told Logan that no magic was necessary? Just direct the energy to where it would do the most good, right?

The priestess settled herself on the ground, Yorke watching from behind a tree. Green eyes closed as Mara concentrated on the gemstone glowing before her. Brilliant images replayed vividly behind her eyelids. Just concentrate, she told herself. Do like Matthew did the first time. Let the energy enter you.

With a thankful whirl of power, the crimson fog exploded into a titanic column of ruby fire and drove into the priestess. An involuntary gasp escaped Mara's lips as the force of the magicks filled her slim frame, sending tingles coursing through her nerves. It was not as she had thought it would be. Such energy she thought would be painful, but it was not the case. The surge of magic was soothing, even pleasurable, but it obviously did not belong in the body of an ex-priestess.

A moment of confusion threatened to shatter Mara's concentration as she wondered where to send the culmination of sorcery. To where it would do the most good, she remembered, but where would that be? Matthew had healed Thromar, added magic to their weapons, then had shot the remaining energy off across the land. But how had he accomplished it? What was he thinking when all that power was grumbling inside him? Did he just say go to where you'd be the most help or did he give it a specific order? The priestess's thoughts stormed in turmoil.

Unexpectedly, scarlet light erupted all about the priestess as the flux of energy dispersed, separating into a hundred small beams and screeching through the forest. Yorke released a yelp as one of the rays shrieked directly over his head, briefly illuminating him in its sparkling red glare before streaking like a sanguine arrow into the blackness. Mara slumped backwards, the sudden discharge of power catching her off guard and momentarily weakening her. A few sparks of ruby brilliance snapped and popped above the treetops as the crimson haze surrounding the Heart fluttered and went out.

The cricket continued to chirp.

Yorke pulled himself to his feet, a stunned expression on his scarred face. "What the *Deil* did ya do?" he exclaimed.

Mara inhaled deeply, watching the last shaft of crimson shriek away into the night. "I'm not sure," she truthfully answered. "I was trying to direct it when it took off on its own."

The rogue took a nervous step into their camp, senses alerted should any of the sorcerous rays decide to come back. "Me mother

always told me t' never stick me nose in a magician's business
'less I like the idea o' never smellin' again," he quipped.

Mara ignored the outlaw and his paranoia as she pulled herself
back into a seated position, gaze locked on the Bloodstone. She
had no idea what she had done—or if she had done anything at
all—but she hoped that whatever came out of her experience was
for the good of the Heart and of the land.

Another cricket joined the first, and their song echoed throughout the night.

Logan stared up at the starless sky, his disposition as dark as the
unnatural night above him. Scythe leaned against a tree, sharpening
the keen edges of his steel boomerangs, his harsh eyes lost in
thought. The only real activity came from Dirge as he scuttled
crablike about Roshfre's unconscious form, administering to her
wounds and muttering emphatically to himself.

Logan's single eye pulled away from the darkness around him
to glance at the still redhead and the rodentlike scurryings of the
necromage. *She wouldn't be there at all if it weren't for me,* the
young man mused sourly to himself. *It's all my fault she's hurt; all
my fault so many men died. Damn me for being so stupid! What
the hell did I think I was doing, anyway? Lead an army! Hah!
I'm an Outsider, remember? I don't even belong here. So what
do I do? I take the trust of over a hundred men and lead them
full-speed ahead into a slaughter. Wonderful. Whatever gave me
the idea that I could win?*

Sadness welled up in the young man's throat, but he denied the
tears that tried to flow from his eyes. *You're an idiot, Matthew,* he
cursed himself, and the despair overwhelmed his senses. *You've
killed practically everyone who's ever tried to help you here.
You'll be lucky if you'll ever be able to accept another offer
for help again after all you've done. Maybe it would have been
better if I had died in the* Daigread *chambers, or, better yet, had
let the Worm kill me, or, even better still, had died in that double
discharge of the Jewel that had killed that thief instead.*

A red will-o'-the-wisp unexpectedly broke through the foliage,
skittering and prancing about the blackness like a scarlet lightning
bug. Logan raised his head to stare at the sudden manifestation of
light when the bulb of ruby energy exploded, spreading a curtain
of minute pinpricks of scarlet magic out across the brush. Scythe
and Dirge both watched in bewilderment as the fine mist of red
melded back together, piecing together purposefully while its glow

of sanguine illuminance spread to the surrounding woods.

"What in Imogen's name . . . ?" murmured Scythe, one hand clutching tightly to a boomerang.

Dirge's eyes widened as he gawked at the fine haze and jabbed a bony finger as the sorceries continued to blend together. "Matthew Logan!" exclaimed the necromage. "I do believe it's you!"

Confusion dampened the depression ruling the young man's thoughts as he peered at the red swirl of magic. At first Dirge's shout made no sense to him, but then Logan saw the distinct, oval shape to the crimson glimmer and the oddly distorted features built up from a million motes of theurgy. His surprise was understandable when the young man realized he stared into a mirror reflection of his own face created by the multitude of magical flecks.

"What . . . ?" sputtered Scythe. "How?"

Logan's first reaction was to deny everything. "I had nothing to do with it!" he declared, a weird fear gnawing at his innards as if to remind him to never take credit or blame for anything ever again.

Dirge's eyebrows narrowed. "Lelah's beauty," the magic-user breathed. "It's Natural magicks. More potent than anything I've ever felt before; more alive than any person I've ever touched."

As his magically formed image grew clearer, Logan squinted his only focused eye at the sorcery. "It's the Heart," he gaped, recognizing the source before the necromage. "Mara's regulated the Heart."

"Who's done what to what?" demanded Scythe. "What in Agellic's Gates is going on?"

"The Heart," Logan hastily explained. "It needed regulating and Mara—or someone—did it. But . . . But why's it here? Why this?"

Dirge scrambled to his feet, tangling himself in his robe in his haste to greet the source of energy. "Regulation of the Heart," he mumbled. "Regulation. Regulation. Ah ha! Sorceries released to go where they'll do the most good. This is obviously where they'll do the most good, eh?"

"By creating an image of me?" Logan cried in disbelief.

The necromage was momentarily befuddled, as even that didn't make sense to his somewhat crazed mind, gaping at the crimson portrait as it slowly started to drift away from them, retaining its mask of Logan.

"Where's it going?" Logan wanted to know.

"There's only two ways to find out," Dirge responded. "Either ask it or follow it."

"Follow it?" Scythe yelled. "What *is* it?"

Neither Logan nor Dirge answered the magic-wary rogue as the scarlet imposter wafted gently eastward on the harsh winds. Robe aflutter, Dirge quickly slung Roshfre over the back of his dead horse and started following the retreating form of red. Logan paused only fleetingly as he threw a questioning look at Scythe before trailing the necromage into the dark forest. Miscellaneous doubts crossed the young man's mind as he kept his eye on the ruby shade of himself, pondering the reason behind the Heart's odd apparition.

A perturbed grumble sounded behind Logan as Scythe drew himself into his mare's saddle, shadowing the two men from a safe distance. A snarl was drawn on his lips as the blackness of the night closed in about them.

Out of habit, Logan glanced at his watch. The infinite darkness that met his curious eye sent a jab of fear through his system. Now more than ever the blackness had hold of this world. Judging from his own sluggishness, Logan surmised it was somewhere near ten or eleven in the morning after their defeat—meaning they had spent a good part of yesterday fleeing the conquered town of Plestenah and all the night pursuing a sanguine image of himself. Nonetheless, ebony filled what should have been a morning sky.

Constant mutters betraying his unease spilled from Scythe's lips as the outlaw followed warily behind Logan and Dirge, nervously tugging at the strap of steel boomerangs he wore diagonally across his chest. The strap of weapons burned another image into Logan's skull, and the young man pondered Moknay's fate, or the fate of Thromar, or Nightwalker, or even Mara. Although this ruby-faced picture was undoubtedly the Heart's magicks, no one said it had to have been Mara's doing.

"What if it's a trap?" Scythe probed from horseback.

"No trap. No trap," Dirge waved him off. "It's the Heart."

"That doesn't mean dung to me," the rogue spat. "Who says it still can't be a trap?"

"I says," Dirge responded. "If the Heart had fallen into the hands of the enemy, it would not remain in existence long enough to engineer a trap."

Scythe refused to give in. "So where's it leading us?" he demanded. "And for what purpose if not to blast us into so many little pieces when we get there?"

"Stop being so damn pessimistic!" Logan snapped at the cut-throat, realizing instantly that he was being hypocritical. "Just follow it and shut up, okay?"

"Oh, I'll follow it," remarked Scythe, "but I won't shut up. I want to make sure something memorable comes from my lips before I get the dragon droppings blasted out of me!"

Logan was going to bark another reply but caught himself. There was no sense firing tension between the three of them—four, if you counted Roshfre. For all the young man knew—and this was being overly heavy on the pessimism—they were the only four who had made it out of Plestenah alive. And that brought another complexity to the young man's mind: If they were the only survivors—or if only a handful of survivors remained—what were they to do now? There was nowhere else they could go for help before the Darkness-clad Reakthi destroyed both Eadarus and Debarnian.

Hoofbeats sounded through the darkness, and Logan looked up, his single eye alert. Dirge's own head jerked up with birdlike swiftness and a smug smile painted itself on his thin lips.

"To the north," the necromage predicted. "The Murderer."

Logan pivoted just as Moknay's grey-and-black stallion leapt the underbrush, trampling to a halt before the young man. Gloved hands instinctively reached for the daggers across his chest but just as swiftly jumped away as the Murderer recognized the young man on foot. A grave smirk lifted the left side of Moknay's lip, and his trim mustache went with it.

"I should have expected as much," the grey-eyed outlaw commented. "Your doing, friend?"

Logan raised ignorant eyebrows at the Murderer's query before he noticed the second scarlet visage hovering beside the first. Unexpectedly, one of the mystically formed images dispersed, its Loganlike picture shattering outward, then regrouping into a laser-thin stream of power. With a warbling screech of raw sorcery, the quarrel of magic rocketed westward, shrieking through and around the darkened foliage of the woods. Scythe and Stearck both flinched involuntarily.

"Not my doing," Logan finally answered Moknay, his one eye trained on the retreating blast of energy.

"Whoever's idea it was, they've got good taste," Halette said with a grin, winking in Logan's direction. "And I'm glad to see you're taking care of my sister."

"I'm no tracker," the blacksmith, Fjorm, remarked, "but I'd say it's heading us in the direction of Debarnian."

"If the sun would rise, perhaps we'd know where we were," Thumbs weakly groaned from the back of Halette's cart.

"If the sun still exists," Stearck apprehensively added.

Grey eyes reflected the scarlet glare as Moknay clucked his horse forward. "Wherever we are or wherever we're going, I'm not one to lightly put my trust in sorcery," he sneered. "This time, however, I think it's our only recourse."

Logan couldn't help but feel the stab of guilt return to his breast at Moknay's mention of trust. It was in the young man's image that the small band now placed their trust, and, as Moknay had said, many of the group would not have done so beforehand. Neither would many of the men who now lay dead in the deserted streets of Plestenah, Logan mused.

The horses and cart started eastward once more, trailing the crimson glimmer that imitated Logan's features. In an hour, faint shafts of sunlight began to pierce the voidlike blackness of the sky, and the golden rays of day tried to chase away the dark. Odd shadows splashed the forest as the ebony refused to be dispersed, scattering into cloudlike formations snaking and coiling across the heavens. Tendrils of darkness churned and waved as the arctic gale persisted in howling through the afternoon, touching the small group with its wintry cold.

More horsed men—injured and uninjured—began to join the small group, each following their own magical phantasm of Logan. Steadily, the band grew larger in number until some fifty survivors accompanied them, and Logan frowned at the state of most.

Pale faces from loss of blood or absolute terror marked their features, and bloodstained clothes told of wounds, hidden and unhidden. Even the rogues and outlaws of Eadarus showed visible shock at their brutal defeat, and Logan could not shrug off the feeling that many looked in his direction for either guidance or blame. Surely blame was the better of the two, the young man decided, for his guidance would only bring more death to these men.

A surprised voice woke Logan from his detached thoughts, and he blinked his eye to see Yorke standing before them. "Woulda never've believed it wit' me own eyes if I's hadn't've seen it fer meself," the rogue declared.

As darkness started to return in its unnatural dusk, the last image of Logan went screaming off into the trees.

Scythe dismounted, approaching his companion with something of a skeptical mien on his face. "Believed what?" he asked. "Are you at the bottom of all this?"

"Me?" Yorke exclaimed. "Ya know me's better than that, Scythe! Was that priestess! She did some fancy magiclike stuff and . . . voom! People start joinin' up wit' us right aways. Yer the last o' them."

Mara! Logan thought happily to himself. It *was* her! It was her doing! Then she was alive! She was safe!

Overcome by relief, the young man bolted in the direction Yorke had come, charging into a wide clearing filled with the survivors of war. Logan didn't even scan the multitude of fighters, reserving his halved vision for the slim red-and-black-garbed woman who had to be around. A happy cry sounded from one side of the clearing, and Logan saw her. All guilt, sorrow, and soreness swept away from the young man's mind as he raced through the crowds of people, horses, and carts. Eager arms entwined about Mara's waist and held her close, thanking whatever gods the people of Sparrill worshipped that she was unhurt.

"Are you all right?" he queried, the concern so deep it almost hurt.

"Of course I am." Mara beamed back, her smile ravishing. "What about you?"

The young man grinned in response. "I'm here, aren't I?" he replied. The somberness of the rest of the camp began to creep into the pair's reunion, and Logan risked a glance at those about him.

There were perhaps one hundred men in the camp, maybe less, many wounded, many others still weakened. Handfuls of horses stood about the clearing, nervous snorts escaping them as the freezing gale moaned through the foliage. Weary, despair-filled eyes locked on the young man as he surveyed the area, the guilt and depression returning. Not even the sight and touch of Mara could beat back the harsh reality of their plight. They had started off with the population of two towns and had been decimated to less than one hundred and fifty men. And the Reakthi menace followed? There was no hope.

"We didn't do so good, did we?" Logan mumbled softly, unable to face Mara with his failure.

"We tried," the priestess answered. "That was as much as we could do."

"But we didn't win," the young man retorted. He clenched his hands in frustration as he stared at all that was left of his army. "Where's Nightwalker?"

The sudden silence from Mara prodded an ominous tension in Logan's stomach as he looked briefly at her. Her downcast eyes and quietness answered better than any words.

"Oh, shit," Logan breathed. "He's not dead. He can't be."

The nod from Mara confirmed the young man's fears. "He . . . Well, he just kind of faded after the battle," she tried to explain. "But he said something about a book. Groathit wasn't at Plestenah—he went westward with some book of some sort that Nightwalker said we have to get. It's the only way to restore Balance to the Wheel."

"What good is Balance when we've lost?" Logan despondently asked.

Mara's grip on him tightened. "We haven't lost!" she argued. "Nightwalker said this book would help us save the Light!"

"Did he say anything else?"

The priestess nodded, her dark tresses bouncing about her shoulders. "He said we had to go eastward," she recalled, "but I'm not sure what he meant. He said something about the Purity itself helping us near Debarnian."

Logan screwed up his face, trying to decipher the Shadow-spawn's last enigma. Near Debarnian? he mused. There wasn't anything near Debarnian at all but forest. Yet surely Nightwalker didn't mean that, did he? Why near Debarnian if the Purity could help us here? Or why not even near Plestenah if the Purity could help us at all? So what else could it be? The Heart? No, if Mara saw him before he died, then Nightwalker would have been able to say something about the Heart itself if that's what he meant. Not even he would be that mysterious when he was dying, would he? Damn, it *was* Nightwalker, and he *never* gave a straight answer, so what the hell Purity was near enough to Debarnian that it could help these scragglers of a rag-tag army?

The expression that crossed Logan's features startled Mara as he pulled out of their embrace. "The Roana!" the young man shouted. "Nightwalker had to have been talking about the Roana!"

The priestess blinked in her bewilderment. "But how . . . ?" she started.

Logan interrupted. "Remember when the Worm had those Demons chasing us for Launce's staff?" the young man queried. "When they attacked us at the Roana, the river helped us on its own. Maybe the Heart'll make it do likewise."

Or maybe the Purity didn't do anything at all and you did it all yourself, Logan's dark side gravely mused. While we're so busy remembering things, remember what Dirge told you. Magic's an unconscious force. Maybe *you* had the river help you since Natural magicks are your forte—or will be, if you keep using them so much.

Logan paled at the sudden revelation but tossed the pessimism aside. That was only speculation, he told himself. Only one of the possible explanations for what happened before at the river— and, besides, now that the sprites aren't held captive by any *Deil*, maybe they themselves will help.

A grim wish of good luck echoed deep inside the young man's mind as he turned away from Mara and sought out other familiar figures in the groups of survivors. It was now imperative they set up some kind of plan that would not fail them as their hastily devised strategy had at Plestenah, and, for that, Logan would need the more experienced in their little force of fighters.

And the guilt of their defeat started to soak in once more.

Steel flickered in the Murderer's eyes as Moknay turned away from where Thromar sat to glare deeply into Logan's eye. "I've never seen him like this," the grey-eyed brigand remarked. "Upset, yes. Even depressed a few times, but never so despondent that he wouldn't formulate a battle plan."

A frown crossed Logan's face that mimicked the sneer on Moknay's lips. It wasn't as if the young man blamed Thromar for not wanting to take part in their effort to save Debarnian from the pursuing Reakthi—if Logan had his way, he'd have nothing to do with it either—but, where his guilt was founded as the leader of all those men who had been killed, Thromar's guilt stemmed from the fact that he was the one who had devised the plan that had so fatally fallen through.

"Maybe we shouldn't ask him, then," the young man decided. "Maybe it would be better if we figured it out for ourselves."

Anxiety sparked in Roshfre's blue eyes. "We're thieves and cutthroats," she stated. "Our tactics do not mesh very nicely with full-scale warfare."

"She's right," agreed Moknay. "We need Thromar's experience."

Reluctance filled the young man from Santa Monica as he turned his halved vision in the direction of where the Rebel sat. Even though he was such a large figure, the fighter had retreated to a small corner of their makeshift camp, alone and looking very small. Whispering voices of guilt continued to plague Logan as he stepped away from the apprehensive group around him and toward the silent warrior so loyal to Sparrill.

Thromar spoke without even turning around. "I know what you're going to say, friend-Logan, but it will do no good. I am unfit to lead an army."

"Who said anything about leading?" Logan queried, trying desperately to keep a tone of lightness in his voice and failing dismally. "I'm the one leading the army. We just need some kind of plan."

"Discuss it among the others," the Rebel responded sullenly. "I cannot make such decisions properly."

"Who says?" questioned Logan.

Thromar extended a meaty palm toward the remaining clusters of soldiers. "Does not this sorry sight speak for itself?" he asked. "It was my strategy that has decimated our troops—I shall not make that mistake again."

A growing unease began to eat its way through Logan's courage, trying to break down the young man's will and force him to run and surrender. Thromar's reluctance was so much like his own that Logan feared he, too, would be overwhelmed by his own despair—but then that would mean Groathit had won not just the battle but the war after all. If no one retained the courage to fight—held onto their determination—the spellcaster had triumphed.

"You can't run away," the young man softly said, speaking as much to himself as to the Rebel. "Oh, sure, you can try—not take any more responsibility—but you really can't run away. Whatever happens will still have an effect on you, whether you helped, hindered, or ran away. Then you'll always wonder what might have happened if you had helped devise a battle plan, or helped fight in some other way, but those'll just be thoughts of regret. Always wondering what could have happened—never knowing 'cause it never did.

"I found out that mistakes play a very important part in our lives, Thromar," the young man went on, lost in his thoughts. "Remember when we were looking for the Smythe? Boy, I made some real dumb ones there. I actually ran into Zackaron and almost gave him the Jewel! Talk about a dumbshit! But—if I hadn't have made that mistake—Groathit would have stolen the Jewel from us and there would have been no one to oppose him."

Thromar's beady eyes remained bereft of their glimmer. "Yet that mistake cost no one their life, friend-Logan," he observed.

The guilt encompassing the young man strengthened as old memories came back to haunt him. "No, but I did kill Launce," he replied. "And the ogre. And I was the one who led all those men into battle. They were following me! And I caused the death of over half of them."

"It was my plan . . ." the Rebel protested.

"It was my leadership!" Logan harshly interrupted. "Hell, I didn't even sound the retreat! I was too busy looking for Groathit to be worried about all the people dying."

A frown spread beneath Thromar's beard. "I cannot believe that," he said. "You were only trying to do what needed to be done—for your own good *and* the good of Sparrill."

Logan glanced up and fixed the Rebel with his single eye. "What did you say?" he wondered.

"Those men died for a cause," Thromar repeated. "They knew that—though I know it doesn't make you feel any better. You had to try to do what you had to do."

Inadvertently, the young man had pulled the fighter out of his own depression by venting some of his own. "I hope you're listening to yourself," Logan told the Rebel, "'cause the same thing you're saying to me goes double for you."

Thromar stopped speaking and screwed up his face as he recalled his previous words. A look of perplexity, followed by a frown of thought, crossed his bearded features before his eyes rested firmly on Logan. A faint twinkle returned to their blackness.

"You've tricked me, friend-Logan," he grumbled.

A small smile stretched across Logan's lips. "I did nothing of the sort," he returned. "It's just that if I've got to keep my position as leader of this sorry excuse for an army, I want someone who I can trust as my tactician."

The large fighter got to his feet, a brawny hand resting on his sword. "In that case, friend-Logan, I will do it . . . for you."

Logan tried not to flinch at the profession of loyalty. "Do it for Sparrill," he suggested, and the two approached the area of camp where the others awaited their leadership.

*   *   *

Servil shuddered at the memory but continued speaking: "When I scouted for Fraviar, the Darkness moved in first, but it was not so when the Reakthi attacked the town. Their forces came first."

Moknay stroked his mustache, eyes aglitter. "So we may have a chance, then," he murmured.

Fjorm grunted at the Murderer's skepticism. "Sounds to me like we've more than just a chance," the blacksmith declared. "We'll send them bastards to Gangrorz's Tomb after all!"

"Maybe, maybe not," Thromar stated, caution dampening his usual enthusiasm. "All this rides on the hope that the Reakthi advance across the river first."

"An' if they don't?" Yorke queried.

"We all meet the same fate as Marcos," Roshfre answered.

"What about the magical aspect of things?" inquired Xile, and Logan did not like the fact that everyone looked at him.

The young man shrugged, feeling both helpless and angry. "I don't know," he admitted. "This was Nightwalker's suggestion— and even then we're not sure about that. The magic might help us, or, then again, we might be on our own."

"You can't do anything . . . ?" Xile started.

Moknay cut off the thief, knowing Logan's reluctance to work magic. "Don't worry about the magic," he informed the others. "If it helps, it helps."

"Oh, it'll help. It'll help," Dirge declared, his head bobbing up and down in eager agreement. "Not quite the magic you're talking about, but it'll help, nonetheless, eh?"

"What are you talking about?" growled Scythe.

The necromage pointed an animated finger in the direction of the pursuing Reakthi, his eyes wild with scrambled emotions. "That Darkness is too powerful," he said. "Don't you understand? It has never been before—at least not in written history—taken such a physical form as ourselves. If no one else noticed but me, I can understand your ignorance, but all our Reakthi foes are gradually deteriorating from the inside out. Comes from the Force burning inside them. Why, I estimate the first of these troops should wither away in two days' time."

Thromar peered hard at the half-sane magic-user. "Are you sure of this?" he demanded.

"Sure of what?" Dirge asked back. "The deterioration or the two days' time? Oh, yes! Yes! These shells will certainly deteriorate! Whether it's in two days' time or three—or maybe even four or five—well, that I'm not quite certain about, but, then again, who is, eh?"

"It's something we'd better not put our trust in either," Moknay declared, and Logan wondered if it was the Murderer's unease of magic or his usual cautionary measures that spoke. "I think our best chance lies with Thromar's preliminary plan."

"A moment ago it was just a chance," Fjorm chuckled. "Now it's our best chance."

Thromar pointed to the hurriedly scrawled map before them. "The Roana isn't the ideal place for an ambush, but, with this group, and with a row of archers just within the foliage along the banks, we should be able to cut down a good number of men as they ford the river. Imogen knows *these* Reakthi won't have the sense to retreat, so if we just keep shooting into them, by the time they do get across the river, it'll be very likely we'll have slightly evened the odds."

"Yeah, from a thousand to one to a hundred to one," Hach complained.

"If we march first thing tomorrow, we should reach the Roana possibly by nightfall—or what used to be nightfall," the Rebel continued. "We'll dig in along the eastern banks and wait. Servil, are you still willing to act as scout?"

His expression stern, the lean tracker curtly nodded.

"All right, then," Thromar concluded, "let's all hope to Brolark that we can make up for losing Plestenah and keep Debarnian from the same fate; someone's got to remind these Reakthi whoresons that Sparrill belongs to no one save Sparrill. Oh, and Dirge, find a new horse. Yours is starting to really reek."

It no longer lurked in the bushes awaiting the proper time—now it ran with thunderous footsteps toward the gurgling, rushing beauty of the Roana. Now, it knew, was the time to act. The bad magic was coming eastward—pursuing those who were friends. The other friends, therefore, must be told. They must be warned: The bad magic was coming. The bad magic would be here soon. Now was the time to act.

A bird took to the unnaturally dark sky, shrieking not in fright but in response to the hurried footsteps below. Spread the word! seemed to be its cry. Spread the word! Bad magic nears! Bad magic comes! The time is now!

Somewhere close by, a wolf howled in answer, and the trees came alive with activity.

Reinforcements

Matthew Logan clung to the bow as tightly as he did to his last, waning shred of hope. A freezing, biting gale tore through the leaves of his hiding place, and an unholy darkness filled what should have been an early morning sky. Anxious murmurs wafted up from the surrounding foliage, and the young man could glimpse others crouched in the brush as he was, hands clutching bows and crossbows. Before him, dimly illuminated by its own crystal-blue waters, the Roana River flowed gently northward, water plants calmly bobbing atop the soothing, methodical ripples.

Logan's attention returned to the western bank; he felt the arctic wind sail through his body and snatch the courage from inside him. It has to work, he thought, trying to console himself. If they failed here, there would be no stopping the horde of Darkness-controlled Reakthi. This was the young man's final test—the last *Daigread* ritual forced upon him. If he won here, he at least won the opportunity to converge on Groathit's forces. If he lost the upcoming battle—or won but at the expense of too many men—he failed and was condemned to Sparrill, and, probably shortly thereafter, death.

There was a sudden blur of motion from the western bank, and Logan swung his impaired vision upward to catch sight of Servil, his lengthy mane of brown-gold hair billowing in the freezing winds. With an ease that made Logan gape, the lean scout jumped through the water of the river and scrambled across to the opposite shore. As Logan watched, Mara moved alongside the young man, momentarily distracting him. He gave the priestess a worried look as he remembered her presence in the lineup of archers, but a second glance at the heavy Binalbow in her hands helped ease some of his fears. When he turned back to the river, Servil was beside him in the shrubbery.

"Are they coming?" Logan questioned.

The scout nodded once. "And there is good news," he reported. "They stay on course and travel on their own."

Logan blinked his good eye. "What?" he wondered. "What do you mean?"

Servil smiled fleetingly, jerking an eager thumb at the western bank. "The Rebel leads them a merry chase through the forest," he explained, "and right for our little trap. In addition, the Darkness has deserted them."

Logan still found it hard to believe the words he was hearing. "Deserted them?" he repeated.

"Just as I said," responded Servil. "It abruptly returned westward as if answering an unspoken summons. The Reakthi force travels on its own."

"Groathit's doing," Mara put in.

Logan released a dumb nod, his optimism kept in check by his darker side. "So at least our ambush should work," he decided unsteadily. He cast his uncovered eye westward, concern etched on his face. "Are you sure Thromar's all right?"

A short chuckle escaped Servil's lips. "He moves like a chomprat on *skelmp*," the scout merrily reported. "They'll never catch him."

Logan nodded in feigned satisfaction, but still feared for the fighter's safety. All right, so maybe Thromar *did* formulate the plan that had fallen through at Plestenah—and it was understandable that he'd be reluctant to formulate another—but why had Logan so stupidly agreed that any heavy risks would be taken by the Rebel himself? As leader, Logan should have pulled rank on him, but then Thromar would never have returned to his usual boastful self—their defeat striking him a personal blow and the loss of Fraviar as an added wound to his pride. The Rebel had always introduced himself as the greatest fighter in all Sparrill—maybe he had to prove that self-appointed title to himself once again.

Logan frowned. A fat lot of good it'll do if he gets himself killed.

Silence filled the forest, disturbed only by the howling of the polar wind. Minutes that passed like hours caused Logan's fears to grow, and the young man nervously fidgeted with the quiver of arrows slung across one shoulder. All along the riverbank, Logan knew thieves and cutthroats from Eadarus knelt side by side with merchants and shopkeeps from Debarnian, long-range weapons poised in an uneasy quiet. A few yards behind the archers—in a line just as long—waited the remaining fighters, ready to confront the Reakthi once they finally reached the eastern shore. Logan only hoped that when that occurred the archers had done their job and had sufficiently reduced the number of chestplated soldiers.

Hoofbeats shattered the stillness, and a red-and-black mare splashed headlong into the Roana. Her massive rider flailed his blood-caked sword high above his head, the arctic gale streaming through his reddish-brown hair.

"Darkness or not," Thromar roared to the forest behind him, "you Reakthi are still a pitiful lot!"

A wild grin stretched beneath the Rebel's beard as Smeea trudged across the river. With a hurried leap, the mare pranced free of the water and bolted into the greenery. Flakes of snow dotted her red mane, and a fine sheen of ice glittered across Thromar's unsheathed blade.

"Stupid chestplated bastards," the Rebel muttered happily. "They almost lost me twice in their own darkness." Tiny eyes scanned the dark foliage to his right and left. "Everybody in position?" he asked Logan.

The young man shrugged in his uncertainty. "I hope so."

"As do I, friend-Logan," Thromar answered.

Logan felt Mara shift beside him, leveling her Binalbow at the clearing of the riverbank. Servil nocked an arrow into his bow, and the young man pulled an arrow free of his own quiver. Focusing his attention on the coming battle, Logan returned his single-eyed gaze to the Roana and slipped his arrow into his bow. He hesitated before drawing back the bowstring as the dark brush on the opposite bank shuddered and the first of the Reakthi stepped out into the clearing.

Flakes of ice danced across the shore as the dark-eyed warriors stalked free of the forest, a freezing wind screaming at their backs. Logan felt his last feeble spark of hope die as row after row of Reakthi marched stiffly for the Roana, energy crackling from their empty sockets. An odd contrast of shadows flickered across the riverbanks as the Darkness-consumed soldiers threw a hideous shade of ebony against the light blue brilliance of the river, and the more powerful glare of blackness made Logan want to throw down his bow and run for his life.

Bowstrings twanged all across the eastern shore, and the air was filled with shrieking shafts of wood. Withered flesh gave way before iron-tipped quarrels and steel arrowheads; yet no blood flowed—no soldier fell. The Reakthi swarm steadily advanced, the first of the booted feet splashing into the Roana's beauty. Gnarled, shriveled hands flexed spasmodically as fatal sparks of magic leapt from bony fingertips, and a few of the chestplated figures reached for their weapons, faces impassive and eyes aglow.

There was another volley of arrows that riddled the oncoming mass, and two of the Reakthi went down. A sudden bout of hope flared in Logan's breast—accompanied by a cheer from the concealed archers—and the young man loosed the first arrow in his bow. He hastily reached over his shoulder and plucked free another shaft, placed it, and fired. It wasn't necessary to aim, he told himself. With so many of the Reakthi on the western bank—and more still coming from the forest behind them—any shot under six feet would strike something.

The young man's dark pessimism had not fully retreated: With so many of them? it ominously repeated.

Logan tried to ignore the shudder of fright that passed through his system as he kept himself busy with the rapid firing of Thromar's bow. Beside him, the Rebel watched with an inquisitive eye as the chestplated soldiers plodded onward, wooden shafts protruding from their gaunt, gangly frames. Major and minor wounds from their previous conflict crisscrossed their scrawny forms, their withering flesh slashed to reveal the ebony gleam that radiated from within.

The first of the Reakthi emerged on the eastern bank and Logan instantly swung his bow on the warrior, fighting the panic that rose in his throat. Immediately, the chestplated figure was the target for nearly fifty archers who slammed their bolts and arrows into the soldier's body. Repelled by the sudden force of the multiple blows, the Reakthi toppled back into the river and was carried off by the current.

Logan fought down the urge to join in the cheering as two more Reakthi took the first's place on the eastern shore. Already the muscles of the young man's arm and shoulder were tired from constantly drawing the sixty-pound bow, and he began to feel the weariness of their march and earlier defeat return.

Mara's green eyes narrowed as she noticed a line of ten Reakthi halt on the opposing bank. "Matthew," the priestess hissed through clenched teeth.

Logan jerked his head where Mara pointed her Binalbow and confusion filled his good eye. More soldiers still strode from the woods, so why had this single line of ten stopped? What was the Darkness inside them planning? Had it finally understood the blatant stupidity of walking headlong into a blizzard of arrows? No . . . the rest of the Reakthi continued their mindless march into the Roana and the screeching arrows. So what was the purpose . . . ?

Black sorcery streaked from the ten Reakthi and stabbed into the foliage of the eastern bank. Screams of hidden archers split the unnaturally dark morning. Logan released an audible curse as one stream of jet-black fire seared the air near his left shoulder, and Thromar threw himself to the forest floor as another blast narrowly missed his head.

"They're onto us," growled Servil, directing three simultaneous shots at the ten Reakthi.

Freezing wind shrieked as energy tore through its arctic blast. Unnatural power raced from withered hands and screeched over the heads of the Reakthi fording the river, exploding into the forest of the eastern bank. More dying screams pierced Logan's ears and the surge of guilt made it impossible for the young man to draw back his bowstring. It was only a sudden flare of determination to return to his world—a world where battles like this never happened—that kept the bow in his hand.

Four more Reakthi waded onto the eastern shore, and Logan immediately directed his bow for the chestplated quartet. The bowstring twanged harshly in the young man's ears as the arrow leapt free, but there was an answering grumble of energy from the western shore. Bursts of velvet magic sprayed around the four Reakthi from their comrades on the opposite bank, cindering the arrows and quarrels that headed toward them. Logan flinched as one of the rays screamed over his head and splattered against a tree behind him.

"Damn them!" Thromar cursed. "Friend-Logan, we have to pull back!"

With the screams of the dying still echoing in his mind, Logan nodded swiftly. "Okay," he answered. "Sound the retreat."

"Wait," Servil interrupted. "If we scattered our forces to the north and south, they'd have no targets. We'll have them trapped in a crossfire once the Reakthi cross the river and start into the forest."

"And save the rest of the men until then?" Thromar mused, thoughtfully stroking his heavy beard. "It's worth a try."

"Pass the word, then," the scout responded, scurrying into the foliage. "Scatter the archers so we're not such an easy target— either seen or unseen."

We're improvising again, Logan thought darkly to himself. The exact same thing that defeated us at Plestenah. But we can't stay here! Those blasts would wipe us out just by continuously pelting the forest! If we didn't scatter to the sides as Servil suggested, we'd have only retreated to the east.

Logan and Mara ducked through the greenery, their weapons clutched in their hands. Other archers weaved and scrambled around them, scrabbling for cover from the shrieking bolts of darkness. There was a scream from somewhere off to Logan's right as another shaft of sorcery ripped through the forest and struck a human being. Perhaps it was the young man's imagination, yet he thought he smelled the stench of burning flesh sweep past him on the gale.

"Scatter!" Logan cried out, hoping to save as many lives as possible.

Roaring blackness exploded on Logan's left, throwing him bodily into the air. Thromar's bow flipped out of his grasp and landed lost somewhere among the shrubbery. Dark flames crackled to life as the young man skidded to a brutal stop, stars blazing behind his eyelids. With a dazed mumble, he pulled himself into a seated position and tried to shake the blurriness from his good eye. He could barely make out the armored forms fording the river to his left or the ten figures across the Roana, their hands flaring with blackness . . . a blackness that steadily made its way into Logan's skull and cast him into unconsciousness.

Someone was shaking him; trying to rouse him out of a sound sleep. A disturbed groan fled Logan's lips as he tried to roll away from the persistent shake at his shoulders. Leave me alone—I don't wanna go to work today.

"Matthew! Get up!"

The sound of Mara's voice and the fear that tainted her words caused the young man's eye to spring open. Black flames still roared nearby, and the cacophony of battle thrummed throughout the forest, muted only by the howling of the wind.

"Huh? What?" Logan exclaimed, jerking himself awake. "What happened?"

"I thought you were dead," Mara admitted, taking in a deep breath of relief.

Dim memories of an ebon eruption flashed briefly across Logan's mind. "How long was I out?" he wondered.

"Not very," responded Mara. "All the Reakthi have crossed the Roana, including the ten or so using magic, but . . . but we can't hurt any of them! They've formed some kind of shield that destroys our arrows."

Squinting—trying to ignore the throb of pain at his temples— Logan glanced through the foliage to spy the final ranks of the dark-eyed Reakthi. A thin, misty veil of power surrounded the soldiers, and Logan watched as an arrow streaked from the forest and dissolved against the wall of magic.

"Shit," the young man swore. "Where's Thromar?"

"Probably with the others," the priestess guessed. "We split up, remember?"

Logan nodded slowly, attempting to piece together events that the sudden blast of sorcery had befuddled. In the two or three minutes he had been unconscious, the Reakthi had crossed the Roana and continued their steady advance eastward. And now there was no way to get at the chestplated warriors through their curtain of magic unless someone wanted to test their shield's strength against flesh and steel.

If only there was some way to get to them, the young man thought with a frown. *Maybe my sword might pierce their shield since I endowed it with some of the Heart's magicks, but I seriously don't want to try it. Besides, only four of us out of our whole army have magical weapons.*

An unexpected bellow ripped through the dark morning sky, and, at first, Logan attributed it to the insistent dizziness lurking in his brain. Then his impaired vision caught sight of the flutter of leaves as a towering, light blue form smashed its way through the trees, titanic, sledgehammerlike fists pounding into the last line of Reakthi and disrupting their crackling black mist.

"Fiiiiiight!" the light blue ogre thundered, and the woods came alive with dark-furred creatures.

Logan blinked in surprise at the mass of monkeylike animals that dropped down from the treetops into the midst of the soldiers. Beady, black eyes filled with rage, and tiny, yet sharp fangs gouged out chunks of withered flesh from the inhuman warriors. Daggers and sharpened sticks stabbed beneath armored limbs, and the high-pitched barks and snarls of Munuc's people filled the icy air.

Arrogantly, the Darkness-consumed Reakthi ignored the small creatures, but when three of their number fell beneath the combined onslaught of the ogre and the little beasts, dark eyes turned on them and power screamed. A dozen anthropoid figures splashed

backwards, fur aflame with ebony sorcery. The freezing wind
howled with nefarious laughter as the tiny corpses blasted back
into the foliage from where they had come, smoke billowing from
their limp bodies.

"*No!*" Logan screamed.

Leaping to his feet, the young man bolted directly toward the
mass of Reakthi, his sword jumping into his hand. Somewhere—
many miles away perhaps—Logan heard Mara call out his name
in concern, yet he did not answer her. The light blue ogre was
alive and helping with Munuc's kind, and the young man would
no longer sit idly by and "lead" while everyone else died for
his cause.

Crimson flared along the edges of his blade as Logan charged
the horde of chestplated warriors. Silver and scarlet merged in
the darkness of the morning, and Logan's Reakthi weapon drove
through a withering throat. Black energy sputtered as the sword
cut through muscle and bone, severing the head from the neck.
Vague, feeble grasping gestures afflicted the headless soldier like
an epileptic seizure when the unearthly dark glare from inside its
gangly frame guttered and choked. Logan's good eye went wide
as the Darkness attempted to strengthen itself and accidentally
burned through its physical shell.

The foul odor of charred meat forced its way into Logan's
nostrils as ebony fire blossomed into life, instantly consuming the
lanky framework of flesh and bone. A misty outline of blackness
hovered momentarily in space before rocketing skyward in what
Logan suspected to be confusion.

A dozen eyes filled with unholy energies trained on the
young man, and a fist swaddled in dark magicks swung for
his head. Blindly, Logan dropped to the ground, his sword
jutting out. He could feel the sudden jar of a body impaling
itself upon his blade, but there was still movement. Something
like freezing warmth neared his cheek, and the young man
opened his eye to see nothing but blackness descending for
his face. Unexpectedly, the black glare flickered and dropped
to the ground as the clawing hand abruptly separated from
the wrist.

Mara frantically pushed Logan to one side, her sword and dagger
in her hands. "Matthew!" she shouted. "What are you trying to do?
Get yourself killed?"

"Dirge was right!" the young man yelled over the wind's cry.
"They're using up their bodies!"

Mara's sword was a blur of silver and red. "Only not fast enough!" she replied. "We're going to get killed!"

A shrill note tore through the forest, and Logan jerked to his left in wonderment. A tide of armed men rushed out of the shrubbery to his aid, Thromar's mighty bulk leading them. Archers hurried out from every side of the battle, striking the Reakthi on unprotected flanks. More and more bodies in gold and bronze chestplates crumpled to the forest floor, devoid of the energy that had animated them. Others still evaporated from overuse, leaving disoriented flares of man-shaped blackness to flee westward.

Deadly black bursts of Darkness ripped through the woods, catching men and anthropoid beings alike in their fatal streams. The temperature dropped to intolerable levels as the wind screamed louder, knifing the armies with icy talons. Frost littered the trees and bushes, and clumps of snow settled on the corpses of either side.

A familiar voice suddenly sprouted at Logan's back. "Hoo hah!" Yorke exclaimed. "I's do believe we're winnin'!"

Hach blocked a descending mace and gave the optimistic rogue a sneer. "Don't swing your sword until it's forged," he growled. "We've lost once before."

Xile ducked a bolt of magic and lunged upward. "Don't mind Hach," he said. "It's his job to complain."

"Complain later!" Logan shouted. "Fight now!"

There was an upheaval of darkness between Yorke and Hach and both men flipped backwards. Logan was spattered with gore as the flesh of Hach's face was torn forcibly from his skull and scattered across the battlefield. Bile rose in the young man's throat as he relentlessly swung his sword back and forth, trying not to think of the faceless corpse that lay somewhere at his feet.

"Dung!" Logan heard Yorke curse at his back. "Wot in the name of Imogen hit me?"

Weapons glinting silver, Xile fought his way to Logan. "They still have the advantage," the thief observed. "Even with your friends"—he waved a hand at the monkeylike beings and the ogre—"they'll defeat us."

Mara nodded, her long hair whipped by the harsh wind. "We need to fight their magic," she declared, and the implication in her voice was obvious.

"No!" Logan furiously snapped. "There's got to be another way!"

Another chorus of screams rang above the shrieking of the wind.

"The Purity *has* helped us," Mara cried, indicating the ogre, "but it can't fight alone! That's the reason you were brought here! That's why that wind picked you up! The Purity needs someone to fight for it!"

"I didn't want it to be me!" Logan yelled back, a sense of betrayal brewing in his stomach at the words that Mara spoke. They were the words the young man hated the most to hear—and they were even more hated coming from the lips of the woman he loved.

"Whether you like it or not, you've got to face facts," Xile put in, his bandana snapping in the winds. "Our forces alone can't stop them so long as they still have their magic."

"We can try!" Logan howled in frustration.

"We can also die!" Xile argued back, narrowly avoiding a fist of raw energy.

A soft touch fell on Logan's arm. "Matthew," Mara breathed, green eyes locking on his eye, "you know I wouldn't ask you to do this unless it wasn't absolutely necessary. But we have a chance! We have a chance of beating them! The only thing stopping us is their magicks!"

Logan pulled away before he was caught up by the emotions released by those beautiful emerald eyes. There was reluctance in Mara's gaze—as if she deeply understood his dislike to use magic. And why shouldn't she? She of all people knew him best. So why was she asking him to do this? Why was she asking him to risk his normal life back in Santa Monica? Selfishness? To keep him to herself?

The young man frowned deeply at his cruel suspicions. Shame on you, Matthew, he scolded himself. You know Mara better than that. That sounds like something Cyrene would have done—not Mara. So why would Mara ask him to do the one thing he really hated to do unless she believed it would help? But who was to say she would be right? For all his magic, Logan might not be able to help win the fight. So where would that leave him? Defeated—just as before—but only that much closer to imprisonment in Sparrill forever.

And who was to say that Mara wasn't right? another portion of his mind queried. Remember what you were telling Thromar: " . . . you'll always wonder what might have happened . . . but those'll just be thoughts of regret. Always wondering what could have happened—never knowing 'cause it never did." You're a big talker, Matthew, but maybe you just don't have the guts to do what you say others should do.

Logan took his single eye away from the battle, eyebrows narrowed. "I'll need to get through to my horse," he told those gathered around him.

The smile that briefly stretched across Mara's lips—and the look of hope that sparked in Xile's eyes—did nothing to help calm the young man's fears and anxieties concerning magic. Magic was the one thing that had pulled Logan out of his usual mode of life and had contributed added complications with his passive accumulation of it in Sparrill. Because of that, Logan had a loathing for sorcery that rivaled any rogue's.

"Get up, Yorke," Xile instructed, extending a helpful hand toward the dazed outlaw. "We've got a battle to win."

Yorke staggered to his feet. "Tell the ground t' stop spinnin' and I will."

A grey-and-black blur among the chestplates of the enemy, Moknay glided through the swarm of Reakthi. Cold eyes locked on the four figures that struggled purposefully eastward, and an eyebrow rose in silent thought. The expressions etched on the faces of Xile and Mara told the Murderer of a determination that drove them through the horde of warriors. The expression on Logan's face was a mixture of so many conflicting emotions it was impossible to read, and Yorke's face spoke of one injured in battle and fighting solely on his instincts to survive.

With an agile spin, Moknay turned away from a group of dark-eyed Reakthi and slid into the shadows of the unnaturally dark morning. Grey eyes locked on a single form stanced nearby, and a gloved hand clamped down on Scythe's shoulder. Before he could lash out at the owner of the hand, Scythe was spun effortlessly around and forced to face the Murderer.

The rogue snarled at the interruption. "Hey!"

"Shut up and do as I say," Moknay retorted, and the icy glare in his eyes silenced even Scythe.

A dagger stabbed in the direction of Logan and the others. "What do you see?" the Murderer demanded.

"A blasted war," Scythe barked as his dark green eyes swiftly scanned the men, Reakthi, anthropoid beings, and corpses filling the forest. "What the *Deil* else am I supposed to see?"

Moknay gripped the rogue by his collar and redirected his gaze. "Now what do you see?"

Scythe's eyebrows shot up as he spied Logan's group. "They're heading somewhere, aren't they?" he understood.

The grey-eyed Murderer nodded grimly. "Question is, where to and what for?"

Scythe avoided a sword and kicked the attacking Reakthi backwards. "What'd you have in mind?" he questioned sardonically. "We can't ask them—we're too far from them. I'd sooner sprout wings and fly."

Gloved hands expertly extracted daggers laced with ruby light from his cheststrap. "We can make sure they get there," the Murderer replied. "Just how good are you with those things?"

Scythe glanced down at where Moknay's gaze pinpointed his steel boomerangs. "Good enough," the rogue responded, grinning wickedly.

Silver flashed in the blackness of the morning, both daggers and boomerangs whizzing through the fray. Lean, chestplated bodies toppled under the sudden thunderstorm of blades, clearing a path for the four battling eastward. Both men kept an eye on their own surroundings, stopping their deadly barrage only to protect themselves. An impressed eyebrow lifted on Moknay's forehead as Scythe danced back a step, lopped off a Reakthi's hand and followed through by hurling his glittering weapon into the leg of a soldier blocking Logan's way.

"Interesting," the Murderer mused, nodding gravely at the rogue's own weapons strap. "What do you call those things, anyway?"

Scythe smiled a grim smile. "Scythes," he answered.

Logan flinched as a dagger lodged in the arm of the soldier before him, briefly unbalancing the Reakthi. With a snarled curse, the young man swung his sword in a half-controlled, half-uncontrolled arc that severed the head from the neck. Something of a low moan escaped the gaunt corpse as the Darkness inside wafted skyward, fleeing its destroyed host and vanishing into the blackness of the morning.

"We're not going to make it," Logan shouted at those behind him.

"Keep trying!" Xile encouraged.

Keep trying, Logan snorted to himself. That's all I've been doing since I came to this damn place. Trying one thing, then another when the first one falls through. So what the hell am I going to do if this falls through? Die, probably.

A sudden blur of red billowed in the wind near Logan, and the young man jerked his one-eyed gaze about to spy Roshfre fight her way to his side. Blood soaked the right side of her chest, yet the bandit leader seemed as unaware of the wound as the Darkness-controlled Reakthi were of theirs.

"Where to?" the redhead questioned, her mace a flash of wood and metal.

Logan barely avoided a glaring black hand. "We're trying to get to my horse," he replied.

"Any particular reason why?"

Logan ignored the query as he drove forward, knocking three Reakthi backwards, their frail, underfed bodies weighing less than a hundred pounds each. It was a wonder they just weren't blown away by the wind, Logan thought.

A sudden shout sounded in his ears.

"This way!" Roshfre yelled, flailing her mace high above her head.

There was an answering boom of shouts and warcries as the redhead's elite group of outlaws instantly obeyed her command, striking from all sides to clear an easterly path for Roshfre and Logan. The other thieves and men from Debarnian joined in, praying and hoping that whatever the leaders of their ragtag army were up to would help them keep the upper hand and possibly defeat these inhuman, chestplated creatures.

Darkness exploded in a night-filled blast, and Logan almost lost his balance. Shrieks of dying men and monkeys filled the woods, raising a plume of odor that brought tears to both of Logan's eyes. The young man recognized one of the bodies flung backwards as the lapidary, Baynebridge, his blond hair streaked with blood. A number of tiny bodies lay strewn about the tree trunks, three of Munuc's people dying for every one of Logan's men.

Somewhere, mingled with the screams of the polar wind, Logan thought he heard the deep rasp of Darkling Nightwalker:

"Darkness grows. The Balance falters. Shadows fade.

"We are dying."

Barthol clambered down from the seat of the cart and nervously wiped at the perspiration trickling down his brow. He gave the women and injured gathered around the horses and other wagons

an anxious look before returning his gaze to the line of trees and
bushes before him.

"What is it?" Halette demanded, noticing the priest's apprehensive glance.

Barthol's stare flicked uneasily back and forth. "Our forces,"
he said. "They're heading this way."

Thumbs tried to sit up. "Another retreat?" he wondered.

"Couldn't be," interrupted Halette. "There was no signal."

"Then what . . . ?" Liris began.

Barthol pivoted, locking his eyes on the saddlebags of the
yellow-and-green stallion beside his cart. "The horses are with us,"
he stated. "They must want something from the saddlebags."

"Surely not the Heart," Halette responded. "Remember what
they told us happened the last time the Darkness sensed the Heart
was here."

"Why else would our own forces be heading back here without
sounding a retreat unless they had no intentions of retreating?" the
priest shot back. Barthol hefted a sword out of his cart. "I'm going
to help."

Liris's eyes went wide. "Barthol!"

"You're not going alone," Thumbs exclaimed, dragging himself
out of his cart and wincing at the wounds on his chest.

Barthol turned on the injured bandit. "You stay here," he
ordered. "You're not healed."

"You can't fight and carry the Heart at the same time," the
six-fingered cutthroat stated.

"You two are insane!" Halette declared. "I'm coming too!"

Barthol was going to argue but stopped the words before they
had a chance to leave his lips. There was no time, the priest
decided. Three people had a better chance of getting the Heart
to Logan than one. It really didn't matter that those three were
a priest, a whore, and an injured and fingerless thief.

Nodding once at the two, Barthol hurried to Logan's horse and
pulled the skull-sized Bloodstone free of its leather bag. A feeling
of hope sparked within the priest's breast as he clutched the crimson gemstone, sensing the powerful magicks of Nature brewing
inside its faceted form. He only hoped that this was what the army
struggled for—and not the Jewel that Liris still held in her lap.

Barthol passed the Bloodstone to Halette and reaffirmed his
grip on his sword. Beside him, Thumbs lifted a flail in his right
hand. With a whoop, the outlaw charged into the brush, priest
and prostitute behind him.

A deep foreboding filled Barthol's stomach, and the hilt of his sword felt odd in his hand. He was a disciple of Agellic—not a fighter. The closest he had come to a real fight was when Logan had first visited his church and Groathit had attacked him there. That was the reason he had hired Goar—to fight his battles for him. But a sense of worthlessness had plagued him; he felt useless unless he could physically help win the fight. And now . . . now he was doing just that . . . so why did he feel so scared?

Noise assaulted the trio as they burst out into the battle, abruptly blocked by fighting men and Reakthi. Teeth clenched, Barthol drove into the closest of the dark-eyed soldiers, trying not to guess at what his blade pierced and tore. Revulsion shot through his chubby frame as the stabbed Reakthi turned on him, blackness gleaming in its eye sockets. Too stunned to react, Barthol gaped as a withered hand burning with magic reached for his chest but was unexpectedly stopped by a powerful blow from Thumbs's flail. Hardly discouraged, the Reakthi turned its attack on the thief, its glaring fingers reaching for his face. Silver flashed as Barthol brought his sword down on the warrior's collarbone, splintering bone and flesh. Weak legs crumpled beneath the blow, and the Reakthi collapsed to the ground, its ebony eyes blinking out like an extinguished candle.

Trying to clear his head of his fright and astonishment, Barthol trailed after Thumbs, knowing now that he was not useless.

Sweat poured down Logan's face as he hacked time and again at the scrawny, gangly soldiers barring his way. Faint streams of sunlight began to pierce the curtain of darkness overhead, and bizarre shadows scampered about the woods. A unified force now fought its way eastward, still outnumbered by the dark-eyed warriors, and Logan could not help but wonder if they were doing the right thing.

So we might beat them, he mused. A fat lot of good it'll do us if they steal the Heart from us. Not only that, we'll be leading them right to where our supplies and injured are in the carts. Now that is certainly *not* a smart thing to do! Maybe I just want excuses so I won't have to use the Heart, but I can't help feeling we're risking a whole hell of a lot on this one chance.

A confused mumble sounded in the young man's ear and he turned to see a perplexed look scrawl across Roshfre's features.

"What the *Deil* is she doing?" the redhead murmured to herself.

Questioningly, Logan glanced up and saw a mane of red hair similar to Roshfre's own. Through the chaos of battle, he thought he recognized Halette, but his surprise was increased when he spied the injured Thumbs and sword-wielding Barthol before her. A number of Reakthi turned their attention on the trio, and blackness flamed in their eyes.

A whispering chorus of voices seemed to emanate from around the dark-eyed soldiers:

The Purity.
It is here.
Do not let it escape.
Destroy it.
Destroy the Purity.

Mara's hand was suddenly on Logan's shoulder. "Matthew, what's Barthol . . ." she started.

"They've brought the Heart," the young man answered, not knowing whether to be glad or upset.

Blinding black light suddenly engulfed Logan's impaired vision, and a shock wave of tremendous force knocked him to the ground. There was a scream somewhere to the east as Barthol and Thumbs disappeared in the ebony eruption, and a number of Reakthi dissipated with them. Black flames scorched the nearby trees, and terrified barks sprouted from the panicking furry beasts that hid in them. Thunder seemed to fill the heavens as the deafening boom of the blast resounded over and over again, and burning afterimages replayed themselves behind Logan's closed eye.

Halette felt the ground pull out from beneath her, invisible quakes of air throwing her back toward the carts. Velvet sparks snapped and popped, and the half-melted remains of Barthol's sword landed beside her. A persistent ringing filled her ears, and she could not shake her head free of the bewildered lightheadedness that had resulted from the nearby explosion. She still gripped the Heart tightly in her arms, yet somehow sensed the Darkness would soon be upon her.

Eyes blurred, Halette jerked her head up to spy three Reakthi converging on her, their empty eye sockets ablaze with embers of blackness. Bony fingers clawed for her arms—for the scarlet Bloodstone in her grasp. She tried to scream, yet her voice was dumb, and her legs would not obey the commands to stand up and run.

Silver glinted. White armor suddenly intervened between Halette and the advancing soldiers. An expertly wielded sword dismembered the approaching warriors, sending misty black outlines retreating westward. More men in armor marched around the stunned prostitute, weapons slashing at the inhuman creatures. Confusion piled upon Halette's already befuddled state, and the redheaded whore tried to stand but failed miserably.

A friendly hand from a man in black armor guided her to her feet. "You are uninjured?" the silver-haired man inquired politely.

Halette gaped at the Imperator standing before her, a benevolent smile beneath his trim silver mustache and goatee. In horror, she turned and fixed her gaze on the armored troops marching in from the east, their blue-grey chestplates gleaming in the faint sunlight that penetrated the darkness.

The redhead swung back on the Imperator and his white-chestplated Reakmor, her hand leaping for her dagger in uncertainty. That was when she finally passed out.

"I's don't believe it," Yorke muttered behind Logan in amazement. "Reakthi fightin' Reakthi. Who'da thought it?"

Logan squinted his good eye at the chestplated horde, trying to focus on the white and black chestplates of their leaders. Steel flashed as Reakmor Osirik drove his troops forward, pushing their way through weary rogues and merchants to stab at dark-eyed soldiers. Imperator Quarn led his men around the right flank, downing figures in bronze and gold chestplates. It was only the shock of the sudden reinforcements that quelled the joy blooming in Logan's chest. They were doing it! he realized in dumb silence. They were winning! Without magic! Without the Heart! They were winning!

A thunderous bellow of victory went up from the light blue ogre as it hurled a gangly Reakthi in bronze armor into four of its inhuman comrades, and Munuc's people bounded up and down in unconcealed merriment. Mistrust was put aside as the fighters of Eadarus and Debarnian battled alongside the Reakthi of Quarn's fortress, their numbers finally overwhelming the Darkness's soldiers. A pitiful howl went up from the freezing gale as the Sparrillian forces renewed their attack, and the cold chill seemed to vanish from the winds.

The last of Vaugen's Reakthi crumpled to the dirt, and the Darkness fled.

Logan joined in the cheers of triumph.

*   *   *

Imperator Quarn's light blue eyes scanned the battlefield, diffused sunlight streaming in through the treetops. Thick, acrid smoke mushroomed skyward from unnatural fires that still burned, but all else was still. Grey-chestplated Reakthi sat and ate with the rogues and shopkeeps of Sparrill, conversation passing sparsely among them. Monkeylike creatures danced and leapt about the humans, the light blue ogre in their midst. To Munuc's kind, there was little difference between the fighters—those armored or not. All had fought off the impending Darkness, so, therefore, all were to be hailed as friends.

"There is no love between them," Quarn said thoughtfully, watching the warriors, "yet they know better than to let past aggressions come between them and victory. Perhaps it will not be so after Vaugen's defeat, hmmmm?"

Logan shrugged, his own gaze wandering the campsite. It was still hard for the young man to believe that they had defeated the forces Vaugen and the Darkness had sent against them—and he had done it without invoking the magicks of the Bloodstone.

"Last report said the others were headed for Prifrane," Reakmor Osirik proclaimed. "Do we follow?"

The answer was out of Logan's mouth before he knew he was speaking: "Yes."

A silver eyebrow raised on Quarn's forehead. "You sound quite certain of that," he noted. "Any reason?"

The young man got to his feet, hands clamped protectively about the Heart. "Those bastards are going to die," he growled, and stalked away from the black-chestplated Imperator.

A flaring desire for vengeance sparked in Logan, recalling all previous mishaps caused by the conquest-hungry Vaugen and his spellcaster. Now the *Daigread* rituals were over, the young man concluded. Now came the final battle. They weren't playing preliminary games any longer—this was the one that decided it. This was the one that had to end in death—either Logan's or Groathit's. Either way, it would soon be over.

A dark form suddenly matched Logan's stride, and uncertainty flickered in Moknay's grey eyes. "Can we trust them?" he inquired, nodding toward Quarn.

"We have to," Logan replied.

The Murderer nodded curtly. "What about that book? The one Mara said Nightwalker mentioned?"

"We'll get it," Logan snarled with angry conviction. "We'll get it or die."

A grave smirk stretched beneath Moknay's mustache. "You're beginning to sound like me, friend," he observed.

Logan halted. "So?" he demanded.

Moknay shrugged, his smirk vanishing. "I don't know if that's good or bad."

Like a shadow, the Murderer turned away, leaving Logan alone in the center of the camp. *Either way*, the young man's thoughts repeated, *it will soon be over*.

The cold returned to the wind.

·14·

Theft

No feeling of elation accompanied the victory. Despair filled his eyes as Ridglee swept his gaze across the destroyed town of Prifrane, wincing inwardly at the carnage surrounding him. Light flakes of snow drizzled into the village, hissing in protest as they were consumed by the black flames that feasted throughout the town. Limp, lifeless bodies—half-blanketed by snow and ashes—lay about the cobblestone streets.

Darkness roiled overhead in its disembodied state, and soldiers with dark eyes stood like pillars among the dead of Prifrane. Only the hiss of evaporating snowflakes filled the village, and Ridglee threw his gaze farther down the street to the half-burned church that Groathit had made his temporary quarters.

The spellcaster stood on the entrance steps, living blackness radiating from his emancipated form. Ghastly black light from the unnatural fires flickered eerily off the church's facade, painting shadows on the marble wall behind Groathit and Vaugen. In the gloom of the snowfall—and the waver of black light—the Imperator's distorted features matched the foul smirk drawn on the sorcerer's face.

Groathit waved a bony hand at the conquered village, blackness forking from his fingertips. "Well, my Imperator," he leered, and the title was an insult, "did I not say that Prifrane would be ours?"

Imperator Vaugen nodded, dull grey eyes hard and cold with lack of emotion.

"And did I not say that Plestenah would also fall?" Groathit smugly inquired.

Vaugen nodded again.

The wizard's smile widened, drawing the flesh taut around his skull. "Then you know that Matthew Logan will soon be here—as I foresaw."

"In the meantime, you waste precious time on your petty vendettas," the Imperator rasped, a sneer drawing across half of his lips.

"Nothing I do is petty!" roared Groathit, darkness arcing about him. "*I* conquered this town! *I* conjured the Voices! I shall have my revenge!"

"And what am I to do should Matthew Logan arrive before your return?" Vaugen snarled in question. "Ask him to stay for dinner?"

The spellcaster's skull-like smile returned to his withered features, and blackness spat from his left eye. "In a token of my compassion, I shall leave the Voices' soldiers with you," he offered. "Myself and the Darkness will go after the sorcerer—but that must be now. If I wait, the snows may block my passage."

"And hinder your return," Vaugen added, and neither Groathit nor the nearby Ridglee could tell whether the Imperator sounded pleased or perturbed. Surely, Ridglee mused, there was still a deep hatred between the two men, accented by their mutual descent into madness, yet Vaugen knew he was no match for the Outsider, Matthew Logan. That may have been a glimmer of fear in the Imperator's grey eyes, yet Ridglee could no longer be certain. The soldier had given up trying to read the expressions of the insane.

Groathit stepped away from the church and out into the streets, the falling snow snapping into blossoms of steam as they touched the nimbus of energy encircling him. "One last bit of advice," the spellcaster informed Vaugen, and the tone of his voice reeked of threats. "I have ordered two men to guard this building. They will obey no other command but that—and they will not allow anyone to enter . . . not even you. I suggest you do not try to attempt either."

Ridglee's eyebrows raised in wonder as the wizard stalked away from the partially destroyed church. The spellcaster's threat had been so menacingly worded that one would think Groathit's very lifeforce had been stored inside—and, with the extent of magicks the sorcerer now possessed, who was to disbelieve? Ridglee turned to watch the spellcaster stride toward the northern end of town and the Hills of Sadroia.

The snowfall grew heavier, yet the fires of Prifrane would not burn out.

* * *

Logan huddled closer to Mara, the blanket draped over them keeping the rain off their heads. The forest was filled with the heavy patter of raindrops, accompanied by the low wail of the polar winds. Through the infinite darkness of the unnatural night, Logan could barely make out those clustered around him, shoulders hunched and cloaks and cowls drawn up tightly about their necks.

"How much further?" the young man queried.

"Two or three days, perhaps," Imperator Quarn answered, recognizable in the dark only by his silver hair. "It depends on how long this storm lasts."

"We were making good time until the rains started," Osirik put in.

Thromar's voice sounded from the darkness: "I doubt the Reakthi whoresons are going anywhere . . . Vaugen's Reakthi whoresons, I mean. Not yours."

A faint smirk spread across Quarn's lips. "Understood, Rebel," he nodded.

"So wot's the plan?" Yorke asked on Logan's left.

Logan bit his lower lip in thought. "I'm not sure yet," he truthfully answered. "We need to find out more about this book that Nightwalker mentioned. Somehow we've got to get our hands on that before we attack."

"Why?" Roshfre questioned. "Why not attack and get the book then?"

" 'Cause we don't know where it is," Logan told her. "For that fact, we don't even know *what* it is. All we know is that Nightwalker said it was important to get."

"So you do everything this Nightwalker says?" asked Servil.

"You never met him," Mara told the scout lightly. "If he ever came out and said something in simple terms, you did it immediately and never asked any questions."

The humor in the priestess's voice sounded strained to Logan's ears and he threw her a swift glance through the unnatural night. She had taken Barthol's death extremely hard at first, but suddenly her grief had vanished to be replaced by an unusual—and most probably faked—lightheartedness, almost as if she didn't want anyone to see her sorrow. Deep down, however, Logan could still feel the pain of Barthol's death eating her away from the inside, and he wished she wouldn't torture herself that way.

"So what do you suggest?" came Moknay's voice as the Murderer himself was all but invisible in the rain and darkness.

Logan sensed the query was directed at him. "I'm not sure," he repeated.

"I could always enter Vaugen's camp under the pretense of friendship," suggested Quarn. "Pretend I was interested in joining forces . . . that sort of thing. Find out where this book was kept."

"Not on your life," Thromar growled suspiciously. "What's to stop you from actually joining forces?"

"Damn your thick hide, Rebel!" Osirik snarled back. "If it weren't for us, you'd be fodder for the carrioncrows."

"Hah!" Thromar barked. "The day I admit to needing a Reakthi's help is the day I die."

"That can be arranged," the Reakmor threatened, and Logan heard more than one weapon start to slide free of its sheath.

"Enough!" Moknay snapped at Thromar.

"That will do!" Quarn told Osirik.

The Reakmor and the Rebel grumbled in response at the double orders, fixing mistrusting glares on the other through the storm.

"Stupid, it is," came the high-pitched cackle of Dirge's voice. "Both of you are the same. I can see that, but, then again, I *am* a necromage, eh? Yet both of you are made up of the same parts— the same body magicks. Why treat one another like different creatures?"

There was no answer from the surrounding darkness, and Logan could almost feel the tension brewing among the raindrops. Why treat one another like different creatures? the young man thought. The same reason the people of my world treat one another like different creatures . . . bigotry and racism. As Quarn had said, there was no love lost between the Sparrillians and the Reakthi . . . hell, Logan himself didn't like the chestplated bastards! But Quarn and his men were different. They had helped the young man defeat the Worm and had now rescued his forces, dispelling the need for magic. Nonetheless, ever since their march toward Prifrane began, the unease and decades-long rivalry returned. Perhaps the men of Logan's ragtag army gradually forgot the fact that these chestplated soldiers had helped them win a decisive battle, and the Reakthi were beginning to notice this simmering mistrust and react with an unfriendly suspicion of their own.

Moknay's calm voice broke the stillness. "I don't think it would be a good idea to try to fool Vaugen," he said, responding to

Quarn's suggestion. "Those shreds of Darkness that controlled the bodies went somewhere, and I'd wager it was back to Groathit."

"So he would know I had helped you." The silver-haired Imperator nodded. "What other alternatives do we have, then?"

"I can sneak in myself and find out," Moknay replied. "Maybe even steal the damn thing."

Terror exploded in Logan's breast. "No way!" he argued, his concern for the steely-eyed Murderer causing a cold lump of fear to settle in his stomach. "It's too dangerous."

"We have no other choice," Moknay evenly responded.

"We can do what Roshfre said," the young man sputtered. "Attack and hope we find it."

"I don't make it a habit to hope," said a grim Scythe.

"According to Nightwalker, too much is riding on this to leave it up to hope," Moknay remarked. "Besides, half of this little army of ours is made up of men and women whose primary trade is stealing. What could go wrong?"

"The same thing that killed Marcos," Xile retorted, and Logan was grateful for the backup. "We're forgetting that the Darkness can see through tricks that the Reakthi on the ground can't—like at Plestenah."

"So we're back to attacking and hoping we can find it," Roshfre shrugged.

Moknay nodded through the gloom. "So it seems," he gravely replied. "Not that I like it."

"Maybe it will not be so," Servil stated. "Maybe once we arrive, the situation at Prifrane will be to our advantage."

"I hope so," Mara said.

"I don't hope," Scythe reminded them.

Even if there was any sunlight the following day, it could not push its way past the impenetrable blockade of stormclouds filling the sky. Rain still spilled lightly from above, and the arctic wind howled mournfully in between the droplets. Water trickled down Logan's face, and the young man shivered as the icy bite of the wind swept past him. Mara clung tightly to his waist, teeth chattering as their mount plodded slowly through the mud. Around them, their impromptu army marched on, their pace slow and tedious through the rain and mire.

Thromar pulled Smeea to a halt, a meaty hand signaling the others to stop.

Moknay's gloved hands leapt to his daggers. "What is it?"

The Rebel cocked his head to one side. "Heard something," he reported, then went silent.

Mud squished as the large fighter dismounted, his shoulder-length mane of hair plastered to his scalp. Without a word, Moknay followed, his cape fluttering in the cold wind. Quiet encompassed the ragtag troops, and Logan strained to pick out the sounds Thromar had detected. Only the constant patter of raindrops reached the young man's ears, and his halved vision could not hope to pierce the curtain of rain and foliage around him.

A sudden plop that was unrhythmically out of sequence with the rainfall alerted Logan's senses, and he slid cautiously off his horse. The light blue ogre was instantly at the young man's heels, its brutish face screwed up at the sudden silence of the men. Mara started to follow, but a curt warning glance from Logan stopped her. He would be all right with the ogre behind him, his gaze assured her. Nonetheless, the priestess unslung her Binalbow and waited.

"What is it?" Roshfre hissed.

Dirge jerked his head in birdlike fashion to the left. "Men," the necromage said, not bothering to keep his voice low. "To the south. About a score of them."

Thromar withdrew his heavy blade. "Friendly or unfriendly?" he demanded.

The gangly necromage shrugged with his whole upper body. "I can't tell that from just hearing their heartbeats, now can I, eh?"

"Good enough," the Rebel responded. "At least we know what's out there. Friend-Logan, Moknay, Roshfre: Follow me."

"Hey!" Osirik protested. "I thought Logan was in charge."

Logan blinked at the Reakmor. "Right," he remembered. The young man nodded his head in Thromar's direction. "Thromar, Moknay, Roshfre: Come with me."

Replacing Thromar at the head of the group, Logan carefully stepped into the shrubbery. Accumulated moisture pelted the young man from the trees and bushes and soaked through his already damp sweatsuit. The heavy steps of the ogre behind him helped quell his anxiety, and Logan peered curiously around a tree. Another mud-muted footstep sounded somewhere ahead of him.

"Be careful, friend-Logan," Thromar warned.

Placing his hand on his rain-slicked hilt, Logan took another delicate step into the muck. He could hear more noises over the wet slap of raindrops, and the polar breeze threw the warm, hearty smell of stew in the young man's direction.

The abrupt move at Logan's back should have reminded the young man of the inevitable reaction.

"Fooooood!" the light blue ogre bellowed, thundering forward through the mire and almost knocking Logan down.

Frantically, the young man tried to stop the hunger-driven ogre but only managed to grab one brawny arm. With a surprised yelp, Logan was jerked off his feet and carried forward by the light blue creature, mud splashing about its enormous feet. No wonder the ogre was still alive! Logan realized in bewilderment. It had probably outrun Vaugen's troops and hidden safely in the forest. For all its bulk, Logan had underestimated the light blue creature's incredible stamina and speed.

The light blue ogre unexpectedly skidded to a halt in the mire, twisting its squarish head to peer at the twenty or so men leaping to their feet in surprised response. Swords glittered with rainwater, and Logan released his grasp on the ogre, trying not to show the terror that scrawled on his face. Oh, shit! the young man swore to himself. Guardsmen!

A smile of pleased shock registered on one of the uniformed Guards. "Bless me backside!" he exclaimed. "The Outsider!"

A younger Guard behind him placed a restraining hand on his companion's shoulder, sheathing his own blade. "Put away your sword, Tarttan," he instructed. "They'll be no fighting among friends."

Mud squished beside Logan as Moknay and the others caught up with the ogre and the young man. "You're no friend of mine," the Murderer sneered, and the burning hatred in his eyes startled Logan. It took a moment before the young man remembered the Guards had so dubbed Moknay "the Murderer."

"By Harmeer's War Axe!" Tarttan blurted. "The Murderer *and* the Rebel! You're not going to let them just walk away, Aelkyne! Please, tell me you're not!"

The sandy-haired Aelkyne grinned beneath his beard, patting his companion on the back. "Of course not, Tarttan," he responded, taking a muddy step toward Logan. "I'm going to offer them something to eat. I was beginning to think we were the only living things left."

Logan felt Roshfre's eyes on him. "He seems to know you," the redhead noted.

"As well they should," Moknay growled, daggers ready. "Fat old Mediyan sent every single man in Sparrill out after Logan and ourselves."

"And then some," Aelkyne added. He lifted the spoon out of the pot of stew. "Sure you won't have some? It's not much on taste, but it'll quiet the monsters in your belly."

A sudden burst of recognition hit Logan upside the head and he blinked his good eye at the sandy-haired youth. When trying to get the Jewel to the Smythe, Logan had been captured by a troop of Guardsmen. He would never have succeeded in completing his journey unless a band of Reakthi and the understanding ear of a young Guardsman hadn't have intervened. So this was the same young soldier . . . But he had hardly been a commander when Logan had last seen him. How was it he now ordered other men obviously of higher rank?

For the first time, Logan looked at the other Guardsmen. Blood-soaked bandages covered most of them, and the weary, pale faces reminded the young man all too much of the sorry state of his own army after their defeat at Plestenah. Only Aelkyne appeared to be uninjured, and perhaps that was where his sudden rise in rank came from.

The ogre stepped around Logan and approached the stew and the young Guardsman. Eagerly, the light blue creature took the offered spoon and inhaled the steaming food. Moknay, Roshfre, and Thromar watched with apprehension as Logan took a step closer, his wonder aroused by the injured Guardsmen around him. No wonder Aelkyne refused to capture the young man and his friends—none of his men would be capable.

"What happened?" Logan asked in puzzlement.

Aelkyne forced a laugh. "We used to number close to fifty men," he stated, "before those black-eyed Reakthi ran into us. Absolutely slaughtered us. Cut us down to half our forces before we even realized we were being attacked."

"Just like that?"

"Just like that," Aelkyne agreed.

Logan scanned the pale-faced men once more. "Any idea why?"

"I think because we were in their way," guessed Aelkyne with half a shrug. "Imogen knows we stayed well away from the others."

"Others?" Thromar interrogated. "There were others?"

"Caught sight of them heading west," Aelkyne replied.

The black-bearded Tarttan grabbed the younger Guard by an arm. "These are enemies to the Throne," he barked. "Sworn outlaws by proclamation of the King. Why are you helping them, Aelkyne?"

Aelkyne turned on his comrade and his friendly, smiling facade crumbled. "Because there probably isn't a throne or King left, damn you!" he shouted. "We saw what happened to our own forces! None of our messages are being returned! Doesn't that tell you something, Tarttan? Doesn't that give you some kind of clue as to what's been happening? Have you ever known Commander Eldath *not* to respond to a message even if it's just to correct the damn spelling?"

The larger Guard went silent, the expression stretched on his face reflecting the grief he had tried to hide. Logan watched in a hushed awe, recognizing the despair and sorrow that had accompanied his own troops after their retreat from Plestenah. Was it very long ago that we had to face facts just as harsh? the young man asked himself. Was it any easier once knowing you were fighting alone with no celebration feast to mark your victory? This war Groathit had started involved so much more than just possession of the land—it involved the existence of everything related within the Wheel's spin, and such simple things as homeland and separate towns had to be looked over. It had to be understood that such minor things would be undoubtedly lost in such a Cosmic fray.

Real happy endings only occurred in the movies.

Logan hardly realized he had reached out a reassuring hand and touched Aelkyne's shoulder until the contact shattered his thoughts. "There's still a chance," the young man said.

"Still a chance for what?" Aelkyne bitterly responded. "To stop them? How? I'm sure not even the infamous Outsider, Rebel, and Murderer could stop such a horror. Not even with our help."

"Is that an offer?" Logan queried.

A perplexed look crossed Aelkyne's features. "They've killed my friends and march toward my homeland," the Guard answered solemnly. "If I thought there was any way of stopping them, I would gladly help."

"First Reakthi and now Guardsmen," Thromar muttered unhappily. "At the rate we're going, there's not going to be anybody left to fight *against*!"

They had no range of emotions or instincts, Ridglee noticed, watching the dark-eyed soldiers stanced about the ruined town of Prifrane. Even the body that used to be Ithnan's lacked the basic responses that had made him human. It was as if the young soldier had died and had left behind some withering imposter who neither smiled nor frowned. Perhaps the Darkness felt it unnecessary to manipulate the facial muscles to express human emotions, yet these warriors also lacked the basic battle senses a Reakthi spent over half his life learning and perfecting. While Ridglee was able to sense an impending trap, or judge an opponent with a wary eye, the Darkness failed to do either. Maybe, like expressions, it was an unnecessary task for the Voices to perform, but the usage of these skills, Ridglee knew, could change the outcome of a battle.

For example, Ridglee had felt invisible eyes watching him. Not the same preternatural terror that sparked his brain when the Darkness loomed overhead, or when the Voices' soldiers glanced expressionlessly in his direction. It was more a military reaction to a hidden enemy—a gentle paranoia that whispered to the Reakthi that spies lurked on the outskirts of the conquered town; the inhuman soldiers betrayed no such feelings.

Nonetheless, Ridglee did not bother to bring his war-trained instincts to Vaugen's attention. Excluding the Imperator himself, Ridglee was now the last man in Prifrane to retain possession of his humanity, and he no longer cared what happened to himself or those around him.

The beings surrounding him were no longer Reakthi—and, perhaps, neither was he.

Logan nervously fidgeted with the buttons on his watch as he tried to ignore the freezing gusts of wind that swept down from the snow-capped Hills. Clusters of men grouped around the young man in small circles, each to their respective classes. On Logan's right sat a group of Quarn's Reakthi, behind them a gathering of Guardsmen; to Logan's left a handful of Eadarus's rogues huddled together, and near them sat some of Debarnian's fighters. At least no serious fights had broken out, Logan thankfully mused. Aside from an assortment of unfriendly glares, all four groups knew they needed the others—however distasteful that may have seemed.

The shrubbery rustled against the arctic wind, and Servil quietly stepped into the camp, his long hair sprinkled with snowflakes. Nearly indistinguishable from the shadows, and outlined only by the light carpet of snow, Moknay stalked behind the scout. Thromar strode at their backs as they approached Logan.

The members of Logan's army all turned to watch.

"Wot's the news?" Yorke asked from the Eadarus section.

"Both good and bad," Moknay responded, eyes flickering in the snow's reflective glare. "The Darkness is not at Prifrane."

"Is that the good part or the bad part?" Osirik wanted to know from Quarn's area.

"Both," the Murderer answered bluntly. "If it's not there, we can launch the sneak attack we were hoping for—but, since it's not there, we can assume that Groathit's not there either."

"So where did he go?" Roshfre wondered from her own group. "He certainly didn't head eastward; we would have seen him."

"He's a sorcerer," Servil reminded the redhead. "He can go anywhere he damn well wishes."

Logan felt his hopes crumble. "And wherever he went, he probably took the book with him," the young man sneered.

Logan cast his single-eyed gaze downward and stared darkly at his watch. Living, throbbing blackness radiated from the timepiece and cast an ominous shadow across his features. It wasn't fair, the young man concluded. They had come so far and been through so much to find absolutely nothing at the end of their destination. It was like following a treasure map to the X and then discovering there was only an empty chest buried in the sand.

"There's something I don't understand, though," Servil admitted. "There are still soldiers in the town."

"So?" Xile queried.

"So," Servil went on, "the town was destroyed. They can't be protecting a destroyed town."

"No, indeed," agreed Quarn. "If these were human soldiers, I might think they were establishing a foothold—but Prifrane is hardly an advantage, militarily. The closeness of the Hills offers some sanctuary for a northerly retreat, but also leaves the town wide open to an attack from above."

"So what were they doing?" Aelkyne puzzled.

"We guessed they were waiting," Moknay put in.

"Waiting for what?" Fjorm asked from the Debarnian group. "They've got all the men they're going to get."

Mara jerked her head up in comprehension. "They're waiting for Groathit to return!" she exclaimed.

"My thoughts exactly," Thromar nodded, wiping snow from his beard. "If we can strike before he gets back, we can take the town and give that scumcaster the surprise of his life when he returns."

"*If* he returns," quipped Scythe.

"I see no reason why he shouldn't," Moknay returned. "After all, the Voices can't do anything without physical forms—unless Groathit's found some way of using their energies himself."

"That would be madness," Dirge chirped from the darkness. "To attempt such a mastery over magicks beyond the Force of the Wheel would certainly consume him . . . if not in body, then in mind. Only a man of unshaking bravery or utmost stupidity would dare try such a thing."

A grim smirk crossed Logan's face as he listened to the necromage, recalling a similar comment made by Halette before the ritual of *Daigread* had been mentioned. Maybe bravery or stupidity did choose the course of many people's lives, but that had not been the case when Logan had been in Eadarus. What had driven the young man to risk his life by defying Roshfre and accepting *Daigread* was his desperate need to gather an army and stop Groathit—and the young man knew that same drive pushed the Reakthi spellcaster deeper into the Darkness.

Sunlight pierced the misty curtain of falling snow, and Logan squinted his good eye at the remains of Pifrane. Burned and ravaged buildings stood out like charred corpses beneath the white covering of snow, and hazy shapes and silhouettes stood like pillars in Prifrane's streets. At first, Logan couldn't understand why anybody would have columns in the middle of the road until one of the pillars cocked its head, and blackness flared from its empty sockets.

"You see?" Servil whispered, and his voice was no louder than the moan of the wintry wind. "The Darkness is gone."

"Wonderful," Scythe impatiently sneered. "When do we attack?"

"Wait a bit," Yorke informed his companion. The rogue pointed with his broken-wristed hand, and Logan tried hard to follow its defined point. "Look there."

A gloved finger stroked his mustache as Moknay said, "You're right."

His uncovered eye narrowed, Logan was unable to spot anything out of the ordinary. Fortunately for him, he did not have to admit to his inability to see.

"Right about what?" Aelkyne wondered, squinting through the snowfall.

"Two soldiers posted outside a church," Moknay explained.

Roshfre raised her eyebrows, her cold, blue eyes narrowed. "Guards?"

The Murderer nodded. "Could be."

"Guards for what?" Osirik blinked.

Yorke gave the Reakmor a gaping grin. "Fer th' book?" he suggested.

Thromar growled uneasily. "It would be too much to hope for," he snarled. "Maybe it's prisoners or booty."

"You're thinking on the wrong scale, Rebel," Quarn corrected the fighter. "Vaugen and Groathit are no longer interested in mere conquest. They want nothing short of the utter annihilation of Sparrill."

Grey eyes flashing, Moknay threw a swift glance at the men behind him. "Dirge," the Murderer ordered through clenched teeth. "Get over here."

The gaunt necromage pushed his way through the troops to the forest's edge and stood behind the dark-clad outlaw. Questioningly, Logan looked first at Dirge, then at Moknay, then swung his blue eye toward Prifrane.

Moknay looked away from the necromage. "You can detect heartbeats, right?" he demanded. "Can you tell if there's anyone inside that Church?"

Dirge bobbed his head up and down enthusiastically, his face lighting up like an eager child's. "Oh, yes! Most certainly!" he declared.

Thromar winced at the exclamation. "Keep your voice down," he snapped, "and just do it."

Dirge's frantic nodding trailed off, and the wild eyes gradually closed. A few beads of perspiration formed along the lean necromage's balding brow as he concentrated, and Logan could almost see the invisible strands of energy that must be flowing out from the magic-user's body. Abruptly, Dirge's eyes snapped open, and a look of confusion filled his features.

"Most odd," he muttered softly to himself.

"What is it?" Mara asked. "Is there someone inside?"

Dirge blinked the wonder out of his gaze. "Hmmmm? Oh, no! No one inside. In fact, there's no one in the village at all—no one save those soldiers and two men."

"Two men?" echoed Logan.

The necromage nodded. "I'm picking up two heartbeats," he explained. "One near the western edge of town, the other to the south. The soldiers, as you know, don't technically have heartbeats, but I can still sense them. Any living thing—magically animated or not—is not beyond my powers."

Osirik glanced at his Imperator. "Two heartbeats?" the Reakmor mumbled. "Vaugen and Groathit?"

Quarn shrugged, fixing his light blue eyes on Logan. Instantly, the young man could feel other gazes falling on him, and the responsibility that accompanied those looks felt like heavy weights that would crush him into the snow-dusted earth. Imploringly, Logan directed his sight toward Thromar and Moknay.

"I've got a feeling that whatever's in that church could help us," the Murderer mused out loud. "Logan, I'd like to take Xile and Scythe and find out."

Logan blinked in surprise. What the hell was Moknay asking permission for . . . ?

Realization hit the young man, and he nodded silently to himself. To the differing factions of his army, Logan was the only one they'd jointly follow—Reakthi wouldn't follow Guardsmen, and Guardsmen wouldn't follow rogues, and rogues wouldn't follow townsfolk, and townsfolk wouldn't follow Reakthi. Nonetheless, all of them had placed some degree of trust in Logan and—no matter how unsettled that made the young man feel—it was up to him to keep the peace in his own forces so they could launch their attack on Vaugen's.

Logan nodded once at Moknay, hoping the Murderer knew what he was doing.

"We'll charge them from here," Thromar suddenly stated, eyes locked on the town. As Logan's tactician, the Rebel had authority the Murderer did not. "That way Moknay can get into the town safely from the west."

"They're mostly new shells," Dirge responded in warning. "It will be fighting like in Plestenah."

Logan swallowed hard, forcing himself to speak regardless of the anxiety burning in his throat. "No, it won't," he said. "If Moknay does find the book, we can pull out as soon as they're clear."

"We'll enter and exit from the west since all their attention will be on the east," Moknay decided, one hand on his strap of daggers. "We'll signal you once we're out—with or without the book."

Scythe flashed the troops a reckless smirk. "With or without our lives," he added.

An icy shiver forked up Logan's back as the three cut-throats vanished into the foliage. The young man frowned as he peered through the snow toward Prifrane—here we go again.

"Forward!" Thromar thundered, and steel slid free of leather all along the rows of fighters.

Logan jerked his own weapon free and flinched as the bellowing voice of the light blue ogre sounded close to his ear: "Fiiiiiight!"

What followed were blurred moments of confusion as the young man joined in with the crazed rush toward Prifrane, sword flailing above his head. The next thing he knew, blackness confronted him and dark-eyed Reakthi blocked his way. Red flamed from around Logan's blade as the young man cut in at the nearest soldier and drew a bloodless gash across the creature's throat. *No horses and acting as decoys,* the young man thought despairingly to himself. *I only hope Moknay knows what he's doing.*

But—like Scythe—Logan was beginning to see the futility of hoping and feel the hurt of murdered dreams. Perhaps it was better just to estimate the best and the worst of outcomes and be satisfied with that, the young man concluded. *Okay, that means either we get the book and win, or we die.*

Moknay better know what he's doing.

Scythe ducked a snow-spattered branch without missing a step. "What's your plan?" he asked the grey-caped form ahead of him.

Moknay's expression was grim. "I don't have one."

The rogue faltered. "What?" he blurted. "What do you mean, you don't have one?"

"Just what I said," the Murderer sneered, a flash of grey among the white of winter. "I don't have one."

Bandana snapping, Xile added: "Moknay's notorious for his gift of improvisation."

"Gift of . . . ?" sputtered Scythe. "Look, I don't care if you're Agellic himself, I'm not following you in there unless we've a plan."

Moknay's sprint slowed to a brisk jog as the Murderer rounded the western corner of the village. Eyes flickering cautiously across the landscape, he could still see the steeple of the church closer to the eastern edge of the small town, and there also appeared to be more soldiers here. His mustache twitched as his upper lip rose in a perturbed sneer.

"All right," the Murderer snarled in Scythe's direction, "here's my plan. We get in, get to the church, and get out." A villainous stare fell on the rogue. "Satisfied?"

Scythe knew better than to challenge Moknay's glare. "Sounds good to me," he sheepishly replied, shrugging.

Xile half grinned. "Do we go in together or one at a time?" he asked the Murderer.

Moknay scanned the destroyed village, watching quietly as the dark-eyed Reakthi started a slow, unconcerned march toward the sounds of battle to the east. Dark energies sparked from their hands as the chestplated warriors turned down the cobblestone streets and vanished from view.

"Together," Moknay answered Xile.

Like three dark ghosts, the trio of outlaws glided into Prifrane. Unnatural shadows from the wisps of blackness that lingered in the afternoon sky aided the three as they slid from shadow to shadow, only the silver of their weapons betraying their presence. A small group of soldiers passed close to the bandits—and one cast crackling eyes in their direction, yet continued on. Swiftly, Moknay sprinted across the street and darted around a half-burned hostel. Steel blazed in his eyes as he spied the church a few yards to the east, men and Voices battling close by.

"The guards are still there," Xile noted with surprise. "Whatever's inside must be damn important."

"All the better to get in there," Scythe remarked.

A faint smile flickered briefly across Moknay's features. "There's no one at the back door," he said with a smirk.

"How do you know there's a back door?" inquired Xile. "You don't strike me as a religious man, Murderer."

"I had a close friend who was," Moknay replied, and Scythe thought he heard remorse color the words.

"So all we've got to do is sneak in the back?" the rogue questioned. "Dung bugs! You'd have thought it was going to be more exciting than that."

Moknay threw the cutthroat a sardonic look. "You could always hope things pick up."

Questioningly, Ridglee stepped out of the tavern he had been using as his own quarters and surveyed the town. There was no mistaking the sounds of combat that rang from the eastern edge of Prifrane, and the Reakthi smiled smugly to himself. Someone *had* been watching the town, he realized, and, while he had suspected as much, the Darkness had let themselves be ambushed.

Ridglee released the grasp that had so instinctively attached itself to his sword's hilt. This was no longer his fight, he decided. These were no longer the reasons he had sailed from his homeland. The insanity of Groathit and Vaugen had warped those noble ideals—transformed them into hideous mockeries of everything Ridglee stood for.

The Reakthi way was violent—they were a fighting people, living in a harsh land where only the strong survived and the ruthless flourished. But this . . . this horror that the disfigured Imperator and maddened spellcaster had unleashed went beyond those aggressive traits. It went beyond the honor of battle and the conquest that proved Reakthi superiority—it threatened to destroy everything Ridglee understood and appreciated about life—and it had started by transforming the soldier's friends and comrades into lifeless, emotionless husks of sorcery.

Trained eyes caught the sudden blur of motion to his right, and Ridglee swung about. Three men ducked around the corner of a building, all garbed in clothing so dark that the Reakthi had at first thought them pure manifestations of Darkness returning without Groathit. A curious furrow creased Ridglee's brow as he stared after the trio, wondering what damage three lone men could do while armies clashed to the east.

Intrigued, Ridglee stepped stealthily after the men, hand on his sword.

"Keep your head down!" Logan heard someone yell, and the young man narrowly ducked a shaft of howling blackness.

Sword and dagger gleaming crimson, Mara fought her way to Logan's side. Snow sprinkled her long hair, and a bloody gash was torn down her left arm. "Matthew!" she cried. "We can't hold them!"

Logan gritted his teeth as he cleaved open the skull of a soldier in front of him. "I know that!" he shouted back; he barely avoided the returning swing. "But we don't have to!"

"What?" the priestess called, both surprised by what she heard and wondering whether she heard correctly at all.

"We need to keep them distracted," Logan explained. "If we get pushed back, we get pushed back. That still keeps them away from Moknay."

An explosion of dark magicks screamed on Logan's right, throwing men and rubble skyward. Dust and gore joined the drizzle of snow as Logan continued hacking his way through the soldiers of the Voices, feeling the strength drain from his muscles as the hope had drained from his spirit.

"Come on, Moknay," the young man murmured desperately to himself. "Hurry up."

* * *

Uncontrolled fury raged in the dull grey eyes as Imperator Vaugen clutched his sword in his right hand. His maimed left hand curled into a gnarled fist as the disfigured commander turned away from the battle raging down the street and fairly shook with anger.

"The impudent worms!" Vaugen cursed, ire filling his face with red. "How dare they attack me now! How dare they turn Reakthi against Reakthi!" A mindless smile tried to spread itself across the Imperator's fused lips. "But vengeance shall be mine," he chuckled wildly to himself. "Gloat while you may, little sorcerer, but—while you waste your time and magicks in the Hills—I shall be the one to slay Matthew Logan."

Sunlight flashed off the ebony chestplate as Vaugen spun about on his heel and marched defiantly toward the fighting. A sudden flicker of movement from the church caught the Imperator's eye, and he spied the guards leave their posts to halt the advance of the enemy who had drawn too close. A nefarious scowl crossed half of the commander's features as he redirected his course and stomped for the church, deciding his vengeance could wait on Matthew Logan and be transposed instead to the vile little spellcaster who had dared refuse to carry out Vaugen's orders.

Shadows greeted them on the inside as Moknay slipped through the doorway, his boots treading noiselessly on the marble flooring. Xile and Scythe trailed in like silence, all three alert and wary. A few beams of sunlight slanted in from shattered windows and the half-demolished roof, casting intense spots of illuminance that filled the church with golden light. Some snow had made its way inside, and the wind screamed softly as it passed through the broken windows, wounding itself on the shards of glass.

Xile winced as the smell from a decaying corpse lying near the front doors reached his nose, and he cast an unpleasant look at the cadaver. It seemed to be the body of a priest, robe awash with dried blood. A look of shock and horror was on the man's face, frozen into an eternal mask. Behind him, on a podium splattered by blood, rested a thick book.

"Moknay," Xile rasped, tapping the Murderer's shoulder.

Moknay nodded curtly, striding down the marble aisle and inspecting the leatherbound volume. Gloved hands flipped open to yellowed pages, and alien words came into sight.

A primeval fear seeped into the Murderer's system. "This doesn't belong here," he declared.

"Is it the right one?" Scythe wanted to know.

"We won't know that until we can find someone to translate it," Moknay replied, shutting the book and dissolving the unease its otherworldly print had caused.

"Translate it?" Xile wondered. "Where the *Deil* are we going to find time to look for a translator?"

Moknay tucked the book under one arm and began back down the aisle. "We'll have to make time," he retorted.

Without another word, the trio bolted back toward the exit. A muffled explosion sounded from outside the church as Scythe flung open the back door. An unexpected shriek of rage and fury took all three men by surprise, and none of them saw the flicker of steel until it was too late.

Blood splashed the church door as Vaugen's sword plunged through Xile's chest and pierced Moknay's arm behind him. With a painful shout, the Murderer stumbled backwards, almost dropping the book. Steel screeched against bone as the Imperator drew his sword backwards, ripping the blade free of Xile's corpse and catching Scythe across the face. Crimson blurred as the rogue crashed to the streets, his lifefluid staining the snow.

"Maggots!" Vaugen shrieked. "Victory is mine! Vengeance is mine! You shall not deprive me of what I deserve! Laugh on, little sorcerer, as I take the life of Moknay the Murderer!"

The Imperator's bloodied sword descended.

·15·

Spy

Now began the culmination of months of searching—the final few moments of warfare that would satiate the revenge flaring behind the ebony chestplate. With a twisted smile, Imperator Vaugen looked down in disdain at the wounded Murderer tensed before him, their grey eyes locked in a bond of mutual hatred. Wind and snow shrieked as the Imperator's sword sliced downward, flashing for the outlaw's skull. Warm blood spilled down the weapon's blade and onto Vaugen's maimed and scorched hands, and a wild mirth bloomed in the Imperator's eyes. Vaugen knew there was no escape for the man called Moknay the Murderer. All possible routes to safety were out of reach—barred by the descending blade—and even the Murderer's far-famed speed and agility would not save him from at least suffering a wound on his leg to add to the wound on his arm.

Vaugen's blade bit deeply into the Darklight grimoire as Moknay dodged to one side, thrusting out the book to take the brunt of the Imperator's attack. An animallike yowl of rage tore from Vaugen's lips as he jerked his sword free and swung again, his fury growing to intolerable levels. This was his moment of triumph! Why was this man not dying?

"You will not escape me!" Vaugen roared out loud. "I will have my revenge!"

Moknay half staggered, half jumped to one side, the Darklight volume still in his hands. The Reakthi sword slashed the air at his back, and Moknay felt the fabric of his cape tug backwards. The sudden jerk unbalanced the Murderer, and he threw himself forward in a desperate somersault.

Vaugen leapt, sword high above his head. The outlaw was down and still without a weapon in his hands—too concerned with the

spellcaster's stupid little book to defend himself. It was time for
him to die!

A grey boot lashed out and caught Vaugen on the chestplate,
momentarily knocking the wind from his lungs and pushing him
back a step. The Reakthi sword almost fell from the Imperator's
maimed hand as he groped frantically for his balance, righting
himself and allowing the rage and madness possessing him to take
full control. Howling in mindless fury, Vaugen launched himself
at the Murderer, his blood-smeared sword sweeping downward.

Moknay barely rolled out of the way, hearing the wicked stab of
Reakthi steel against cobblestone. Pain flared across his wounded
arm as the grey-eyed outlaw spun to one side, leaping expertly
to his feet, the Darklight volume still clutched to his chest. A
curse slipped from his lips as Moknay realized the mystic tome
prevented him from reaching any of his daggers strapped across
his breast.

An insane wail of rage exploded from Vaugen as the Imperator
lunged again in his wild, madness-induced frenzy. Reakthi steel
ripped the air inches above Moknay's head as the Murderer made
a wild dive downward and to the side, scrambling frantically away
from the church doors. Never before had the outlaw faced such
an unbridled anger as the hatred that flamed in Vaugen's eyes.
Even the mad servant-boy Pembroke had not attacked with such
unrelenting persistence and inhuman speed—although he had certainly come close.

Steel screeched, and Moknay dodged. With a predicting cackle, Vaugen's maimed hand shot out and caught the Murderer a
glancing blow on the shoulder. Agony screamed through Moknay's
wounded arm and tripped him sideways, almost knocking him to
the ground. Cursing, the Murderer barely blocked another blow
from the Imperator with the heavy book in his grasp and sprinted
back three steps.

A smug smile pulled halfway across the Reakthi commander's features. "You cannot escape, Murderer," the Imperator
declared.

A sneer crossed Moknay's lips. "Maybe I'm not trying to," he
snarled, and a grey boot lashed out with lightninglike reflexes.

Vaugen shrieked furiously as the boot slammed into the base of
his wrist, jarring the blood-drenched sword from the Imperator's
grasp. The weapon clattered to the streets with a metallic clap, and
Moknay scrabbled hurriedly backwards. The enraged scream that
followed after the Murderer caught him completely by surprise,

and he whipped around to catch a fleeting glimpse of the man in the ebony armor flinging himself forward, a glittering dagger held in one hand.

Steel flashed; crimson splattered. Twisting awkwardly, Vaugen reeled backwards, an agonized yowl wrenched from his fused lips. In question, Moknay's grey eyes noticed the sudden glimmer of crescent-shaped metal that embedded itself in the Imperator's unarmored arm. An abrupt hand fell upon Moknay's shoulder, and the Murderer wheeled to glare into the harsh green eyes of Scythe.

A smirk blurred by the bloody gash on his cheek spread across the rogue's face.

"I thought you were dead," Moknay admitted.

Scythe shrugged. "I've cut myself worse while shaving." He gave the village a cursory glance. "Might I suggest we depart? We've got what we came for . . ." Delicate fingers touched his wounded cheek. " . . . and then some."

Grey eyes aflame with steely fire, Moknay scanned the town of Prifrane. A single nod answered the rogue's question, and the two outlaws turned in the direction of where the Darkness-endowed troops were steadily pushing back Logan's ragtag forces.

The dying scream of the man on Logan's right sent a shudder of terror through the young man's system as he spun to defend himself, his glimmering Reakthi sword severing the magically swathed fist racing for his head. Flesh gave way before steel, and the flickering hand crashed to the street in a bloodless heap. With draining strength, Logan followed through with his attack, pushing his sword tip through the empty socket of his attacker. Black energy hissed like a perturbed serpent as the weapon drove through the Reakthi's skull, cleaving through bone and finding no brain. Dark power sputtered as the soldier's head practically split down the center, and yet, Logan barely avoided the angry sweep of the creature's left hand.

Mara's sword dismembered the Reakthi's arm in a scarlet glitter of magicks.

"Thanks," Logan breathed.

Mara responded with a curt nod, dark hair flying as she turned to engage another Reakthi. Logan watched her in wonder, sensing that something was wrong with the priestess. Maybe it was still Barthol's death that ailed her, the young man considered, or maybe it was something else. Maybe it was something between the two of them; he couldn't be sure when the girl kept quiet about it. That made things worse than if she just came out and said what was bothering her. After all, it was certainly easy thinking up all sorts of problems when the actual cause may have had nothing to do with the two of them. But how could he be sure unless Mara said something? Until she did, the young man's paranoia would just go on creating more and more possible explanations for the priestess's silence.

Blistering heat from the soul of utter darkness clipped the preoccupied young man across the face, searing his body with fire and ice. With a scream of the dying, Logan pitched backwards, falling away from the groping hand that had struck his cheek. Scalding hot magicks melted through his flesh, and stabbing tendrils of liquid nitrogen speared his brain. So intense was the pain that Logan hardly felt himself crash to the cobblestones or hear Mara cry out his name in concern. For that brief moment, Logan's entire life centered around the seething agony in his cheek and everything else seemed to fade from existence.

The dark-eyed Reakthi advanced on the fallen Logan.

There was a deafening whirl of power, and blood-red light exploded outward from Logan's sword. Snow fizzled into steam as the spiraling shaft of scarlet spumed from the Reakthi steel and slammed through the body of the converging Reakthi. A scream from a hundred thousand whispering voices gripped the city by its foundations as the human shell crumpled inward, trapping and crushing the dark flare within it. Purity roared, and the chestplated soldier disintegrated, leaving behind a small pile of grey-black ashes that joined the snow on the arctic gale.

There was no shade of blackness left.

Gigantic but gentle hands helped Logan to his feet, and the young man turned a blurry eye on the light blue ogre, its brutish face scrunched up in worry. Mara was also at the young man's side, a frightened hand on his arm.

"Matthew," she said, "are you hurt?"

Logan reached up tentative fingers to where he was certain bone showed through the melted and fused skin of his face. His befuddled state of mind amplified when he felt nothing wrong with his features . . . not even the red and blistered mar of a burn.

"I . . ." he sputtered. "What happened?"

"Maaaagic," the ogre breathed in awe, its eyes wide with astonishment.

Mara's hand helped steady the young man's faulty balance. "You destroyed a part of the Darkness," she said. "Matthew, how much magic did you put into our weapons?"

The confusion churning inside him mutated to ire as Logan heard the familiar questions of sorcery directed at him . . . questions that he didn't know the answers to and didn't plan to know. Damn Dirge! the young man swore. He *was* using the magic unconsciously—just as the necromage said he could. How much magic had he put into their weapons? And had he been the one to release that blast? Like during *Daigread* when the ealhdoeg had first attacked? Logan had assumed his sword was acting on its own accord. Damn! Damn! Damn!

The young man's temper dissolved as the rasping death-rattle of the Voices filled the town:

The Purity.
It is here.
It brings banishment.
The stench of banishment.
Destroy it.
Destroy the Purity.
Destroy its Champion.
Destroy Matthew Logan.

Logan tried to suppress the fearful chill that crawled its insectlike way down his spine and sent an icy explosion of terror through his brain. Just the mere mention of his name from the hideous whispering Voices seemed to steal what little strength was left in the young man's body, and the stigmatic inhumanness of the words ignited a natural instinct to run and hide.

Logan trained his good eye on the battle raging around him and noticed how many of the dark-eyed warriors turned on him. With a frantic look toward the town, the young man fixed his single eye on the half-burned church looming ahead of him. As questions of Moknay's progress flashed past his mind, the young man spotted the two dark figures that suddenly bolted around the corner of the structure, blurs of black and grey among the whites of winter. Logan's relief was abrupt, however, as a third form in blackness darted around the church, its Reakthi sword still dripping gore.

Logan momentarily forgot all about the Reakthi menacingly advancing on him and directed all his concern for the fleeing outlaws. "Moknay!" the young man screamed so loudly his throat hurt. "Behind you!"

Regardless, Logan knew he could not be heard.

*   *   *

The crunch of snow underfoot warned Eadarus-trained reflexes, and both Moknay and Scythe dropped to the street. Vaugen's sword screeched overhead, its wielder howling in fury as his wild swing missed both men. Blood still streamed from the Imperator's wounded shoulder, and Scythe's razor-sharp boomerang remained lodged in the Reakthi's flesh. The pain, however, only fueled Vaugen's insanity as he drew back his blade and chopped downward, striking for Moknay's skull.

"He doesn't know when to give up, does he?" Scythe queried, spearing out a leg and catching the Imperator in the kneecap.

A startled shriek ripped from Vaugen's lips as the Reakthi sword leapt like something alive, changing direction in mid-descent and screaming for Scythe. With an exclamation, the rogue hurdled out of the way, wincing as the tip of Vaugen's sword nicked his right leg.

Moknay managed to pull his throwing knife from his belt. "He's mad," the Murderer grimly stated, eyes locked on the slavering Imperator.

"Mad?" echoed Scythe. "I'd say he's pissed."

"Carrion!" Vaugen spat at the pair. "Vengeance is mine! Who has won now, little sorcerer? I have won! *I* have won!"

Blood-streaked steel flared, and Moknay rolled to his feet. As the Murderer cocked back his arm to throw his knife, pain flickered anew in his wound. The three-bladed throwing knife spilled from his hand, and his footing faltered in the snow-covered cobblestones. A wrathful cry of triumph pierced the town of Prifrane as Vaugen's sword slashed downward. The cry turned into a howl of pure rage as Moknay once again deflected the blow with the enormous volume in his hands. Screaming, Vaugen tore his blade downward, jerking the book from Moknay's grasp and ridding the Murderer of his makeshift shield.

Moknay lunged for the Darklight grimoire skittering across the cobblestones.

"No!" Scythe warned. "Don't be a fool!"

Vaugen drew back an arm as the Murderer left himself open to attack.

Steel rang against steel as another Reakthi blade interfered with the Imperator's strike, and Moknay flinched, abruptly realizing the danger he had placed himself in. Grey blurred as the Murderer swerved, leaping to his feet and expertly freeing twin daggers.

Vaugen snarled like a rabid beast, saliva spewing from his fused lips as he turned on his new attacker. Aided by the madness of its wielder, the Imperator's sword pushed past an experienced defense and caught Ridglee in the gut just beneath his golden chestplate. Unexpectedly, grey-gloved hands struck the distracted Vaugen on either side of his neck, driving glimmering red-bladed daggers deep into the Imperator's throat.

Moknay watched with a sneer as Vaugen swayed unsteadily on his feet, hands locked around the golden hilts lodged in his throat. Rivers of crimson babbled from the Imperator's neck and down his ebony chestplate as the insane fury in his dull grey eyes dimmed and went out.

Imperator Vaugen toppled to the street, dead.

Moknay retrieved the Darklight grimoire and turned a curious eye on the dying Reakthi. Already a heavy red stain formed in the snow about the soldier's body, yet the warrior showed no discomfort as he struggled to sit up, one hand clutched around his wounded stomach.

Ridglee peered through eyes bleary with the nearness of death at the grey-eyed man before him. The coppery smell of lifefluid filled the soldier's nostrils, and he knew his life was escaping him as rapidly as the blood that flowed from his body.

The Reakthi managed one last intake of air. "End this madness," Ridglee forced out, his dying voice a whispering plea.

The grave nod from the caped outlaw before him imbued Ridglee with some of the determination burning in the steely-grey eyes, and the Reakthi knew he had done the right thing in blocking his Imperator's swing. Reassured, Ridglee lay back in the snow and closed his eyes.

In time, he no longer felt the cold of winter around him.

A blaring note from a warhorn split the snow-filled air. "The signal!" Thromar roared happily. "I knew that untrustworthy, murderous, conniving bastard wouldn't let us down!"

"A fat lot o' good it'll do us," Yorke frowned from close by, striking continuously at the pressing tide of Reakthi.

"We can break off the attack," the Rebel stated. "Friend-Logan, what do you suggest?"

Logan's glimmering sword drove through an advancing Reakthi and barely pulled out in time to block another on his left. "What do I suggest?" the young man angrily thundered, his strength depleted and his attack fueled by his rage. "Why the hell are you asking me?"

Thromar's blade knocked back two dark-eyed soldiers. "You lead us, friend-Logan," the fighter remarked. "Do we pull back?"

"And go where?" the young man yelled. "We still don't know where Groathit is!"

Furiously, Logan chopped his Reakthi weapon sideways, catching a warrior and knocking it to the ground. There was no way they were going to be able to defeat the forces Groathit had left at Prifrane, the young man knew, but if they retreated they would have lost their last chance and Groathit would be free. Oh, maybe they'd have his book—and possibly a way to even banish the Voices—but the spellcaster himself would still be alive. So long as that happened, there would be nothing to stop the wizard from formulating another attack, and Logan would never get back home. No, Logan had already come to the conclusion that if things were ever going to end, Groathit had to die. So where did that leave him now? Between a rock and a hard place again!

"Ain't gonna make it through this one," Yorke was saying darkly. "Carrioncrows are already watchin'."

Logan ignored the rogue's pessimism and cut down another of the Voices' shells. What to do? What to do? If they retreated, they lost what they fought for: a chance at Groathit. If they stayed, they lost, period. Dammit! They had the book . . . now what?

Logan questioningly scanned the destroyed village with his good eye, frowning at the number of dark-eyed Reakthi that remained. The whole other half of Vaugen's men filled the town, most of them just recently given to the Voices. Maybe if they pulled back, the Reakthi wouldn't follow them. They were, after all, obeying Groathit's order to stay in Prifrane. That meant maybe if the young man and his troops retreated, the inhuman soldiers might not pursue. Not that that was a hundred percent true . . . but there was the chance. That way they could return to their vantage point around the town and wait until Groathit returned. By then, the book Nightwalker had thought so important might have yielded something of some value to them.

Like a depressing specter of death, Logan's eye caught a glimpse of the large, black, hawklike bird Yorke had noted beforehand.

"It's no good," a grim voice sounded behind Logan. "We need a translator."

Logan risked a quick look over his shoulder at the grey-garbed Murderer and the heavy book in his hands. "What language is it in?" he questioned.

Daggers flashing, Moknay shrugged. "Too old to tell even that," he replied. "Nightwalker probably would have known."

"Nightcreeper probably wrote the damn thing!" Thromar snorted unpleasantly.

"What about Quarn?" Logan asked, hopes failing. "He's been studying . . ."

The somber shaking of Moknay's head cut the young man off. "Too old," came the grave answer. "I asked him on the way toward you." A flicker of steel lit the Murderer's eyes. "The only person I knew who could have translated this magical claptrap would have been Barthol."

And Barthol's dead, Logan mused sourly to himself. Great! We've got the book but can't read it and—even if we could— Groathit's not here to use it on! Shit! Why the hell does everything have to happen to me? Why couldn't we just open the damn book to the section on destroying spellcasters, read the damn entry and go home? But noooo! Things have got to be complicated! Things have *always* got to be complicated! Damn! Why the hell would Nightwalker send us after a book that none of us could read?

A sudden gleam of hope twinkled in the young man's blue eye as he looked down at the heavy tome. Wait a minute, he thought. Nightwalker knew he was dying. Why would he tell us about something we couldn't use without him? That just didn't make sense . . . unless there was something Mara had left out when she . . .

Logan spun on the dark-haired woman fighting beside him. There was still a hidden sadness inside her that dampened the glitter of her green eyes, but Logan thought he finally recognized the expression. It was one of uselessness and inadequacy . . . the feelings Logan suffered from when he had first arrived in Sparrill— the way he had felt when constantly blaming himself for the death of Druid Launce. Mara blamed herself for the death of Barthol— or at least her inability to have made things different—and that was why she had retreated in on herself. Her false front of humor had died as the guilt had built, and the return of the ogre had worsened things by making her an unnecessary aid to Logan like when he had approached the Guardsmen's camp. Mara had always known she was outclassed in strength and skill, and her own worth had been sorely in doubt. And now . . . now she was their last chance.

"Mara," Logan inquired, "can you read this?"

The priestess didn't even turn away from the fight. "Probably not," she answered. "If Quarn can't . . ."

"Damn Quarn!" the young man snapped. "You told me yourself the only thing you had that Thromar and Moknay lacked was all the studying you had done! Can you read this?"

Eyes filled with despair glanced briefly at the alien script. "It's too old," she responded, her tone without emotion.

"Look at it, damn you!" Logan howled. "Don't try to hide under all that guilt! *I've* done that too often to let you get away with it!"

A spark of anger erupted in the emerald eyes, and Mara fixed a challenging glare on Logan. Desperation held the young man's one-eyed gaze solid, and the truthfulness in his words broke through Mara's shielding of self-pity and guilt. While the others kept the dark-eyed Reakthi at bay, Mara reached out and took the Darklight grimoire from Moknay's hands.

A thoughtful frown crossed her lips. "It's old, but . . ." Her voice trailed off; she was unable to commit herself.

Logan decapitated a soldier. "But what?" he demanded.

"I might be able to," the priestess said softly, fearing her own ability to fulfill her words.

A secret smile crossed Logan's lips. Too many times he had felt as Mara had—afraid and incapable of much, too scared to give his word loudly. Fears that the young man had discovered he had no time for were now haunting the priestess, and he knew they were as unfounded as his own. Why was it a person doubted their own worth the most even when they had proven time and again that they were worth something? Even Logan . . . yeah, even Matthew Logan himself was capable of doing something right! And, damn the Voices, Groathit was gonna lose!

Logan looked up in defiance at the dark bird perched above the village, and the faint tug of a memory sparked in his mind.

"That's no carrioncrow," the young man abruptly whispered.

A few curious eyes fell upon him.

"It's a spy."

Yorke blinked. "Beg pardon?"

New strength began to flow through Logan's system. "It's one of Groathit's spies," the young man repeated, more sure of it now. "If we catch it, it can tell us where Groathit is."

"It can talk?" Yorke queried in shock.

"The first one could," Moknay answered, nodding approvingly.

Logan started an impulsive advance toward the tree where the dark-feathered creature perched. If Mara could translate the book—and they learned Groathit's location from the spying bird—the young man's ploy might just work. There were still a lot of unknowns at work, but—and Logan couldn't keep the malicious smirk off his face—Logan was an Unbalance . . . and the Unbalance thrived on unknowns.

The young man pushed through dark-eyed Reakthi and men alike in his frenzied charge for the tree. A gaunt form fleetingly appeared in the sea of figures, and Logan's blue eye fixed staunchly on the lean necromage.

"Dirge!" the young man shouted. "Dirge!"

The wild-eyed mortician threw a perplexed gaze in Logan's vicinity.

"That bird!" Logan commanded, jerking a finger skyward. "Get its heartbeat!"

Dirge's eyebrows went up with surprise. "Excuse me?"

"Just do it!" Logan screamed frantically.

Through the snowfall a crowlike caw sounded that tried to quench Logan's sudden drive for success. "Heartbeat! Heartbeat!" the bird squawked as it launched into the heavens.

A half-strangled cry of loss and despair ripped from Logan's throat as he watched the bird wing its way through the snow and wind, losing itself in the wintry curtain of mist and ice.

"Got it!" Dirge abruptly exclaimed. "It's heading into the Hills!"

A relentless fire fanned to life in Logan's chest. "Follow it!" he ordered. "And don't lose it!"

Puzzled stares trained on the young man as Logan ordered his troops to break off the attack and head northward. A forceful drive Logan could only recognize as the desire for revenge and the longing to go home filled his veins, replenishing the strength he had lost in battle. Cautious eyes from the men behind him doubted the young man's sanity and murmured rumors that they now tracked a carrioncrow into the Hills only strengthened their suspicions.

The heavily bearded Tarttan threw Aelkyne a look of immense displeasure. "I believe your Outsider friend has gone daft," the Guard snorted. "He's got us chasing birds."

The younger Guardsman scratched his own beard, worried eyes set in the direction of Logan and the snow-capped Hills. "There's a reason for it," Aelkyne remarked.

"Aye, an insane one," Tarttan grumbled, trudging obediently through the snow and leaving the town of Prifrane behind.

Darkness began to spread across the heavens.

Torches crackled through the light snowfall as Logan followed the dark path that wound naturally through the mountains. Plumes of mist escaped the young man's mouth as he clambered steadily upward, slipping now and then on the snow in his haste to reach the summit. The cold of the unearthly winter bit into his face and hands, and the perspiration that formed on his brow seemed to instantly turn to ice, adding to the sting of the snow.

"Friend-Logan," Thromar pleaded, "we're going to have to stop for the night."

Logan kept up his pace. "We can't," he answered. "We'll lose it."

"Dirge can keep an eye on it—as it were," the Rebel protested.

The gangly necromage threw the fighter a glance. "Well, up to a point," he remarked. "Can't hear a heartbeat forever, eh? Not even my ears are that good."

Logan exhaled, and his breath froze into clouds of mist. "See?" the young man responded. "We've got to keep moving."

"The men are tired and cold," Thromar continued, "and the supply carts won't be able to go much further up these slopes. Sooner or later we're going to have to leave them behind. We've outdistanced Vaugen's Reakthi by at least half a day's march— we deserve the rest."

"All right, fine!" Logan retorted. "You rest; you stay. I'm going on."

The large fighter reached out imploring hands. "Friend-Logan . . ."

Logan suddenly halted, spinning around. His footing on the hillside placed him a few inches higher, bringing him nose to nose with Thromar. "Stay with the men," the young man suggested. "I'm not going to need them anyway. It's going to be just me and Groathit."

"And the Darkness," Moknay solemnly reminded.

Logan turned his single eye on the Murderer. "So what?" demanded the young man. "It's not going to be able to do anything to me. All its bodies are behind us—following us like goddamn zombies. Wherever Groathit is, he doesn't have any soldiers with him."

"Or so you hope," Moknay scowled.

The young man from Santa Monica released an exasperated sigh which fled his lips in puffs of icy cold. "Look," he said, "stay here. Stay with the men. I'll keep going."

A saddened frown stretched above Thromar's beard. "Is that a direct order, friend-Logan?" he queried.

Logan's patience was all but nonexistent. "Yes!" he yelled angrily. "I'm going to keep going! This is my last chance, and I'm not gonna blow it!"

An almost tangible depression swelled up from around the Rebel. "Very well, then." Thromar reluctantly obeyed, turning to the troops massed behind them. "We stop here!" the fighter called to the weary soldiers.

The grateful mutters from the battle-worn and ragged forces caused Logan's ire to increase. The young man felt the same fatigue they felt—suffered from the same cold they endured. Why couldn't they see that stopping would tear asunder the last hope that book and bird offered? If things worked out right just for once, the young man would find Groathit's location either by catching the bird flying somewhere ahead of them or by simply trailing it back to its sorcerous master. If in that time Mara found something useful in the massive tome she continuously pored over, Logan would have the advantage Nightwalker felt he would need and—coupled with the Bloodstone—Groathit would be no more.

And to think, he was supposed to give up all that just for a night's rest?

As tired and shivering warriors settled down to a well-deserved rest, Logan marched defiantly through their ranks. "Going somewhere?" a voice holding no hint of weariness inquired.

Logan glanced swiftly at the shapely figure outlined by the torches. Red-yellow firelight danced gleefully through the drizzle of snow, glimmering alluringly off the mane of red hair that spilled down Roshfre's back.

"I'm going on," the young man curtly responded, not caring to stick around for the bandit's answering comment.

Logan was slightly surprised when the redhead matched his stride. "I'll come with you," she offered.

"You don't have to."

Roshfre shrugged as amply as her sister. "Let's just say I'm as eager to see this thing through as you are."

Logan nodded once in the outlaw's direction as he continued his purposeful pace toward the supply carts. Maybe a few people to help out wouldn't be such a bad idea, he decided. After all, he'd need Dirge's help to keep tracking the bird and Mara's help to translate the book. Maybe Roshfre could come in handy in case Groathit *did* have a few men with him.

Shoving aside these thoughts as unimportant at the moment, Logan approached the wooden carts and horses. He hurriedly flipped open the saddlebags of his yellow-and-green stallion and extracted two empty pouches. In the first he placed the Heart, securely tying the leather straps closed and then attaching the pouch to his sheath's belt. In the other sack he placed the Jewel, taking the golden gemstone from Liris and eyeing it questioningly before hiding its xanthic flame in the leather pouch. The young man wasn't sure why he was taking the stone except as an added measure of defense should the Bloodstone not be enough. As a last thought, Logan picked up the tin of powder that controlled the Jewel's fluxion and started back toward the front of his army's ranks, Roshfre at his back.

A snide voice sounded in Logan's ear as he returned to his friends. "Yer not thinkin' o' walkin' out on us?"

The young man looked over at Yorke and Scythe, the latter's expression even more menacing with the loosely bandaged gash running down his cheek. "I'm not walking out on anybody," Logan replied matter-of-factly.

"Yer leavin', ain'tcha?"

Logan was in no mood for the rogue's banter. "That's what I've been trying to do since I got here," he snapped. "Look, if you're coming, just say so. If not, get out of my way."

The two cutthroats exchanged malevolent grins and fell into step behind Logan and Roshfre, torches crackling above their heads. Mara and Moknay glanced up as the four stepped closer; Dirge stood off to one side, insane eyes trained on the ebon sky.

"We ready?" Logan queried.

"Thromar's told Quarn and Aelkyne what we're doing," Moknay reported. "The three of them will stay behind and keep Vaugen's men off our backs."

Footsteps sounded through the blackness north of the Murderer, and Servil clambered his way down the slopes. "There's a small footpath up this way," the scout advised. "It seems to cut directly northward."

Logan didn't need to ask if the long-haired archer was coming with them. "Then let's go," the young man urged. "We're wasting time. Dirge, can you still sense it?"

The necromage stiffened, straining as if listening for a far-away noise. "Heading north ... northeast," he stated. "Hasn't stopped yet."

Logan climbed up the rocky slope, joining Servil on the footpath while the twin jewels at his belt bumped bothersomely against his legs. The other six followed, Scythe and Yorke retelling to one another their tales of the previous battle in hushed mutters and with nefarious grins. Logan threw the two rogues a questioning glance as he scuttled his way up the mountainside, thoughts roiling through his mind. Eight of them—nine counting the ogre that loyally followed the young man—against the Reakthi spellcaster and the Voices, the young man mused. Plus they had the Heart, the Jewel, and Groathit's book. It was against Logan's nature to ever feel overly optimistic concerning anything—no matter how much things were in your favor—but the dying flicker of hope had started to burn brighter. Staying safely pessimistic, Logan knew they had a pretty good chance of at least banishing the Darkness.

The wind howled in fury—bringing with it an odd twinge of disagreement that lightly brushed past Logan's face—and its frigid cold shrieked throughout the Hills of Sadroia.

The campfire wavered in the current of harsh winter winds that swept through it, sparks leaping into the pitch-black sky and fluttering like lost fireflies into the night. Half-asleep, Logan watched the faint pinpricks of light bob off into the darkness around them, mesmerized by their intense yellow-orange gleam.

Eagerly, the night swallowed them whole.

"I don't like following something I can't see," Scythe muttered beside the young man.

Logan pulled his good eye away from the fire and looked at those gathered about him. "Is it still there?" the young man directed at Dirge.

The necromage swiveled his head up and down. "Still there," he parroted. "Still there. Can't see it through all this darkness, but I'd wager it's perched just about a spear's throw above us, if one of us had a spear, eh?"

"Then why don't we's just knock a few tailfeathers loose and get it down t' our level?" queried Yorke.

A sneer was on Moknay's lips as he retorted, "Because in this blackness we're lucky to see the fire in front of us, let alone be able to hit a damn bird as dark as the night itself."

Scythe feigned a look of shock. "Agellic's Gates," he jested. "You mean to say there's something Moknay the Murderer can't hit?"

Moknay's sneer indicated he found no humor in the cutthroat's sarcasm. "I've wasted daggers on the first of Groathit's spies," the Murderer remarked, "and *that* was during the day." The outlaw stepped away from the campfire and instantly melded with the blackness. "Take advantage of the brief rest," he suggested as an afterthought, "because I am close enough to see you."

Logan caught himself dumbly nodding as his eye stared once more into the dancing sparks of the fire. Fortunately for them, Groathit's bird also needed to rest, and the young man had eagerly plopped to the ground. He hadn't realized beforehand how sore his arms were, or how heavy his legs were, not to mention the bruise on his cheek from that blast. It was just like the blow from the snakelike *Deil* on the banks of the Jenovian River that had knocked Logan from his horse. It had hurt like a bitch, yet Logan had been able to get right up without so much as a singed hair. Questioningly, Logan's memory replayed the events on the riverbank, and his single eye trailed to the light blue ogre seated across from him, its brutish face passive. They had heard Demons in the bushes only seconds before the *Deil* had attacked, but the creature had sprung out at them alone. How long had the ogre been following them? How many times had the light blue beast saved them from dangers that had lurked just ahead of them? Or had it been following them at all?

It was strange, mused Logan. If the Darkness was such a powerful Force and all that—why was it so limited? Something to do with the Wheel's spin, perhaps? And how could the ogre slaughter God knows how many Demons and intimidate a *Deil* into attacking? Because the ogre was a Natural being—a creature of Purity and Nature like Munuc and similar to the sprites? Maybe. So why was Logan getting bruised by Cosmic Forces from beyond the influence of the Wheel while others—like Barthol and Thumbs—were instantaneously obliterated? Because he also came from outside the spin of the Wheel?

At the thought of the chubby priest, Logan's eye flicked from the ogre to the motionless form beside it. Her long dark hair splayed about her, Mara had succumbed to sleep, her head resting on the open pages of Groathit's book. Sleep had erased the guilty and weary expressions carved into the priestess's beautiful features, and a small smile stretched Logan's lips. It was good to see her sleeping, he concluded. At least her conscience allowed her that much. And—in a way—it was fortunate Mara was the only one capable of reading the tome stolen from the Reakthi spellcaster. Maybe now she'd be able to disperse the guilt she felt by aiding the young man more than anyone ever could . . . by finding the passage that would destroy the unnatural darkness that embraced them and restore the Balance to the faltering Wheel.

Wincing at the aches in his limbs accented by the cold, Logan lay back and went to sleep.

Shrieking like the arctic gale, the cloud of churning blackness descended on invisible wings, its triumphant howls and peals of laughter filling the night with a hundred million echoes. Terrified, Logan whipped about, grabbing Mara's hand and pulling her toward the green-and-yellow horse nearby.

"We've got to get the hell out of here!" the young man cried over the Darkness's screams. "I've got to get back to my world!"

Ice filled Mara's veins as the priestess leapt into the saddle, her arms grasping tightly around Logan's waist. She could feel the unearthly, unnatural cold of the dark horde behind them, and its very nearness sent a shiver of nausea through her system. This horror did not belong in Sparrill, she knew. It was a disease . . . a disease that should have been cut out like most diseases. And— like most diseases—the longer it stayed, the more powerful and dominant it grew. Staying as she had in Agellic's Church, she had seen the sorry state of some townsfolk who had lost limbs to infected cuts or illnesses. Although these incidents were rare in the magical abundance of Sparrill, the Darkness now made those disfigurements little in comparison.

Mara screamed as an ebony tentacle reached around the front of the yellow-and-green horse and ripped its legs out from beneath it. The world flipped in a spiral of sentient blackness, and the priestess crashed headlong into the foliage, concerned more about Logan's well-being than her own.

Logan jumped to his feet, a flaming red shaft of uncontrollable magicks in his hands. "Mara!" he called to her. "Run! I can take care of this thing!"

The priestess's eyes went wide. "No!" she warned. "Matthew! Don't! You need the book!"

Logan's flaming weapon transformed into the heavy, leather-bound volume but its sudden change did not surprise Mara. "I've got it!" the young man yelled at her. "Now go!"

Scrambling to her feet, Mara tried to run toward Logan, but her legs would not obey her commands. She watched in horror as the young man swung the massive tome like a sword, the screaming Darkness sweeping down toward him. "But that's not the way to use it!" the priestess screamed. "I need to translate it!"

Logan turned a nasty glare on her, and blackness flickered deep in his uncovered blue eye. "So you can do for me what you did for Barthol?" he inquired with a whispering rasp seeping into his voice. "So you can sit back and watch me die?" Living Darkness exploded outward from Logan's skull in a geyser of twisting limbs and writhing appendages. "I don't think so."

The cry that spilled from Mara's lips was mimicked by the tide of ebony boiling toward her, and the Darkness-filled Logan released a villainous chuckle as his squirming tentacles coiled about the priestess's throat and squeezed. Something far off in the distance groaned in its death-throes and somehow Mara could sense it was the final restraints on the Wheel shattering and giving way before the Voices' undeniable victory.

The ground split under her feet as the Balance ruptured entirely, and the Darkness greedily consumed everyone and everything.

Perspiration winding down her face, Mara jerked herself rigid, green eyes wide as she surveyed the camp about her. Figures huddled in a tight circle around her, all still with sleep. Only the lean necromage remained awake—or, at least, his eyes were open—as he peered resolutely in the direction of Groathit's spy. A sigh of relief fled the priestess as the nightmarish visions of her subconscious faded and she ran a shaking hand through her long, dark hair.

"Frightening, wasn't it?" Dirge chirped from his vigil.

Mara blinked. "What was frightening?" she wondered.

"Your dream," the necromage replied, the polar wind billowing through his yellow-white hair. "The way his head exploded like that."

"How in Imogen's name do you know what I dreamed?" the priestess asked, more surprised than angry.

Dirge smiled his half-mad smile. "Body magicks," he explained. "An offshoot of sorcery from our minds that work almost like messenger birds—almost like the bird we're chasing, eh? I can read these messages when I want to—or when they're as strong as yours were."

Mara looked down at the thick book she had been sleeping

upon, its yellowed pages buffeted by the freezing gale. Her mind was grappling with the abilities of the gaunt man near her when she caught sight of a word flashing by on one of the pages turned by the wind: *Enys'vksiay*—roughly translated to mean the Wheel's Balance. Hurriedly, the priestess fought the gale and flipped back the pages, her eyes scanning down the length of the alien words. A muted sense of triumph burned through her breast as her green eyes locked on the familiar word and the line accompanying it.

Enys'vksiay hygFwsim toLhw'zir, Mara read. *The tilting and restoration of the Wheel's Balance.*

The guilt and self-pity fled, and not even the unnatural cold of the wind could dampen the sudden warmth of success that flowed through Mara's body.

·16·

Incantation

Through the impenetrable blackness and flurry of windblown snowflakes, the dark eyes remained locked on the east. Ignorant of the cruel wind that raked icy claws across his face, Zackaron peered out into the unnatural darkness, his lean form tottering in the gale. Somewhere, the sorcerer recalled, there had once been beauty. Somewhere there had once been green. For as far as his eyes could see, green had stretched endlessly in all directions. Now . . . now all that remained was darkness . . . living, vile darkness that perched atop the world like a carrioncrow atop its meal. The stench of decay was strong in the spellcaster's nostrils, and horrible pains wracked his body. What the land felt, so did he. He was Zackaron . . . master of the Jewel and one with Nature. When the land died, so did he.

He was dying.

The gaunt sorcerer weakly pulled himself back into his cavern home, his scrawny legs barely supporting him. The wind blew long strands of his brown and grey-streaked hair into his face, yet the wizard paid no attention. The hurtings inside him were growing . . . becoming intolerable. For a fortnight he had heard the dying wails of the land . . . knew that not even the Purity could hold up much longer under the invading Darkness. And her Champion? Where was he? Why had he not saved her? Why did he allow this to continue? Why did he let it hurt so much?

Zackaron limped feebly to his chair and sat, his strength depleted. It came for him. To the southwest . . . it was coming in all its nightmarish glory. The hurtings he felt were not enough—there would be more. More hurtings until the land died . . . and when the land died, so did he.

Where was his Jewel?

The sickly magician tried to stand but lacked the strength. A trembling hand reached out and absentmindedly stroked the glimmering orb that stood in the middle of the cave. Tiny pinpricks of energy jumped at the contact but were instantly extinguished as if falling into a void of no magic. The magic, too, was dying, and when the land died, the magic died. And when the magic died, so did he.

A tiny gleam sparkled in the sorcerer's dark eyes, and his hand flickered with a brief golden flame. A similar fire turned the orb a pleasing yellow, and the cave was momentarily filled with vibrant magicks. Then, drained, Zackaron collapsed back into his chair, the faint smile that had fleetingly crossed his bearded features succumbing to exhaustion. It was done should the Unbalance arrive. Would he bring clay like he promised?

Zackaron's dark eyes closed as a jab of pain lanced through his chest. The land was dying.

So was he.

Dark eyes visibly filled with his mistrust of magic, Yorke watched the thick book near him like he would a poisonous snake. "Now what I's don't unnerstands is why in Imogen's name would a wizard be usin' a book wit' the means o' defeatin' the thing he's controllin' in it?"

"In case it ever got out of control?" suggested Mara. "Does it really matter? What does matter is that I've found the passage we need to right the Wheel."

Scythe blanched. "What do you mean, *we*?"

"Besides," the priestess went on, "we don't know for certain whether or not Groathit was really using this book. All Nightwalker told me was that he had it and we had to get it from him."

"Maybe he had it to stop us from getting the incantation, eh?" Dirge put in.

Mara gave the necromage half a nod, tapping the elderly volume on its worn and ragged cover. "Now, one of the things that makes this language so difficult to translate is its ambiguity. The title itself is *Rkhbs'wmnf* which can either mean Darklight or Lightdark."

"So how do you know you've found the right spell?" queried Roshfre. "What if you've translated it one way when it was meant to be translated another?"

Mara threw the redhead a confident smile. "Trust me," was all she said.

"It's not you I don't trust," Roshfre muttered. "It's the magic."

Moknay lifted the thick tome and leafed through its wrinkled pages. Grim grey eyes flicked upward with the accuracy of one of his daggers, and the Murderer pinned his gaze on Logan. The young man remained unaware, staring distantly into the campfire, a million unreadable thoughts passing through his uncovered eye.

"Well, friend?" Moknay questioned. "Can you do it?"

Logan pulled his gaze away from the flames and looked briefly at the Darklight grimoire. A feeble shrug shook his shoulders. "I'm not sure," he admitted. "I don't know what to do."

"Most incantations only require the user to read the spell, backing each word with magic," Mara explained. "Certain words are more important than others—I'll point them out as we go along."

Logan returned his one-eyed stare to the fire. Well, he told himself bitterly, here we are. Mara's found the passage I need to right the Wheel and chalk up one point for our side . . . so why the hell am I hesitating? Because I finally realized how much magic I'm going to have to use? So now what? Now I don't want to do it? No, that's stupid. Of course I want to do it . . . I want to go home, don't I? It's just that . . . well, shit! I'm afraid. Everything—hell! More than everything—is riding on this one! If I read that passage right, Mara said that will restore the Balance to the Wheel—how many times have I screwed *that* up before?—and it will leave the Voices open to banishment. That was one of the things that had made it so easy for Groathit to summon the Darkness into Sparrill in the first place—the Balance had been so severely distorted in the Darkness's favor what with the resurrection of Gangrorz and my own goof-ups with the Jewel. So if I right the Wheel, the Balance returns to neutral and the Voices' hold here weakens considerably.

But the magic . . . How much magic is this going to take? Probably lots. We're not talking about *Deils* or wounds now . . . we're talking Cosmic Balances and Macrocosmic Forces. Say . . . I wonder if restoring the Balance will bring back the Blackbodies? Maybe even Nightwalker . . . ? Awww, come off it, Matthew . . . they're dead. They've been dead a long time and if you don't do something soon, everything else will be just as dead.

Logan reached out a tentative hand and took the Darklight from Moknay. The alien words blurred before his single eye as apprehension gripped his mind. "So now what?" he wondered. "I just read it?"

Mara got up from where she sat and repositioned herself behind the young man, her chin resting on his left shoulder. A slender finger pointed at the bizarre words. "Right here," she instructed, " '*Gu oud f'nwib . . .* ' That's where you want to start. Don't worry about the pronunciation . . . the magic'll react regardless how you say it."

Logan hated the ominous foretelling of failure fluttering about his stomach. "How am I supposed to summon magic when I'm reading?" he wanted to know.

Dirge responded, "Let it come unconsciously. When least expected, you are most powerful. The blessing and the curse of an Unbalance, eh?"

A snarl sounded in Logan's throat as he remembered earlier fears about overdoing his subconscious abilities. With his anger boiling in protest, the young man looked down at the incantation before him and started to read.

" '*Gu oud f'nwib oudcy eui. Ehuim. W'rkcy eui . . .* ' " His voice trailed off.

Green eyes filled with wonder, Mara looked at Logan. "What's wrong?"

Logan halfheartedly shrugged. "Nothing's happening," he said. "There's no magic."

Dirge waggled a long finger at the young man. "You were consciously blocking your subconscious," he accused.

Logan sneered at the necromage. "Well, excuuuuuse me!" he retorted. "I'm no spellcaster! I don't even know what the hell I'm doing trying to right the goddamn Wheel!"

"Spellcaster or not," replied Dirge, "you must restore the Balance."

Must! Must! Must! Logan thought foully to himself. Everything's a big must! I *must* do this! I *must* do that! I *must* save the multiverse from utter destruction even though I don't want to! Why can't I just *must* myself home?

"Would an outside source help?" Moknay asked Dirge.

"Outside source?" Roshfre shot back. "What in Agellic's Gates are you talking about, Murderer? You're no sorcerer."

"Never said I was," Moknay returned, "but I noticed a small glitter from the Jewel when Logan read those first few lines. I may not be a spellcaster, but I've been around magic enough to know there's a very definite link between the Wheel and the Jewel."

"The Equilibrant," echoed Dirge, bobbing his head up and down vigorously. "Yes, Matthew Logan, focus your concentration on the

Equilibrant and it will do the task for you."

Logan brightened, pulling the Jewel free of its pouch. A hundred thousand reflections looked back at the young man from the faceted gemstone, and the golden glimmer of fire that burned at its infinite center sparked brighter in Logan's hands.

Dirge's head kept bobbing up and down. "Now read the incantation," he instructed.

The Jewel cradled in his lap, Logan returned his one-eyed gaze to the Darklight tome. " *'Gu oud f'nwib oudcy eui. Ehuim. W'rkcy eui. W'rkcy muiz luhekhr kir swcyr.'* "

As the alien words came unsteadily from the young man's lips, the yellow-gold flame inside the Jewel leapt higher. Golden streaks of theurgy shot upward from the glittering facets, and a crackling aura of power enveloped the Jewel in a yellow veil of illuminance. Yorke and Scythe both scrambled backwards as sporadic bursts of energy sprang from the gem's smooth surface and stabbed into the night.

An abrupt jolt of pain seared through Logan's leg and the young man released a pain-filled yelp, pushing the Jewel away from his lap. Red-hot fire seared the flesh of his left hand as the young man batted the flaring Jewel off his body and crawled backwards, not stopping until some distance was placed between himself and the gem.

Snow melted in a two-foot radius as the coruscating Jewel blazed into the rock of the mountains.

"Ouch!" Logan complained. "Damn thing burned me!"

The young man threw a questioning look at those around him. The sizzle of melting snow harmonized with the howl of the wind as Logan noted Scythe and Yorke watching him from behind an outcropping of rock, their usual roguish bravado stolen by the Jewel's wicked flare-up. Roshfre and Moknay had also backed away, their cold eyes locked on the gemstone. Only Servil, Dirge, and Mara remained at the young man's side; the ogre cowered behind a boulder scarcely large enough to protect it.

Dirge's wild eyes filled with speculations. "The tilt is far too severe," he surmised. "It will take a staggering discharge to correct the Balance. Are you up to it?"

Logan blinked at the necromage. "Shit, no!" he exclaimed. "I'm not going to try that again! You saw what that thing did to Barthol's Church!" Not to mention what I've seen it do to a thief stupid enough to steal my horse, Logan added to himself. It's bad enough using magic—it's another thing altogether to wind up a bleached skeleton in the Hills of Sadroia!

The ogre's awed rumble came from the darkness: "Maaaaaaaagic."

Moknay took a cautious step back toward the campfire and the gleaming Jewel. "Now what?" he queried. "Is there a chance any other incantation will work?"

Mara shook her head. "No."

As its halo of energy dissipated, Dirge lightly lifted the Jewel from the melted snow. An almost comedic expression of confusion crossed his lean features. "Perhaps there is a chance," the necromage murmured to himself. "Perhaps if I hold the Jewel and numb the sensations in my hands I may bear the brunt of the magic."

"Ya'd probably stick yer head in th' campfire if ya thought it'd do us any good, too," Yorke snorted.

Logan rubbed at the twin burns on his body, his anger and anxieties dampened by the brutal suddenness of his injuries. "No," he told Dirge, "we need you to track Groathit's spy. If something happens to you, we'll have completed only one-half of the job."

"So what are we going to do?" asked Mara. "There's no one here who can control such forces without getting hurt."

"Who says we've got to hold it?" asked Scythe. "Why don't we leave it on the ground and get the *Deil* out of the way?"

"Magic needs guidance—a focus—or else it is only so much wasted energy," Dirge explained. "Human or nonhuman, some living creature must direct the flow. Setting the Jewel on the ground will accomplish very little . . . unless you want to dig a very deep hole, eh?"

Logan got to his feet, a frustrated rage eating away at his heart. So close! he cursed. So damn close! The right incantation, the right source of magic, and no one powerful enough to direct it. Damn! Why'd it have to be the Jewel? The Heart he could control; Logan knew that much. But the Jewel . . . the young man remembered the words of Barthol when they had first started their search for the Bloodstone: " . . . the Jewel of Equilibrant is the most powerful item in the world—in the entire multiverse," the priest had said, "but too powerful for the likes of us. Look at Zackaron. He only released a small portion of the Jewel's energies, and it drove him mad. Can you imagine what would happen if someone tapped into even more power?"

Musing, Logan stared into the infinite night. Zackaron, he recalled. The insane wizard wielded powers that bordered on godhood, but he lacked the common sense to use his magicks for anyone's benefit . . . even his own. Still . . . the Jewel had been in Zackaron's care for God knows how long—years? centuries?—before Logan accidentally stole it from Pembroke. If there was anyone who knew the workings of the Jewel, it was Zackaron . . . and the sorcerer made his home in the very Hills they were in.

"There might just be a chance," Logan mumbled out loud, turning to what he hoped was the east and slightly tilting his head skyward.

To the others, it looked as if Logan strained to pick out a noise that had not yet been made.

Bitter cold sank its fangs into Logan's uncovered eye, drawing the moisture out of his contact lens. Icy fingers stroked through his black hair, and the flesh of his cheeks grew numb as he defiantly faced the arctic gale. He was rewarded by a disorienting flux that originated somewhere to the northeast. A faint smile pulled across his lips as the young man turned away from the biting wind and glanced at his companions.

"I think there's someone who can help us," he declared.

"Who?" wondered Mara.

Logan's eye gleamed in the firelight. "Zackaron."

The cluster of rogues—with the exception of Moknay—shuddered. "Yer mad," Yorke concluded. "I's mean . . . he's mad . . . but yer mad fer suggestin' it. I's heard it said that if there's anything worse than a sorcerer, it's a mad sorcerer."

Logan looked at the Jewel in Dirge's grasp. "Look," the young man said, "the Jewel was his. He probably knew the damn thing inside out before he tapped into it."

"But that was centuries ago!" protested Roshfre.

"It's the only chance we've got," Logan retorted. "Or would *you* like to try to hold it?"

The color drained from Roshfre's face as she took a cautious step backwards.

"There's only one problem," Scythe quipped. "Where the *Deil* are you going to find him? Last I heard he was living on the eastern shore of Dragon's Neck."

"He's moved," Moknay remarked. "He's holed up in these hills."

Yorke, Scythe, and Roshfre all displayed another serious twinge of discomfort. "Still," Scythe went on, "there's an awful lot of hills."

Logan allowed a small smile to cross his features. "Don't worry about finding him; you leave that to me," he explained. "The only problem I can think of is us. How can we get to Groathit *and* find Zackaron?"

"Split up?" prompted Servil. "It's not a good idea should the storm get stronger—but it seems our only chance."

Nodding grimly, Logan studied the eight before him. "Dirge," the young man instructed, "you're the only one who can follow Groathit's spy. I'll take Mara and Moknay with me to Zackaron; the rest of you, go with Dirge. When you find where Groathit is, send Servil to look for us. We'll be somewhere northeast of here."

"There's an awful lot of hills," Scythe repeated ominously.

Logan shot the rogue's pessimism a nasty glare before training his eye on the long-haired scout. "Is that too hard?" he demanded.

Servil hesitantly shook his head. "It all depends," the archer replied. "If the storm worsens, it may cover your tracks to the point where I can't follow you at all."

"We'll just have to hope it doesn't," Logan stated.

Scythe's sardonic smirk grew wider. "I don't hope."

"Then you can come with me to Zackaron," Logan snapped at the cutthroat.

Scythe shut up.

Dirge looked away from where Groathit's bird nestled in the snow-draped trees. "Perhaps we should catch the spy now, eh?" the necromage asked. "Get the information?"

"Too much of a risk," Moknay said. "Groathit's birds are fast. If we miss, it'll head even faster to wherever the spellcaster's hiding. If that happens, Groathit will be expecting us."

"What's to say he isn't expecting us now?" Roshfre frowned.

"Nothing," Mara answered, "but right now it feels safer to assume he isn't."

Logan scanned the people gathered about him. So few of them against such magicks. The idea of splitting up did not sit well with the young man—he seemed to get into more trouble by himself than with friends—but he wouldn't be alone, would he? He'd have Moknay and Mara to help him find the others, and Servil trailing them once Groathit was found. Between the scout and the Murderer, they shouldn't lose track of one another . . . and the ogre was pretty damn good at following people as well.

Logan took the Jewel from Dirge and replaced it in its pouch. Golden pinpoints of magic still pranced about its faceted surface, yet the scalding temperatures that had burned Logan's hand and leg had vanished. Frowning at the mind-staggering power he carried at his belt, Logan tucked the Darklight grimoire under one arm and started to the northeast.

"Hopefully we won't take long finding him," he told the other group. "And whatever you do, don't take on Groathit. He's mine."

Yorke almost laughed at the thought. "An' yer welcome to him!"

The disturbance fluttered past on the winds once more and Logan turned, allowing the warplike distortion to pull at him like a magnetic force on iron. Then—teeth clenched in determination— the young man stalked into the mountains, nervous hands gripping the Darklight volume so tightly that his knuckles turned as white as the snow.

From its perch, Groathit's spy watched with glistening black eyes.

Like the bubbling of tar, an infinite chorus of rasping whispers resounded through Groathit's skull and from a million places around him.

The Purity.
It draws nearer.
Nearer.
It must be destroyed.

The Reakthi spellcaster pulled himself up the rocky slope, his black robe billowing about his lean frame. A vile grin marred the wizard's wrinkled features as he threw a gaze upward at the boiling sea of blackness suspended in the wind and snow. The darkness of his left eye flared with eager anticipation.

"Did I not tell you it would be so?" smirked the sorcerer. "Matthew Logan will come . . . and the Purity shall come with him. Then both shall die."

Only the Darkness may banish the Light.
Only the Darkness.
You are not powerful enough.
Your form limits you.
Other forms must be prepared.
For us. For the Darkness.

Other forms.

Groathit sneered at the roiling cloud of Darkness, yet held his emotions in check. It was useless to rage at the intangible mass of evil floating above him—the Voices held no concept of true emotions. It said what it believed to be so and nothing more—although Groathit would have thought himself far more than capable of slaying both Matthew Logan and banishing the Light. Nonetheless, the Reakthi spellcaster cared little for the magical Bloodstone the young maggot carried. Only Matthew Logan's blood staining the snow red would satisfy the chestplated sorcerer's fury; if the Voices wished to shatter the Heart, it would be theirs.

Who destroyed the Bloodstone meant nothing to the wizard. Groathit would still be an ultimate Force in the Dark universe that would rise up to replace the Wheel's multiverse. He would be a god—the only extension of the Darkness retaining its physical form—limited in some ways; far more powerful in others. The entire realm of Darkness would be his kingdom . . . where no upstarts like Matthew Logan would ever dare threaten his reign.

"I have already prepared other forms for you," the wizard told the seething mass of blackness, "so that you may carry out the destruction of the Purity." A rigid, threatening finger lanced heavenward. "But remember, Purity's Champion dies at my hands alone—Matthew Logan is mine."

Squirming tendrils of living ebony writhed across the sky. *So be it*, answered the choir of hissing Voices.

Ah, our forms approach.

They approach.

Darkness will prevail.

Groathit turned and peered through the drizzling snow, smiling at his own ingenuity. He should have thought of this earlier and saved himself the trouble of Vaugen and his petty whinings. Men? Bah! What use were men to the Force of Darkness? Men were weak, frail little creatures. Only beings birthed from the very heart of blackness itself deserved the right to be pawns of the Voices—only beings of tainted magicks and corrupted Nature could consume and control unimaginable quantities of sorcery.

Groathit's smile widened into a leering, skull-like grin as the shrill, soul-wrenching shriek of a Demon split the quiet of the Hills, and a vast armada of dark shapes came winging their way westward.

*   *   *

Faint beams of sunlight battered against the blackness filling
the sky, transforming the heavens into a mottled canvas of grey
and black. What little light did reach the ground reflected back
brightly off the snow, forcing Logan to squint his uncovered eye.
Instinctively, the young man glanced at his watch and shivered at
the blaze of sentient darkness that thrived there.

"It doesn't look like there's going to be any daylight," Mara
noted nervously, brushing her windblown hair out of her face.

Moknay's grim mien appeared. "Be thankful for what we have
now," he advised. "It's not likely to last long."

Logan frowned at the despair in the voices of his friends and
felt his own hopes sink lower. Constant doubts plagued the young
man—whispering voices of his own telling him that he went to his
death. Who was he trying to kid? He was going after something that
blotted out the sun, and his only weapon was a jewel no bigger
than a football. How could he even possibly see a glimmer of
success there? And what if he did succeed . . . had he thought
of that? What happened if he won? He used the Heart and went
home, right? And, in doing so, he left behind every person who
had befriended him and helped him in Sparrill—left them like
he had only tolerated them to begin with. But that wasn't so,
was it? He had grown to more than just tolerate Sparrill—Logan
had grown to actually enjoy moments of his stay . . . and he had
certainly grown attached to those he now called friends . . . and
some attachments were stronger than others.

A half-mumbled curse broke the young man's silence, and he
blamed the harsh wind for the spot of moisture that formed in
his eye.

Another twinge of sorcerous vertigo jerked Logan out of his
thoughts and he adjusted his stride, struggling to find footholds in
the snow-dusted rocks. The bagged gems at his waist continued to
bounce against his legs as if reminding him of their existence and
of his own importance. Logan reaffirmed his grip on the Darklight
grimoire with an irritated murmur and looked up at the landscape
before him as if he could spot the unusual aura of Zackaron's
insanity-tinged magicks.

Moknay scanned the winter-shrouded hills with cold grey eyes.
"Is it much farther, friend?" the Murderer inquired.

Logan shrugged. Once before he had purposely homed in
on the sensation of Zackaron's magic, and once—not quite so
purposely—had allowed the feeling to draw him onward. That

almost resulted in giving the Jewel to Zackaron instead of the Smythe, and now that was just what the young man was going to do: give the Jewel to Zackaron. He hoped that what he was doing wasn't a very big mistake . . . Logan excelled at making big mistakes.

Moknay halted, senses alert.

"What is it?" Mara queried.

The Murderer's upraised palm silenced the priestess, and she and Logan both remained still and quiet; even the light blue ogre cocked its head quizzically to one side. There was a questioning eyebrow raised on Moknay's forehead as he swung grey eyes flecked with puzzlement on the three with him.

"What is it?" Logan tried again.

The Murderer sneered. "Not sure," he responded. "Had the feeling we were being followed."

Logan threw a worried look over his shoulder at the white-clad mountains at his back. Deep valleys encircled them, littered with snowy carpets, and the freezing, unearthly wind howled on every side of them. The beauty of what should have been a panoramic view, however, was blurred by the drizzle of snow and voidlike blackness. Abruptly, a weak tug of Zackaron's abnormal sorcery pulled at Logan's arm and the young man turned to the north, rounding an outcropping of rock. Even through the unnatural gloom of the Darkness, he recognized the narrow cleft dissecting the mountainside that came into sight, yet icy fear filled his veins when he spied the inhuman silhouettes stanced outside. Horrified, Logan threw himself backwards, ducking back behind the outcropping of rocks. Sweat broke out along the young man's brow, and his sudden intake of air was a strained hiss between his clenched teeth.

Moknay instantly held two daggers. "Trouble?"

"And how," nodded Logan. "Someone's already beat us here."

Mara blinked. "Who?"

"Looked like Demons."

Moknay peered cautiously around the corner, grey eyes narrowing at the shadowy forms guarding the entrance to Zackaron's cavern home. An unsettling wrench affected even the Murderer's composure as he noted the flaring blackness that burned in the enormous eye sockets of what were once Demons; a quick glance skyward informed Moknay that the Darkness had arrived.

The Murderer replaced his daggers. "We've got to get out of here," he declared in a hushed voice. "If they sense the Heart . . ."

"What about Groathit . . ." Logan started.

Moknay cut the young man off. "The Balance is still in their favor," he said. "You can't fight them now."

Maybe I can't fight them at all, Logan gravely told himself. If I saw what I thought I saw, the Voices now possessed the most powerful shells they could. Demons were distorted creatures of Nature—made by Gangrorz and capable of wielding magicks they stole from any other source of power. If the Darkness had filled them with energy, these bodies wouldn't burn out like the Reakthi—this was the exact purpose for which they were made, and that alone made them undefeatable.

Mara risked a glance around the outcropping of stones. "How are we going to get through to Zackaron?" she wondered.

Moknay's cold eyes flashed with steel. "There probably isn't a Zackaron left," he answered grimly. "Groathit's probably turned him to dung."

"We don't know that for sure," Mara protested, an emptiness welling up inside her as their plan slowly tore apart.

The Murderer shot her a pitiless glare. "What do you want to do? Go on up there and ask them if Zackaron's still alive?" he snapped in a gruff whisper. "We're four against the Voices with even the damn Wheel opposing us! I'm Moknay the Murderer . . . not Moknay the Suicidal!"

Mara lowered her gaze as the futility of their situation descended on the quartet. Unless they could restore the Balance to the Wheel, they could never hope to banish the Darkness—and unless they could get through to Zackaron, they could never hope to restore the Balance to the Wheel.

Trying to resist the hopelessness swelling in his breast, Logan tightened his grip on the Darklight grimoire. He would not let the frustration building inside him eat away at what little determination and courage he had left. So long as they still had the book and the two jewels, there was still a chance of stopping Groathit. There had to be!

The light blue ogre's massive hand suddenly fell upon Logan's shoulder, and the enormous creature pointed a curious finger on his other hand toward the ebon-filled sky.

"Biiiiiird," the ogre said.

Logan looked up questioningly. He almost didn't see the black form swoop down out of the darkness and streak into the opening of Zackaron's cave, its feathered wings cutting through the veil of snow. A moment of uncertainty clouded the young man's brain—probably caused by the complications suddenly facing them—and he realized too late what the bird's appearance meant. Fear exploded in his gut as he bolted to the edge of their protective outcropping in time to see Dirge push his way through the snowy mist, oblivious of the Demons half-hidden in the gloom.

" . . . believe it's stopping," the necromage was saying to those behind him.

Dark sorcery crackled. Gangly creatures imbued with blackness and still screened by the curtain of mist swung flaring talons toward the five. Logan's blue eye went wide with horror as he expected to see his companions—companions that *he* had sent this way—get cut down by the Voices' Demonic pawns.

The young man charged Zackaron's cave. "*No!*"

Velvet sorcery erupted as Logan's warning cry rebounded off the hills around them. Snowflakes vanished in an abrupt burst of steam as ebon shafts of power lanced through the winter, catching the rocks beside Dirge's head. Yorke and Scythe immediately ducked to one side, Roshfre reacting just as swiftly. Servil dropped to one knee, bow out and arrow nocked; Dirge threw himself forward, scrawny arms draped over his balding head.

Inhuman eyes seared away by Cosmic energies drew away from the five and fixed on Logan, rounded mouths twisting into obscene mockeries of smiles. Disembodied Darkness stormed overhead as the young man jerked free his sword, forcing himself to stand his ground. He wouldn't allow the terror boiling up inside him take control—the Darkness knew he was here now and Logan knew it would not let him escape . . . not that there was anywhere to escape to.

The Purity, the Voices rasped.

It has come.

Destroy it.

Silver launched from Moknay's hands, deadly blades screaming through the drizzle of snow. "Go!" the Murderer shouted at Logan. "Go for Zackaron! Get inside!"

Logan nodded once, charging for the cavern's opening. Cold moisture seeped through his Nikes as he leapt through the thin layer of snow, and he let the chill of the mountains dampen the fear that assailed him from inside. He dodged a clawed hand bursting with

magicks, stumbled in the snow, regained his footing in time to duck
another Demon. His sword speared out, catching one Demon in the
solar plexus. Its soul-shattering scream of anger pierced the young
man's nerves, and he wondered why the Demon's acceptance of
the Darkness did not blot out its previous persona as it had with
the Reakthi . . . Probably because the Demons were used to using
powers that didn't belong to them.

Hampered by his halved vision, Logan skidded to a halt, jerking
to his left. The entrance to Zackaron's cave was within ten feet of
where he stood, and he caught sight of some of his friends nearby:
the ogre flailing brawny arms at the Darkness's Demons, Mara's
sword and dagger combination glinting red in the unnatural night,
Scythe's metallic boomerangs screaming through the polar gale.

Logan hurried to the opening of Zackaron's cavern and barely
avoided the black shape that vomited from the mouth of the
cave. Razor-sharp claws sliced the air near Logan's nose, and a
daggerlike beak clacked in avian fury as Groathit's bird banked
sharply and dove again.

"Die! Die!" the bird crowed, a streak of black against the white
of the falling snow. "Matthew Logan! Die!"

Logan threw himself to the ground, sword jutting upward. Scarlet
magicks sparked and Groathit's spy screeched as the young man's
blade drove through its breast. Black feathers wafted across the
hills as the hawklike bird twitched spasmodically, hanging limply
from the point of Logan's weapon. In disgust, Logan shook the
corpse free and dashed for Zackaron's cave.

A howling stream of Darkness exploded from inside the cave and
blossomed at Logan's feet, throwing the young man backwards.
Red-hot pain tore across his face as Logan smashed up against a
wall of rock, warm blood dribbling down his eyepatch. Stars went
supernova behind his eyelids as the young man lost his footing in
the snow and crumpled to one knee, the Darklight grimoire and
his sword knocked from his grasp.

Logan thought he heard Mara cry out his name.

Wiping blood and snow from his cheek, Logan tried to shake
away the fuzziness that invaded his skull. Blurred images from
his uncovered eye sent warning messages to his muscles, yet the
young man found he could not respond. Fingers numb with cold
fumbled for the pouches at his belt as the gaunt form of Logan's
attacker stepped free of Zackaron's abode, blue-grey hair blown
by the shrieking winds.

A confident smile stretched across his withering features,

Groathit stepped nearer. His left eye crackled with the Darkness of the Voices. "It's time, Matthew Logan," the spellcaster leered. "It's time to die."

Blades of darkness screamed from the sorcerer's bony hands, and Logan leapt blindly to one side. The explosion of dark sorcery behind him riddled his back with sparks of icy flame and shards of rock scattered across the mountainside. The reverberating thunder of the explosion's echo deafened the young man as he stumbled to regain his balance, and blinding power momentarily threw his halved vision into the blackness of blindness.

Friendly hands caught Logan and helped him stand upright, rescuing him before he teetered too close to the mountain's edge. The young man had no time to thank whoever stood behind him as a high-pitched wail split the mountain air and leathery wings threw up gusts of snow. A clawed hand gloved in blackness lashed out from above and ripped one of the bags from Logan's belt, almost knocking the young man to the ground again.

Darkness boomed with triumphant laughter as the Darkness-controlled Demon glared down at the bagged Heart, scarlet light burning dimly from within its leather pouch. In response, black energies coalesced in the taloned hands and engulfed the glimmering Bloodstone.

The land screamed.

Darkness

Like the death-rattle of the world, the Darkness's rasping laughter filled the black skies above the Hills of Sadroia. Desperately, Matthew Logan lunged for the Heart in the talons of the Demon hovering over him, yet the gangly monster danced back upon the arctic winds, a grotesque smirk on its circular mouth. Vile, Dark sorceries churned in the creature's empty eye sockets, and the polar gale screamed over the peaks and crags of the mountains, shrieking in the land's agony.

A heavy, blood-caked sword unexpectedly shot out over Logan's head from behind him, its blade catching the Demon in the chest. No blood flowed, but a startled screech of surprise ripped away the creature's monstrous smile, and one powerful beat of its leathery wings sent the Demon gliding backwards. Scarlet light flickered dimly as the Bloodstone fell from the taloned grasp, black plumes of smoke still billowing from the charred leather pouch that once contained it.

Eye locked on the Heart, Logan jumped. Icy fire burned through his sweat jacket as he fell across the Bloodstone, but the young man knew what would happen if another Demon got its claws around the gem. This time it wouldn't be the leather sack that was destroyed—it would be the Heart itself.

Befuddlement finally seeped into the young man's thoughts, and he wondered who had so timely rescued him—from both falling over the edge of the mountain and forcing the Demon to release the Bloodstone. Logan's confused look became one of shock as he turned and was greeted through the blur of snow by the yellowing smile of Thromar.

"Thromar?" Logan blurted. "I thought I told you . . ."

"I never could obey a direct order," the Rebel chuckled, swinging again at the angry Demon.

Logan tried to blink the astonishment from his uncovered eye as he spotted the lines of troops pushing their way up the slopes. Scores of fighters from Eadarus and Debarnian mingled together with clusters of Guardsmen and Quarn's Reakthi made their way up the steep mountainsides and engaged the dark-eyed Demons atop the hills.

Thromar's heavy blade lopped off the head of his opponent. "Hah!" the fighter roared. "Dark eyes or not, Demons are still a puny lot!"

Rumbles of fury bellowed from the living Darkness overhead and Logan flinched, his surprise cut short. At any second he expected a forking shaft of black lightning to come streaking out of the ebony mass above him, and he huddled at Thromar's feet like a frightened child, the Heart wrapped protectively in his arms.

Dummy! Logan berated himself when no strike came. *The Voices can't do things like that . . . thankfully! But it's only a matter of time before their pawns start firing blindly in the direction of the Heart. That was how Barthol died.*

Logan scrambled to his feet, snatching up his sword which lay half-buried in the snow nearby. A glinting black claw almost raked his shoulder, yet Thromar's huge sword cut through the wind and snow and severed the fingers with a bloodless pass.

The Rebel peered at Logan through the gloom, flakes of snow lost among his mane of reddish-brown hair. "Is the Heart damaged?" he asked seriously.

For the first time since rescuing it from the Demon's hands, Logan inspected the ruby jewel in his grip. Red light still pulsed weakly from the Bloodstone's interior, a dying heartbeat in the frigidness of the Hills, yet its soothing warmth splayed across the young man's injured face, and he tucked it carefully under one arm.

"Not that I can tell," he answered Thromar, swinging clumsily with his own sword at an advancing Demon.

A grey shadow slipped between Thromar and Logan; and Moknay the Murderer pointed a glinting dagger under the former's nose. "I *thought* we were being followed," the outlaw snarled with just a hint of humor in his grim voice.

"Have you ever known me to miss a battle, Murderer?" Thromar boomed indignantly. "I? Thromar the Bold? Strong of limb? Sharp of wit?"

Moknay sneered. "Long in breath," he added. "Now shut up and help get Logan to Zackaron."

"Zackaron?" echoed the Rebel. "How the *Deil* did *he* get involved with all this?"

Daggers flashed from Moknay's hands. "Just do it!" he snapped. The Murderer suddenly turned on Logan with a swiftness that startled the young man. "Oh, and you dropped this a while back, friend. I thought you might want it returned."

Logan had to squint through the snow and unnatural darkness before he recognized what Moknay held out toward him. A wave of relief washed through the young man's innards as he took the offered Darklight grimoire. In his frantic attempt to save the Heart, Logan had forgotten all about the tome and its importance. The relief he felt tried to transform into a giddy, lightheadedness, and Logan had to suppress the bubbling enthusiasm growing inside him.

It's not over yet, the young man's darker side warned him. So you got lucky for once in your life—big deal. Don't get all optimistic now. Just because the Heart and Darklight are still in your hands now doesn't mean they will be three minutes from now . . . or three seconds from now.

Logan heeded his pessimistic side and forced down the joy that took root inside him, emphasizing his dark thoughts by scanning the area about him. On every side, battling figures were everywhere—partially lost among the gloom. Every now and then the young man would spot the glimmer of grey metal from one of Quarn's Reakthi or the glimpse of a Guardsman's uniform half-buried in the murkiness . . . but where was Mara? And the ogre? Was Dirge still alive? How was Yorke faring?

A familiar voice of grating steel rose in pitch above the howl of the wind and the cacophony of battle, and Logan couldn't fight the shudder of fear that raced through his system.

"Show yourself, Matthew Logan!" Groathit's voice split the Darkness. "Show yourself!"

He is there, the Voices responded.
There.
He has the Purity.
Destroy him.
Destroy the Purity.
Destroy them both.

Logan's grasp on the Darklight and the Heart tightened instinctively as he battled with the preternatural horror the Voices caused within his mind. He was going to fight this? Alone?

No! That was just what they wanted him to think! They were just Voices! Like their servant, Gangrorz, almost half their Power came from the mysterious, impenetrable Darkness in which they thrived. What you could not see was all that much more frightening—but these foes were not physical. So they can see where the young man was among the throng of battling figures . . . so what? They couldn't even point a finger in his direction.

Logan threw an apprehensive glance at the mountain cliff surrounding him. "I'm never going to get past Groathit," he muttered. "The Voices may not be able to point me out, but he'll spot me if I try to get to Zackaron."

Grey flared in Moknay's eyes. "Hmmmm," the Murderer mused, a nefarious smirk pulling on his mustache. "I have an idea."

"Uh-oh," jested Thromar. "Last time he said that, I wound up stuck in a maze of blasted secret passages."

Ignoring the jovial Rebel, Moknay took the Darklight back from Logan and flipped through its yellowed, elderly pages. Questioningly, Logan watched, momentarily forgetting about the war that raged on around him. What the heck was Moknay planning?

Moknay's smirk widened as gloved hands neatly tore a sheet of parchment from the Darklight's leather binding. Mischief swirled in the Murderer's glare as he handed Logan the single page.

"What . . . ?" Logan started.

"That's the incantation you need," the cutthroat interrupted. "The one Mara found. Take it and get to Zackaron."

The young man from Santa Monica gave the spell in his hands a bewildered glance. "I still won't be able to get past Groathit," he repeated.

Moknay tucked the rest of the ancient tome under his arm. "Leave that to me," he quipped, slipping into the darkness before Logan had a chance to protest.

Logan's half-strangled shout of disapproval died in his throat as the grey-garbed outlaw melded with the unnatural night. Anger at Moknay's recklessness rose to replace the astonishment. "He's going to get himself killed," the young man snarled, Nikes kicking up snow as he bolted after the outlaw.

Hoping he was heading in the right direction, Logan sped through the murky snowfall. He tried to ignore the trickles of blood that still wound their way down the sides of his face from what must have been nasty gashes on his forehead. It was probably the cold that numbed the pain, but that also worked against him. His hands grew colder, and his fingers felt like they were expanding

into thick, clumsy digits. Worriedly, the young man shuffled the
Bloodstone in his arms, cradling it like a football player held a
football. The single page of the Darklight grimoire flapped noisily
in his left hand, small shreds of the elderly parchment breaking off
and scattering to the wind.

A warbling howl sounded close to Logan's ear, and the young
man ducked a taloned hand that grabbed for his arm. Answering
shrieks of Demonic rage resounded all about the mountaintop, and
Logan prayed the Heart's weak pulse was not sufficient enough to
home in on. The Bloodstone's magic was very unique, the young
man remembered, yet it was also very elusive. With a little luck
the Voices' Demons might not even sense the presence of the
jewel as Logan moved through their ranks.

The young man frowned. If anybody needed luck right now, it
was probably going to be Moknay.

Feet barely sinking into the carpet of snow, Moknay the Murderer swerved through the press of fighting bodies. Grey eyes familiar
with the darkness, Moknay peered through the unnatural night and
locked on the narrow opening in the hillside. Steel tainted with the
glow of red magicks diagonally raced across his chest as he came
to an abrupt halt, gloved hands clamping tighter around the leather
volume in his grasp.

A fine line of perspiration appeared above Moknay's brow
when his gaze fixed on the scrawny form in the silver chestplate
blocking Zackaron's cave. It was almost unfortunate the Murderer
had accompanied Logan on his adventures. Back in Eadarus—
when life had been relatively simple—Moknay had been blissfully
unaware of magic's capabilities. He had known a few sorcerers
before—even heard the rumors that some items were said to
perform Cosmic upheavals—but a little magical trickery had
never unsettled him as it had some of Eadarus's night crew.
Yet that had been before he had seen rivers unnaturally swell,
or resurrected *Deils* warp Nature, or had actually held the flaring
Jewel of Equilibrant.

Agellic's Gates! He had actually *held* the damn thing! And
now . . . now where had Imogen taken him? Not less than two
months ago his unease of magic had heightened to where it
shattered his concentration and set his nerves on edge—now
he was going up against a Reakthi spellcaster who had made
a pact with the Voices? A spellcaster who, when less powerful,
had shrugged off a well-placed blow to the neck and had hurled

the Murderer across the streets of Eadarus?

That had been a long time ago, that.

Moknay sneered at his doubts. What was it Thromar had said? "Magic may have its mystery and danger, Murderer, but so do you." Had to admit it—sometimes Thromar did have a point.

Moknay planted his feet in the snow, the Darklight held brazenly before him. A snarl of defiance marred his grim mien, and he boldly faced the one-eyed spellcaster, who still screamed Logan's name to the winds.

"Wizard!" the Murderer barked, and the scorn was blatant in his voice. "I have something that belongs to you!"

Crackling black energy turned away from the murky gloom and riveted on Moknay like an ebony ember. Enraged veins stood out on the spellcaster's neck as Groathit's bony hands swung upward and writhing blackness arced from his fingertips. "You dare?" the sorcerer shrieked. "You dare touch something that belongs to me? You will die, Murderer! You will die and so shall your friend! Matthew Logan shall die!"

Moknay leapt expertly to his left, escaping the ebon blast. At least he had learned the grimoire was still important to the sorcerer—or at least important enough to distract him.

Moknay jumped again as a second blast of Darkness spumed from Groathit's fingers and ruptured a wall of stone. A grim smile spread across the Murderer's lips as a third blast caught a Demon across the back and sent it toppling over the mountain's edge, its wings bent and broken. The wizard was allowing his anger to ruin his concentration and was lashing out in an infuriated, impatient pattern. So long as Moknay kept moving through the battle about him, he could easily evade the unaimed blows.

A Debarnian fighter unexpectedly backed into the Murderer, his arm accidentally jarring Moknay's wounded shoulder. Pain flared anew through the outlaw's chest and his balance faltered in the snow. It was instinct more than anything else that twisted Moknay back around toward Zackaron's cave.

Howling rays of Darkness streamed from Groathit's palms.

Logan inched stealthily along the mountainside, cruel rock jabbing into the flesh of his back. He tried his best to blend in with the unnatural blackness around him—tried to keep his full weight off his feet so he made as little noise as possible while walking, but his efforts seemed too clumsy.

Damn! Moknay made it look so easy!

The young man winced as a body smashed into the hillside, splattering him with warm droplets of blood. Bile rose in his throat, but the young man forced it down. That was why he had to succeed, he told himself. That was why he had to make it to Zackaron's cave unseen and restore the Balance to the Wheel—'cause people were dying. Dying all around him. Right now. Right that very instant. And the longer he took, the more people died.

Logan made a wild dash for the cavern's opening and flinched as a stray bolt of magic struck the wall where he had just been. Shards of stone and sparks of sorcery pelted the young man as he dived frantically into the cave, stumbled, forced himself to scramble onward on his hands and knees. The eerie green glow of Zackaron's chamber seemed unsettlingly dim, and the young man pulled himself to his feet, his hold on the Heart weakening.

The stony home of the insane spellcaster remained much the same. Odds and ends decorated the shelves, and the disagreeing flux of Zackaron's unbalance radiated outward from the crystal orb situated in the center of the room. Still, Logan felt his last hope wither as his single eye fell upon the motionless form lying on the cold, stone floor. A titanic, overpowering wave of frustration crashed down on the young man, swamping his courage and draining his strength, and a futile howl of rage escaped Logan's lips and rebounded endlessly off the rock walls.

Damn him! the young man swore to himself. Damn Groathit! He had beaten him! Beaten him at every damn turn! Every damn time it looked like things were going good, Groathit was on hand to fuck things up! Damn him! Damn him! Damn him!

Logan swung a furious eye back toward the entrance, clenched fists shaking at his sides in an impotent rage. "You're dead meat, asshole," he vowed.

"Unbalance?"

Logan wheeled around, his fury snapping into surprise. Curious eyebrows raised beneath the blood smearing his forehead, and his hand hesitantly touched the hilt of his Reakthi blade.

"Unbalance?"

The young man directed his halved vision at the lifeless form crumpled near the iron-wrought pedestal of the glimmering orb, watching for any telltale sign. It couldn't be, he despondently told himself. He's dead. He's not moving . . . he's not breathing. He must be dead.

The sudden change of color in Zackaron's orb caught Logan's eye.

"Unbalance?"

Apprehensively, Logan approached the glittering orb. "Zackaron?" he queried, questioning himself as much as the globe before him.

The green glow melted into blue. "Ahhhh, Unbalance," the voice of Zackaron said from the orb. "Hoped you would come. Hurt badly, am I?"

Logan blinked at the motionless body. "You're dead."

A mindless snicker sounded from Zackaron's orb. "No, no, not dead," he corrected. "I am hidden. I am hiding. I am hid. Yaaagh! Deformity! Freak! Outcast! Unclean! Inside here I hide. Fooled the fool, did I not? Thought me dead, did he not?"

"Yeah," answered Logan, "but so did I."

Zackaron giggled. "Not so. Things were prepared should the Darkness come, and come they did. And now you are here. Here you are. Have you come to lessen the pain as before?"

Logan looked down at the wrinkled page in his hand. "Yeah, but I need your help."

"My help?" parroted the globe. "My help? Not much help I'd be. You must help me first."

A swelling pressure of anger built up inside the young man, and he almost threw down the Bloodstone in his ire. There was that damn word again! Must! Must! Must! And what kind of help did Zackaron want? There was a goddamn war going on outside, and Logan was in no mood to do anybody any favors!

"Look, people are dying out there!" the young man snarled at the talking globe. "Just what the hell kind of help do you want? I don't have time to run out and get you some goddamn clay!"

The blue flame of Zackaron's orb drifted into a misty purple. "I do not want clay now, Unbalance." The wizard's voice sounded hurt. "I want to help you, but may not do so in this position. I need your help to get back to my body."

Logan paused, embarrassed by his outburst, yet his fury did not vanish. Twinges of anger laced his words as he retorted, "What the hell am I supposed to do? I'm not a spellcaster."

"Lift the orb and place it in my arms," Zackaron explained. "It is as simple as navigating a plowhorse through a sheet of moon's dirt."

Logan screwed up his face at the sorcerer's rantings. Okay, so maybe he wasn't making any sense, the young man concluded, but maybe—somehow—the wizard might be able to reanimate his body. Watch it be my kind of luck to have him forget how to reverse the process!

Shuffling the Heart into the crook of his arm, Logan cautiously lifted the glimmering orb from its iron-wrought stand and grunted in sudden surprise to find it far heavier than he thought it would be. On the pedestal the globe shimmered with a delicate fragility, yet in the young man's hands the orb weighed him down with the force of its magicks.

The violet glow of Zackaron's orb winked into an alarming red.

"Unbalance!" came the spellcaster's frantic voice. "Behind you! Darkness speaks! Voices shout! Behind you!"

Logan whipped around to catch sight of a dark-eyed Demon launch itself into the cavern. Wild blades of Darkness shot from its inhuman hands, and Logan threw himself backwards, crashing into a bookcase and tumbling to the ground. Protective hands clutched desperately around the Bloodstone and Logan was unable to stop his fall, his already injured forehead smacking painfully into an overturned chair.

Zackaron's sparkling orb spilled to the ground and shattered into a million crystalline shards.

Exploding ebony sent shock waves of deadly force radiating outward in all directions, threatening to bring down mountaintops of snow with avalanchelike results. Invisible ripples of power knocked Moknay backwards, snapping the Murderer's head back with a painful, concussive jolt and jarring his balance as well as the snow beneath his feet. Rumbling echoes gripped the mountain range as huge slabs of snow fragmented underfoot, sledding downward and shooting off the mountains' edge, taking men and Demons with them. A curse slipped from Moknay's lips as the snow below him tried to carry him off the cliff and he was forced to make a wild leap to the right.

Agony burned through the Murderer's arm as he slammed into an outcropping of rock, a pain-filled cry tearing from his throat. Warm rivulets of blood seeped through his grey clothing as he fell heavily to the ground, his arms still locked around the Darklight volume.

Groathit took a menacingly confident step toward the downed Murderer, his bony fingers drawn up like claws. "As you die," the spellcaster wheezed, "so shall Matthew Logan die."

Moknay's eyes glowered with hatred. "I'm not dead yet," he sneered.

A ghastly smile on Groathit's withered features was the only warning Moknay had before blistering streams of Darkness forked out for him. The Murderer swiftly somersaulted backwards, throwing out both arms and hurling the Darklight into the center of Groathit's attack. Leather burst into black flames and cracked parchment turned to ash as the ancient book was caught in the maelstrom of ebony power.

The Darklight grimoire exploded.

Ignoring the pain in his shoulder, Moknay freed two daggers, and silver blazed through the murky night. Gaping as he was at the destroyed Darklight, Groathit screamed in rage as twin blades sank into the flesh of his unprotected arm. A distasteful frown scarred the spellcaster's expression as he jerked one of the daggers free, watching with a morbid fascination at the dark, pulsing glare that emanated from beneath his skin. Only a weak trail of bloodlike ichor dripped from the wizard's wounds, and the smile returned to his wrinkled features as Groathit swung his crackling black eye on Moknay.

"I'm not dead yet," the sorcerer mimicked, and Moknay's own dagger came screaming back at him.

In an attempt to release the frustration and fury growing inside him, Matthew Logan lunged for the nearest weapon and threw the iron-wrought pedestal in the Demon's direction.

"Goddamn you!" the young man yelled, succumbing to the insanity of overwhelming anger as he hurled Zackaron's chair. "Goddamn son of a bitch!"

Screeching, the Demon's eyes flared darkly and reduced Logan's makeshift weapons to slag and splinters. Undaunted, the young man clambered to his feet, all sense of self-preservation lost to the undying rage brewing within him. All that mattered was that he had been so close . . . so damn close! He had made it to Zackaron! He had done it! Then this . . . this bastard interrupted and made the young man drop Zackaron's orb! And it was gonna pay! Boy, was this goddamn son of a bitch ever gonna pay!

Crimson flickered up and down the length of Logan's sword as the young man charged, his furious warcry filling the rocky chamber. What might have been surprise glinted briefly in the Demon's expression before magic-swathed claws lashed out for Logan's head. Scarlet magicks and Reakthi steel met the hand halfway and sliced through flesh, muscle, and bone. A perturbed squeal escaped the Demon's rounded mouth as it swung its other hand.

Controlled by the inhuman rage flooding his muscles, Logan ducked, bringing his sword straight up. The diamond-shaped point of the young man's sword skewered the Demon's lower jaw, ripping up into its circular mouth and severing its tongue. A garbled shriek of pain fled the monster's lipless mouth, and the creature tried to pull away, tearing its own lower jaw apart to escape Logan's sword.

Logan jerked his sword away and hacked sideways. Razor-sharp steel drove through Demonic flesh, and the gangly creature screamed in irritation. A wild hand shot out and caught the base of Logan's hilt, knocking away both sword and young man. Blackness flared in the Demon's empty sockets as the Bloodstone fell out of Logan's grasp and what would have been a smile tried to stretch across the monster's slashed flesh and shattered bone.

The hatred and ire urging the young man on died abruptly as Logan saw the glaring Heart tumble from his grasp. Terror drove its fangs into his courage. Logan tried to dive for the fallen jewel, yet his anger-spawned strength had fled. Once more the aches and pains from his wounds stabbed at his nerves, and the weariness descended upon him like a fog. He watched in exhausted horror as the Demon's sticklike legs sent it springing across the cavern and toward the Heart.

A sudden figure blocked its way.

Dark eyes blazing with insane fury, Zackaron clamped hands on either side of the Demon's throat. Spitting, crackling energy encircled the sorcerer like a magical nimbus, and his eyes reflected the fire of theurgy.

"You broke my ball," the spellcaster snarled, and all his energy erupted from his hands.

Unable to scream, the Demon burst as Zackaron's magicks punched through its frail body. Blackness and golden sorcery clashed in mortal combat, and even the Darkness inside the Demon scattered before Zackaron's might. An answering moan of anguish ripped the heavens outside the cave from the Voices, and Logan jumped to his feet, his weakness chased away by the hope once again alive inside him.

A disgusted look on his lean features, Zackaron wiped his hands on his robe. "Foul creatures," the wizard stated. "Foul, putrid, revolting creatures. I would sooner dip my mother in dragon dung than taste the stench of Wormy sliminess."

Logan picked up the Heart, the thunder of Voices from outside coaxing him to hurry. "Whatever," he responded. "Look, I don't know how the hell you survived, but we've got to restore the Balance. We . . ."

"How the hell I survived?" parroted the spellcaster. "Quite simple! Simple, quite! I said I needed to get out. One way was to touch the orb to my body. That would have worked just as nicely. Just as nicely. But this . . . ! This! *He broke my ball!*"

Logan flinched as the blinding aura of sorcery returned to encompass the insane magician, and he gave the bagged Jewel at his waist a queasy look. *I'm going to give him this?* the young man asked himself in astonished fear. *I'm going to give the craziest man in all Sparrill the most powerful item in the multiverse?*

The young man's darker side answered with a macabre shrug of humor. *Sure, why not?* it queried. *That way if you beat Groathit, you'll still have to worry about Zackaron destroying the world.*

Logan frowned at his own black humor and untied the pouch. "We need to restore the Balance," he explained again, hoping there was some semblance of reason left inside Zackaron. "You were going to help me, remember?"

The lean sorcerer cocked his head to one side in a confused move that reminded Logan of the light blue ogre. The halo of magic surrounding the magician died to a flicker, and a naive, innocent expression of childish ignorance spread across Zackaron's face.

A cold knot of fear formed in Logan's stomach as he freed the Jewel and held it out toward Zackaron; the spellcaster accepted it quizzically.

Logan picked up the single page of the Darklight grimoire and glanced briefly at the alien words. "I'm going to read this, and I need you to control the energy it releases," he said. "Can you do that?"

When the young man looked up, he did not like the wild, maniacal look burning in Zackaron's eyes and the golden, answering gleam at the Jewel's heart.

Voices filled the sky like thunder:
The Purity!
It burns!
The Equilibrium resists us!
Banishment!
The stench of banishment!
Groathit threw the sentient blackness overhead a villainous scowl. *A distraction!* the wizard snarled to himself in realization. *The accursed little maggots dared try to fool him?* While he wasted

time with the Murderer, Matthew Logan went on unhindered! But
no more! Matthew Logan would die—and the Purity would die
with him! Then all would belong to the Darkness! Then all would
listen to what the Voices had to say!

The wizard turned his Darkness-enhanced vision toward the
grey-garbed Murderer and frowned as Moknay avoided the dagger
thrown at him. A pity, Groathit mused. It would have been a fitting
end for the Murderer to die by his own weapon.

Robe flapping, Groathit turned away from the outlaw and stalked
through the snow. Matthew Logan was somewhere—somewhere
hidden in this curtain of darkness and snow. But he would not
be for long! The whelp had dared too much, and his time had
come!

A mystic pass of Groathit's gnarled hand threw men and Demons
aside, and the sorcerer's dark eye scanned the mountainside. Hide
all you want, worm, the wizard growled to himself. I will find
you. You know I will find you. I am Groathit, greatest of all
Reakthi spellcasters—greatest of all spellcasters! None are left
to oppose me! The Smythe! Zackaron! All are dead! And you,
Matthew Logan . . . you, too, shall be among their number to fall
beneath the might of Groathit!

The wizard spun around, and the wind screamed in his fury.

The cold fear tripled inside Logan's gut as Zackaron fixed
wild, dark eyes on the young man, a look of utter insanity on the
sorcerer's features. The Jewel burned in the spellcaster's hands,
and golden-white illuminance filled the cavern chamber with livid
energy.

Oh, shit, Logan swore to himself. What the hell have I done?

Zackaron's eyes flicked to the coruscating Jewel. "My Jewel,"
the sorcerer breathed, and his voice was a whisper of awe. "My
Jewel. I have you back."

Logan almost ran when the spellcaster's eye swung back up
and met his. "I must thank you, Matthew Logan," Zackaron
declared, and the awe remained in his voice. "For eons I have
been a prisoner of my own power—master of magic, yet mad.
And now . . . now the Unbalance operates once again; now my
pain and wounds work against the Dark."

Logan blinked at the disturbing calm that filled Zackaron's
voice.

"I am sane, Matthew Logan," the magician proclaimed, and a
fleeting smile drew beneath his trim beard and mustache. "I am

sane, and I have you to thank. Quickly now, we must prepare."

The young man failed to blink the wonder out of his system as Zackaron wheeled about, blazing tendrils of golden-yellow light zigzagging from his fingers and reconstructing the shattered orb.

"Wait a minute," Logan sputtered, words failing him. "What the . . . ? How . . . ?"

Zackaron looked away from his repaired globe, impatience tingeing his moves. "There is no time, Matthew Logan. No time," the wizard interrupted. "Suffice to say all that has occurred has severely acted upon the Balance of both the Wheel and the multiverse. Your gift of the Jewel has restored the sanity burned away previously by my lust for power, and I am now in control. Do you know what I say? I am now in control."

This is too weird, Logan concluded. I do one little good deed in my life, and suddenly everything's moving too fast. Zackaron's insanity is cured—or can you even cure insanity? Anyway, it's gone . . . and somehow it's because *I* gave him the Jewel after all the nasty stuff *he* went through with Gangrorz and now the Voices. So now what? Now he's in control of all that magic he took from the Jewel and is just as eager to restore the Balance as I am. But there's still a war going on outside, and we're still not exactly sure about how we're supposed to banish the Darkness, and Groathit's still out there somewhere, and . . . Whoa! Hold on a second! I've gotta catch my breath!

Zackaron tapped impatient fingers across the face of his glittering orb. "We cannot restore the Balance if you insist on standing around," the sorcerer scolded. "Quickly, get the incantation and hold on tightly to the Heart. We will use both it and the Jewel. That way the Voices will never be able to stop us."

Logan tried shaking his head, hoping maybe that would straighten out his befuddled state of mind. "Huh? What?" he said. "I could have used the Heart for this?"

"No, no, not by yourself," Zackaron replied. "Not without the Jewel. You and I will use the Heart and the Jewel. You see, the Jewel is the Wheel's Equilibrant, but the Heart is Sparrill's magic—between the two of them, their magicks will work together to right the Wheel and banish the Darkness." The wizard strode hastily toward the cavern entrance. "Hurry. This way."

"Back out there?" Logan exclaimed, knowing the risks of letting the Darkness spot the Bloodstone.

"We cannot confront our enemies from here," Zackaron returned. "We must face them directly. We are Champions,

Matthew Logan. Champions of the Balance and the Purity. And you are the Unbalance—everything and nothing rests solely on your shoulders; all and none are in your hands. It would not be fitting to triumph while hidden from view. Come!"

Logan felt the uncertainty build inside him as Zackaron stepped purposefully for the cave's mouth. Not befitting, the young man grumbled to himself. Everything and nothing! All and none! On my shoulders! I liked it better when this guy was insane. At least then he wasn't crazy enough to walk into the middle of a full-scale war!

The sounds of battle and the howl of the freezing wind did nothing to calm Logan's anxieties as he hurried after Zackaron and stepped back out into the darkness of the Hills.

·18·

Unbalance

The wind raked icy claws across Logan's face as he stepped out into the snow and away from the protection of Zackaron's cavern home. In his hands the Heart of Sparrill beat with a waning pulse of scarlet light, a blatant contrast to the fearful pounding of Logan's own heart. The sounds of battle once more assailed the young man's ears, made all the more frightening by the unearthly gloom that engulfed the Hills and hid the source of the noise. Demonic screams, human cries, and the crackle of Dark sorcery all sprouted from within the blackness, their echoes thrown far into the mountain range. Roiling, sentient ebony writhed through the murkiness of the snow-filled sky, inhuman, unintelligible whispers coming from its impenetrable interior.

Logan forced himself to ignore the shiver of fright that crawled its way down his spine and fixed his single eye on the gaunt sorcerer beside him. "Now what?" the young man queried, yelling to be heard over the wind.

Zackaron's dark eyes remained downcast, locked on the Jewel in his hands while his lips mouthed voiceless words. Logan blinked in befuddlement when the Bloodstone in his own hands flickered to life, mimicking the rhythmic glow of the Jewel. The two gemstones began to simultaneously strengthen their respective brilliance, casting mixed shadows of red and yellow across the hills.

"We must be on guard now," Zackaron warned Logan. "I have linked the Jewel to the Heart and the Heart to the Jewel. Both will respond in kind to the incantation—but now they are an even greater threat to the Voices. The Darkness will be upon us shortly. Quickly—perform the spell before we are overwhelmed."

Logan fumbled with the Heart and incantation while his gaze kept nervously flicking back and forth. Hurry, he tells me, the young man grumbled to himself, still trying to get a firm grip on both the Bloodstone and the page of parchment. He tells me everything he's gonna do five seconds after he's done it and then expects me to react calmly and rationally! What the hell does he think I am? A superhero?

Logan made a sour face. No, he probably thinks I'm a spellcaster.

Beads of sweat formed on the young man's brow as he finally held the page with the incantation right side up and cradled the Heart tightly against his chest. Trickles of perspiration joined the trickles of blood winding their way down his face as Logan anxiously bit his lower lip, squinting his uncovered eye through the gloom to read the alien script.

A high-pitched squeal of fury stopped the young man before the first word passed his lips. A Demon dived out of the gloom above them, black energy roaring about its talons, its bestial scream tearing into the heart of Logan's courage. In reply, golden force exploded outward from the Jewel's in Zackaron's grasp, striking the Demon. Pale flesh ignited, and bone and sinew were reduced to grey-black ash. Even the living Darkness inside screamed in agony as the yellow-gold sorcery slashed through its blackness and scattered it to the arctic winds. The dying howls of the ebony were echoed by the cloudlike mass of blackness overhead.

Pain! a hundred thousand rasping voices moaned. *We feel pain*!
The Equilibrium burns!
It burns!
It must be destroyed!
Destroyed!
Destroy the Equilibrium!

A hint of urgency twinged Zackaron's words. "Quickly, Matthew Logan," the wizard coaxed. "There is not much time."

Trying to ignore the butterflies in his stomach, Logan looked away from the once-mad spellcaster and returned his gaze to the remaining page of the Darklight grimoire. Out of the corner of his uncovered eye, the young man caught sight of a dozen winged silhouettes pushing their way through the snow and wind, blackness sparking in their empty eye sockets. Squirming, thrashing Darkness snaked about their talons, and soul-searing screams escaped their rounded mouths.

"Hurry!" Zackaron commanded, the urgency mounting.

Logan's eye focused on the ancient print, and his voice trembled with fear. " '*Gu oud f'nwib oudcy eui*,' " he read once again. " '*Ehuim. W'rkcy eui. W'rkcy muiz luhekhr kir swcyr*.' "

Sorcery radiated outward from both the Jewel and the Heart, splashing crimson and flaxen spotlights across the hillsides. In immediate response, jet-black streams of magic yowled from the approaching Demons, riddling the landscape around Logan and Zackaron. Black explosions ripped apart the mountainside, melting rock and snow and scattering sparks of dark energy. Logan tried hard not to flinch—to keep his attention riveted to the incantation before him—but that was nearly impossible with someone hurling bolts of sorcery at him. The young man made an instinctive jump to one side and barely avoided a blast that impacted between himself and Zackaron.

With a convulsion of fiery ice, the explosion of Darkness threw Logan backwards and right off the side of the mountain.

Blood splattered the snow as glowing black talons tore through flesh. With half his throat ripped away, the wounded Guardsman pitched forward, a garbled scream caught in his shredded vocal cords. Yorke winced as the soldier collapsed into the carpet of white and lay still, his lifefluid staining the snow red.

"This isn't working," Roshfre rumbled from nearby.

Yorke lunged at a Demon. "I can see that," he retorted.

Dark magic flamed and caught one of Quarn's Reakthi. The metal of the soldier's chestplate splashed to either side in a molten spray of liquid steel, accompanied by a hideous rainfall of blood. Yorke tried to duck the shower of crimson but was only half-successful. Warm spatters struck the outlaw's face and were lost within his hair, and he felt his stomach twist in protest. He had seen a lot of nasty things before, but nothing had compared with the beating they had taken at Plestenah . . . until now . . . until this.

They were being slaughtered . . . regardless of the forces that had arrived with the Rebel. Nothing they seemed to do stopped these dark-eyed Demons. They kept on coming . . . relentlessly . . . endlessly. No amount of fighting seemed to stop their progress, and Yorke's trepidation grew as he noticed how the number of men fighting about him had been replaced by the gangly creatures with the dark eyes.

A brutal shove pulled the rogue from his thoughts. "Get your head down!" Roshfre barked, pushing Yorke to one side.

Both outlaws narrowly avoided flaming black claws.

Yorke pivoted, driving a dagger deep into the Demon's solar plexus with his right hand. He had learned a long time ago to ignore the pain of his broken wrist, and concentrated solely on the battle around him. One moment of careless musing, and he was so much carrion . . . not that that seemed to matter, the bandit thought. Something had to be done or that's what they'd end up as: worm fodder. Something had to be done that could change the inevitable outcome of this war. Something that could at least save Yorke's neck.

"We's got t' do somethin'," the rogue declared.

Roshfre's mace tore the flesh away from a Demon's face. "What the *Deil* can we do?" snapped the redhead. "We're not like that Logan fellow!"

Yorke looked up, half a smile spreading across his scarred features. *That* was how he could stay alive. "'Xactly," the rogue grinned, "so's if we's want t' do somethin' about stayin' alive, what would you suggest?"

Comprehension erased Roshfre's confusion. "Find Logan," she understood.

What was it Logan had said? "Bet yer ass," Yorke nodded. "'Sides, he still has me whip."

Darkness peered through Darkness, and blue-black vision etched the scene into Groathit's mind. He saw men outlined in dark blue— Demons in violet-black. The gloom of the Hills was nonexistent, its darkness cancelled by the darkness of Groathit's crackling eye, but still, the Reakthi spellcaster could find no trace of Matthew Logan.

You always were good at running, worm, the sorcerer sneered to himself, but it will not help you this time. This time you have nowhere to run where you will not be caught—nowhere to hide where you will not be found.

Groathit scanned the mountainside, bony hands clenched angrily at his sides. He was Groathit! Why could he not find the wretched little cur that was Matthew Logan? Surely the maggot had not escaped him again? No . . . his friends still fought his war—guilt would keep the whelp here. So where was he? *Where was he*?

A sudden cry of pain resounded through the spellcaster's mind and reverberated across the mountains: *Pain!* the Voices screeched. *We feel pain!*

Groathit scrambled up an incline, the crackling orb of blackness that was his eye surveying the fight below him. Something had hurt the Darkness, and there was only one thing capable of accomplishing that: Matthew Logan.

The increasing glare of yellow-black light caught the wizard's attention and he swung his gaze eastward. He sensed the familiar aura of Balance—the kind of magic he had felt emanating from the Jewel when he had wrested it from Logan's grasp. Then a second glare pierced the wizard's eyesight—a blinding white light of such intensity that it hurt Groathit to look at it. This, the sorcerer knew, was the Purity; that was where Matthew Logan was.

Howling black tendrils of power lanced from the wizard's gnarled hands, stabbing through the curtain of snow on their way toward Logan. At the last instant, the young man leapt aside, escaping the bolt. Darkness flamed as the blast struck the ground where Logan had been, and even Groathit's Darkness-enhanced vision was momentarily blinded. As his blow rocked the hillside, Groathit lost sight of the pure white light of the Heart.

Frail, skinny legs ascended the mountain, and a ghastly smile stretched on Groathit's wrinkled features. No matter, the Reakthi told himself as he climbed higher for a better view. There is nowhere he can hide . . . nowhere he can run.

Today Matthew Logan dies.

I'm gonna die.

Freezing air whipped itself into a frenzy at Logan's back as the young man pitched over the side of the mountain and dropped like a stone. Abrupt pain knifed into his back and his skull banged hard against snow-clad rock as he landed roughly on a ledge some ten feet down. Stars blossomed behind his eyelids, and he fought off the encroaching unconsciousness. Somehow his befuddled mind understood that he had not fallen far enough to splatter at the base of the mountain, but that he *had* come to a stop. Dazedly, the young man from Santa Monica pulled himself into a seated position and looked to his right.

Sparrill stretched out below him, cloaked in darkness.

Logan reached a gentle hand behind his head to feel for the bump that was undoubtedly sprouting on the back of his skull and touched warm fluid. Repulsed, the young man drew his hand away to see it smeared with blood.

Blood? His muddled brain reeled. *His* blood?

The gloom of the mountainside blurred, and Logan had to fight off another bout of impending unconsciousness. At least I didn't fall all the way down the mountain, he told himself while waiting for the dizziness to leave. And I didn't lose the Bloodstone or the incantation. I've probably got a concussion and a few broken bones, but hey! I should be thankful, right?

The young man's sarcasm was lost in the steady throbbing ache of his head, and he forced himself to clamber to his knees. He had to get back to Zackaron and finish the incantation . . . but what if Zackaron was dead? What if that blast had killed him or knocked him off the other side of the mountain? And be reasonable, Matthew, you can barely stand, let alone fight your way through a dozen Demons. Let's just stay here and rest . . . too bad we can't read the incantation from here.

An idea forced its way through the pain and dizziness of Logan's mind. And who says I can't? the young man questioned himself. No one ever said Zackaron and the Jewel had to be near me. Dirge said I needed a focus . . . well, if I focus everything on the Heart, that should work, shouldn't it? Didn't Zackaron say he had linked the Jewel and the Heart together? Hell! What have I got to lose? Just the entire known multiverse.

Through vision blurred by the agony in his head, Logan began reading the ancient passage from the Darklight grimoire. Ruby energy swelled upward from the Bloodstone, filling the young man's precarious perch with vibrant, crimson magic. The frigid bite of the unnatural wind died as the Heart's soothing warmth took its place, caressing Logan's body with an almost physical embrace. The painful throb in the young man's skull faded away as the crimson gleam intensified, and he could feel the hurt and discomfort from his many wounds dying under the buildup of Natural magicks.

As more of the alien words stumbled from his lips, Logan sensed the almost electric charge of power in the snowy air about him. A blazing halo of scarlet fulgor encompassed the Bloodstone that rested in Logan's arms. Whatever he was reading—whatever he was saying—it was working! The Heart was building up a discharge of energy. The young man only hoped the Jewel was doing the same.

The last trace of dizziness fled Logan's cranium, and he jumped spritely to his feet. More and more power flowed outward from the Heart, creating a blood-red nimbus of energy that chased away the gloom and added strength to the young man's limbs. This is it! Logan told himself. This time it is going to work! This time he was going to be able to control the discharge and restore the Balance! This time he was gonna win!

A scream of rage broke the young man's concentration, and Logan jerked his head skyward. A Demon came streaking off the mountain's ledge toward him, blackness spuming from its claws. Silver unexpectedly flashed in the light of the Bloodstone's flux and sliced effortlessly through one of the creature's wings. The Demon's scream of anger became one of shock as its flight was disrupted and it fluttered helplessly against the freezing gale, missing Logan's ledge and bouncing down the mountainside.

Logan heard its bones snap when it finally struck another ledge and rebounded off, continuing its fatal roll down the hill.

Blue eye filled with wonder, Logan stared up at the ledge above him. He raised his eyebrows when Yorke peered down at him, grinning a grin that lacked certain teeth.

"Yer a hard man t' find," the rogue stated.

Logan breathed a sigh of relief; at least someone had seen him go over the edge. "Yorke," the young man called back up, "I need to get back up there. I'm a sitting duck down here."

The outlaw blinked. "Yer a what?"

"An easy target!" Logan shouted back. "The Demons can come at me from above and from the side!"

Yorke eyed the flood of scarlet luminescence from the Bloodstone that outlined Logan with a fiery red flame. "Can'tcha fly?" the rogue inquired.

Ire sparked in Logan's uncovered eye. "I'm not . . ."

"I's know! I's know!" interrupted Yorke. "Yer not a spellcaster! Well, I'll tells ya what. Ya still got me whip? Throw it up here and we'll use it like a rope. Sound good?"

Logan glanced hurriedly at his belt and was grateful to see Yorke's whip still coiled at his waist. Surrounded in crimson light that continued to waver about him, Logan unraveled the weapon and hurled it up the side of the mountain. Yorke caught the whip's handle expertly and anchored himself securely in the snow. As Logan drew himself up, renewed vitality flowing through his system, scarlet sorcery trailed its way up the length of braided leather.

Yorke gave the glowing red whip an apprehensive look and resisted the instinctive urge to let go and hide from the obvious magic coming toward him. What if it burned his hands? It was bad enough fighting with a broken wrist—what would happen if sorcery seared the flesh from his fingers? Not even he would be able to fight with no hands! But . . . if he let go, Logan fell. What was more important? His fingers or his life?

Yorke tightened his grip and pretended to ignore the crimson energy filling the leather of the whip.

Logan pulled himself up over the mountain's edge and rolled quickly to his feet. Ruby light bathed the immediate area around the young man, and a number of Demons swung their bulbous heads in his direction.

Logan waved a shimmering red hand at the Demons. "Keep them away from me," he ordered Roshfre and Yorke. "I'm almost finished."

"Almost finished with what?" Roshfre wanted to know.

"Almost finished with the incantation!" barked Logan. "Keep 'em back!"

The young man frantically looked back at the sheet of yellowed parchment still in his grip. He had come so close to completing the incantation, and the Bloodstone still pulsed with the energy it had accumulated. Did he have to repeat the whole thing again or just take up where he had left off? What he wouldn't do to have Mara here with him now! Oh, hell with it! Read the whole thing!

" '*Gu oud f'nwib oudcy eui. Ehuim. W'rkcy eui. W'rkcy muiz luhekhr kir swcyr. Oud'rkcy suubyr vkab rwyr. Enkf oud mkcy'd ewss iyczh vy oudhg kmkwi. Luus.*' "

Sanguine sheets of power shot up from every angle of the Heart, adding to the already blinding aurora of blood-red color. Falling snow turned to steam as the Heart's staggering flux magnified, and Logan could hear its unspoken query—sense the magic's desire to aid the dying land the best way it could.

Go, the young man commanded the sorcery. Go balance the Wheel! Go!

Crimson blazed. A hundred sporadic shafts of theurgy lanced through the murky sky, joined by the golden spears of force that came from the Jewel. The entire mountain range was lit by the eerie combination of red and golden suns as the Jewel and Bloodstone coalesced in unison and discharged as one.

A million screams of fury and pain wracked the Darkness, and the Demons echoed their cries. A growing rumble sounded beneath Logan's tennis shoes, and the hills began to quake, reminding the young man of previous earthquakes during the first imbalance of the Wheel. However, while those quakes proclaimed the tilting of the Wheel, these quakes declared the opposite.

A sudden voice sounded in Logan's brain. "*Now, Matthew Logan,*" came Zackaron's disembodied command. "*The rest of the magic. Set it free. Direct it at the Darkness; banish the Voices!*"

Logan needed no prompting. The air around him was alive with energy, and he sensed the terrific pressure building up inside the

Bloodstone's interior. It was far greater than any other flux he had felt before—almost as if another source of energy backed it—and Logan understood what Zackaron had meant by the Jewel and the Heart working together. Only the Jewel could restore the Balance, just as only the Heart could repel the Voices. Somehow the bond Zackaron had set up between the two gems allowed them to aid one another in their respective tasks—just as the Heart had assisted in the righting of the Wheel, so would the Jewel aid in the banishment of the Darkness.

Cold fear shot through Logan's gut as he looked up and spied the sheet of living blackness writhe and coil angrily in his direction, vengeful thunder booming from its depths.

The Purity! the Voices roared. *It still exists!*

It works with the Equilibrium!

The Equilibrium!

Destroy them!

Destroy them both!

Darkness descended.

Groathit jerked about, a scowl on his wrinkled face. A deep dread not of his own filled his scrawny frame, and he flinched as blazing streams of white light stabbed through the heavens. The Purity! The sorcerer blanched. In such force? Impossible!

The acrid taste of the Equilibrium set Groathit's stomach on edge, and the Reakthi wizard squinted his crackling eye at the battle sprawled out below him. Somehow the Jewel and Bloodstone were working together—how Matthew Logan had been clever enough to engineer *that* was beyond the spellcaster, yet it had happened. What that discharge had proved befuddled the sorcerer since it had no target. Nonetheless, Groathit knew something was happening . . . the twin flux of both the Jewel and the Heart, the threatening rumble in the ground beneath his feet . . . The whelp was up to something.

Blue-black vision locked on a form seen in dark blue color, yet its shape was unmistakable. It was the girl . . . the one with the long dark hair who had grown so attached to Matthew Logan . . . and he to her. She would be the perfect means for his downfall. She was a means of exploiting the young fool's many weaknesses and stopping whatever it was Matthew Logan dared to attempt. With her in the wizard's clutches, the maggot dared not release another iota of sorcery for fear of causing her untimely demise. Which really was a pity . . . after all, she was as dead as he was.

The horrid smile returned to Groathit's face as he started a brisk run across the mountaintop to where Mara struggled side by side with Servil and Reakmor Osirik against the Darkness's Demons.

As the Hills of Sadroia shuddered about him with terrifying force, Logan dropped the Darklight's last remaining page and gripped the Bloodstone in both hands. Determination carved itself into his expression, and a defiant sneer turned up the young man's lip. Complete, total Darkness enveloped him, trying to overwhelm him with its eon-old horrors and blood-freezing cold, yet Logan stood fast. The scintillating nebula of magic still encircled his body, and his terror was burned away by the soothing warmth of the sorcery surrounding him. Only the slightest twinge of anxiety raced along his nerves as the young man turned away from the Darkness swallowing him whole and looked into the glaring center of the Heart.

Raw, unimaginable energy as great as Sparrill's expanse looked back at the young man, crackling, spitting, waiting for his command. Sparks flashed like minute red comets, piercing the curtain of complete ebony, drawing burning crimson gashes of light across the blackness. Slowly—gradually—Logan took in the fluxion of Natural magicks, feeling the warm tingles of power bring goosebumps to his flesh. Mind-staggering quantities of sorcery flowed from the Heart into Logan's body through an invisible bond, and Logan swung his uncovered eye up at the Darkness encasing him.

"You're history, sucker," Logan gritted through clenched teeth.

Purity exploded from the Heart in a three-hundred-and-sixty-degree circle.

Zackaron jumped back as the golden Jewel of Equilibrant blazed to life of its own accord, impaling the gloom with an unexpected upheaval of dazzling sorcery. Intense heat blew a warm blast of wind into the spellcaster's face as he tried to regain control of the gemstone, yet there was no way. The Jewel was releasing an uncontrollable blast of Cosmic proportions that would probably be sufficient to take off the entire top of the mountain.

For the first time in what must have been centuries, Zackaron felt fear.

Golden-yellow theurgy vomited from the coruscating Jewel, winding in on itself to form a twisting, writhing column of energy. Surprise replaced the fear in Zackaron's eyes as he realized someone was controlling the Jewel. Impossible as it seemed, Logan must have reached out through the link between the Heart and the Jewel and taken command of both gemstones!

There was no doubt that he was the Unbalance!

Zackaron held the flaming Jewel out at arm's length, and a smile bordering on the insane crossed his lips.

A tremendous shock wave of scarlet and gold tore through the Darkness in a complete circle about Logan, stabbing the blackness with ruby-yellow knives. Mind-numbing screams fluctuated throughout the ebony as the wall of blood-red and golden energy punctured the Voices' heart, scattering shards of sentient ebony across the hillside. Blown backwards by the expanding shock wave of red-gold magic, the Darkness spread thinly over the mountains, parts of it dissipating like a heavy fog before a harsh wind. Agonized screams sounded from the Darkness's interior as it dispersed in shreds, trying futilely to resist the wavelike sorcery that splayed outward from around Matthew Logan.

Teeth clenched, Logan kept up the barrage of theurgy, sending out bursts of magic that expanded outward like ripples in water. Faint sunlight began to pierce the weakening veil of gloom as the young man's bombardment continued, hurling the Voices backwards through the heavens.

The first of the Demons was caught in the red-gold ripples that radiated from the young man, and its scream was ripped harshly from its throat. Pale flesh tore from its bones, and muscles and internal organs burst in gold and red flames. As the skeletal remains of the Demon crumpled into ash, dying howls still echoed about the Hills. The Darkness inside the Demon shrieked once as the tidal wave of magic speared into it and sent it fragmenting in all directions.

Banishment! the Voices wailed. *The stench of banishment*!

The Purity assails us!

We are undone!

No!

Noooo!

The sky came alive with an inferno of crimson and golden sorcery.

Groathit swung to his left, disbelief swelling in his gut at the sight coming toward him. The Darkness! his mind reeled. The

Darkness succumbed to an overpowering wave of gold and red magic! It cannot be! It must not be!

The sorcerer whipped back around, his fingers curling into makeshift claws. The girl was nearby, he thought. There was still time . . . still a chance to grab the bitch and defeat Matthew Logan. The whelp had not won yet! So long as Groathit remained alive, Matthew Logan would not win . . . would *never* win!

Thunder blasted through Groathit's eardrums, and the spellcaster wheeled about. A massive wave of scarlet and golden fire reached out toward him, its Purity searing the Darkness of his eye. A single cry of defiance and rage went up from the Reakthi wizard as he hurled a blast of blackness at the onrushing force of magicks and felt the pleasing warmth of Nature swamp him with its Light.

The entire mountaintop volcanoed as Darkness met Purity and Equilibrant; Groathit screamed as his world disintegrated in a blinding conflagration of golden and sanguine radiance.

Mara flinched as the mountaintop behind her exploded, showering splinters of Darkness and shards of rock across the heavens. A few grey clouds lingered in the afternoon sky—and the sprinkle of snow persisted—yet the Voices' unnatural hold on the firmament had been broken. A warm wind filled the air as the yellow-red waves of sorcery expanded out past the Hills, reaching out in every direction, dispersing all traces of the Voices and their accursed Darkness.

A swelling pride filled the priestess's breast as she spotted the lone form of Logan outlined brilliantly by the collective force of gold and ruby resplendency. Waves of mingled theurgy continued to stretch out from about the young man, pushing the Darkness backwards, scattering the remains of its already diminished form. Even the Demons around the priestess had crumbled to ash, the ebony inside of them shattering like crystal and blinking out of existence like the sparks of a torch.

A weary smile stretched across Mara's lips as the Voices' screams died to a whisper. They had done it! They had won! Matthew had won!

Scythe instinctively shuddered as the concussive blasts of magic passed over him, reducing his Demonic attackers to nothingness. A pleased smirk twisted Dirge's gaunt features as he threw the injured rogue a devilish glance, amused by Scythe's uneasiness.

"You have nothing to fear," the necromage told the rogue. "The sorcery is controlled by the Unbalance. It has been commanded to do nothing more than banish the Darkness—fear not, it will not take you with it."

Scythe shook as another ripple of energy swept over him, its soothing breeze dampening the ache of his wounded cheek. "That's easy for you to say," the cutthroat snarled apprehensively, squinting as the afternoon sun turned the carpet of snow into a blinding covering of white. "You don't mind magic or dead people."

Aelkyne looked up, staring wide-eyed at the bands of ruby-gold sorcery that splashed across the mountainside, chasing the unnatural gloom from the sky. A small bird hidden in the foliage nearby began to twitter experimentally, its song filling the air of the Hills. Scarlet-yellow shadows flickered across the mountaintops as the ripples of energy continued their outward movement, rupturing the blackness wherever they touched. Even the wicked burn on the young Guardsman's side felt better as the pulse of gold-red magic passed overhead.

"What . . . What in Imogen's name is going on?" Aelkyne sputtered.

Imperator Quarn leaned wearily on his blade, his silver hair spotted with the blood of fallen comrades. "It appears we have won," the Reakthi commander concluded, inhaling deeply.

The light blue ogre gave the circular waves of sorcery a cautious glance. "Maaagic," the creature breathed in awe, worry sparking in its eyes.

"Indeed, my large friend," Quarn answered the ogre. "I believe our Outsider friend has done what he set out to do."

The Debarnian blacksmith Fjorm let his sword drop into the snow. "Just like that?" the stocky man demanded, his expression showing disbelief. "One moment we're being cut down—the next, we've won?"

Quarn's pale blue eyes settled on the blacksmith and glinted with a frightening knowledge of mystic things. "Magic is capable of much," explained the Imperator, "and what we fought was a battle on both the physical and mystic planes. We could not have won one without winning the other." The man in the black chestplate looked questioningly southward. "I'd even suspect the remnants of Vaugen's troops have been crushed by Logan's impressive attack."

Aelkyne suppressed a shiver. "And to think," the young Guard mused, "I was made to think he was the enemy. I'm glad we're friends."

The ogre smiled crookedly. "Frrrrriends."

The last screaming fragment of Darkness spun helplessly backwards, buffeted by the crimson-yellow gale. There was a final boom of thunder as an implosion split the heavens and the blackness was torn out of existence. Fading rumbles threw their echoes to the Hills as the gentle fall of snow ceased and all went quiet. A few birds chirped their greeting to the sun, and the sun replied by bouncing warmth off the snow-covered ground, yet there was a stillness in the air. Things were not quite resolved . . . there remained one last task. One last action.

Logan let the Heart of Sparrill spill out of his hands and tumble into the snow, its flaming aura of scarlet power winking out. An overpowering fatigue suddenly gripped the young man by the temples and he dropped to one knee, the vision of his single eye blurred even with its contact lens. He had the sensation of having just run a ten-kilometer run in just under twenty seconds and not feeling any ill effects until after crossing the finish line. Tingles of sorcery still trailed their way up and down his body as Logan collapsed into the snow, letting the white flakes draw the warmth from his body and return normal sensation to his limbs.

Gentle hands lifted the young man and set him upright.

"You did it, friend-Logan!" Thromar boomed happily. "You defeated the Darkness! I wouldn't have believed it if I hadn't have seen it with my own eyes! And you say you're not a spellcaster!"

Logan pulled himself away from the Rebel's crushing embrace, strength returning to him as a familiar anger built up inside him. "I'm not a spellcaster," the young man spat, enjoying no pleasure from his triumph. "I'm not a spellcaster and I never will be!"

A sincere smirk of admiration was on Moknay's usually grim features as Logan turned away from Thromar and suddenly faced the Murderer. "We owe you a great deal, friend," the grey-garbed outlaw stated.

Logan waved him off impatiently. "You don't owe me anything," he sneered. "I did what I did because I had to." He let his weariness fan his ire. "I didn't do it because it was the right thing to do; I did it so I could get the hell out of here. Now, where's Zackaron?"

"I am here, Unbalance."

Logan pivoted and found the dark-eyed sorcerer standing beside Thromar, a blank expression on his gaunt face. The Jewel still faintly glowed in the wizard's grasp and Logan picked up the Heart, pushing it out toward Zackaron's hands.

"Here," Logan snapped, "take it."

Without a word, Zackaron accepted the skull-sized Bloodstone. There was something in his eyes, Logan noticed. Something he wasn't telling . . . but what else was new? *Ever since I have come here there was always something I didn't know about . . . something somebody was keeping from me until it was too late.*

Hurried footsteps sounded in Logan's ears, and the happy cry of Mara almost broke the young man free of his anger. Teeth clenched, Logan steeled himself for the priestess's embrace and tried not to let the warmth and happiness return to his system . . . *not now . . . not for what he was about to do.*

"You did it!" Mara cried, holding him tightly. "I knew you could! I always knew you could!"

Logan frowned, the happy cheers running through his army and the closeness of Mara dampening his ire. *No!* he warned himself. *Don't give in! Don't feel what you want to feel! So you've won . . . big deal. You can't let it get to you.*

Mara noticed the coldness in the young man's response. Green eyes filling with concern, she asked, "Matthew? Is something wrong?"

Logan pulled himself free of Mara's arms, eye downcast. "No, nothing's wrong," he retorted. "It's just . . ." *It was getting to him.* "I can't . . ." *How the hell was he supposed to keep this up? It wasn't going to work. Not when . . . not when he loved this girl so damn much.* "I'm trying . . . aw, shit! Mara, I . . ."

The dark-haired woman understood. "You want to go back," she said softly.

Logan could barely stand the depression in her voice. "I *have* to," he tried to explain, his facade of anger crumbling. "I . . . I don't belong here. I never did. I'm not like the Smythe. I didn't want to get pulled out of my life. On Earth I knew what I was doing . . . knew what I was supposed to do. Here . . . Here I'm just so damn confused! And all those people . . . Everyone who died trying to help me. And all of you . . . All of you who did everything you could to stop me from tripping over my own damn feet! I messed up so much of your lives."

A smirk stretched Moknay's mustache. "We didn't do it because it was the right thing to do," the Murderer commented, using Logan's own words. "We did it for our own personal reasons as well."

"I was still a burden," protested Logan, "and even if you say I wasn't, I can't help feeling I was. I just want to get back to *my* way of life. *My* world. I . . . I like this place—I can see why the Smythe wanted to stay—but my staying seems to do nothing but endanger you. And . . . And you're my friends. I don't want to hurt you in any way."

A frown appeared above Thromar's beard. "But then things will get boring, friend-Logan," the fighter responded. "What will we do for fun without you?"

Mara held up a slender hand, halting the Rebel's words. Her expression betrayed the emotional sorrow she felt, yet she held her composure, refusing to give in to the tears that wanted to burst from her eyes. "We have no right to tell Matthew what to do," she told Thromar in a steady voice. "He's the one who makes his choices . . . not us. If he wants to leave, that's his decision—we can't force him to stay . . . that wouldn't be right."

The priestess faced the young man, her green eyes delving deep into his single eye. "I was a disciple of Lelah," she said, and her voice trembled slightly with sadness. "I remember Barthol telling me the key to love was giving. Not just giving *to* one another . . . but giving up. That was the truest test of love—to want to give the one you loved anything they wanted . . . even if it meant losing them forever. It's not easy for me, but I know it's what you want."

Mara looked away, unable to finish.

Logan swallowed hard. She was letting him go, he realized. She was telling him that she cared so much about him that she would do anything for him to be happy . . . even if it meant never seeing him again.

The young man from Santa Monica felt the doubts and second thoughts rising and forced himself to face Zackaron. Quickly, he told himself. Do it now while you still have the courage . . . Do it now while your friends are still alive.

Logan's voice was a strained whisper: "Send me back."

The look in the spellcaster's eyes became recognizable: despair . . . pity. Something was not right.

"I am sorry, Matthew Logan," Zackaron answered. "I cannot."

There was a hint of sadness in his icy grey eyes as Moknay spun on the sorcerer. "Perhaps you didn't hear my friend," the Murderer sneered, "but he wants to go home."

Zackaron nodded, slowly. "I know, Murderer, but I cannot send him back. No one can. He has absorbed too much magic . . . become too powerful to reenter a world such as his own that has no magic. It would never accept him even if he could break his ties with Sparrill. He is trapped."

A deep feeling of emptiness took root in Logan's stomach.

He is trapped.

"His abilities are astonishing," Zackaron was saying. "Never before have I seen such power—except for myself—which indicates it has been some time since he has grown to the level of spellcaster. There were probably signs . . . clues that told he had taken in too much magic.

"I am sorry, Matthew Logan, but Sparrill needs her Champion of Purity."

Signs . . . clues . . . Logan mused, the emptiness inside of him growing. The blow from the snakelike *Deil*; Logan had shrugged it off. Was that why Nightwalker had looked at him so strangely? And his "talk" with the ealhdoeg. That hadn't been natural, had it? Logan had caused it. Just like he had caused his sword to flare and the communication to be established.

He is trapped.

Logan's ragtag troops atop the hill had gone quiet, and the emptiness inside the young man increased. The entire mountain range seemed to join in his sorrow.

A scratchy chuckle broke through the silence.

Logan swung his impaired vision to the west and spied the gnarled figure clumsily staggering back up the demolished mountaintop, black-red gore spattering its lean frame. The afternoon sun blazed off its silver chestplate, and the wrinkled, withered features were drawn back in a hideous, eyeless mask of macabre humor. The faint breeze of the Hills fluttered past the tattered black robe and through what remained of the spiky, blue-grey hair.

No one made any move toward the grisly figure as it crested what used to be the hilltop and towered above them all, a ghastly visage among the destruction of the mountain's peak.

"Then I have won, hmmmm?" Groathit leered, empty sockets scanning the people below him. His wounded and ravaged body swayed precariously in the gentle breeze. "There is no victory here," the spellcaster jeered.

Logan looked down at the ground. Lost. Empty.

He is trapped.

Groathit's sightless gaze seemed to seek out the young man. "I could have sent you back, Matthew Logan," the Reakthi mocked. "I could have returned you to your world the first day we met, but you resisted me. You fought me. You refused to come with me and damned yourself to Sparrill forever."

The emptiness ignited; anger blazed into life.

"There is no victory here," the spellcaster repeated. "Your success in destroying the Voices has destroyed your only chance back. Your triumph has spelled your doom, Matthew Logan, and even your victories are your failures."

The fury grew.

"All that I have worked for was your defeat, Matthew Logan," Groathit went on, "and even as I die I know now you have won nothing. I failed to stop you from becoming the next *spellcaster* of Sparrill, but I succeeded in stopping you from attaining that which you wanted the most. At least in that I was triumphant . . . and knowing that is a far greater satisfaction than watching you die."

The rage exploded.

Logan jerked his head up, crimson light highlighting the intense anger that swirled in his uncovered eye. "*I am* not *a spellcaster!*" he screamed, and scarlet energy thrust outward from his hands.

Groathit howled as the entire mountain range flared with the blood-red brilliance of Nature's magicks. Unbelievable quantities of sorcery shrieked from Logan's arms and enveloped the Hills, blotting out the sun with a blinding, crimson glare. Brackish ichor spumed from Groathit's body as he was caught in the maelstrom of Natural energies, his withered flesh seared by ruby flames.

Consumed by the unquenchable anger burning inside him, Logan channeled all his fury and frustration through the power screaming from his hands. An angered cry escaped the young man's lips as red and silver theurgy streamed endlessly from his fingertips, creating a blood-red and metallic sea of color around him.

As Groathit's dying shriek faded away into echoes, the Hills of Sadroia disintegrated and the explosion of rock and stone dimmed as an unsettling buzz infiltrated the young man's skull, blinding him with its sudden burst of pain. An abrupt jar threw Logan to the muddy ground and the wind was knocked from his lungs, leaving him gasping for air. An overwhelming weakness gripped his body from the release of sorcery, and it took great effort just to lift his head in question toward the place where Groathit had died.

Bewilderment broke through the vertigo and weakness Logan felt when his single eye focused on the blue-and-white sign above his head:

Santa Monica Boulevard.

He was home.

Epilogue

"Matthew, where are you going?"

Matthew Logan gave his mother a distasteful sneer. "Out," he snarled, and shut the door behind him before she could reply.

The young man stuck his hands in his jacket pockets and stepped quickly down the walkway of his parents' house. A cold breeze blew in from the Pacific Ocean to the distant south, ruffling its wintry fingers through Logan's black hair, but the young man was oblivious of the weather. He was lost in thoughts that were as grey and as bleak as the clouds filling the Southern Californian sky.

He had been such a fool, he thought, condemning himself while walking. Whatever had given him the idea that things would end happily ever after? That he could ever go home again? God only knows how he had had the arrogance to think that his world . . . his *real* world would wait for him. It hadn't waited for him . . . it didn't wait for anybody. It had kept on going along fine without him, making a few adjustments here and a few changes there to compensate for Logan's mysterious disappearance.

Maybe I was expecting some kind of time warp, Logan frowned at himself. Some kind of temporal displacement or something technical like that. Something that had made every month in Sparrill only a minute on Earth . . . but no, things had run almost the same, time-wise. In fact, he had been gone over a year, Earth-time, in comparison to the seven months or so spent in Sparrill.

Logan scanned the cloudy heavens, his new contact lenses swirling behind his eyelids. I wonder what happened to Moknay, and Mara, and Thromar, and all the rest, he mused sadly. I wonder if they think I'm dead. Or maybe Zackaron explained what had happened.

The young man looked down at the pavement as he meandered

slowly down Lincoln Boulevard. What exactly did happen? he wondered. Somehow he had allowed his anger to tap into all that magic Zackaron had said he had accumulated—the magic that was trapping him in Sparrill. Through his fury, he had probably released it all . . . or enough of it . . . directing it straight for Groathit. But what had happened then? Had the discharge of magic been so great that he had been propelled home? That had to have been what happened. Subconsciously Logan must have been thinking of home—blaming Groathit for never being able to get back—and the magic had responded as he bombarded the Reakthi spellcaster with all of his rage.

Most powerful when least expected, Logan laughed to himself. Hah! Dirge didn't know the half of it!

Logan turned down another corner and continued his walk, sneering when he saw a police car drive by. Police, the young man snorted to himself. It had been the police who had picked him up when he returned . . . and they had treated him roughly because he had no answers for all of their questions. It had been at the police station that Logan had discovered his apartment was now rented out to somebody else, that someone else now had his job, and that he had been on the missing persons list for over a year and presumed dead. Plus they had confiscated and impounded the weapons given to him by Moknay and Thromar and were all set to send him to the nearest mental institution if the young man hadn't thought of calling his parents to properly identify him. Not that he really blamed the cops. His world had continued on without him and had filled all the vacancies left by Logan's vanishing act— making him an unidentifiable figure wearing a sword, dagger, and eyepatch, and that alone stretched the imagination of more than one—if not all—of the police officers the young man had talked to.

He hadn't even bothered to try to explain where he had been.

So now where was here? Jobless, living with his parents, and unable to tell anyone what had happened to him without being branded a paranoid schizophrenic. No one would have believed him anyway, but it was infuriating to notice the curious stares following him out of the room and catch the nervous whispers behind his back: "What do you think really happened to Matt . . ." "He hasn't been the same since . . ." "Probably went nutso . . ." "Poor guy . . ."

This was the normal life he had wanted to return to? It had been bad enough in Sparrill to be looked at as different, but on Earth it was even worse. At least in Sparrill people accepted you for what you were, not for what you had been. On Earth there was always someone poking into your past—never letting you leave behind what you once were or what you once did. And I used to think Earth was a better place!

Logan stopped his aimless stroll and looked up. There was a business office to his left, and he couldn't understand why it looked so familiar. Abruptly, he recognized the area and realized he had returned to the spot where he had originally been picked up by the mysterious red-and-silver wind. Only now the empty field had been replaced by a business office and a gas station, and Logan's depression heightened.

Everything's changed—even the damn field.

I wonder what Moknay's doing right now?

The young man wandered past the office building and through the gasoline station. What was the sense of coming back to a way of life when that way of life no longer existed? he asked himself sourly.

I wonder what Thromar is up to?

Logan jerked to a halt, narrowing his eyes at a lone figure near the restroom doors. There was nothing particularly interesting about the figure: he was a middle-aged gas attendant in dirty jeans and a striped shirt; it was his odd actions that sparked Logan's curiosity. He was looking about him as if plagued by a swarm of invisible insects, and Logan blinked when he saw what appeared to be a very powerful wind billow through the attendant's hair.

Logan turned and faced the south: There was only the slightest of cold breezes filling the air.

Releasing a wild yell, Logan launched himself forward, charging his despair into adrenaline. A shrill shriek like grating metal split through the noise of the gas station, and red-and-silver light winked into existence, coiling toward the puzzled attendant. An exclamation escaped the man's mouth as Logan smashed into him, knocking him away from the miniature tornado of crimson light. A secret smile was on the young man's face as he dived headfirst into the spiraling vortex of color and felt reality wrench itself around him. He didn't even feel the vertigo or discomfort like before as the scarlet-and-silver funnel of sorcery swallowed him up and sent him spinning end over end through the multiverses.

Heck with it, Logan concluded. Sparrill needed its Champion

of Purity, and it might as well be me. It would be back to the old disagreement, but at least this time I'll know what mistakes *not* to make.

The young man smiled. I wonder what Mara's doing?

STEVEN BRUST

__ATHYRA   0-441-03342-3/$4.99
Vlad Taltos has a talent for killing people. But lately, his heart just hasn't been in his work. So he retires. Unfortunately, the House of the Jhereg still has a score to settle with Vlad. So much for peaceful retirement.

__PHOENIX   0-441-66225-0/$4.99
Strangely, the Demon Goddess comes to assassin Vlad Taltos's rescue, answering his most heartfelt prayer. But when a patron deity saves your skin, it's always in your best interest to do whatever she wants . . .

__JHEREG   0-441-38554-0/$4.99
There are many ways for a young man with quick wits and a quick sword to advance in the world. Vlad Taltos chose the route of the assassin and the constant companionship of a young jhereg.

__YENDI   0-441-94460-4/$4.99
Vlad Taltos and his jhereg companion learn how the love of a good woman can turn a cold-blooded killer into a _real_ mean S.O.B...

__TECKLA   0-441-79977-9/$4.99
The Teckla were revolting. Vlad Taltos always knew they were lazy, stupid, cowardly peasants...revolting. But now they were revolting against the empire. No joke.

__TALTOS   0-441-18200/$4.99
Journey to the land of the dead. All expenses paid! Not Vlad Taltos's idea of an ideal vacation, but this was work. Even an assassin has to earn a living.

__COWBOY FENG'S SPACE BAR AND GRILLE
0-441-11816-X/$3.95
Cowboy Feng's is a great place to visit, but it tends to move around a bit — from Earth to the Moon to Mars to another solar system — Always just one step ahead of the mysterious conspiracy reducing whole worlds to ash.
